A Five Thousand Year Old Prophecy

Cael turned the last page of the ancient tome. And there, in remarkable bone-chilling clarity was the fourth and final prophecy. He felt as if scorpions were crawling on his flesh as he read. When he finished, he had to force himself to breathe. Then he read it again.

The words on the page were impossible. Cael shuddered so hard his bones felt like they were rattling.

His mind reeled. Did his grandfather know about this?

He read it again.

It couldn't be true.

He wanted to cry.

Never in his life had he felt more lost and alone.

SECOND CATACLYSM
Cult of Yex Saga: Part I

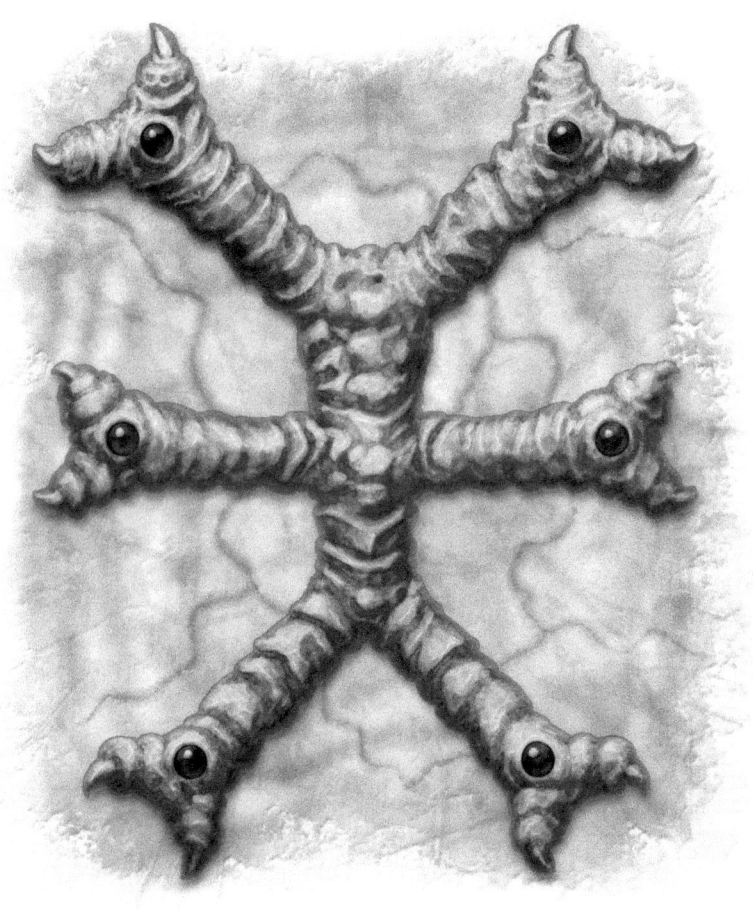

Jason F. Smith & C. Parker Garlitz
www.cultofyex.com

*We dedicate this book to our families,
for all their love and support.*

TABLE OF CONTENTS

Prologue

"It is said that one man saved the world in ancient times. During the darkest hours when it seemed certain that the Cult of Yex would emerge victorious, Adirak, Wizard of Taglyon, stood strong. His unflinching leadership crushed the Cult and his cunning tactics imprisoned the great demon himself in the astral realm.

Adirak was crowned King of Taglyon. He spent his reign vanquishing remnants of the cult and establishing safeguards to ensure that its pernicious evil could never rise again. Despite his efforts, Adirak feared that a residue had somehow managed to elude him, awaiting a time of rebirth. But nary was a whisper heard from the Cult for thousands of years. But for the occasional rambling prophecies of madmen, the Cult was almost forgotten and the few who feared resurgence grew complacent.

If Adirak had lived a thousand lifetimes, he never could have predicted the manner in which the Cult had hidden itself. In his most fevered dreams he could not have imagined the demonic arcana that abetted them, nor their patient scheme to rise again and unleash their demon master."

-Prologue to the as yet unwritten Return of the Cult of Yex, by Caed the Chronicler

CHAPTER ONE

Afterimage

*Letharchenel, the fanatical Captain of the King's Guard, depart-
ed Bystle Vale on orders of King Tharchelon himself. He carried
a list of four names: Cael, Needle, Brynn and Mallet. His mission? Kill them.*

-Return of the Cult of Yex, by Caed the Chronicler

*1st Day of Summer – 5:30 AM – Boxxaway's Cottage in the Low-
er Steppe - 20 Hours Before the Earthquake*

Sixteen-year-old Cael Hotheway could hear his own shallow uneven breathing and the *thip-thip-thip* of his blood pooling
on the dusty floor. He sat with his cut wrist dangling over the
viscous pool, his elbow resting on his knee. The metallic smell
of blood mingled with dust rose to his nostrils. His right hand
held the now bloody knife.

Cael rocked softly back and forth, his head feeling fuzzy
and his brain light in his skull. He watched the slow-moving
pool laboriously swallow the fine desert dust on the floor. The
shiny edges of the puddle crawled over each tan-white speck,
entombing them in a crimson hue.

Cael felt a cold stickiness coat his face as he listened to the
drips of his blood falling off the tips of his trembling fingers to
feed the growing pool. His mouth opened in despair, threads
of spittle creating webs between his lips. Tears filmed over his
eyes and dropped to mingle with their sister fluid.

He loosened his grip on his tool of choice, the rusted knife.
It clattered on the floor and came to rest on the ground to the
right of his wobbly, four-legged stool. Both knife and stool
looked more like the ancient artifacts he regularly found in

the desert with his grandfather than functional items used in a proper home. An equally shabby table stood to his right. A single tallow candle on the table flickered near the nub. Cael raised his hand to hold his forehead.

It was early in the morning in the windowless back room of his grandfather's cottage in the desert city of Demon's Bluff, half an hour before the desert sun would begin to peer into every corner of the landscape. It was the coolest part of the day, but still quite hot. Cael was fully dressed in light linen trousers, leather boots with black flaxen laces tied up to his skinny knees, and a white short-sleeved tunic. His sweaty mop of brown hair spilled over his head, concealing his bloodshot blue eyes and the dirty rivulets left by the tears as they dropped down his face. The pale flesh of his cut wrist pulled back into a demented smile, allowing his blood to well up and out into the dry morning air. Fresh blood, his blood, spilled to enhance the magical power of the enchanted spectacles he used to see into the past.

He was a wizard, or at least an apprentice. As an apprentice, Cael did not have the power to see into even the recent past; much less sixteen years ago, but the enchanted spectacles somehow afforded him the ability. He had fiddled with them all night since he found them lying outside the door to the small back room of their cottage. Most likely a hidden treasure found by their old dog, Dheke.

Cael found that when he donned them, he was able to catch glimpses of what had transpired in this room, days and even weeks ago. Mostly he just saw himself reading in the cramped space by candle light, as was his usual habit. The room had been abandoned for all other uses except this. Cael's and his grandfather's bedrooms, his grandfather's painting room and the kitchen made up the rest of their meager home.

He knew that he had been born in this room and it occurred to him as he played with the glasses that his newfound spectacles might give him the chance to see what his parents looked like. There was nothing more he wanted than to see his mother's face.

Eight Years Earlier – Lake Balankov

"Little chub, what you doing?" Uncle Danilus asked affectionately.

Eight-year-old Cael looked down into the murky water of Lake Balankov and shivered, his face bent over the side of their rowboat.

The lake water was filtered with dark green algae and ripples of white as beams of sunlight penetrated it. Beneath the dancing beams of light, the green hue faded into utter blackness.

"Chub!" Danilus called again.

Cael jerked his gaze away from the water and looked to his beloved Uncle. Danilus wasn't his actual uncle, but a desert ranger who looked after Cael from time to time for his Grandfather Boxxaway. Cael's time spent fishing with Danilus was almost as memorable to him as practicing magic with his grandfather. Sometimes he pretended the red-headed desert ranger was his father.

Cael smiled. "Sorry, Uncle."

Danilus grinned back. "No worries chub." He looked at the cane fishing poles trailing long lines in the water. The bonebacks weren't biting this evening. Danilus stretched his arms above his mop of red hair while looking at the setting sun. "You still feeling spooked by what you saw this morning?"

Cael jerked as if a spider had crawled up his spine. He looked into the cold depths again and imagined that he heard the distant clanking of chains. Earlier this afternoon, they came across a series of wooden buoys floating in a wide circle marking a section of shallow rocks.

"Why don't those buoys float away?" Cael had asked.

Danilus rowed over to one. "Take a gander under it."

Cael leaned over and grabbed the buoy. He tilted it sideways and what he saw froze his blood. Attached to the bottom of the buoy was a metal chain, grown over with green algae. It descended from the buoy until it disappeared in the foreboding blackness below.

Nothing in Cael's young life had prepared him for the feeling of seeing that chain descending down into the depths. He squeaked and fell back into the boat.

Danilus hooted with delight when Cael explained his reaction. *"Chains wrap round your soul... and drag you into darkness!"* he sang an ancient rhyme meant to frighten children. Cael realized his terror at seeing the chain wasn't rational, but his reaction had been visceral and terrifying nevertheless.

The part that haunted Cael the most was Danilus' phrase *drag you into darkness*....His imagination obsessed on what lurked below.

"I was just foolin' with you," said Danilus, "Joking about them chains. I didn't know it would spook you so bad."

"Did you know my parents?" Cael asked.

Danilus was surprised by Cael's question at first but then grew pensive. "No Cael, I didn't. I came along after. That what got you all wrought up about the water? Your parents got sent down the river when they died..."

Cael looked back over the side of the boat. "They died *on* the river. That's what Grandfather said." He peered over the edge of the boat again.

"You reckon they drowned?" Danilus asked. "But you can swim, can't you?"

Cael nodded. "Grandfather made sure I could swim early. Tossed me in the river since I could walk."

"Reckon I know how you feel," said Danilus, rubbing his bearded chin. "I lost my parents too. I reckon I don't know if they are dead or alive."

"Some of the kids in the street of the city," said Cael, "they--they tease me because I've got no parents."

Danilus grunted. "You got to remember something Cael, and hear me well. You got your Grandfather, and you got me."

Cael smiled. "They died when I was a baby. It's just... I don't even know what my mother looked like. Or my father."

Danilus nodded. "I reckon it ain't unnatural wonder about them."

"I wish could just meet them. I'd do anything to go back and change things," said Cael.

Danilus reached out, his big hand took Cael's shoulder and pulled him into an embrace. "We all wish some things were different, Cael, but it's a fool's game. You just can't change the past. You listen to me little chub. I know it hurts not knowing your parents, but what's done is done. Hear me well, for sure-- you just look forward. Ain't no use ever looking back."

1st Day of Summer – 5:30 AM – Boxxaway's Cottage in the Lower Steppe - 19 Hours Before the Earthquake

Try as he might, Cael couldn't get the spectacles to provide more than brief glimpses of the very recent past. He could feel the magic in them, but he just couldn't coax more out of them. In desperation, he finally resorted to blood augmentation to enhance the magic. This was something his grandfather had warned him repeatedly to never try, but the thought of seeing his parents was far too compelling.

Shedding his blood seemed to help. He was able to see a blurred, dim physical outline of a woman. He focused on the image trying to make the afterimage as clear as the day it happened.

Cael mustered one single pinpoint of desire, to see his mother. His mother whom he had never touched or hugged or even heard her voice. He willed a searing focus on the one day of his life he had *known* her: his tiny toes, his furious red face at birth. His vision had traversed backward in time, seeing the sparse events of this room, until....

He could still see it replaying in his mind, as if he were there right now. He had seen this very room... there against the wall, a bed with a straw mattress covered by old stained linens. A beautiful pregnant woman, her face slick with sweat from strain, lay in the bed. A man sat on the very same stool Cael sat on in the present. He was bent over the woman, washing her face with a wet cloth. These were his mother and father.

He saw all this as if he were hiding in the room's tiny closet, peering through the gaps in the planking of the closet door.

Suddenly, Cael was jerked out of his memory and into the present by the sound of a loud bang. "What are you doing in here, Cael?"

The door to the room opened in a cloud of dust. His grandfather, Boxxaway Hotheway, shuffled in from the hall, ducking to avoid hitting his head on the low lintel, almost causing his long white beard to drag in the dust. His red wizard robes, tattered like a much-loved patchwork quilt, swirled around him like a cloud of insects.

From beneath bushy eyebrows, he looked hard at Cael, first at the spectacles propped up on his head, then at his bloody wrist. "What in the hells? Where did you get those?"

"You hid it from me." Cael choked between breathless sobs. His uninjured forearm reflexively swiping across his lower face to remove an accumulation of snot, spit and tears.

Boxxaway's robes collapsed down around him, making him look thin and emaciated. "We need to stop that bleeding. You can't augment the magic in a device. Cael, you damn fool." Boxxaway dropped to his knees, tearing at his robes and tying a makeshift bandage around Cael's wrist.

Cael stared at his wrist. The blood was warm and sticky as it ran over his palm.

Boxxaway glared at him, his eyes hard. "How many times have I told you *never* to use blood to augment a spell? Did I ascribe to you an intelligence you do not possess? Or did you deliberately ignore what I have taught you? Magic burns your life force away as it is. Look at me! Start augmenting with blood and you'll be as old as me in a few months."

Cael felt his ears turn red.

Four Years Earlier – The desert just northwest of Demon's Bluff

"Can I just try the *hold* spell?" Twelve-year-old Cael asked again, pulling the sleeve of his grandfather's robe.

The old man wobbled, almost losing his footing on the

treacherous sandstone. "Careful here, Cael!" he said, leaning on his staff to stabilize himself.

"Can I? The *hold* spell?"

Boxxaway surveyed the ascending slope that led up to the opening of the abandoned copper mine. It was early morning, the sun having just risen over the dunes across on the east side of the Demon River. Cael and his grandfather hiked across the rocky hillside on their long weekly walk. Part lecture, part practice, there was nothing Cael loved more than this time with his grandfather learning the mysteries of the arcane arts.

Cael skipped ahead and scrambled up the slope, stopping inches in front of a mound of squat, thorny bushes.

"Cael!" Boxxaway called out, stern and commanding. "What did I tell you about being cautious? There are crag rattlers out here! Now get back and work on the *sparker* spell again!"

Cael's shoulders slumped. "But I'm sick of the *sparker*! I can do that in my sleep!"

Boxxaway's old face lit into a grin, then he laughed as he hitched up his robes and sat down on a rock, catching his breath and dabbing a mist of sweat from his brow. "We've been over this, Cael," the old man said. "Why do we spend so much time on the *sparker*?"

"It's the best way to practice forming magic without spending very much of my life," Cael sighed.

"The small spells barely age you at all," Boxxaway said. "Mere seconds or minutes. Unlike me, you have minutes to spare."

"But when do I get to try a *real* spell?"

"A wizard must be disciplined, Cael, restrained," his grandfather said, fixing him with a serious look. "Use magic carelessly and you'll spend away your life far too quickly and end up like me. The first rule a wizard must live by is *never use magic if you don't have to.*"

Just down from where Boxxaway sat, a red and black-winged butterfly flitted around a thorny scrub brush that managed to take root in the cracks of the sandstone slope. His grandfather tracked the flying insect with his eyes until it finally lit on a long thorn. "You think you can *hold* that butterfly?" he asked.

"But you said..." Cael trailed off in disbelief. Was his grandfather finally allowing him to try? They had discussed how to form the magic of a *hold* spell for many an hour, but the old man never had relented to let him actually try it.

"Yes, I know," Boxxaway said. "You're now an appropriate age, I suppose. Do you know why a butterfly is a good candidate to practice on?"

Cael's excitement made it hard to think. He just shook his head as he approached the bush where the butterfly flitted.

"Because," Boxxaway said, "the smaller the creature, the easier it is to *hold*. It requires less magic and that means you spend less of your life."

"Really?" Cael asked. "It's okay?"

"Yes, Cael," Boxxaway said. "If, that is, you really think you can do it."

"You don't think I can?" Cael said with mock indignation.

"One little butterfly?" Boxxaway teased.

Cael whirled. "Watch me!" He reached out to start gathering in magical energy.

"Breathe," his grandfather called to him.

"Oh," Cael said. "Yeah." Cael set his feet further apart and locked his eyes on the butterfly. It had begun to flitter about the bush again. He breathed slowly and carefully into his diaphragm, feeling out into the surrounding area with his senses. Ah--there it was: the *Arcanus Navitas*. A rich tapestry of energy. He closed his eyes and felt the eddies and tides of the unseen magical flow.

"Don't just grab at it," Boxxaway scolded. "Invite it in."

Cael nodded. The energy was right there around him. He needed to be patient--needed to *allow* it to come to him. To tease it, invite it, entice it.

Cael breathed in slowly. The energy finally began to flow toward him and into him, spreading its peculiar warmth through his body, moving up his spine and into his brain. It was odd mixture of pleasure with a hint of pain.

"Yes," Boxxaway whispered proudly. "Now, form the image."

Cael opened his eyes, saw the butterfly as it landed on a small orange desert blossom, its wings opening and closing slowly. He formed an image of the butterfly in his mind's eye that was frozen, unmoving.

"Yes," Boxxaway said. "Now merge the two."

Cael felt his heart thump with excitement as the arcane energy swirled in his head. The two images merged in his mind.

"Now!" Boxxaway whispered. "Send it out."

The vibrant intensity of the magic was strong and felt good, but it was also getting a bit wily and unmanageable.

"Send it out!" Boxxaway whispered again.

But just then the butterfly started to flutter into the air, breaking Cael's concentration. Cael's image of a frozen butterfly disappeared just as his spell fired. The eldritch energy flashed from his outstretched palm, where it flew apart and dissolved uselessly back into the *Arcanus Navitas*.

The butterfly flew away to another flower, mocking Cael's attempt at the *hold* spell.

"Hells!" Cael swore, as he felt disappointment and frustration building. Cael couldn't help it as tears filmed over his eyes. The magic always felt so good, so natural, and when he couldn't master it, so frustrating.

"You almost had it," Boxxaway said with a good-natured laugh. "But don't forget, you've likely spent several minutes of your life, even though the spell failed."

"Why does it have to spend your life?" Cael asked, turning to look down the slope. He did not want his Grandfather to see his tears.

Boxxaway chuckled. "Everything has a cost, my boy. The magic comes into your body, but when it leaves, it takes a piece of you with it. It's just the way it is. Look at what it did to me."

Cael looked back at his grandfather. The man was ancient beyond belief, pale, wrinkled and bent. But he still had a smile on his face.

"How old are you, Grandfather?"

"Use magic judiciously, Cael. *Never use it unless you have to.*"

"Wouldn't blood magic keep us from getting old, Grandfather?" Cael asked.

"No no no!" said Boxxaway shaking his head disapprovingly. "Blood augmentation is the *last thing* you ever want to do. Listen to me, Cael," the old man continued, "I don't know where you heard such a thing, but blood magic replaces the *Arcanus*

Navitas, and it amplifies the amount of your life it takes with it. Blood magic is a very dangerous technique. Besides, there is ample power in the *Arcanus Navitas*."

Cael nodded.

"The circumstance would have to be extreme," Boxxaway said. "Besides, blood augmentation makes it more difficult to focus the energy. Right now, you have access to more power than you need. Your failure with the butterfly demonstrates perfectly what I have been telling you. You need more practice in your ability to *focus* the magic, not gather it."

Cael nodded, but felt a mixture of fear and curiosity.

"Blood magic..." Boxxaway said as he stared off into the distance. "You'd have to be truly desperate for power,"

Cael looked ruefully at the butterfly, perched now in the sunburst yellow petals of yet another flower. "Can I try again?"

Before Boxxaway could respond, a menacing rattle filled the morning air. "Uh--Grandfather, don't move!"

Coiled right up next to where the old man sat was a huge crag rattler. Its body was as thick as Cael's thigh. It was hard to tell its length all coiled up, but Cael guessed it was six feet long, maybe eight. It raised its head and the deadly *rat-tat-tat-tat* sound of its rattle once again filled the dry morning air.

Boxxaway held perfectly still, his eyes fixed on the snake. "Well, isn't this nice," he muttered through clenched teeth. A small desert breeze kicked up, causing his robes and beard to sway. Boxxaway slowly closed his eyes and breathed out through his open lips as he waited for the breeze to die back down. The *rat-tat-tat-tat* got louder and the snake appeared ready to strike.

"Maybe you should try that *hold* spell again," Boxxaway said as he opened his eyes to stare at Cael.

"*Hold* spell. Yeah, ok. *Hold.*" Cael tried to swallow, but found his mouth was dry as desert chalk. He coughed a couple times, then remembered to breathe.

Breathe! Breathe! Breathe! He slowly sucked in the air between his teeth, filling his belly. A strange calm filled him. Yes. Yes, he could do this.

Rat-tat-tat-tat. The sound got louder as the desert wind gusted again.

"Any time now, my boy," Boxxaway said, his voice low and terrified.

Cael felt for the *Arcanus Navitas* and relaxed--inviting it. It flowed in more easily now.

He looked at the snake as it began to rear back for full striking power. *Rat-tat-tat-tat. Rat-tat-tat-tat. Rat-tat-tat-tat.*

He looked up once into his grandfather's rheumy eyes. There was a sad desperation there, and then, a glimmer of confidence.

Confidence in me, Cael thought.

He felt his lips break into a grin, and he looked back at the rattlesnake. He couldn't *hold* a butterfly, but this was different. He had no one else in the world but his grandfather.

The wind gusted. Boxxaway's robes flapped. The snake's mouth opened wide.

Rat-tat-tat-tat. Rat-tat-tat-tat. Rat-tat-tat-tat.

Cael formed the image of the paralyzed snake in his mind and released it as if he too were coiled to strike. Cael closed his eyes and thrust out his palms and released the spell.

Then, silence. Cael creaked one eye open. The snake had stopped rattling and was stock still, posed as if about to strike.

Boxxaway leaped up and away and ran to Cael. "By all the hells, boy, you did it! You did it!" Belying his old broken frame, Boxxaway scooped Cael up in a wild embrace. "I thought my moment had come for sure!"

Cael grinned. "I did it."

Boxxaway put him down and turned back to the paralyzed crag rattler. He lowered his hand and gently squeezed Cael's shoulder. "That you did, my boy, that you did."

1st Day of Summer – 5:30 AM – Boxxaway's Cottage in the Lower Steppe - 20 Hours Before the Earthquake

"And how in the hells did you get my *Lorgnettes*?" Boxxaway indicated the spectacles perched on Cael's head by pointing with his chin as he applied pressure to his wrist.

"They were lying on the floor just outside the door to this room," Cael said. "I couldn't sleep and sometimes I come in here to think. I--I saw them lying there on the floor so I picked them up and brought them in here."

"That damn dog!" Boxxaway muttered. "He is getting worse all the time. Rooting around in every unforsaken niche he can get that big stupid snout into, pulling out every item he can find and then piling them up wherever it tickles his rotten fancy. I've half a mind to send him down the river."

Cael knew that wasn't true. Boxxaway loved Dheke, his old grey mastiff. Dheke had a tendency to get nervous when Boxxaway and Cael were away. Sometimes they would come home to find clothing, blankets and wooden spoons strewn about the cottage. Cael occasionally wondered if Dheke's behavior was less about nerves and more about plain amusement in watching Boxxaway fume over the mess in his home.

"So, I gather you put the *Lorgnettes* on," said Boxxaway. "And couldn't figure out how to use them. The first thing to pop into your thick head is grab a knife and do the one thing I keep warning you never to do."

Cael dropped his head, ashamed.

Boxxaway grew silent and his features slowly softened "And those tears? From the pain of your wound, or something else?"

Cael stood up and stomped to the corner of the room. "This is where the bed was that I saw my mother on!" he accused.
"Oh," Boxxaway said, wiping his bloody hands on his robes and then snatching the *Lorgnettes* from Cael's head. He strode back to Cael's now vacant stool and settled his large thin frame down upon it. As he did so, he deposited the spectacles into one of the many pockets of his robes.

"A wizard always maintains calm, Cael. Take a breath and tell me what you saw. Frankly, I need to know whether I have to kill you or not." Boxxaway's eyes glinted as a slight smile moved across his lips.

Cael was inconsolable. "I feel like dying right now as it is. Maybe you could do me the favor."

"Sometimes it seems dying would be easier than living," Boxxaway admitted, a gnarled finger touching his thin, dry, lips as the smile faded into thoughtfulness. "But it is our duty to live for others, Cael. Not to die for ourselves."

"*Why didn't you tell me this is where my parents died?*" Cael shouted. His heart hammered in his chest and his tongue tasted like tin. "In our own home--in this room? I read and practice spells back here!"

Boxxaway looked pensive, but said nothing, his watery eyes unfocused. Cael didn't expect an answer. Adults didn't actually answer questions.

"I never see you come in here," Cael spat. An unwelcome searing feeling began pounding its way into his cut wrist. The sting and ache made him momentarily breathless, but Cael was quite sure the ache in his heart was worse.

"This room is sacred to me, Cael," Boxxaway said finally. "It's where your father died. Where your mother, my only child, died. I have left it unused out of reverence."

"You never told me the details of how my parents died. I didn't even know what they looked like," Cael said. "Once I understood what these spectacles could do and how to harness some of their power, I--I saw myself being born. Right here!" He pointed to where he had seen the bed in his vision.

"*Lorgnettes* are difficult to use, Cael. I'm impressed that you were able to figure them out on your own. But it was foolish. Such things can be dangerous to the uninitiated."

Cael felt fresh tears spilling over the rims of his bloodshot eyes. "I got to see my mother! And my father. He was helping her. She kept screaming. She was covered in sweat."

Cael paused and then quietly added, "But her face was still beautiful. So beautiful."

"Even in death..." Boxxaway whispered and a film of rheum welled in his eyes.

"Then I was born. My mother's face was slick with tears and sweat. She had the biggest smile I have ever seen. She kissed me over and over and over. Father was crying too as he looked at both of us, squeezing my tiny legs and gently resting his hand on my tiny baby belly. Then... then it went all wrong, Grandfather."

Cael stared down at his hands as if they were somehow foreign appendages.

"A shadow emerged from the closet."

Boxxaway looked up sharply. Cael felt a sudden chill at the memory.

"No, not really a shadow. It couldn't have been a shadow because it was... it was me." Cael looked over at the closet door on the south wall and then back down at his hands. A thick crust of blood trailed down the length of his injured arm.

"Go on," Boxxaway ordered.

"I couldn't see him because I *was* him in my vision. I could see what he was seeing. As if I were looking through *his* eyes."

Boxxaway leaned forward and motioned for Cael to continue.

"He... I... he stabbed Father, but Father fought back, turned the blade on him and stabbed him in his thigh." Cael touched his own thigh absently. "I felt the blunt pain of it for a moment. But it was too late. Father's wound was mortal. He collapsed. There was blood all over my... his hands."

Cael could barely see through the tears in his eyes. His heart thumped in his chest, and he felt like his temples were being squeezed. He put his hand on his chest, then moved it up to rub his right temple for a moment. Cael turned, struck the candle, sending it spinning against the wall. Sparks flittered in the air as the room darkened.

"What happened next?" Boxxaway whispered. Cael could hear his grandfather's labored breathing. He himself could barely breathe, as if there were no more air in the room.

Cael choked and slid down to the floor. Even though the room was now completely dark, Cael could see perfectly the memory of what happened next. Looking through the assassin's eyes, he saw his own hands raise the knife over his mother. She turned to shield her newborn baby son in one arm. She lashed out with her free hand, but the assassin blocked her and plunged the knife into her breast. Blood sprayed everywhere, over the assassin, over the newborn baby. The baby screeched like it had been stabbed itself. He stabbed her, over and over.

Cael told all this to his grandfather.

"And then?" Boxxaway asked.

"And then--nothing. The vision was over and I was back here in the present, with you." Cael felt exhausted.

"So you didn't see me come in after the assassin took your

mother's life?" Boxxaway asked.

Cael couldn't speak. He felt like he had a rag stuck in his throat.

"I came right after your mother died," Boxxaway said. "With the blood everywhere, I'm sure the assassin thought he killed you too. You had stopped crying for some reason and there wasn't a scratch on you. I thank the heavens every day for that, Cael."

"She was so beautiful," Cael said, trying to shake the brutal pain from his head. He had seen his mother and father. He finally knew their faces. For the first time in his life he felt they were real, not just the ghosts of his imagination.

Boxxaway was silent.

After a moment, Cael was able to speak. "You said they died in the river."

"That's not entirely untrue. I did send their bodies down the river. I would have liked a more fitting burial. Dirty Agrabi custom, sending my daughter down the river. But I needed them gone in a rather public way. I sent you down the river, also. At least everyone thought that one small bundle was your tiny body."

"How come the assassin didn't kill you, too?"

Cael heard Boxxaway take another deep raspy breath. Then let it all out at once. "In a way, he did," he finally said. "He fled. His job was done. I scared him away, enough to save you."

Cael understood. His eyes rolled upwards as fresh tears streamed down his face. "I feel like dying now."

"Your parents weren't the poor fisherman I told you they were," Boxxaway said.

Questions were coming to Cael's mind faster than he could process them. His parents were not who he grew up thinking they were? Why where they murdered? Who murdered them? Why had Boxxaway kept it from him?

"I saw the symbol in the vision, the one we have seen on the relics we collected in the desert," Cael said. "I saw it on the hilt of the dagger that killed my parents."

There was a snap and light filled the room. Cael squinted. His grandfather almost never cast spells anymore; he was too old and burned out from using it without prejudice in his youth. Each spell cost him life, and at his age, even a simple illumination spell might age him to death. But now he held out a small wand, nothing more than a twisted stick really. The tip glowed dimly. He pointed it, casting light onto the dusty floor. "Draw it."

Cael had never heard his grandfather speak this way before. The words were unmistakably a command. Even growing up, when Cael did something extremely foolish (which seemed to be fairly often), his grandfather's tone was usually gentle.

"Grandfather, there is nothing to draw! It is the same symbol we have seen a handful of times on the relics!" Cael's pain had reached an overwhelming crescendo. He did not want to draw the symbol.

"Draw it, Cael. I need to know for sure." Boxxaway's voice was still cold and detached.

Cael found he could not disobey his grandfather's order, not that he even wanted to. Holding his gashed arm close to his chest like an injured bird, he moved to his knees. With his other hand, Cael traced the distinctive symbol in the dust.

Even as he drew it, the simple shape filled him with a new foreboding he had not felt previously. Its innocent lines intersected and combined to form a symbol that was unmistakably evil. Cael had seen the symbol several times before. It was the symbol of the *Cult of Yex*. It was an ancient religion of demon worshippers, but the Cult had been destroyed over five thousand years ago. He and his grandfather scratched out a living hunting the desert for Cult artifacts, selling them to wizards and collectors. A few of the relics they discovered displayed that symbol. Before that day, the symbol had simply meant extra money when they sold.

"Very few have ever seen that symbol, Cael, and fewer still know what it means. The good wizards who defeated the Cult eons ago spent considerable energy trying to wipe that symbol from the face of our world. Many a wizard burned themselves out while scrying to find and erase that symbol wherever it appeared."

"I don't understand. Why did the killer carry that symbol? Who killed my parents?"

Boxxaway let out another long breath and looked at Cael with stern eyes. "Your parents were killed because of who your father was. Your parents, your father, was a member of a group called the *Society of Eyes*. They were sentinels, Watchers descended through the centuries. I am not a Watcher, Cael. That legacy came from your father's side. But after your parents were killed, I learned of their deeds, and sought to prepare you to one day assume your father's duties."

Cael's thoughts were a blur as he tried to process the implications of what his grandfather was telling him.

"Watching for what?" Cael asked, even though he knew the answer.

"Guarding against the prophesied return of the cult," Boxxaway said.

"The Cult is still around? The Cult was responsible for killing my parents?"

"And they would have killed you too, Cael," Boxxaway sighed.

"Why did you hide this from me? All the time we were gathering those artifacts? You knew, Grandfather, you knew!" The grief in Cael's voice was now edged with anger.

"I didn't hide it from you entirely. You were protected and prepared. Who taught you to use magic? You know more of the cult's history than you realize. What have we been doing out in the desert? Digging for Cult artifacts. And with each artifact, a lesson, correct? As for your parents, well, I was actually going to tell you tonight."

Cael had never known his grandfather to lie, but he found this too much to believe.

"The psychic afterimages in this room are strong." Boxxaway hacked out in a cough. "To experience your parents' death in that way is something I would never have allowed you to do."

Cael felt a dull pain as his stomach twisted itself into a knot. The pain continued to unfold into anger. The visions flashed in his head. He couldn't stop seeing the knife plunge into this mother's breast, the white flesh gaping open.

He could not stop seeing the blood.

"But a vision like that," Boxxaway said. "It's like living it. When you use *Lorgnettes*, it can be as if you actually experience the past. I fear it may haunt you forever."

"Why didn't you?" Cael asked.

"Didn't I what?" Boxxaway responded, bewildered.

"Tell me," Cael whispered.

Boxxaway closed his eyes a moment as he exhaled softly. When he opened his eyes, Cael could see the dreadful effort it had taken Boxxaway to hold this secret all these years. A new and deeper weariness etched Boxxaway's face and clouded his eyes.

"You are young, Cael. I delayed telling you to protect you. Children shouldn't have to deal with information like that."

Cael slowly nodded. "Where has the Cult been all this time then? Where are they now?"

"Coming," Boxxaway said after a thoughtful pause.

"Well, I'd like to meet them," Cael said with a defiance that thinly covered the pain from his memory.

"You may get your wish," Boxxaway said. "I fear that soon the Cult of Yex will fully emerge from the shadows of eons and make themselves openly known once more. The Cult struck a blow when they killed your parents, Cael. Your father should be carrying this burden, for I am too old and you are too young."

Cael shook his head. "I always thought the Cult was just something from the past. You are certain they never went away?"

"Your parents are witness to that," Boxxaway said sadly. "I'm too old to fight them, Cael, and you are too inexperienced, *right now*. But I have been preparing you."

"For what?" Cael demanded.

"Seers of old were put to death for prophesying that the

Cult would one day return," Boxxaway explained. "And that a great cataclysm would portend their rebirth. The signs have grown clearer of late and I fear the time is at hand."

Cael stared at his grandfather as he tried to cope with the flood of information. "I only care that my parents were killed. I want to find who killed them."

"Welcome to the *Society of Eyes*, my boy," Boxxaway said. "It's not enough to find who killed them. We have to stop them. It is your privilege and your curse to live in the days when the Cult of Yex finally returns after five thousand years of hiding."

"So, what? I am supposed to stop them? What can I possibly do?"

"Well, you can start by seeking out those who can help you," said Boxxaway.

"No. No way. I don't want help from anyone but you," he said.

"Assist an old man into the kitchen," Boxxaway said as he slowly lifted off the four-legged stool. "Besides, your wrist needs a proper bandage."

Cael followed his grandfather from the back room into the hall and down into the great room that served as a kitchen in their little mud brick cottage. As he walked along, the pain thumped back into his wrist with a wicked bite. Cael's breath caught as he gripped his wrist.

Boxxaway stopped in the doorway to the kitchen, his foot tapping rhythmically on the frayed old red carpet set there. Dheke dozed fitfully nearby. Boxxaway was lost in thought.

"Grandfather?"

"You must listen to me, Cael," said Boxxaway, snapping out of his brief reverie. "Tonight is a special night that I have foreseen. I wonder that it is no coincidence that of all days for you to see the past, today was that day. Come sit at the table, Cael."

As Cael slunk into a chair at the table, Boxxaway poured water from a clay jug into a large wooden bowl. He then opened one of the shabby cupboards that lined the kitchen and pulled out a clear bottle. It was one of Boxxaway's many tinctures that he prepared using alcohol and the various different herbs and flowers scattered around their desert home.

Boxxaway settled in next to Cael with the bowl of water,

several strips of linen, and the bottled tincture. Both man and boy sat in silence as Boxxaway gently unwrapped the makeshift bandage he had applied in the back room. Boxxaway then began to carefully moisten the wound and surrounding skin with a wet strip of linen, loosening the crusted blood and caked on dirt. Cael winced at the pain but also felt a deep warmth for his grandfather.

As Boxxaway worked on Cael's sliced wrist, he began to speak softly. "There are three whose destiny is to serve with you as Watchers, even if they don't know it yet. You must bring them here to me tonight. The time has come for the revelation of all secrets. I believe that they, like you, are in danger. Something is soon going to happen, and preparations made long ago are coming to fruition."

"Who are these people? Why do we need them?" Cael asked as he watched Boxxaway continue to mop his arm with the pungent tincture.

"Do you imagine you can take on the Cult by yourself?" Boxxaway asked, eyebrow raised.

Cael rubbed his eyes with the heel of his free hand. His answer was yes, absolutely.

"Their destiny is intertwined with yours, Cael," Boxxaway said. "They will have their own reasons--eventually."

Cael digested that and felt a swell of fear in his gut. "Won't you be helping?"

"I am your guide, my boy, but you must tread the path without me," the old man said. "This is in your hands now. My time is past."

Boxxaway finished tending to Cael's arm by snuggly tying several strips of linen around the red, gaping wrist. He then rummaged around in one of the pockets of his tattered robes. He handed Cael a gold coin. Cael stared in disbelief. A *gold sun!* Where had his grandfather come up with this? They had survived on copper stars and an occasional silver moon from as early as Cael could remember.

Cael opened his mouth to ask, but Boxxaway held an arthritic finger to his lips.

"I know, Cael. There will be time for answers later. That will buy you passage up the cliff to the plateau. If my own divinations are correct, the people you seek should be at the grave-yard at midnight tonight. *Don't be late.* There is a new moon, so you will need to take a lantern. You should spend the remainder of the day resting."

Cael indeed felt tired, down to his marrow, but he had no intention of actually resting. He had just discovered who his parents really were and what they were fighting. He needed to learn more and he knew where he might start looking.

"The three of them are about your age, Cael," Boxxaway continued. "And they will be converging on the Bygrave Mauso-leum, the first pyramid on the right about half a mile down Ga-drax Row. Their names are Brynn and Mallet, who are brother and sister. The third is someone you already know, the child Needle, whose father competed with us out in the desert hunt-ing for artifacts."

Cael frowned at that. Needle? Of all people, not him. He did not like Needle Graji.

"Don't look at me that way," Boxxaway said. "Needle will come in very useful. It's his birthright, same as yours. You must go to them and bring them back here to me tonight. Do you understand?"

Cael looked out the window at the morning sky. It had turned from dark purple to a brightening crimson. The same color as the blood of his murdered parents.

He nodded.

CHAPTER TWO
Stranger in a Strange Land

Five thousand years ago, the Cult of Yex suffered its first major defeat at the hands of Adirak in the Battle of Oar. Many of the cult's battle mages were killed that day. The desperate sorcerers turned to an eldritch restorative from the bowels of the Abyss itself. They were desperate to hold Adirak off long enough to complete the summoning of the great Demon Yex, no matter what the personal cost.

-*Return of the Cult of Yex*, by Caed the Chronicler

1st Day of Summer – 7:00 AM – Outside Boxxaway's Cottage – 18 Hours and 30 Minutes Before the Earthquake

The assassin stood on the dusty road looking at the rundown mud brick cottage that was the home of Cael Hotheway, the first name on his list. Letharchenel shook his head in amazement. The house was so old that the whitewash had mostly flaked off of the dried mud and he was sure the roof leaked. Not that it mattered in this forsaken desert, as it obviously didn't rain here very often. His thoughts wandered again to his own home in the secluded Bystle Vale where the sweet rain drizzled frequently.

He studied Cael's house from a secure vantage further up the lane. He had been watching for over an hour now, long enough to know there were at least two people in the house: a very old man and a teenage boy who he knew was Cael. They had walked past the open airy windows on several occasions. There were also signs of a dog living with them, but he hadn't seen it directly. The dog might be trouble, but he had handled worse before.

As he continued to watch, olive and pale skinned people lumbered by in both directions along with their animals including dogs, goats, donkeys and an occasional gangly humpbacked beast, the likes of which Letharchenel had never seen before. He recoiled in disgust at the awful stench of the creatures.

These desert folk were giants compared to his diminutive height. His people, the Rothkin, were small in stature and slender of build. Letharchanel himself was only four feet two inches, which was tall for his people.

To be able to fulfill his task, he needed a way to blend in. Soon after he had entered the town, he found one.

One Day Earlier

Letharchenel had floated down the lazy Demon River in a makeshift canoe, noting as the landscape changed from cool canyons of forested highlands to boulder-strewn flatlands, onward past a fetid stinking swamp and finally into the arid desert. In his entire life, he had never seen such terrain, but he did not pause to think about it much. Things like this simply didn't matter in the grand scheme of things. The plants were sparse and those that did grow were strange, rugged things that grew spines instead of leaves. The dry grasses and shrubs looked as if they cared not at all if their roots ever drank deeply of cool water. Fibrous trees with stiff dagger-like leaves that grew outward in tufts at the ends of barrel-arms rose worshipfully to the unforgiving sun.

All this was inconsequential, and though the heat and inhospitality was bothersome, it certainly wasn't going to stop him. Finally rounding a lazy bend in the river, the massive mesa he was searching for hove into sight.

When he saw the town, crammed impossibly between the sheer cliff of the mesa and the western shore of the Demon River, he knew it didn't matter how different things were. Here were people and he knew that people were people, no matter where you went. So what if their cottages were made of sun-baked clay bricks huddled together in the flat area down by the water? So what if the larger cottages were built up on the higher land next to the bluff? Were those a lattice work of cat-walks, cave entrances, and even buildings built directly on the face of the sheer cliff?

Not so different than the homes amidst the branches and hollows of the gigantic Bystle Tree. Looking back at the rocky cliffs again, he wondered, were those war machines atop the cliff, designed to hurl projectiles down upon an invading army? Such devices also adorned the highest branches of the Bystle Tree.

There were differences here, true, but also similarities.

The most important similarity was the people, and the fact that no matter who you were, if someone cuts your throat, you bleed and die.

He beached his canoe on the western shore north of town and trudged through farmland and irrigation ditches into the heart of Demon's Bluff.

Soon, Letharchenel spied a clothesline in the backyard of a ramshackle cottage on the outskirts of town. Brown and white desert garb hung from it, swaying in the warm breeze. One set of clothes looked to be a human child's pair of breeches, tunic and tan robes. He loved children. These clothes would fit his diminutive size. He had been about to enter the yard and steal the clothes when the very child who owned those clothes banged out of the back door of the house. He carried a wicker basket as he skipped down the steps toward the clothesline. The child must have only been around ten years old and was clearly obeying the early morning command of his mother. He had begun to pull the clothes down in jerks, wadding them up and tossing them into the basket.

When his basket was filled, he turned back toward the house. So focused on his work had he been, he hadn't noticed Letharchenel sneak into the yard to stand behind him.

"Hello?" the child said, looking curiously at him. They stood eye to eye. Letharchenel loved that look of innocent curiosity. He reached out with his leathery hand and caressed the child's face. The boy smiled in confusion. Letharchenel jammed his dagger into the boy's throat to cut off any scream as he deftly pulled the basket of clothes away from any blood that might stain them.

He eased the boy down to the dusty earth and looking around quickly, he rifled through the clothes in the basket for what he needed. He fled the yard and found a secluded place. He made the change in a kind of rapid manic dance, hoping no one saw him naked. The very thought that someone might see him even in a partial state of undress made him intensely uncomfortable.

He strode happy and smiling into a busy lane wearing a flowing tan robe over the child's breeches and tunic, convinced he now fit right in with the Demon's Bluff population. Hopefully, the other four children, his real targets, would be as easy to find and as satisfying to kill. He loved children.

Suitably disguised, it didn't take long to discover where Cael lived by obsequiously asking questions.

Cael and his grandfather were known in the town and he quickly learned directions to the area they called the Lower Steppe. The house was along the busy road leading west from the market up to what was called the Middle Steppe.

1st Day of Summer – 7:05 AM – Outside Boxxaway's Cottage – 18 Hours and 25 Minutes Before the Earthquake

Letharchenel stood up the lane a pace from Cael's house wearing the airy tan linens, confident that as long as he didn't act suspiciously, no one would think he was anything other than a child himself. The light billowing garb easily concealed his assassin's tools: the hand crossbow at his waist and the slim daggers at his wrists.

He had been vigilantly blending into the crowds using his smaller size and his natural skill at avoiding attention as he observed the mud brick cottage. He had watched long enough; the time for action approached. He just needed the right moment to sneak into the cottage.

Another one of the gangly four-legged creatures passed

close in front of him, and he again yearned for the earthy smell of damp soil and dew-covered grass. Everything here in the desert smelled wrong. The dryness almost made for an absence of odor. The only smells with any power were unpleasant and foreign.

Sand whirled about him as a gust of hot wind skipped up the lane. Grit and sand permeated his clothes and hair and the oppressing dry heat parched his throat and chapped his skin. He could not understand how anyone could live here, much less choose to. Soon, there would be four less living here; even more if anyone else stood in the way of accomplishing his mission.

His mission was foremost in his mind. From the moment he had left the Bystle Vale, Letharchanel was focused on only one thing: killing the four children whose names were on the parchment handed to him by King Tharchelon himself.

The traffic ebbed. Now was the time. He walked nonchalantly across the road, his bare feet itching on the hot cobble stones. He walked up the steps under the porch and listened at the yellow door.

He heard nothing.

He reached out and took hold of the door handle and pushed.

The door opened on metal hinges that barely squeaked.

He pulled his hand crossbow from his belt hook. If there was a dog, his poisoned quarrel would silence him in seconds. If the boy Cael was inside, he would kill him with his preferred method: a dagger thrust through his throat and up into his brain.

He entered the house.

The house was empty. The occupants must have both left out the back door and he had just missed them. Dust on the floor and the table in the back room suggested they had recently been here. A stool was overturned away from the table and a candle had been knocked to the floor. He knelt on the ground and touched a dried black crust of sand. He stroked it with his hand, sniffed his fingers, then tasted it. Blood.

Had they known he was here? Had they fled?

He didn't think so. It was just dumb luck that they left, and dumber luck that they left through the back door. As he made his way back to the kitchen, he made eye contact through the window with an old neighbor woman in the adjacent cottage. She waved at him through her window with a senile smile.

He considered his options. He could lie in wait for this Cael, but didn't he have three other targets as well?

Letharchanel slipped out of the house and back onto the street. He unrolled the scroll of parchment given him by King Tharchelon, and reviewed the next name on his list: Needle Graji.

CHAPTER THREE
Through the Eye of the Needle

When our battle lines finally advanced within sight of the plateau, thousands of olive-skinned indigenous nomads calling themselves "Agrabi" streamed in from all over the desert to join the fight. Our ranks swelled with their fierce warriors. It seems the Cult of Yex left no peoples unmolested.

-Colonel Daereus Beale, 4th Desert Battalion

1st Day of Summer – 10:00 AM – Demon's Bluff Thieves Guild – 15 Hours and 30 Minutes Before the Earthquake

Two brutish goons dragged sixteen-year-old Raju 'Needle' Graji before the man who was sure to be his judge, jury and executioner.

The room that might become his tomb certainly fit the part. It was under the Butcher's Shop, which was really a front for the nefarious Thieves' Guild. A smoky torch sputtered in a wall sconce, casting long, animated shadows over the moldy, blackened sandstone bricks that walled them in. The air was damp and musty, as the room was near the Demon River and seepage occurred. The smell of rat feces filled the air.

A skittering noise reached Needle's ears from the shadows. A chill raced through his body, as if someone had taken a fingernail and scratched him from the nape of his neck to the base of his spine. His empty stomach tightened at the sound. Needle hated rats.

This was a bad idea coming here.

But what choice did he have? Desperation drove him. He needed money. Since his father had disappeared a year ago, he had been alone in taking care of his blind mother. If he didn't find work soon to pay for her rent, she would be cast out onto the streets and forced to beg for alms. But any hope of alms from his own olive-skinned Agrabi people was misplaced. There was no charity in the Kuma.

He had tried everything he could think of to earn money, going door to door, offering to work for a copper star here or a copper star there. Shoveling camel dung, emptying spittoons, burning trash, gutting fish. No job in the city was too low for him when it came to saving his mother, but very few of his own people hired him, and more than once, when the work was done, they cheated him. There were simply too many desperate Agrabi adults looking for work.

Two things his pride wouldn't allow him to do: beg, or work for the Buerdeleise who ruled the city. He wouldn't beg, no sir, he would not. It wasn't in him. And he wouldn't work as a personal fawning servant for the white Buerdeleise. Sure, that might be where the best jobs for his people were (so testified many a lowly servant) but you had to bow and scrape and debase yourself in a way Needle wasn't built for. He'd rather eat dung than say yes sir! no sir! What you need me to do now, sir?

With rent due right now and impending eviction coming, he had been reduced to this last desperate idea: sneak into the Thieves' Guild using skills learned from his missing father and prove his worth to their leader as an apprentice. Asking them directly for a job had borne no fruit, so he felt he needed to prove himself in a more dramatic way.

And it had worked--kind of. He had snuck in successfully and allowed himself to be caught. Now, he hung before their leader in the arms of two goons, hoping his audacity and courage would soon be rewarded

The man in the room spun slowly to face him. When he saw the man's face, all the moisture in Needle's mouth evaporated. His tongue stuck to the roof of his mouth, tasting like tin. The Buerdeleise man's unshaven, rat-like face made him appear dark and sinister. Glittering, almost bulbous, wide-set eyes stared from under a veil of greasy black hair.

The man sniffed the air, his long nose twitching.

"What's this?" the leader asked, his voice nasally and raspy.

The man filled Needle with preternatural terror. Here was

a cold-blooded killer, without conscience. Worse, there was a wicked creativity in his eyes that suggested his lack of decency was sprinkled with a heavy dose of cruel ingenuity. He wasn't just evil, he was ingeniously so.

Needle was filled with a grim certainty that his precious time in this world was about to come to an abrupt and shocking end. He hadn't just made a little mistake coming here. This was a monstrous and calamitous error.

"My name is..." Needle began, despite being terrified. He didn't get to finish. The man lashed out, striking Needle with the back of his hand. Needle's head slammed back and his lips serrated against his teeth. Blood filled his mouth, washing over his teeth and coating his tongue all the way down the back of his throat. His head swam from the blow, and for a moment he saw two of his adversary. One was too many, so he closed his eyes.

"I don't care who you are," the man said. "To me, you are just a scrawny little Agrabi boy. Barely got hair on your sack I'll wager too. A shame you're so scrawny. You won't fetch much I'm afraid, especially if we can't break the defiance in your eyes."

Needle imagined he didn't look good. He hadn't eaten well in a year and he knew his bones protruded all over his body. He had shorn his stiff black hair close to his scalp, as was the custom of his people to keep infestations down. Worse, he knew the linen trousers and tunic he wore, once white, were stained and torn. Besides his old knife, his leather boots were probably the only thing of much worth he owned and they were worn through. He had left his knife at home, thinking the thieves might get the wrong idea if they caught him. But now Needle couldn't imagine their reaction being worse that it was.

The two men holding him had iron grips and his arms were going numb. His hands felt heavy and useless as he tried to clench his fists to wake his fingers.

"He got past the entrance," one of the burly goons holding him said. His voice seemed unnaturally deep compared to the nasal voice of the leader. "Got down the stairs and quite a ways down a tunnel before we caught him."

"I let them capture me," Needle explained. "I wanted to prove my worth to you."

"How in the Abyss does this happen?" the leader demanded of his henchmen. "Did we start advertising for youngsters now like some Taglyon trollop brothel fallen on hard times?

"Hey!" the goon replied, "You go blame someone else. We caught the little bastard, which wasn't easy. Guarding the front door ain't our job!"

The man looked at him and for a second Needle thought he was going to strike him again. Instead, he laughed. "What's a half-starved Agrabi boy doing sneaking in here?"

"Need work," Needle said. "Got my mother to feed."

"Maybe you got hair on your sack, after all." The man shook his head. "How did you know this was the Thieves' Guild?"

Needle knew he had to step up if he expected to save himself and his mother. Didn't matter his stomach was tied in knots, and he was on the verge of pissing himself.

"I had to get your attention and show you what I can do," he started, alarmed at how fast he was talking. But he couldn't stop now. "I snuck past your guards. I need work and I am a good sneak. I can be of value to you. I just need money so my mother isn't kicked out onto the street."

The man smiled and then backhanded Needle again. "I don't care a whit about your momma!" Gods, the man was strong. Needle's mouth exploded again in pain and blood. It spilled over his lips.

"I asked you a question," the man said softly. "How did you know this was the Thieves' Guild?"

Needle goggled at him, trying to refocus his thoughts and stem his panic. He wanted to cry, to beg, but he knew that would only make things worse. He finally took a breath and spoke slowly: "My Father brought me here, years ago, when I was very young."

"A lie," the man said suspiciously, cocking his head to the side in thought. "Nobody brings a kid in here."

"My father did. It was years ago. His name was Kemano Graji and he brought me with him once."

The man's face twisted into an instant grin. Needle immediately understood that he recognized his father's name.

"So, you're Kemano's whelp!" the man laughed. "That explains the nerve you got!"

Was this a good laugh or a bad laugh? Needle could only nod yes, hoping the clouds were lifting. He had to hope. There was nothing left but hope, and it flooded him with relief. Finally he had gotten through to the man.

Then the man shook his head. "You are one stupid kid to come back here after what he done!"

Eight Years Earlier – 23rd Day of Summer – 6:00 AM – Demon's Bluff Thieves' Guild

Raju 'Needle' Graji (before he had earned the nickname Needle) was only eight years old when his father took him to the butcher shop down by the river and he learned about the Thieves' Guild that was headquartered underneath it. That was the day that his father began to teach him the skills that would allow him to one day sneak into the Guild headquarters. It was also when he finally began to understand what his father did for work. Unlike most Agrabi men, he wasn't a common laborer.

"Wake up, my son," Father said. Raju hated being woken up early and tried to roll over on his reed mat. He felt sluggish, like his head was filled with sand.

"Wake up!" Father said again, shaking his shoulder.

Raju peered out from under the thin linen sheet he had draped over his head. The familiar smell of his father's cooking reached his nostrils. "Ugh," was all he could muster. What time was it? No light came from behind the shutters of his small bedroom in their modest adobe cottage in the Abala Ku, which was an Agrabi district of Demon's Bluff. It was still dark out.

"Here are your sandals," Father said, tossing them onto the bed.

Raju blinked in the light of the white tallow candle his father had set on the small wooden bench next to his bed. "Where we going?"

Father smiled at him. He was a short man compared to other men, but he was huge to Raju. He was stocky with a barrel chest and had black hair on his head as thick and coarse as the forests his mother had told him about in stories. His smile lighted Raju's heart, with his white teeth and wide eyes. His nose was huge, twisted into a knotted bulb at the tip. It had been broken more than once.

"I have a secret to tell you."

That got Raju up. He pulled on his tan linen trousers and white tunic and belted them with a worn flaxen cord. "What's the secret? What is it?"

"Put your sandals on," Father whispered with his finger to his lips. "Shhh, I don't want to wake your mother."

Raju pulled on his sandals and wrapped the leather thongs up his calves and over his trouser legs, as was the custom of his people. Now dressed, his father led him out into the open kitchen of their cottage. Just the smell of the kitchen flooded him with a sense of security. Father had the black potbellied stove already fired up, and an iron flat skillet spat with spiced eggs.

"What's the secret?" Raju asked again, sitting on the bench that ran the length of their wooden tavern style table. His father picked the up the cast iron skillet by the handle with a dirty black rag to protect his hand. Taking a pinch of spice from an earthenware jar, he added a bit more to the eggs and nudged some into the hollowed out wooden trencher in front of him. Raju immediately shoveled the eggs into his mouth with a battered wooden spoon. They tasted wonderful. A wooden bowl of figs, dates, almonds and a wedge of hard camel's milk cheese sat to the side. A horn of honeyed mead provided the drink.

"Don't eat so loud, you'll wake your mother," Father said sternly. He sat down next to his son and began eating straight from the skillet.

"Are you going to tell me where you go when you go away?" Raju whispered. "Are you?"

"Better," Father said, and he couldn't hide his smile again. "You're coming with me." His white teeth were startling against the dark tanned skin of his face.

Raju couldn't believe it. He was going with his father on one of his secret trips. Ever since he could remember, his father left for weeks at a time and his mother complained bitterly about it. He had felt both curiosity and sadness, along with a bit of the same resentment his mother had nurtured. Now, he was going to find out where his father had been going. What could it be? His eight-year-old mind conjured a hundred different possibilities. He couldn't help himself, and asked again, "Where are we going?"

His father's smile faded. "My son, what I do is sometimes dangerous."

"But you are careful," Raju said, espousing his simple and complete faith in his father.

Father shook his head. "You are getting old enough and I need your help. Finish getting ready. I will come back to fetch you in a moment."

Young Raju finished his eggs in silence, beaming with excitement and pride that filled him to his toes.

They left their small mud brick cottage and went into the streets of Demon's Bluff. It was not yet midsummer, and even though the sun had just peeked over the eastern horizon, the heat was already starting to build. The sand-strewn mud-baked streets were mostly empty. Lanterns still burned fitfully at every corner as a warm breeze coursed over them. A few men were out, mostly alone or in pairs, silently getting ready for the day's work. Dressed in white linen tunics and trousers or sometimes in billowy robes belted with flaxen cords, they almost looked like ghosts in the murky morning light. The sounds of wagons rolling and horse tack creaking could be heard down a side street.

Raju soaked it in with fascination. He loved Demon's Bluff. Staying in their cottage with his mother was always torture. She preferred to have him indoors, to keep him safe, but he chaffed under that restriction and slipped out as often as he could. He'd walked down these streets a hundred times, playing here amongst the other Agrabi children of Demon's Bluff. But in the cold, grey light of dawn, everything looked different. Haunting lanterns flickered shadows over the old mud brick buildings.

"Where are we going?" Raju asked.

Father didn't answer. They just kept walking north, out of the Abala Ku, which was a section of town heavily populated by the olive-skinned indigenous Agrabi. It was in the Lower Steppe section of Demon's bluff. Further south, of course, than the Buerdeleise areas, but not so far south as the Kuma, which was where the poorest Agrabi lived. In fifteen minutes, they had walked into the Market District.

The sun was now over the eastern horizon and the morning business was well underway, with scores of wagons, camels and other animals filling the street. A small pack of mangy strays, "buck dogs" as his father called them, sniffed about looking for some breakfast.

This was Raju's favorite place in the entire world. A multitude of smells wafted over him, from warm bread baking in clay ovens, to the open air grills starting to cook meat, to the stench of the hide tanners, to the pungent smell of unwashed people trying to mask their odor with scented oils. Minstrels tuned their lyres, street acrobats stretched in preparation for a day of performing and snake charmers were testing their flutes. The apothecary tent offered herbal poultices, which smelled awful and tasted worse. Lepers, banned from the waterholes and the physician tents, gathered mummified in stained white rags begging alms from the merciful. Astrologers and entrails diviners set up their booths, while a long-bearded religious zealot dressed only in a loincloth waved his arms and prophesied certain doom for the unrepentant. Merchants, selling everything from bread to fish to wine to roasted scorpions, began to call out to passersby. Amidst them all was an occasional town guard dressed in their blue tunics over thin mail, leaning on their pole-arms. Beggars rattled their tin cups, street urchins frolicked about, and even amidst the watchful gaze of the town guard, pickpockets surreptitiously plied their risky trade.

This was the center of the universe as far as Raju was concerned, where the pale-skinned Buerdeleise and the olive-skinned Agrabi mixed in a wonderful confusion of sounds, sights, smells and tastes.

They traveled for several minutes through the merchant district before they angled eastward toward the river.

"We're here," Father finally said, tugging his hand and pulling Raju out of his reverie. They stood before a dilapidated mud brick shop, along a row of other trade shops like those plied by masons, coopers, brick makers and potters. A simple sign hung askew over the door.

Meat.

"We're getting meat?" Raju asked, not quite keeping the disappointment from his voice.

Father laughed as he reached out and knocked on the door, rattling the dirty pane of glass set in the wood.

The door opened and a bald-headed Buerdeleise man with high cheekbones and a bruised lip stuck his head out. He was wearing a white apron that was doused in blood. The smell of raw meat was overpowering.

"I was sent by Dagorn," Father said quickly.

The man frowned and Raju took a step back. The man rubbed his temple and Raju noticed the man was missing the pointer finger on his left hand.

"You Kemano?" the man spoke with a bit of difficulty. His fat lip affected his speech.

"Aye."

"Who's this then?" the man said, pointing to Raju with his chin.

"My son," Father said.

"You shouldn't bring him inside," the man said.

Father looked surprised. "You want me to go inside with you? I'm just here to pick up the supplies Dagorn arranged for me. There should be four camels and equipment for a desert expedition."

"They want to talk to you inside, but you don't want the kid to see what's in here."

Raju was thinking the same thing. No way in the world he was going to walk into that butcher shop. The smell alone was enough to make him want to throw up.

"My son is coming with me," Father said.

"I'll stay out here, Father," Raju spoke up. He saw a cart full of dates across the road and a man selling monkeys stood nearby.

"He's coming with me on the expedition," Father said.

"You want to bring him in here, whatever, but you been warned," the man said. He opened the door and waved them in.

The missing finger bothered Raju. It seemed like he couldn't help but stare at it.

Father prodded Raju forward. They walked past the man with the bloody apron and Raju pressed himself against the doorjamb to avoid touching the man's protruding belly. Nausea almost overwhelmed Raju as the smell of the man's sweat mingled with blood and raw meat hit him.

They entered a large square room. The wooden floor was saturated with blood stains. The far side of the room was adorned with pig carcasses hanging from large metal hooks. To the left, there was a bloody table with huge cleavers and butcher knives and a hand crank hopper where the meat was ground. Piles of bone and gristle and a few eyeballs were strewn in the corner.

Raju could not believe how much food there was here. Half a dozen pigs hung here. It was an amazing display of wealth in a world where one sold hog could feed an Agrabi family for an entire season.

"Gods," Father said under his breath.

Raju, never a squeamish child, stared at the blood and gore. His stomach was churning and the eggs he had just eaten were threatening to come up.

The butcher led them to the back of the room through the maze of hanging hog corpses to another door. He knocked on it. A young, tall man with a long nose, dressed in black cloth leggings and tunic, opened the door.

"This is Kemano," the butcher said.

The tall man nodded, turned quickly and signaled for them to follow. He led them down some sandstone stairs and into a maze of dank musty passages.

Where are we? Raju wondered. He had no idea there were tunnels beneath the butcher's shop.

Smoky torches held in rusted iron sconces were intermittently hung along the passages. They were near the river, so that explained why everything was wet. At least it was cooler down here. The man led them through the damp passages to a moldy wooden door and pushed it open.

"Wait inside," he said in a nasally voice as they entered.

The small room was roughly hewn out of the stone. It was also bare, with only a lantern hanging from the ceiling to give light.

"Father..." Raju began.

"Don't worry, Son," Father explained. "I wouldn't normally bring you into a place like this, but believe me; you are safer by *my* side."

Raju didn't feel comforted. He knew instinctively that this was a bad place, and yet, there was something about it that was intriguing. The darkness, the damp, the smells and feels--he just liked it, even though he was scared. He imagined exploring the tunnels with his friends and that seemed like a fine idea.

The door opened and a Buerdeleise man entered, wearing a white sleeveless tunic, brown trousers and black boots. A gold chain with a silver medallion hung around his neck and his clean-shaven face was split into a wry grin.

"Well sir, you are here, right on time."

"Thank you," Father nodded. "But why are we down here? I was told the expedition would be ready at sunup."

Raju gripped his father's hand tighter.

"How did you expect to get across the river?"

"On old man Windle's ferry," Father said.

"Nah," the man said. "The camels are ready to go on the other side of the river. Dagorn told us to take you under the river."

Father's eyebrow shot up. "There's a tunnel *under* the river?"

Raju was thinking the same thing. That was the neatest thing he had ever heard of.

The man nodded, "What do you expect from the Guild? We got tunnels *everywhere*. Follow me. I'll take you through to the other side."

1st Day of Summer – 10:15 AM – Demon's Bluff Thieves Guild - 15 Hours and 15 Minutes Before the Earthquake

"What did my father do?" Needle asked the rat-faced man. "Do you know where he is? He's been missing for a year now!"

The man stared at him, chuckling. "Why would I know where your father is? Your problem isn't him, little whelp. It's that you made the biggest mistake of your life coming here and having me find you."

"I need to feed my mother," Needle said quietly. "I proved myself. I need a job."

"A job?" The man shook his head. "Hells, I'd sooner hire a one-legged harlot with dropsy and decrepitude than hire some Agrabi whelp. But you are right about being worth something to me."

Needle's heart fell and then rose.

The man looked to the goons holding Needle. "Take him down to the barge. We have a load of slaves heading out to Balankov. He'll make a nice addition, not to mention a profit."

Needle paused to digest that for one second, then in an adrenaline-filled panic began kicking and screaming. He had heard what happened to children sold into slavery. It wasn't a death sentence, but it was damn close. It would, however, be a death sentence to his mother. She could not take care of herself. He was her only hope.

His struggles were in vain however. There was no escaping the two goons. They held him in a vice. They grunted and dragged Needle from the room. A few punches to the gut shut him up.

He lost track of where he was. They seemed to be walking down endless tunnels dripping with water. He was near the river, of course, though he didn't recognize the tunnel as the one he had traveled eight years ago with his father. They dragged him up some stone steps and into a large brick warehouse with a dirt floor. Light leaked in from two dirt-caked windows on the east side of the building, revealing rows of wooden crates. It was hot in the vast dusty area and he felt sweat starting to gather on the nape of his neck. One of the men snapped rusted iron shackles onto his wrists. A short chain connected the shackles.

He didn't know what he felt at this moment. Stunned to start with, combined with a mixture of fear and anger. Yet, these emotions hadn't really filled him up yet. Right now, all he felt was a strange numbness.

He knew he needed to shake himself awake. He needed to think quickly, before the terror really took control of him. *There had to be a way to escape.* If his father had taught him anything, there was always a way.

Old pine crates big enough to hold three to four children each littered the dirt floor of the warehouse. The men dragged Needle to one of the crates and pried the lid off with a crowbar. It lifted with a screech of bent nails. They threw him inside where he landed in a tangle of arms and legs amongst three other people.

Slaves.

One of the goons reached in and locked his shackles onto a chain that connected the other slaves in the box. A number of small round holes in the walls of the crate provided a tiny amount of light and ventilation.

The goon then slammed the lid shut and pounded the nails back into place with a hammer, the sound thundering in the small confined space.

"Keep quiet in there! Unless you want a whipping, you hear?" The goon's footsteps faded away.

Needle felt his fear starting to peek up from his belly into his heart. He had to fight it off. He scrambled to find a place to sit. His heart felt clogged with thick immovable blood and struggled mightily to pump. What the holy hells had just happened to him? His mother had warned him. But never in a million years could he have guessed he would get sold into slavery.

One wrenching thought consumed him. If he stayed in this crate, his mother was going to die. There was no charity down in the Kuma where they lived. None at all.

"Move yer feet!" someone groaned. Needle jerked and looked at the slave crowded next to him inside the small confined space of the wooden crate. The dirty Agrabi boy across from him looked to be only 10 years old. Needle looked around. The slave to the right of him was a young Agrabi girl. Not much older than the boy, by the look of it. But the diminutive old man across from him was different.

Dressed in rags that might have once been white, he rested his white-bearded chin on his raised knees. His feet were bare, with long uncut toenails. The man had pale skin like the Buerdeleise, but his features were not Buerdeleise. Needle searched his memory. He had heard of folks like this, little folk, people from the far north.

"You a Rothkin?" he asked, momentarily distracted from the horror of his imprisonment by the funny-looking little man.

The old man looked up with bloodshot eyes. White scraggly eyebrows grew ferociously over his forehead. He nodded; peeling back chapped lips to reveal yellow splotched teeth.

"What you doing here?" Needle asked. He didn't know much about these folks other than what his mother had told him. They lived in a fabled green forest far away to the north. Despite their small size, they were fierce warriors. Occasionally, one of these small folk would come south, usually as exiles from their far-distant land, or as traders of pelts, exotic spices and strange fruits.

The man didn't answer.

The crate was lifted onto a wagon. More goons outside cussed and swore under the heavy load. In a few moments, the wagon began to move and exited the warehouse.

The sun beat down and Needle knew it would get hotter than the Abyss inside the crate. The wagon bumped along for a short ride and then came to a stop. Needle smelled the river and heard the calls of seagulls and herons.

They were unloaded by more burly goons and their crate was set down. Needle peered out one of the holes and could see the river. Their crate was on the edge of a barge which was aligned north-south. They must be pulled up and tied to a long dock, awaiting departure to Balankov.

The girl to his right started bawling. It was the most awful sound Needle had ever heard. He wanted to slap her, but then he suddenly felt what she must have been feeling. What was going to happen to her? He could only imagine what they did to young girls. His own fear was mounting, and this little girl's crying didn't help.

I have to get out of here, he realized. And in a moment of surprising altruism considering his destitute circumstances, he knew he needed to help the girl as well.

Eight Years Earlier – 29th Day of Summer – 7:00 AM – The Valley of Oar

"The Valley of Oar," Father said.

"Whoa--" Raju said.

They had left Demon's Bluff a week previous, traveling east for a few days on the old caravan route known only as "The Road" with their four camels. Then, without a landmark to guide him, Father had turned them northeast into the barren wastes of wide open sand dunes. How he knew where to turn, Raju had no idea. There had been nothing visible except the yellow sand piled into rolling dunes by the endless wind.

This morning, they topped a high yellow dune and looked down at a strange sight. Dark grease surrounded Raju's eyes, to cut down the glare from the bright sun. But here, the glare was gone. He couldn't believe what he was looking at. A few grains of sand, blown by the hot biting wind, skidded down to a hard, black, glassy surface about fifty feet ahead of them. The entire valley was filled with this smooth, black glass. It must be miles across.

"See that gnarled rock?" Father pointed ahead just slightly to the left. Far out into the sea of black glass, Raju saw the hump of black rock his father pointed at.

"That is where the wizard Malevolent came with his army. Over there Black Widow and Blot covered his left flank. Nepharus and Smoulder covered his right."

Raju was completely confused by his father's words. The camels kept plodding until they reached the edge of the black surface, then stopped and looked around, their large eyes blinking slowly. The camel Raju was riding groaned, and then smacked its lips together, showing its huge lower teeth.

Raju ignored the unsettled camel and stared out over the impossible glassy landscape. The sand blew over the edge of it for a few feet, but beyond that it was bare, black and smooth for miles.

"We'll have to go around it," Father said. "It is too hot to ride on, except on cloudy days."

"Who was Malevolent?"

His father didn't answer immediately; he seemed lost in his imagination. "Hundreds of thousands died in this valley, did you know that?"

"And those other names? Black Widow? Smoulder?" Raju asked.

Father snapped out of his contemplation. "The Battle of Oar was fought here. It was one of the largest and most hard-fought battles against the Cult of Yex over five thousand years ago. Malevolent was one of the nastiest, darkest wizards the Cult had, along with four of his apprentices. These guys were hellish apocalyptical giants of their time. Barely human. It is said they functioned on pure hatred."

Raju reflected on the names his father had spoken: Malevolent, Black Widow, Blot, Nepharus, Smoulder.

"All five died here," his father continued. "This was the defeat that forced the Cult's great commander, General Yazak Thuune, to retreat to the high mesa stronghold of the Cult. The mesa of Demon's Bluff is where the Cult made their last stand. It is where they were finally defeated by King Adirak and his companions."

"I don't understand," Raju said, but he wanted to understand. His father's excitement was contagious. A great battle! Terrible wizards! There was something about the place: dark and dangerous.

"They fought the battle against the armies of good, but their hatred was not enough," said Father. "Adirak's armies and his wizards gained the upper hand."

"What happened?" Raju asked breathlessly.

"Malevolent and his apprentices spent their life force to give power to their spells. They believed in their twisted cause so much that they gave their last breath to see it through. They called so much power at once that it created this blasted land you see. They scorched the earth."

Raju marveled. "Why don't the dunes cover it? They cover

everything else."

"Nobody knows for sure, but for thousands of years, the encroaching dunes have left this place alone. Some say that powerful magic still lingers and somehow keeps the sand at bay."

They sat in silence for a few moments, looking out over the amazing scene.

"Have you ever wondered why I dig up artifacts?" Father finally asked.

Raju considered. He had just recently discovered that his father's secret was that he dug up ancient relics from the Cult of Yex. It never occurred to the eight-year-old to wonder why.

"You sell them?"

Father beamed at him. "Yes."

Raju looked out over the black scarred valley. "But for other reasons too?"

Father nodded, his dark face splitting into a grin and those white teeth of his shined in the sunlight. Raju smiled back, understanding on some level the excitement his father felt finding lost artifacts.

"I don't see anything out there," Raju said.

Father shook his head. "All the artifacts here were recovered centuries ago. Or at least the ones that could be reached. No one has ever found a way to dig through this black rock to see what is underneath."

"So, where are we going?"

"Out beyond," Father said, patting the worn leather satchel on his saddle, which contained his papyrus maps. "That way," he pointed east by north east. "But, every good artifact hunter comes to see this valley. Got to feel it. Can you *feel* it, my boy?"

Raju nodded. He *did* feel it. He was too young to analyze what he was feeling, but there was a visceral draw to the place, an excitement that focused all his attention to this one spot. He now understood why his father sought artifacts. If it was anything like witnessing the blasted land before him, he wanted to search for them, too.

Father dug in one of his saddlebags and pulled out a set of shackles. Raju had seen them on prisoners in the city from time to time. Father tossed them to him and Raju deftly caught them with one hand while the other hand held onto the reins of his camel. The shackles clinked in his hands.

"Put those on," Father said.

Raju was taken aback.

"You are plenty old enough now. It's time for you to start learning the skills that will serve you well. My duty as your father is to teach you what my father taught me. Lock those on your wrists and then we'll see how long it takes you to get out of them."

Young Raju dropped the reins, fidgeted with the shackles and managed to bind both his hands in the metal cuffs.

Father nodded. "Now get out of them without the key."

Raju looked down at his bound hands. What in the world had just happened?

They traveled half a day, skirting the vast plain of black rock and then headed back out into the rolling yellow dunes of the desert, heading in a northeasterly direction.

All this time Raju's hands were bound before him. He rode his camel in them, ate in them and slept in them. His father would *not* release him. Every time Raju complained, his father said, "You remind me of me when my father put the shackles on *my* wrists."

He hated his father by the time he figured out how to open the shackles, three days later. He took two iron nails from one of the supply bags and holding a nail in one hand and another in his teeth, he managed to pick the first lock after hours of effort.

"Took me a week," Father said, grinning, when Raju finally cast the shackles down at his feet as they camped for the evening.

"Why didn't you tell me how to get out of them?" Raju asked with bitterness.

"You want to be able to help yourself?" asked Father. "You ever get in trouble, you need to be able to figure things out for yourself. No better teacher than that. Your mother protects you too much, and it's my responsibility to make you strong. Make you tough. This trip isn't just about coming along for the ride, Raju. I'm teaching you things, things my father taught me and his father taught him. These things will seem hard. But you'll learn to carry on the important work of our family. They may save your life one day."

Raju just stared at his father. None of that made any sense to his eight-year-old brain.

"Now put them back on and do it again," Father said as he stirred the pot of porridge he was cooking.

1st Day of Summer – 11:15 AM – The Docks - 14 Hours and 15 Minutes Before the Earthquake

Inside the slave crate, Needle forced himself to think. Somehow, the memory of his father's shackles had calmed him. Peering through the ventilation holes, he could see that several crates were stacked around his, and even on top, except for the one side that faced east looking out over the sluggish Demon River. He could smell the damp and hear the water birds out there. There was only one real avenue of escape: the river.

"Don't try to escape," the Agrabi boy to his left said, sensing what Needle was thinking. "They'll just whip us if we do."

The old Rothkin nodded. "Whipped me good once already, yes sir, yes they did."

"Well, I'm not staying here," Needle said. He thought of his father, that great man who in many ways was bigger in memory than he had ever been in real life. Father would not stay in this crate.

"Better chance of escape once they sell us off to someone," the old Rothkin advised.

Needle shook his head. His father had taught him patience, that's for sure, but right now was *not* the time for patience. He needed to get out now. His mother wouldn't survive two days without him, much less the month it would take him to get back from Balankov.

Only problem: how to get out? He couldn't pry the top off;

too many slave crates were stacked above him. He didn't imagine any amount of screaming or yelling would trick the guards into opening the box to see if everyone was okay. It would probably just result in a beating or a whipping. The only real option was to kick out the side of the crate and swim for it. After examining it carefully, he felt certain he could do it. The wood showed the first signs of dry rot and he still had his sturdy boots on. The other three in the crate all had bare feet. Maybe the goons were supposed to take his boots off and forgot in their haste. Two maybe three good kicks and he might be able open a hole big enough to wiggle through. Just a few feet to the water before the guards had time to react. Besides, it wouldn't be the first hole he had wiggled through in his life. Yet, he was chained to the other three prisoners, one of whom at least, he felt compelled to help.

He examined the shackles on his wrists. Standard locks. No problem, if he could find something to pick them with.

He looked around and spied a possible solution. One of the nails used to hammer the lid of the crate shut had slipped sideways and was protruding through the splintered wood. He might be able to make that work, but it would be an awkward angle. He still needed a second pick.

He examined his clothing. He was dressed in tattered trousers and a tunic, which hung loosely over his bony frame. Needle touched his stomach, feeling his ribs. He hadn't eaten well in over a year, since his father disappeared. Maybe there was an upside to not getting enough to eat. Considering how thin he was, he wouldn't have to kick a very big hole to squeeze through.

However, he had nothing on him he could use to pick the lock.

He looked at his fellow prisoners. The little girl had nothing on her, nor did the little boy. Both were quietly weeping. The old man was dressed even more sparsely than Needle.

Looking at the old man's feet, Needle had a sudden inspiration.

"Hey old man," Needle said, "You do me a favor?"

The Rothkin glared at him suspiciously.

"I need you to bite off the end of one of your toenails. I think

I can use it to open these locks."

The old man didn't move but his eyes hardened.

Needle didn't have time for this. He had suffered through various indignities for a year and he wasn't going to allow slavery to be added to the list.

He reached out and grabbed the smelly Rothkin's foot. The old man looked like he had swallowed a snake, he was so surprised. He yanked his leg back, but Needle was stronger than he looked. He hooked his arm around the old man's foot and leaned against him, holding him down.

The man's foot stank like soured clotted milk. Needle didn't care. Using his teeth, he chewed off a long, hard, yellow sliver of the man's big toenail. The man groaned like he had been knifed, clearly trying to keep his voice down for fear of another whipping from their captors, but all he was missing was a chunk of his overgrown toenail.

Needle spat out his prize into his palm and held it up to the light of a ventilation hole. The jagged shard might just be what he needed.

The old man shrunk away from him as Needle leaned up to the protruding nail. Levering the left lock on his shackles up into the nail, he used the toenail with his right hand.

It was incredibly hot and cramped in the crate, and sweat poured from his brow into his eyes. The odd angle he had to work with made the job very difficult and the salt of his sweat stinging his eyes made it even worse. But he kept working at it.

Suddenly the lock clicked open and his left hand was free.

"Hells, yes!" he said. He appreciated his father's lessons like he never thought he would.

Water splashed through the holes in the walls of the crate. Needle peered out and couldn't see what was going on as other crates blocked any view.

"They are splashing the crates with water to keep us cool," the young Agrabi boy said without emotion.

"They don't want their cargo to die," added the old Rothkin.

Needle turned his attention to the shackle on his right wrist. The cooler temperature made the job easier, and in short order, he had freed himself from the remaining shackle.

"Come here," he said to the little girl, smiling at her.

She shook her head, her eyes wide with fear and anger. She stared at him like he was doing something bad as she retreated further into the corner of the crate. Needle was confused. So he turned to the boy.

"You," he said.

The boy didn't move either, hiding his face in his arms. What was wrong with these kids? Did they *want* to stay slaves? Needle figured they were just too scared. He certainly could empathize. He felt the fear, too.

Needle looked at the old man questioningly. The old Rothkin just glared, shook his head.

Needle sighed. He looked back at the little girl. What could he do but offer her the chance to escape? *I can't force her*, he thought. If she's that scared, she won't go easily and she'll just get me caught again. Same with the boy.

"We can get out of here," he hissed at them all imploringly.

No one moved. Needle grit his teeth and hardened his heart. He had to. Someday, he might regret leaving them here, but right now he had to think about his mother.

He wedged himself with his back against one wall, pushing the boy and the girl to the side. He drew his legs in close to get the maximum force when his heels impacted the side of the crate.

He was about to start kicking when he heard someone yelling. The voices were far away but seemed to be growing. Crewmen seemed to be moving away from them toward the commotion. Time to hurry before the argument out there died down. He launched his adrenaline-fueled boot heels at the side of the crate facing the river and it splintered magnificently. Light poured in from the hole and he could see the muddy river stretching away to the far, green, eastern shore. He also saw a fishing boat bobbing along in the swell downriver a bit. Exhilaration powered his second kick and the hole blew open.

He squirmed through the opening with little difficulty out onto the bulwark of the barge.

He stayed low, and looking left and right, he estimated the barge was at least eighty feet long and the crate from which he emerged was stacked on the aft section. He heard someone call out, "Some damn kid busted out of a crate!" He could see a goon peering at him from down the row of crates to the left, but he couldn't reach Needle on account of all the other crates stacked up impeding the way.

Needle looked back at the girl. He felt a lump rising in his throat. His mouth was suddenly dry. Why did he care about this little girl? He had no idea why, he just knew he did. But he wasn't going to let her stop him from saving his mother.

He heard a man above him, on top of the stacked crates, reaching down for him. He looked to the left and right and saw goons navigating the walkways toward him. Most of the goons were distracted by whatever was happening on the other side of the barge by the dock and were heading that way. Another surge of adrenaline raced through him. It was working! He would make it!

He looked over the edge of the barge at the lazy flow of the river and saw the last thing he wanted to see: *rats*. Three mangy river rats were swimming at the edge of the barge, their disgusting claws scrabbling for a hold so they could climb aboard. Their beady eyes horrified him and he froze.

His heart pounded. The goons were getting closer. But he couldn't move. This was stupid. All he had to do is roll into the river, swim underwater and escape to freedom. But he couldn't. Rats. Filthy, mangy rats. His muscles would not respond. The mere thought of their soggy hair and their wormy tails overwhelmed him. Their filth permeated the water.

The goons were approaching.

Then he thought of his mother. She needed him. And he almost rolled in at that thought, but his brain was flooding with memories from his childhood: Ganger's Tomb, the wizard Boxxaway, that kid Cael, and the rats. Oh, he would never forget the rats.

Eight Years Ago – 43rd Day of Summer –7:00 AM – Eastern Desert

Two hard weeks after leaving the Valley of Oar, Raju still loved every minute of the journey. His father was not a warm man, but he was constantly engaged with Raju, whether telling stories, challenging him, or teaching him new skills.

After getting out of the shackles the second time, he never complained again, though his father devised even more difficult challenges for him. Raju at first hated them, but then began to love them. There was no surer way to get his father's praise than to succeed at one of his challenges.

Success often made his father happy enough to tell a story, and Raju *loved* his father's stories.

"I ever tell you about the first time I met a witch?" Father asked him after another day of searching the desert in vain. They had spent most of the day in the eastern sand with dunes as far as the eye could see. Not a single speck of life, not even lizard tracks graced the beautiful knolls of sand.

"A witch!" Raju exclaimed, shivering. His mother had filled him with witch stories, but the kind that gave him nightmares. Witches used dark and sinister magic. Not like wizards--a distinction Raju really didn't understand. They inscribed insane patterns from the far reaches of the multiverse. Most witches ended up insane after a lifetime of depredations. Their infamous exploits were legendary, at least from his mother's point of view. She seemed bent on protecting Raju from witches by making him afraid of them. But her stories had also created a strange fascination in him.

He had never heard his father talk about witches before. In fact, he had a sudden realization that his father always frowned whenever his mother started in on her stories about witches. This made him even more eager to hear his father's story.

"Well, she was beautiful; let me start off by telling you that." Father smiled. "Not scary like they always say."

That was the last thing that Raju expected his father to say. Beautiful. Not scary. Raju tried to digest that. Of course, they could be beautiful, but only to beguile you. Everyone knew that their true form was ugliness, twisted by the dark symbols they held kin with. Had his father been beguiled? Mother would certainly make that suggestion if she were here right now, delivered in a biting tone.

Unfortunately, he didn't get to hear the rest of the tale about the beautiful witch. It was at just at that moment he noticed something strange on the horizon.

"Father," Raju interrupted, "what's that?" He pointed across the dunes into a depression where the sun was reflecting off of something.

Father sat up in his saddle, squinting. "My boy! That's it! That's what we are looking for! But how did it get uncovered?" He started fumbling with an ancient scroll he kept in his saddlebag. His weathered hands, the backs covered in coarse black hair, shook with excitement as they held the map.

"Look," said Raju, his eyes sharper than his father's. "There's someone there!"

Father put his maps down with a bewildered frown. "Who in the Abyss is that?"

They plodded in silence, the dry heat pressing down upon them. The desert winds had abated and the air was still. Raju felt trepidation. He had never seen his father looked so worried and it scared him.

As they approached, Raju noted two things. First, jutting from the golden sand up to the height of a man was a pyramid of black, polished obsidian. Second, standing next to it was a very old pale-skinned Buerdeleise man with red linen robes and a white disheveled beard that was so long it almost trailed in the sand. A young Buerdeleise boy, who looked to be close to the same age as Raju, with uncombed, short brown hair stood at his side, also dressed in red linens. Three pack camels loitered several yards away near a pitched tent.

"Kemano Graji!" the old man called out in a booming voice that seemed incredibly out of place here in the desert. The old man seemed thrilled, like he had just found a long-lost friend.

Father turned to Raju and whispered, "How does he know my name?" There was confusion on his face. This was no 'old friend', that was for sure.

"You've never seen him before?" Raju replied.

Father bent over close. He whispered, "I *have* seen him with that boy down at the market. Shuffles around like an old codger haggling with the merchants. But I can't believe he made it out here. I thought he was just an old man. I heard tales he was a wizard once, but he burned out. He doesn't spend time with the wizards at the academy, though."

"Name's Boxxaway Hotheway," the old man called out with a broad grin that showed old yellow teeth. He struggled up to them as they reached the black, three-sided pyramid jutting from the sand. He extended a battered sun-browned hand upwards, which was a Buerdeleise custom, not an Agrabi one.

Father reluctantly leaned down and shook it, then warily dismounted.

"And this is my grandson, Cael," Boxxaway said, pointing to the young boy with him. The kid stared at them with a blank face.

"What are you doing out here?" Father asked, clearly trying to keep the edge from his voice.

"Why, I'm here, same reason as you!"

Raju clambered down from his camel, landing on the hot sand with a thud. The boy approached him shyly as his father and the old man continued to talk. "Hey, what's your name?"

"Raju."

"I'm Cael."

"Heard that already."

Cael stepped back with a hurt look in his eyes.

As if Raju would be nice to a Buerdeleise boy. The Agrabi didn't trust them one bit. He looked to his father, who was talking with Boxxaway.

"... and we got here about two days ago," Boxxaway was saying. "And look at this. If you look real close, you can see scratch marks all around the edges near the top. The marks were here already when we uncovered the top of the structure. It looks like someone has tried to break into this tomb. I am guessing they weren't successful."

"Tomb robbers were common in the ancient times," Father said as he hunkered down. He brushed some sand away from the base of the pyramid with his fingers. "Did you notice this?"

It took Boxxaway almost half a minute to get his old frame that low to the ground as he bent down on one knee. He looked in close at where Father was pointing.

"Well, I'll be! I did *not* notice that before! Your eyes are sharp, my friend. Mine are not what they once were."

Raju and Cael eagerly shuffled through the sand to look, and there right where Father was pointing were faint scratches that formed an eerie symbol:

It was the first time either of the young boys had ever seen the symbol, but it surely wouldn't be the last.

"The Cult of Yex," Boxxaway breathed in awe.

"You know of them?" Father asked with a surprised look on his face.

"Of course I do," Boxxaway said in what Raju interpreted as a defensive tone.

"No ordinary grave robbers tried to break into this tomb," Father said. "It was the Cult, and it looks like they left their evil mark when they failed to crack it. These scratches surely date back to near the fall of the Cult over five thousand years ago."

"I thought this tomb was made by the Cult," Boxxaway said.

"Don't you know who is buried here?" Father replied.

"Isn't this the tomb of Ganger?" Boxxaway asked uncertainly. "I thought he was an important figure in the cult."

Raju looked at Cael. The boy was listening intently. Raju had initially disliked him, but now felt a sort of kinship with him. The two children were both confused by all these events, but still very interested. There was something about these histories that fascinated Raju on a level he couldn't explain. And his initial worry over meeting Boxxaway was gone. Father had settled down and so he felt less agitated.

"It is Ganger's tomb, all right," Father said. "He died long before the Cult fell. When the Cult still controlled this territory.

They sealed him here in a tomb befitting a fallen leader of his stature to protect his body for a time when they might try to recall him from the grave. He was the Cult's greatest infiltrator and spy. But when Adirak's forces captured this ground, they sealed his tomb to prevent the Cult from reopening it. It looks as if Adirak's seal has held for all this time. Clearly, the Cult tried to open it and failed."

"I can't open it, either," continued Boxxaway, rubbing his forehead. "I puzzled over it for two days. Ugh! I shouldn't have had any trouble with this. I'm good at opening things, but hells, I can't figure this one out. It's stumping me."

Father smiled. "That's because this tomb wasn't sealed with wizard magic, old man."

Boxxaway raised an eyebrow in expectation.

"Witch magic," Father said with a grin.

Boxxaway took two steps backward, wonderment on his face. "Well, that would certainly explain it," he chuckled. "But, that would mean Adirak had witches working for him against the Cult?"

Raju could see relief on his father's face and felt a burst of pride himself. This old Buerdeleise wizard didn't know half as much as his father did! "Witch magic isn't as bad as you might think," Father said.

Raju wished he had been able to hear the rest of his father's story about the beautiful witch.

"So I presume you know how to open it?" Boxxaway asked.

"How come it's all glass?" Raju interjected.

Father looked down at him and smiled. "It looks like glass, son, but it's not. It's a black rock called obsidian that has been polished until it shines like glass. The Cult of Yex favored obsidian because legend says that obsidian originates in the Abyss itself. It could also be polished to make a slippery surface that would make it difficult for tomb robbers to scale it. The entrance to these tombs is always at the very top. For us, the sand has piled up over the centuries, and we now stand at the top of the vast pyramid. It continues down hundreds of feet below us into the sand."

"This area wasn't always a desert," said Boxxaway. "The desert sands have moved in over the thousands of years since the Cult of Yex was here. I don't think the tomb builders expected it to be buried by the sand. It's good for us, because it would be very hard to climb otherwise."

"You still haven't explained," said Father, "how in the Abyss you came to be here out in the desert. And why."

Boxxaway turned his attention back to Father. "I think we have a common acquaintance up on the Middle Steppe. Dagorn Bygrave hired me to find the tomb."

Raju watched his father's face move from bewilderment, to anger, then back to bewilderment. "He hired *me* to find this tomb. Why would he hire you as well?"

"I think he was just impatient. Probably wanted a backup," shrugged Boxxaway. "Several weeks ago, he offered to pay me a handsome sum if I could bring him something called The *Ring of Dekrys*. He told me everything he knew about where it might be, including that it was hidden in the ancient tomb of Ganger. I have an amateur interest in the history of the Cult, so I took him up on the offer. Don't want to ruffle your feathers. I didn't know you were hired as well."

Father didn't say a thing. Just looked angry.

"So how do you open it?" asked Boxxaway.

Father quickly snapped out of his anger. "How did you find the tomb? Dagorn certainly didn't know where it was."

"It was quite simple, really," Boxxaway said. "Dagorn showed me a map with the locations of other tombs that had already been found. I presume you were the one that discovered them?"

Father waited expectantly.

"Something about the way the tombs were positioned on the map seemed very familiar to me. I took the map home with me, and after studying it for a few hours, it came to me: The Dragon."

Father scrunched up his nose to signal that he didn't understand.

"The stars," Boxxaway said, looking skyward despite it being day. "The location of the tombs were in a pattern trying to form the constellation of The Dragon. Only one star was missing."

Father's mouth opened in utter amazement. He turned and

walked over to his camel, dug through one of the saddle bags, and came up with a bundle of parchment tied with a leather thong. He shuffled through the papers and pulled out a map as he stalked back. "I can't believe I didn't see it before," Father said staring at the map. "I made this map and I never saw the obvious. It couldn't be clearer. Ganger's tomb is the only star missing, and it's right here, exactly where it should be. Unbelievable."

"So, how did *you* find it?" Boxxaway asked.

Father quickly folded his map up as if concealing something. "I have my resources."

Boxxaway smiled, accepting that without argument. "So, how do you open the thing?"

Father grumbled under his breath and went back to his camel. He stuffed his papers back in and took out a flask with a cork stopper. "You need a special concoction prepared by a witch to reveal the hidden markings that protect the tomb."

"How do you know a witch?" Boxxaway asked, narrowing his eyes. Raju was wondering the exact same thing.

Father didn't answer. Instead, he slogged through the sand to the glass pyramid. It was incredibly hot. Sweat beaded on his brow and gathered in his eyebrows. He opened the vial and poured the clear liquid out onto the peak of the black pyramid.

Raju was surprised that the liquid did not behave as it should have. It didn't run down the sides of the three-sided pyramid like water, but instead oozed slowly and was absorbed by the black rock as if the stone were drinking it in.

A bluish glowing horizontal line appeared a few inches down from the top of the pyramid. Raju shifted a few feet to the left and saw that the line continued to wrap around to the second side of the pyramid. He surmised it circled to the third, but before he could check, a symbol appeared below the line, also glowing in blue. The symbol resembled an eye, although it was turned sideways. He shifted to the left again, and sure enough, the symbol appeared on the second side of the pyramid. He walked through the sand to see the third side of the pyramid. Yes, all three sides were inscribed. Raju envisioned that looking at the pyramid from the top down, they would form a connected symmetrical pattern.

Father stepped over to Raju and whispered in his ear while Boxxaway was transfixed by the symbols on the pyramid, "I have been trying for years to find this tomb."

The excitement in his voice bordered on giddiness. Raju couldn't help but be excited too. He just wished Boxxaway and Cael weren't here. It would be much better to enjoy this moment alone with his father. He suddenly wondered what his mother would think if she knew what they were doing, and that his father knew a witch.

"Now what?" Boxxaway asked as he approached the symbols for a closer look.

"Well," said Father, "now that the lock has been revealed, all we must do is open it." He leaned in close to the intricate symbol on the panel nearest him and studied it for several seconds before he reached out and placed his finger on the symbol at a point near the center of it. "Let's see if I can remember how to do this. It's kind of confusing."

"You're the witch!" Boxxaway breathed.

"Of course I'm not," said Father. "But I *do* know one. You don't think I'd come all this way to Ganger's Tomb and then not be able to open it, do you?"

Boxxaway took two steps closer to get a better look at what he was doing.

"Everyone keep quiet for a few minutes while I try to remember how to do the pattern," said Father.

It took Father about a dozen tries as he dragged his finger along the lines of the glowing connected pattern on all three sides of the pyramid before he finally got it right.

With a click, the triangular panels of the pyramid separated with a loud hissing noise as ancient air escaped from the tomb.

Raju staggered backward, wrinkling his nose. "What stinks

so bad?"

"It's just stale air. I've smelled worse," said Father, also stepping backward, but not taking his eyes off the top of the pyramid.

The panels separated from each other and slowly flipped open as if the bottom sides were on some unseen hinge, revealing a triangular gaping hole in the top of the pyramid.

Boxxaway stood transfixed. "What were those symbols?"

Father hesitated slightly, then said, "It's a witch sealing sigil. It is designed to seal the tomb in such a way that only a witch could open it. Or someone who has help from a witch."

"They kind of look like eyes, don't they?" Boxxaway said.

Raju was still very young, but somehow he knew his father was hiding something from the old wizard. Raju had watched Boxxaway's eyes squint almost imperceptibly in reaction to his father's reply. What did his father know about the eye symbols that he did not want Boxxaway to know?

"What about Dagorn?" Father asked.

Boxxaway frowned. "We split the bounty, I guess. It would be the only fair accommodation, I expect. After all, we make a good team. Neither one of us could have done it without the other."

"That's not true," Father said. "I am the one who opened it, and I found the pyramid without you."

Boxxaway shrugged. "But I found it first. That's the point. The only fair option is that we split the bounty."

Father chewed his bottom lip for several moments with a worried look on his face. "I suppose you're right. I guess we don't have any other options, do we?" he said with a resigned sigh.

Boxxaway strode to the edge of the hole at the top of the pyramid and squinted as he peered down into it. "I think we need to drop a torch down there."

Father moved up and so did Raju. Cael was already there.

He looked down. Rusted iron rungs bolted to one wall led down the shaft into darkness.

Eight Years Ago – 43rd Day of Summer –9:00 AM – Ganger's Tomb

"What in the Abyss?" Father breathed. "Now what do we do?"

They were deep under the level of the sand now, inside the tomb itself. They had climbed down the shaft and progressed slowly through narrow passages and vaulted antechambers, making their way carefully lit by flickering torchlight as Raju's father disarmed traps designed to maim or even kill tomb raiders.

Raju paid rapt attention as his father artfully disabled trap after trap. He beamed at his father's confidence and skill. He wanted nothing more than to learn the things that his father knew. He wanted to make his father proud. Boxxaway and his grandson contributed nothing as far as Raju could tell, and that hardly justified their taking half the treasure.

Eventually, they came to a dead end. The passage had ended in a solid wall of thick sandstone, with only a single opening about a foot square in the middle of the wall. It was a thin shaft that continued deep into the rock ahead.

"Maybe we missed something?" said Boxxaway, clearly without an idea of where to go from here. They had not found any treasure at all, much less the *Ring of Dekrys*, which was the most prized artifact that was rumored to be buried in this tomb.

"I don't think so," said Father. "I have been in many similar tombs and I know we didn't miss a hidden door or anything like it. I know how to spot them. But, I've never seen something like this."

"It would take days to chip through that rock, maybe weeks," Boxxaway mumbled.

Father simply nodded his head. He thrust the smoky torch down the narrow shaft, hoping to be able to see further in.

"Wait a minute. I think this shaft opens into a chamber

down there. Maybe fifteen feet in."

"Do you think you can slide a torch all the way into the chamber?" asked Boxxaway.

Father had no trouble shoving the torch all the way down the passage where it disappeared into the chamber at the end, falling in with a shower of sparks. Shadows flickered within the chamber

"Ah!" exclaimed Father's muffled voice. He had stuck his head into the opening of the shaft to get the best view. He removed his head and said, "The chamber looks small. I can see a lever on the far wall. I'm sure we just need to work the lever to open the way. But I don't see a way we could reach it. Even if we had a long pole, we could never get the leverage we need."

"You need a wizard," said Boxxaway.

Father raised his eyebrows quizzically.

"This tomb was clearly constructed so than only a powerful wizard could open it," Boxxaway explained. "I guess the builders assumed that regular tomb robbers would never have a wizard to work that lever telekinetically."

"Well, old man, it's a good thing you are here after all!" exclaimed Father. "Time to earn your money."

"It's not that simple for an old ember like me."

"Ember?" asked Father.

"A burned out wizard. In my youth, I didn't restrict my use of magic as I should have, and I spent myself in the process. Let's just say, I'm not quite as old as I look. I'm afraid I'm not much use as a spell caster anymore."

"How old are you then?"

"Never you mind about that. We should turn our attention to finding another solution."

They were arguing about their umpteenth possible approach when Raju finally proffered what was clearly the only solution. "I can fit through that shaft," he said.

The two men stopped their debate and turned to look at Raju.

Father looked from Raju to the hole, then back to Raju. "It's a good thought, my son, but that shaft is too narrow for even your skinny frame."

"I can fit, Father! I know I can!" Raju said. He straightened up as his own words filled him with confidence.

"Well, I suppose we can let you try it," said Father after several moments of thought, though he sounded unconvinced. "But I'm going to tie a rope to your feet so we can pull you back out of the shaft in case you get stuck in there."

"I won't get stuck! I can make it. You'll see."

Fifteen minutes later, Raju was halfway down the shaft with the rope tied securely to his left ankle. The fit was incredibly tight and he had almost no room to maneuver. His arms were stretched out straight in front of him and he had to lift his weight up on his knees and elbows, which were getting incredibly sore and raw as they scraped inch by inch along the rough sandstone. Raju kept creeping forward without complaint, despite the pain. It wasn't all that different from wriggling free from the ropes in which he had been bound in another of his father's trials. He could imagine his father's pride. He could catch bits and pieces of the conversation going on behind him.

"Look at that!" Boxxaway's voice exclaimed. "The boy looks just like a needle and thread."

"The tomb's architects clearly didn't anticipate a thin Agrabi boy, that's for sure," Father's voice said. "Yep. Just like a needle!"

It took another twenty minutes or so for him to reach the end of the shaft. He hung his arms over the edge and let them hang into the cobweb-draped, dusty chamber as he rested for a few minutes. His elbows were rubbed skinned and bloody. He imagined his knees were the same. He craned his head and surveyed the room.

It was a small antechamber, maybe ten feet square. The floor was only a few feet below from where he emerged into the room and was paved with sandstone tiles. The torch his father had slid into the room still burned, casting eerie shadows on the walls. Several small square holes lined the walls at floor level. The only other distinguishing feature was a large Cult of Yex symbol in bas relief on the wall directly across from the mouth of the shaft; an iron lever was set into the wall in the center of the symbol.

"You okay, my boy?" asked father's voice from behind him.

"Yes. Just resting for a moment."

"Do you think you can pull that lever?"

"Yes I think so, in a minute."

He took a deep breath and slithered out of the shaft and plopped onto the floor of the small chamber, careful to avoid touching the torch and burning himself. He then untied the rope from his ankle.

"What do you see?" asked the old wizard.

"Just the lever. It is set in the middle of a big Cult symbol."

He felt excitement fill him as he walked the few steps over to the rusty lever mounted in the wall. As he walked across the tile, he felt and heard a click. The click was soon followed by a grinding that sounded like stone on stone. The sandstone tile he had just stepped on was a pressure plate and it had depressed about an inch into the floor.

He whirled, looking for something to react to. But nothing seemed to be happening. Then he heard it. It started as just a faint series of clicks, and what sounded like squeaks. They seemed to be coming from the holes that ringed the room.

Then it happened. Streams of rats poured from the small square holes; their eyes burned with an unnatural, hellish glow.

He screamed out, his own voiced echoing robustly throughout the chamber. He recoiled away from the rat swarm, panic filling his chest, but there was nowhere to go.

He could hear his father's voice calling out in a rapid high-pitch, but he couldn't comprehend the words. The rats were almost upon him when he truly began to understand what he faced.

The rats weren't alive.

The army of glowing red eyes that closed in on him was kept alive beyond the capacity of their bodies to sustain life. Bones and ribs showed through holes in the desiccated mangy flesh. Some of the zombie rats weren't much more than simple skeletons with patches of fur clinging to the bones like desert flies on sweaty camel hide. A cheeping, skittering army of undead vermin sustained by evil necromantic sorcery set upon him with mindless focus.

"R-r-r-rats!" was all he could scream as the skeleton-tailed horde began gnawing at the fleshy parts of his feet and toes that protruded through the straps of his sandals.

He had never really been scared like this before. Snakes, snails, spiders, mice, none of them had scared him as a child. But now he felt it. His muscles would not, could not respond. He couldn't think; he could barely breathe. He knew that he must reach the iron lever and jerk it down, but he stood frozen, unable to move.

And still, the rats poured from the holes. The undead creatures had begun to climb up his legs. He could feel their claws poking through his linen trousers, the weight of their bodies pulling downward on the material. His vision was going black. He feared that in seconds he would collapse on to the floor, still unable to help himself. If he was screaming, he was barely conscious of it.

The rats pressed inexorably on, their claws digging into his legs, hoisting themselves up higher and higher.

His paralysis was complete, he couldn't move, but he certainly could feel each bite, claw, and scratch.

He thought of his father. He would be disappointed in him. He thought of his mother. He would never see her again.

1st Day of Summer – 11:30 AM – The Docks - 14 Hours Before the Earthquake

It was the memory of his mother that really saved Needle as he lay on his stomach at the edge of the barge looking into the muddy flow of the Demon River. He thought of his mother and he knew he had to help her. Even if it meant facing his greatest fear and plunging into the rat-infested waters.

The goons were almost upon him. They would lock him back up in the crate, and he would be sold as a slave, after a torturous whipping. He would *not* get another opportunity to escape.

He forced himself to ignore the prospect of rats in the water. He focused on his mother, shut his eyes, held his breath and rolled over the side of the barge. Rats or no, he was swimming for it.

The water was surprisingly warm, but it shocked him nonetheless. He kicked off the side of the barge with his feet and swam away as hard as he could. His scrawny muscles, starved for proper nutrition, just couldn't provide the speed he needed. A searing pain exploded on the top of his head. He swiveled his head to see what had hit him. It took his eyes a moment to focus. One of the goons stood there holding forth a long wooden pole with a hook on the end.

Needle could feel the reverberation of the jarring impact all the way down his spine. The goon was trying futilely to use the hook to get hold of him and pull him back in, but Needle's momentum had carried him out of the goon's reach. Needle reached up to feel the top of his head and his hand was covered in blood. He felt extremely dizzy and struggled to keep his head above water in the lazy current. He felt himself start to slip under the water into darkness.

Eight Years Ago – 43rd Day of Summer –11:00 AM – Ganger's Tomb

Needle's eyes were shut tight, and his arms protected his face as the zombie rats swarmed all over him. Needle's muscles were paralyzed in panic as their icy claws scratched him. He felt the searing pain of dozens of little teeth sinking into the exposed flesh of his feet, his arms and the back of his neck. The pain was intense, but not as intense as the terror that gripped his soul. *He was being devoured alive.*

Suddenly, bright flashes assaulted his eyes through his shut eyelids. To his utter amazement, the rats stopped gnawing on him. The pain of dozens of bites lingered on, but the little zombies had stopped their assault. The bright flashes continued and he could feel the rats falling off of him.

Needle opened his eyes in bewilderment at his miraculous reprieve. A shower of sparks sprayed into the chamber from the opening of the shaft through which he had entered. Countless sparks showered the floor, bouncing and dancing as they impacted until they popped soundlessly in a final eruption. Many of the sparks lit on him and Needle expected to feel the heat, but they were cool to the touch. The zombie rats had scattered to the far edges of the room to avoid the sparking lights that poured in. Many of the rats crammed against themselves as they fled back into the holes and the rest huddled in great clumps in the traffic jam at the exits.

Needle slowly became aware of his father's voice echoing in the room. He was shouting down the shaft, fear in his voice. *"Pull the lever! Can you hear me? Son? You must pull the lever!"*

In a haze, Needle got to his feet. Some of the rats were growing accustomed to the sparking lights and were cautiously turning toward him again.

He didn't hesitate. He lunged for the iron lever set in the wall and jerked it down with all his weight. It creaked, moving slowly at first and then slid free in a rush. Needle lost his balance and impacted the floor. The last thing he remembered before he blacked out was the grinding sound of stone on stone.

1st Day of Summer – 11:35 AM – Demon River – 13 Hours and 55 Minutes Before the Earthquake

Needle struggled hopelessly as he sank below the surface. The muddy water filled his mouth and he could taste the dirt and silt in it. Far off echoes of churning water and faint voices could be heard like distant unremembered sounds in a dream. His mother would die anyway because hadn't been fast enough to escape. The rat-faced man would win. In moments, his lungs would flood with water and that would be the merciful end. If his father had died a year ago, Needle took comfort in the fact that he was about to see him again in the next life.

Blackness descended upon him when suddenly he felt a hand grab the back of his tunic. He felt himself being hauled upward to the surface. Had the goons found a way to capture him anyway? Needle had given himself up for dead. Since his father had disappeared, life had been harder than he could imagine. The ignominy of slavery after a near merciful death was more than he could bear.

He gasped for air as he broke the surface of the river. Sunlight blinded him momentarily as he felt himself being pulled up against the side of a small boat. Arms held him against the side to keep him from sinking back under the water.

"Raju 'Needle' Graji!" a familiar old voice exclaimed. "Seems like every time I bump into you, you need saving!"

Eight Years Ago – 43rd Day of Summer –11:15 AM – Ganger's Tomb

They stood in the hidden burial chamber before the sarcophagus of Ganger himself. The air was cool, humid and smelled stale. Thousands of years of undisturbed dust and cobwebs covered everything.

Sadly, the treasure horde didn't appear as big as Needle had imagined.

"The Cult was under pressure," his father said. "They didn't have the resources to spend lavishly on their fallen. I'm sure the tomb itself strained their treasury."

Together, they all pushed at the lid of the stone casket. It slid slightly and a burst of stale air rushed out. They pushed the lid off to the side and it cracked with a thunderous sound as it struck the floor.

"Ganger himself," Boxxaway breathed, as they gazed at the contents. There was a mummy inside, wrapped in stained linens, many of which had deteriorated badly. The mummified face was visible through the crumbling rags. A complicated pair of wire rimmed spectacles with thick, dust-covered lenses was still perched on the mummy's desiccated nose.

Ganger's burial chamber was adjacent to the lever room where the undead rats had attacked Needle. Apparently, when he had pulled the lever, the rats fled as the huge sandstone block with the shaft through the middle of it descended into the floor to open the way. Needle didn't remember any of this, as he had knocked himself out in his rush to pull the lever. It also lowered another sandstone block on the left, revealing a passage that opened into where they now stood: before the sarcophagus of Ganger himself.

"You did it, Son!" Father had said to him as he regained consciousness. Needle felt ashamed because he had frozen when the rats came. He did not deserve his father's praise.

"Where did the sparks come from? They chased away the rats."

Boxxaway piped up. "That was my grandson here! Cael here is my apprentice. Sparking like that is an exercise in focusing magic that all apprentice wizards start with."

"We made a good team," the boy said.

Needle felt conflicted about Cael, even though the boy had saved his life. Needle knew that that last comment was made simply to justify their taking half his family's treasure. Needle was furious with himself for giving these two interlopers an excuse to help and justify their thievery.

Father had smeared an herbal salve that smelled of honey from a shallow clay pot on his wounds and they had stopped aching. "We need to get those bites healing up right away my boy. It won't do to have your mother worrying about your battle scars." Needle could see his father swelling with pride he didn't deserve. "She'd never let you come out here with me again."

Once Needle had been cared for, they all turned their attention to the crypt. Ganger's sarcophagus was obvious; it was the only one, and was the central focus of the room.

"The *Ring of Dekrys* is supposed to be here," Father started to say as they all bent down and peered at the mummy in the stone coffin. It smelled like old people. An odor Needle hadn't smelled since he was very young at his grandmother's. He was curious and disgusted at the same time and couldn't believe he was really standing in an ancient pyramid. There was a sense of awe and sacredness to the occasion that he would never forget.

"Indeed," Boxxaway nodded and moved toward the head of the mummy.

Needle saw his father lock his gaze with Boxxaway, and

then both men reached for the mummy. Father reached for the right hand of the mummy and began tearing away the bandages. He revealed a desiccated hand, but no ring.

Father moved to the left hand and started tearing at the bandages when Boxxaway said: "Aha!" The old man had been digging around the corpse's head and neck, and he held up a golden chain with his right hand as he adjusted his robes with his left. Upon the chain hung an onyx ring.

"The *Ring of Dekrys,*" Boxxaway breathed.

"What is it?" Needle asked.

"Ganger was a master spy for the Cult of Yex back when they were at the peak of their power," he explained to them. "That was just before they tried to summon their master into this world. He had a rare ability, a curse some would have said. He could control his shape. He could look like and impersonate other people. It made him a very effective spy."

"How do you know this is really him then?" Cael asked.

"It doesn't really matter," Boxxaway said. "What matters is that we have the ring. It was said that this ring allowed him to control his changes. Without it, he was wild. And it is this object that Dagorn wants so badly."

Needle saw the exultant look on Boxxaway's face and felt anger that this old goon would take half his family's bounty, not to mention he had the ring itself. He looked to his father and saw a curious thing. As Boxxaway was transfixed on the relic, his father continued to dig at the wrapping on the left hand of the mummy. Needle saw his father's hand move so fast it was a blur. When he straightened up, there was nothing in his hand. But hadn't Needle seen a silvery glint? Or was it a trick of the dancing torchlight in this horrific tomb?

He looked at his father's face. It betrayed no hint of emotion. But that in and of itself was a clue that even eight-year-old Needle picked up.

1st Day of Summer – 11:35 AM – The Demon River – 13 Hours and 55 Minutes Before the Earthquake

It took Needle several moments to realize what was happening. It wasn't one of the goons that had pulled him from the edge of drowning. It was the old burned-out wizard Boxxaway Hotheway. His mind was still trying to grapple with the improbability of what was happening to him. He remembered the slavers and looked quickly to the barge.

Three men, the two goons and one large barrel-shaped man with a black ratty beard and a red sunburned face stood on the side of the barge. Boxxaway's skiff was drifting toward the barge and one of the goons managed to hook it with the long pole and pull it up alongside. With Boxxaway's help, Needle managed to pull himself into the boat, almost overturning a small clay jar filled with wriggling worms, next to a cane fishing pole.

"That's my slave," the large man said.

Boxxaway frowned. "I didn't foresee this," he muttered. Then louder to the man, "I don't suppose an argument about the illegality and immorality of slavery will persuade you to let this child go?"

The big man just smiled, a wicked smile that confirmed Boxxaway's supposition.

Boxxaway shrugged. "I didn't think so."

"We'll take the boy," the man said, stepping forward again.

Boxxaway looked around. No one was near. It was an old man and a half-drowned kid against a huge man and his two cohorts. Not good odds.

"How much do you want for him?" Boxxaway said, pulling a small black pouch from his robes.

The man paused, looking at Needle briefly. "He's scrawny but he'll fetch eight silver moons in Balankov."

Boxxaway sighed. He seemed angry underneath his resignation. He tossed the pouch into the air and the big man caught it. The man opened the pouch, and began counting the coins.

"You'll find twelve in the pouch. A premium price and no cost of transport."

The man watched Boxxaway with intense eyes.

Needle studied the man's face as he considered his options. Greed won out and Needle realized that the man meant to take him anyway and keep Boxxaway's money. It was after all, three against two. And Boxxaway was an old man and he, a mere boy.

At exactly that moment there was a sound from behind the men on the barge, and a voice called out, "What in the Abyss is going on here, Vosc?"

The big man turned, startled. Boxxaway, faster than Needle could have imagined, reached out and unhooked the boat. He shoved off from the side of the barge and grabbed the oars in their locks and started rowing down river. The captain and his goons were too preoccupied with whoever had confronted them.

"That was close," Boxxaway breathed as they swept out of sight of the barge.

"What in the holy hells are you doing here?" Needle asked, his hand pressed against his bleeding scalp.

"Fishing," Boxxaway said flatly, pulling Needle's hand away from his head. "Ah, it's just a scratch. Scalp wounds bleed heavily." Boxxaway replaced Needle's hand. "Keep pressure on it for a while, while I think of a way around the new problem in my plans. I needed those moons to get you to the top of the mesa tonight."

"You knew I was going to be here?" Needle asked. It was common knowledge that wizards could use divination, but it was still jarring to think the old man could know something that specific.

"We need to find a way to make eight silvers for you, and fast," Boxxaway said, still pulling at the oars. He looked worn out.

The day couldn't get worse. It started when he got caught sneaking into the Thieves' Guild, got beaten and sold into slavery and almost drowned. The only thing worse than that as far as he was concerned was to be rescued by this old wizard. After all, it was his fault that his family had begun the slow descent into poverty in the first place.

"You got anything to eat?" Needle asked.

Eight Years Ago – 43rd Day of Summer –1:15 PM – Ganger's Tomb

They had loaded the *Ring of Dekrys* and the other artifacts from Ganger's tomb onto the pack camels and the four of them caravanned home together through the roiling desert. Needle's father was uncharacteristically quiet for most of the journey home and Needle sensed his concern. One night as he and his father lay on their bedrolls in their tent, Needle asked him what was wrong.

"There weren't as many artifacts in Ganger's tomb as I had hoped. That, coupled with having to split the bounty on everything with Boxxaway, I won't make as much as I needed."

"I don't understand, Father."

"Don't worry, Son. I'll just have to find more artifacts."

"I'll help you, Father."

"I know you will, Son. I know you will."

But things would never be the same for Needle's family. Father, in an effort to earn back his losses, went on more expeditions. But Boxxaway continued hunting for artifacts to sell to Dagorn and the increased competition made it difficult for his father. The losses mounted, as did his father's humiliation at losing treasures to the old wizard.

They lost their cottage in the Abala Ku, needing to sell it. It was only the first of a series of moves, each one to a smaller cottage. By the time Father had disappeared a year ago, they were living in the Kuma, the slum of Demon's Bluff. It didn't get worse than that.

And since his father's disappearance, it had fallen to Needle to support his mother. Needle also knew the sting of shame and humiliation his father had felt, for he too had ultimately failed in his duty.

Things couldn't get much worse. Needle had been desperate for money and it had all started with Boxxaway.

1st Day of Summer – 11:40 AM – Boxxaway's Dinghy – 13 Hours and 50 Minutes Before the Earthquake

"Why didn't you just let me drown?" Needle asked. This was Boxxaway, after all, the man who had showed up with his snotty grandson in the middle of the desert and stolen half the bounty in Ganger's tomb.

Boxxaway seemed to read his mind. "It wasn't me, Needle. You have to understand we were on the same side. It was your father who turned it into a rivalry. But I can help you, just like I tried to help him."

Needle knew that any help Boxxaway gave him would come with a price too high to pay. Just like at Ganger's tomb, help from Boxxaway just made things worse in the long run.

But what choice did he have? He was starving, his mother was starving, and death was a real possibility if things didn't improve soon.

"How?" Needle asked.

"This isn't about you," Boxxaway said, his voice kind and soft. "This is about something much bigger. Perilous times are upon us. I am going need your help soon, Needle, in ways that you can't comprehend."

Needle laughed. "Go ahead and tell me, old man!"

Boxxaway frowned. "You'll find out, tonight. I have figured out a way I can help you out with money. In exchange, I need you to be at the Bygrave Mausoleum on Gadrax Row on the top of Demon's Bluff at midnight. It's in the old section of the cemetery."

"If I left now to hike the back way to the top of the plateau," said Needle, "I'd never make it by tonight, even if I believed you!"

"You'll just have to ride the lifts then, won't you?"

"Ha!" exclaimed Needle in a sharp burst. The old man had clearly gone mad. A ride on the lifts to the top of the mesa cost eight moons. The wizards at the academy had created the lifts to transport themselves and wealthy patrons up and down the cliff face, but at a price that common folk could never pay.

"Needle, look at me. It is important that you be there tonight at midnight. Yes, it's expensive to ride the lifts," said Boxxaway, "but I can get the money for the lifts for you, and more."

1st Day of Summer – 12:45 PM – Warehouse in Demon's Bluff – 12 Hours and 45 Minutes Before the Earthquake

"You know I can't afford any of this," Needle said to Boxxaway an hour later as he looked at the treasures piled in front of him inside a dusty old warehouse. Boxxaway's old dog sniffed about lazily as they spoke.

Holy hells, he had never seen such a trove in his whole life, even after spending years with his father in the desert. His eyes bulged with envy. His father would have been speechless if he could have seen this. It wasn't gold, or silver or jewels. It was better. There were spearheads blunted and splotched with rust, dull knives, a short sword with a broken hilt. There was a small buckler marked with the symbol of the Yex, a helm with a dragon symbol on it, greaves and other implements of war and several panels of pounded brass with etchings in a language Needle did not recognize. Ceremonial goblets and small braziers and more dotted the pile. Needle was stunned. Clearly, Boxxaway had made finds that he never told Father about. Needle flushed in anger at the old wizard as he realized that even a fraction of this treasure trove could have kept his family from poverty.

"Afford it? I told you, boy. We're making a trade," the old man said, coughing into his hand. His breath smelled of medicinal tea. "I'll pick out some of the pieces for you to take in a gunny sack. Take it to Dagorn and sell it to him. It should get you more than the eight moons you need to get to the top of the mesa. The rest, use it to help your mother."

Needle looked at the old man to detect some deceit in his face, but Boxxaway just coughed again. Was that a spot of blood in his spittle, caught in the grey wisps of his white beard?

"You stole all this from my father," Needle accused.

"Can I help it if I am good at finding artifacts?" the old man smiled and those yellow teeth flashed.

"But my family has been finding the treasures for generations, "said Raju."It's how we eat. And you come along and take it away from us. Like every other Buerdeleise, you take what the Agrabi found first."

"I know you blame me for your family's hardships, but you're wrong to think that way."

"I blame you for my father's disappearance," said Needle hotly.

Boxxaway shrugged. "Please, Needle. What could I have done to your father?"

"He wouldn't be missing if we hadn't been poor, and he wouldn't be poor if it weren't for you." Anger washed over Needle, and he almost lunged at the old man, but restrained himself.

Boxxaway just looked at Needle kindly, but Needle didn't want to see any kindness. Needle wasn't sure why he was so upset with the old man. He was offering to give Needle a fortune in relics, and yet Needle was resisting.

"You're feeling guilty!" Needle said, though honestly he could get no read on Boxxaway's emotions from the look on his face.

"I don't have time for guilt," Boxxaway replied. "Even if I had done something I should feel guilty about."

"What happened to my father?"

"I don't know, Needle," Boxxaway said.

"He's still alive," Needle said.

Boxxaway just shook his head with a sad expression on his face. "Needle, you must face the facts. If your father were coming back, he would have come back already."

Needle shot Boxxaway a hateful glare. "I'm not taking your stuff. This is just like that first time I met you. You used my father to open the Tomb of Ganger. And that is what you are doing now. You are just using me!"

"Hating me hasn't helped you put food on your table, has it?" Boxxaway asked.

Needle felt his eyes bulge and clenched his fists.

"When you hate someone, you just end up hating yourself," said Boxxaway, swallowing. "It's not a healthy way to live. Look, Needle, there is true evil out there in the world. Listen to me. I know you are angry, but control yourself. A real enemy slithers out there in the world, something dark and utterly horrifying. This is why I need your help. I need you to be on the mesa to-night."

Needle glared.

"There are trying times coming, Needle, of which you know absolutely nothing." Boxxaway's tone had changed. It was som-ber, quieter. "You think in simple terms, only about your imme-diate situation. But the world is much larger than you realize. You make assumptions about things, and I can understand that. A boy loves his father. But you don't know everything. A great evil is rising. Wicked wheels set in motion thousands of years ago are rolling toward a nefarious goal. I need your help, Needle. You need to make peace with me, with yourself. I am not your enemy, nor am I responsible for all the misfortune for which you blame me. Sell these artifacts. Buy a lift passage to the top of the mesa and care for your mother with the rest. Promise me that, Needle."

"You mock me! You made my life a thousand times harder, and now you want to buy my forgiveness? You can't see past your crooked nose, you old selfish man!"

"You'll change that point of view soon enough," Boxxaway said. "Time grows short and I have much to do. We will have time to sort our differences later."

Needle stared at the treasure. He had grown up hunting artifacts like these, digging in the desert, in the ruins and prod-ding the deep mud at the edges of the river. Despite his hard-ships, these were the fondest memories of his youth, working with his father. Not many people knew of the Cult of Yex and the Alliance of Adirak and their great battle here 5,000 years ago. But the artifacts left behind weren't just normal artifacts. While many small collectors on the hill wanted old relics from times past, only a few wanted Cult of Yex artifacts. Only one of those wanted the truly rare items from the Cult and that was Dagorn.

But why was Boxxaway offering these items to him? So that he would go up to the plateau tonight? It didn't make any sense. He still could not get away from the idea that he was being used, as his father had been used many years ago. But he also remembered his father's stoic look after he lost half the bounty of Ganger's Tomb. Father never spoke much of it after, and when he did, it was without malice.

Needle considered that maybe his wariness of Boxxaway was misguided. Besides, even if the old man was using him, the artifacts he offered were a miraculous solution to his immediate problems. He and his mother would feast tomorrow.

"Okay," he decided.

Boxxaway smiled kindly as he tossed him the gunny sack that Needle began stuffing with the treasures Boxxaway had chosen.

"You ought to be able to get over 20 moons from Dagorn for that." It was more than Needle could make in years of labor. Maybe a lifetime.

"Promise me, Needle. Promise that you will go to the Bygrave Mausoleum on the plateau tonight."

Needle stared at Boxxaway's face, desperately looking for a clue as to his true intentions. But he was unreadable. "Sure," he sighed.

1st Day of Summer – 2:05 PM – Needle's Home in the Kuma – 11 Hours 25 Minutes Before the Earthquake

Needle's recent deal with Boxxaway had baffled him. The old man had traded his promise to go to the top of the plateau for a wealth of treasure. It wasn't a fair trade and Boxxaway was getting the short end of the stick. That made Needle feel the old ember was using him in some way he didn't yet understand. It made Needle resentful as he slogged through the heat of the unpaved dirt roads of the Kuma. He shifted the weight of the gunny sack full of artifacts he had slung over his skinny shoulder as he rounded the turn into the heart of the Kuma, headed to where he and his mother lived in their rented hovel.

The impoverished feel of the Kuma presented an equally negative series of emotions. Open sewage pustulated through the winding ditches of the Kuma, the fringe district that extended south from the city of Demon's Bluff like a shameful appendage. Dilapidated mud homes squelched in the desert sun. The dry desert wind and sand blew from the west and bored into the unprotected souls of the poor Agrabi who lived there. Most of Demon's Bluff was protected from the worst of the wind by the huge mesa. But the Kuma was too far south to enjoy the windbreak.

He lowered his head against the wind-propelled sand, holding his mouth against his ragged sleeve. He trudged through what people called "the lane," the main artery through the Kuma. What once might have been paved with cemented cobblestones now resembled a dry and dusty river bottom. The Buerdeleise rulers of Demon's Bluff were slow to maintain the Agrabi areas of town and they flat out ignored the Kuma.

Needle hurried past the ragged inhabitants who clogged the sides of the alleys leaning against the walls of their mud hovels, clinging to any shade they could find. Old Agrabi elders scarcely looked up from their tile games as Needle passed them. They played in silence as they waited for the mercy of death. Needle wondered what they would be doing if the Buerdeleise had never come so many eons ago. The sun was well past noon, but its heat refused to abate even a few degrees. Needle imagined that the Abyss itself couldn't be worse than the Kuma's heat, wind and sand. Needle imagined demonic faces in the stares of the few who looked up at him. His once proud people were infected with the same spiritual rot that plagued the structures in Kuma.

Needle refocused his attention on the task at hand and quickened his pace. He needed to get home and tend to his mother.

Their home stood against the wind, a conglomeration of mud and sticks in such poor condition that the wood jutted from the walls and corners where the sand had blasted away the dry mud. Yet it seemed the home persisted seemingly against time itself.

Resigned, he entered the hovel and found his mother dead.

Of course, after all that, she had died on him. He couldn't believe it. She sat unmoving, slumped over in her favorite rocking chair which, like everything else they owned, looked as if it were on the verge of collapse. Mother weighed next to nothing, and by the beams of sunlight peeking through the small openings that served as windows in their mud hut, he could see the brittle bones of her hands poking anxiously against her dark furrowed skin. A veil of thin wispy grey and white hair covered the sheath of skin on her face. Years of living in poverty and hunger had worn her out decades ahead of her time. She had finally succumbed here in the heat of this one-room hovel.

"I'm not dead yet, if that's what you're thinking," Mother said suddenly. Only her lips had moved.

Needle wasn't sure if he was shocked, relieved or angry. Maybe he was all three.

"Enough!" she said as if she could read his mind. She opened her eyes and stared at him with blind eyes frosted over so badly only a hint of an iris or pupil remained. She had not been able to see for almost a year now.

He waved his hand in front of her face.

"Stop waving your hand in my face. I can feel the wind! Did you catch any fish?"

"The trotter I set out was clean," Needle lied. He hadn't fished at all today, of course. "I think someone found the line and worked it before I came back to it."

"I told you to stay and watch it!"

Needle didn't respond. He felt dejected, and he knew what she was going to say next. He pulled the gunny sack off his shoulder and deposited it on the table.

"Looking for your miserable father again?" she said bitterly.

"He's out there somewhere," he insisted. "But I was looking for food and copper stars."

"If he's dead, he's on to the next life, and he'll be a lot happier than I am, but if he's alive, he abandoned us, and he'll be destined for the Abyss."

Needle didn't move. "He's alive. I know it." He hated having this argument with her. While he was risking his life to get them food, she wouldn't allow him the simple belief that his father was alive somewhere.

His mother's tone changed to the loving tone he remembered from years ago. She didn't use it much anymore. "Your father was a good man, Needle. He wouldn't abandon us. You have to find your peace with his passing."

"That's how I know he's in trouble," Needle said pleadingly.

"Poor sweet Raju," Mother said, shaking her head from side to side. "You sure got the faith, but there comes a time when faith hurts more than helps."

Needle knelt before his mother and looked into her blind eyes. She smelled like home.

"You're a good boy," said mother softly, "and clever enough. But you stay away from the people your father dealt with, you hear? You stay away from his work or it will be the death of you, too."

Bam! Bam! Bam!

The noise at the door brought Needle out of the reverential memories of his father.

"They've come to turn us out," Mother said, the resignation in her voice clear.

"But I paid the keeper three coppers last week," Needle said.

"That's only half!"

They both looked toward the door.

Bam! Bam! Bam!

"Ain't no use avoiding it," Mother said.

Needle felt a wave of heat reflecting off the dry clay of the alley as he opened the door. The keeper stood in the doorway. He was a hard-faced Agrabi man, with craggy skin that made him seem even crueler than he was.

"You only paid half," The keeper said. He jerked a grubby thumb toward the street. "You go."

"But I can't put my mother in the street," Needle pleaded.

"Not my problem. Get out. I got paying customers."

Needle knew the keeper could throw them out by force if he chose, but he was not going to allow him to put his mother out into the desert. It would be the death of her.

"I have the money," Needle lied. "I can have it for you tomorrow."

The keeper looked at Needle long and hard, with squinting

eyes almost shut by a lifetime in the sun.

"You paid half. That means tomorrow is your last day. You come and bring me the money tomorrow. Otherwise, I got tenants moving in tomorrow. Before dark."

The keeper turned and walked away. Needle just watched him go. His mother said nothing. They had no food and no money, and now his mother was about to be thrown out into the street.

"So, what you going to do now?" Mother asked as Needle slowly shut the door. "You wasted your time looking for your father. How you going to get copper? Steal it? No son of mine!" she bellowed.

"No," Needle said resignedly. He had tried joining the guild earlier in the day and he was trying to forget how it had ended. "Boxxaway Hotheway gave me some relics. I am going to sell them tonight."

"Boxxaway!" his mother sputtered. "Take them back."

"It's all we have," Needle said. He opened the gunny sack and began to carefully lay out the treasures on the table.

"No, no, no! He's a bad man," she said. "He gave me at least twenty moons worth of artifacts," Needle said. "We can eat right. Forget about just paying the keeper, we can get out of Kuma, get back to the Lower Steppe. Maybe even better."

His mother reached out to him and he took her gnarled old hands. "Nothing good can come from that man. I heard your father speak of him for years, and it was all bad. He is up to something. How can you be sure that the stuff he gave you isn't worthless?"

"This isn't junk. I know junk. I worked with Father many years."

Bam! Bam! Bam!

Needle jumped. A second time this afternoon someone knocked on the door. He looked at his mother, who was shivering despite the heat.

"This is bad," she whispered.

What could be worse than Boxxaway Hotheway? What could be worse than the keeper sending them out into the street? What could be worse than today?

He was about to find out.

CHAPTER FOUR
Intrusion Detector

We thought we had defeated them at the Battle of Oar, but we soon realized it wasn't over. When we reached the bluff, we were dismayed to find the Cult of Yex had gathered to make their last stand. To our dismay, their remaining arch wizards were still potent and were using the same source of unholy magic as the wizards at the Battle of Oar.

-From *The Lost Journal of King Adirak of Taglyon*

1st Day of Summer – 2:00 PM – Boxxaway's Cottage - 11 Hours and 30 Minutes Before the Earthquake

Boxxaway detected the faintest of odors. He had just returned home after his meeting with Needle when he caught the whiff. Was he imagining things? That odor should not be here. Dheke was aware of the intruder, too. He immediately started snuffling at the floor toward the back room. Boxxaway quickly surveyed the various rooms. Nothing seemed to be missing. Not that there was much to take, but the important things were right where he had left them.

He inhaled deeply and slowly through his nose. No doubt about it. The odor was distinct. He remembered it clearly from his younger years. It was the pungent aroma of Bystle Fruit, which permeated the halflings from the forested lands up north.

CHAPTER FIVE
Can I Play With Madness

There is a magic beyond my understanding, whose power comes from ancient patterns and not from the flow of eldritch energy so well understood by those of arcane training. The patterns are passed from mother to daughter and seem comprehensible only to those of certain families. Such magic could prove useful.

-From the *Lost Journal of King Adirak of Taglyon*

1st Day of Summer – 2:15 PM – Needle's Home in the Kuma – 11 Hours and 15 Minutes Before the Earthquake

Brynn Bygrave stared at the mud hovel. Was she crazy, or was there almost no mortar between the irregular mud bricks? *What's holding it together?*

She looked left, then right. She knew it wasn't smart for a sixteen-year-old fair-skinned Buerdeleise girl to walk alone anywhere in the Kuma, much less all the way through it, to one of the very last cottages on the edge of the incinerating desert. Yet, here she was.

She walked up to the loose planks that served as a door. To knock might cause the whole thing to fall apart. She balled her hand into a fist and took her chances.

Thunk, thunk, thunk.

The door rattled on its hinges. The sound reverberated much louder than she had intended, and she felt her teeth reflexively grit together as if the tension in her body could somehow muffle the hollow knocking sound. She looked around again. More than a few seedy eyes watched her curiously. She wore a tattered brown robe she had nicked from one of her father's Agrabi servants. She had pulled the hood up high in the hopes of obscuring her pale face and auburn hair, but her brain was screaming: *It's not working! You're as obvious as a bloody toe on a woven rug!* Her eyes fixed on a thin, toothless Agrabi man with merciless eyes sitting on the porch of another hovel up the lane. She quickly looked away.

There was a shuffling sound from the other side of the door. Good. Risking a trip here once was bad enough. She dreaded the possibility that she might have to return to try again.

More shuffling from the other side of the door, but it still didn't open. The toothless fellow had stood up. Was he skulking toward her? She knocked again, harder this time.

Thunk, thunk- and the door opened.

"Please can I come in?" she hissed hurriedly. Her voice slid past her teeth in a panic she wished she could hide. She pulled back her cloak.

A lanky Agrabi boy about her age stood before her, clearly puzzled and seemingly offended at her presence. The kid obviously hadn't been eating regularly and she could see the protruding bones on his wrists, eye sockets and cheeks. She had no doubt his entire rib cage was visible beneath his ratty, brown, stained tunic. His trousers seemed to dance around his slender waist, one slight breeze away from pooling around his ankles. Only his boots were of any quality at all. His hair was black and cropped short, eyes were wide and very dark, with a hint of defiance in them, or "flint" as her mother might have said. He might have been handsome, in a rugged kind of way, if his face hadn't been so lean and his teeth so yellow.

"You're not the landlord," he said in confusion.

"You have a firm grasp of the obvious," she said, as she twirled the hair at the side of her head. She flicked her eyes to the ground. *Get ahold of yourself, Brynn. This is too important.* She cleared her throat and re-established eye contact. "You must be Needle," she said as she began to unintentionally bounce on her toes. It seemed her body invented this 'I have to pee' dance to convey her urgency to this boy. It wasn't working.

He was not the person she had come to find, but he would have to do. Her desire was to find a man named Kemano Graji, but the people she had talked to suggested he was dead. However, she learned he had been survived by a widow and a young son, about her own age.

"I'm Needle," the boy admitted. "But who in the Abyss are you?"

"My name is Brynn. I know this must seem odd, but I'm here to inquire about your father. I think he knew my mother."

A voice spilled from the shadows inside the shack, "Who is that, Raju?"

"May I come inside?" Brynn asked looking back over her shoulder. The tall toothless Agrabi man was definitely skulking directly toward her. Brynn couldn't help feeling as if the entire Kuma was closing in on her. Panic began to swallow her from the bottom up and she decided not to wait for Needle to permit her entry. She shoved her way past the Agrabi boy into the mud hut, his bony shoulder innocently punching into the flesh of her upper arm.

"My father?" the boy said as he stumbled backwards, shoving the door closed with the tips of his fingers. "You know about my father?" He didn't seem to be at all bothered by her intrusion. He was studying her face greedily, as if trying to find the answer to an unspoken question.

"Well, yes. No. Sort of," was all Brynn could get out, as her eyes adjusted to the dusky dark space that surrounded her.

What a sorry place this was. She could see a few pieces of furniture that were nothing more than random boards nailed together in clumsy forms and shapes. *Barely useful.* On a rickety, splintered table was a neatly-organized display of what looked like old weapons and other trinkets. The neatness conveyed a certain reverence for the hunks of crafted metal and wood, in stark contrast to the grubby surroundings. Some of the artifacts were remarkably well kept, and there were a number of well-crafted weapons among them. Brynn peeled her eyes away from the table to look back at the rest of the brown light-filtered space. Her gaze landed on an equally ancient-looking old woman perched in a twig-stick rocking chair. The wrinkly lady squinted back at her through cloudy eyes.

"Who is it? Describe her!" the old woman demanded.

Needle shifted, uncomfortable with the task of verbally sketching this girl for his mother. "I think it's a Buerdeleise girl, from up the steppe."

"And...?" prodded the old woman.

"And..." Needle dragged out hesitantly, "she is a bit taller than me, reddish-brownish hair. I guess. I don't know. She has pale skin, green eyes?" Needle's discomfort rose in his cheeks as bright red flares.

"Huh," said his mother "Sounds hideous." The old woman opened her mouth, showing teeth as patchwork as the house. She released a squealing titter.

Once recovered, she asked with pointed curiosity, "What in the world you doing here?"

Brynn decided not to like her. She didn't like Needle much more at the moment, but he was better than the old woman. She ignored the old woman's question and turned to Needle. "I came here looking for your father, Kemano, but a man I asked said he was dead. Like I said, I think your father and my mother knew each other."

"Been dead a year," the old woman said in a nasty sing-song voice at the exact same time Needle shook his head and said: "He's not dead."

Brynn looked at the old woman. As Brynn's eyes became increasingly adapted to the low light, she noticed for the first time that the ancient lady's pupils were completely clouded over with opaque white. She was blind.

"My mother died about a year ago, too," said Brynn as she turned back to face Needle. "She was murdered."

"My father is not dead and certainly wasn't murdered," Needle said, his dark eyes flashing with vehement defiance. "He's alive. I just don't know where."

Brynn considered before she spoke. She had no idea if the man was still alive. Hopefully he was; she wanted to speak to him. Still, she had an odd feeling; call it an instinct, which said he was cold and that she needed to focus on Needle instead.

"I think I may know something about him. Maybe we can help each other," she said, plowing forward despite Needle's resistance. As she spoke, a dog started yip-yapping from somewhere behind the hovel. The annoying sound came in clearly through the back window and ended as abruptly as it started. Probably from one of the packs of mangy dogs that Brynn had seen patrolling the Kuma. Needle and his mother paid no attention whatsoever.

"You are mistaken," Needle said, as if coming to some sort of conclusion. "I don't see how you could be right. Why would your mother have anything to do with an Agrabi?"

Brynn didn't like being challenged but she kept it from showing. "I recently learned about them. Any interest in hearing about what I found or would you prefer I leave?" Brynn really hoped she wouldn't be asked to leave.

Luckily, there was an intense need in his dark eyes, a craving for information about his father. Brynn could see that the boy so wanted to believe his father was alive and she had a moment of connection. Briefly, she understood him. She too had those moments when she wished her mother was alive, wished it so hard she almost believed it was possible. Wished it until a hard knot would form in her throat and then bubble out of her mouth in hot, heaving sobs of grief and loss.

Despite the moments of heartsick wishing, Brynn's mother was dead. She had watched as her body, wrapped from head to toe in bandages, was lowered into the cold stone funerary box with her personal items for the journey into the heavens. She saw the lid sealed shut with a scrape and a thud in the Bygrave family mausoleum.

"And if your father is still alive," she continued, "I think I might be able to help you find him."

"This girl is mad," the old woman chuckled. "She's not used to the heat." Brynn decided to dislike the old crone even more.

"How?" Needle demanded, incredulity plain on his face.

Careful, Brynn thought. She had to proceed slowly here. She would not believe her own story if she herself had not lived it. What she had planned was even more outlandish, and now she saw clearly that she would need this Agrabi boy's help. Hopefully, the letter she had tucked in the pocket of her robe would make him understand.

One Week Earlier – 84th Day of Spring – 7:15 PM – Brynn's Bedroom

Pearls and pink. Frothy lace. Extravagant frills. Disgusting. No, downright vomitus. Her stockings were tight and constricting, her toenails already beginning to poke rebellious holes in the light gauze that imprisoned them. And the corset--who in their most demented moment would have ever created such an evil device? She was desperately trying to ignore the python squeeze and rub-raw dig of this whalebone prison. She was fine the way she was, thank you very much and she had no desire to do herself up for anyone, much less some suitor arranged by her father in one of his calculated political maneuvers. But she had decided that she would do as her father asked; she would do almost anything for him. Had her mother been alive, she would not have approved of his attempt to marry her off, nor the way he had the servants preen her.

Brynn relished a daydream-y moment, her mother striding across the bedroom floor, deftly unraveling the ribbon of the corset and flinging it to the floor; nothing but flint and mother's love in her eyes. The daydream faded along with Brynn's wistful smile as a whalebone drove into her side.

Brynn looked up into the mirror and cringed. Rose-red rouged cheeks and lips to match. Her naturally wild russet mane, slicked and pulled back by the teeth of a shimmering comb, inlaid with mother-of-pearl imported from Taglyon. Her feet, used to feeling grass and the heave of horseflesh as she dug in for a ride, were infernally crushed in heeled shoes.

A doll on display, she thought and then sighed as she envisioned being plucked off a bedroom shelf by a small girl. Brynn preferred a subtle, more natural approach to beauty, just like her mother.

She turned her thoughts back to the events of the evening. She had met her suitor years before at a dinner of nobles in Balankov. Wenlock Boricov, the eldest son of a Duke of Balankov. She had not felt anything about him one way or the other at the time. He was nice enough and also happened to be quite friendly, verging on charming. He had talked to her the majority of the evening and had even draped his coat over her shoulders in a cordial gesture as the night grew cooler. But now her brain was deftly rewriting memory. She was convincing herself that he was deserving of nothing but her utmost distain.

To show off her suitability as a bride, her father had arranged for her to cook dinner for Boricov. Brynn took great pride in following her mother's recipes with exactness and did so not only with her mother's memory in mind but with the desire to comfort and connect with her father. Brynn cooked the meal with exuberance, imagining her mother by her side, laughing as the flour sifted across the stone floor and the plums popped under the force of the knife. Her mother symbolically joined with her in singular concentration as they wove the braided bread together and basted the golden-brown goose. It was the closest Brynn had felt to her mother since her mother's death and she only hoped the meal would bring the same echo of joy to her father.

Wen was clearly impressed with Brynn's meal as he dug into the pastries, baked fruits and savory goose. He smiled at her with unabashed appreciation and complimented her skill in the kitchen. He really was a good person and seemed to lack the need to hook into her with empty praise. Brynn liked that, but he was far from her primary concern.

Throughout the evening, she had watched her father closely. He, on the other hand, was clearly watching intently to see how things had progressed. His focus seemed to be the political inroads that this meal may or may not be making for him. A union between the Bygraves and Boricovs most certainly would benefit them all. Brynn knew all of this, but hoped this meal was awakening something deeper in her father; something that perhaps scabbed over when her mother passed. Brynn had never truly known her father well. She and her mother were thick as thieves and he had always allowed them their distance. She was not sure why that was so, but it was. In her childish way, Brynn had always imagined that when her mother and father went behind closed doors, he would drop into the role of the doting and dedicated husband that every little girl believes her father to be. She believed he loved her mother with a fierceness that could not, for whatever reason, be shown in public. She also believed the death of her mother had broken his heart so wide open he was lost. She was sure that she was the only one who could eventually, hopefully, retrieve him.

Brynn knew that on the surface her father was trying to improve the lot and station of the family. That was a noble goal taken by itself, but the intensity with which he rushed forward to achieve this end was hurtful to Brynn. At times, it felt like he only wanted to advance his grand political strategy. Brynn held onto the belief that his relentless maneuvering was his way of dulling the pain he felt over the loss of his wife. He was a powerful man, not accustomed to showing any emotion; so of course, he was going to bury his pain in the day-to-day of his work. Brynn believed he wanted her to be happy, that his primary goal was her happiness and that political advantage to the family was only secondary. She had to believe that, even as she glanced at the dour expression etched into his face which only lightened as he leaned in to chat with Wenlock.

For the most part, Brynn would have to say the dinner was successful. She and Wen had a nice conversation despite the suffocating corset. The food was delicious and left her swimming with memories of her mother. Her father seemed pleased, no, maybe not pleased, but at least he enjoyed discourse with Wen. After dinner, she was excused by her father to return to her chambers.

Wen smiled and stood, bowing slightly as he said, "G'nite, Brynn. It was a pleasure dining here tonight and even more of a pleasure being in your company." Brynn nodded at him and felt a silly rush of blood in her face.

Her father also stood. "Not exactly your mother's cooking, but good enough, I suppose. Good night, Brynn." At this Brynn felt the blood recede from her face as quickly as it came. She turned and left the dining hall.

Brynn launched into her chambers, tears welling in her eyes. She had imagined that her mother's food, deliberately crafted with her hands, would perhaps begin to melt her father's heart. Brynn was embarrassed and utterly distraught. Two Agrabi serving girls stood in the corner of her bedroom, staring.

Brynn shouted at them, "Get out, you stupid hens!" and

chased them into the hallway, slamming the heavy wooden door behind them.

Off came the dress: tear drop polka-dots and smears adding new texture to the already embellished material. It had been a gift from her father and she hated it as it flumped to the floor. She wrestled with the corset, finally managing to wriggle out, bending and distorting it in her struggle. The heels, kicked off blindly, skittered across the floor. The stockings ripped and shredded. The comb pulled out and hurled against a far wall. Brynn's face was wet with tears and her eyesight a complete blur as she pulled on a comfortable black silk robe and fell on her bed, hugging her pillow.

There was a knock at the door.

"I want to be alone," she said in a desperate voice.

The door opened anyway. If it was one of those skulking Agrabi servants... She looked around for something close at hand that she could throw.

"Dear, dear, Brynn, what is with these hysterics?" Her father, Duke Dagorn Bygrave said as he stepped into the room. "So the meal was bad but certainly not worth crying over. So you just don't have the same knack your mother had. The Boricov family is one of the wealthiest in Balankov. You can just have the servants do all the cooking."

Brynn stared at her father, speechless. He too had changed out of his formal clothing from the dinner party, and was dressed only in a dark blue silk robe. Barefoot, he held a fine crystal glass, filled as usual, with red wine. It was rare these days to see him without his goblet in hand. His black hair was combed back and hung just above his shoulders. Every third hair was grey or white. A life of scheming and worry had begun to take its toll on him. His salt and pepper goatee broke into a smile, causing the crow's feet around his steely gray eyes to become more pronounced. "I don't think that boy cares one way or another whether you can cook or not." Her father chuckled while lifting the glass to his lips.

"I... I." Brynn was reeling. She had no idea what she was trying to say, and then screamed: "I made that meal for *you*. It was one of Mom's special recipes. I am sure I followed it to perfection, nothing was out of order. I...."

"Hmm, that is cute, sweetheart, but your mother clearly had talents that did not wind their way down the family tree." Her father said this last bit with a cruel smugness that Brynn did not fully understand. "It's not your fault."

He walked across the room and sat on the edge of the bed next to her. He took another sip from his drink, closed his eyes and ran a hand through his graying black hair. "No harm done. Even if he does have concerns about your cooking, I can smooth it over." Another gulp from his glass.

Brynn felt as if someone had kicked her in the guts, not just the stomach but the guts where you actually had to dig to get at them. Her father had been distant and more or less cold her entire life, but this was different. Was he just thoughtless or deliberately cruel?

"Father, are you angry at me? Did I do something wrong?" was all she could squeak out.

"Go to sleep, my dear. I will see you in the morning." Brynn's father turned to leave and then added, "And Brynn, it is not as bad as you think. At least your mother was not here to taste that roast goose. She would have eaten it with a smile." He left the room, closing the door with a convincing clunk.

Brynn was numb for a few seconds. And then it came, at first like a slowly creeping vine and then like a stampede--heart-shredding grief. Why was her father being so savage? What had she done to deserve this? Would her mother really have hated the meal? Brynn curled into a fetal position, a motion innately designed to protect her soft insides from further attack. She rocked and rocked and rocked. Rocked until her thoughts calmed.

Brynn took a deep breath and began to unfold as she rolled over onto her back and dangled her head off the edge of the bed. She replayed the maddening events of the evening in her head, trying to place them in a more logical order--assigning stories and supporting evidence to explain her father's awful behavior. He had put effort into insulting her, but she chose to let it go for now. The remaining tears drizzled up her forehead and into her hair.

As she lay there, she allowed her eyes to focus and unfocus on the decorative patterns stenciled on the wall by her bed; a mindless game to try and take her attention off of what had happened.

Slowly, a tune started playing in her head, bubbling up from the past. It was a tune she had not heard for well over a year--her mother's favorite song. Her mother had taught her to play it on the harp, and she had hummed it to lull her children to sleep. Mother had whistled it as they cooked together. It certainly was an odd, almost exotic, tune. Now that she thought about it, it was a rare day that her mother was not humming or whistling that tune when they were together.

She un-focused her eyes again. She imagined that she could see faces and shapes in the randomness of the decorative patterns. The tune stubbornly started over again in her head.

She focused her eyes again on the patterns.

She stopped.

She blinked.

She un-focused and re-focused again. Her heart skipped as her entire body erupted in goose bumps.

The pattern in the decorative stenciling! It was clear: nested within the scope of the larger design, upside down and unmistakable. She kept her head hanging over the edge of her bed as she scanned the decorative stencil as it repeated itself over and over. Though the stencil pattern repeated itself, only in this one instance was the pattern nested inside the stencil. The other repeats were similar, but this one here, on the wall by her bed, it was unique. Her mother's song repeated itself again irresistibly in her head. She started whistling it almost involuntarily. It was incredible that she had not noticed this nested pattern before, right here by her bed.

Dozens, perhaps hundreds of memories of her mother flashed through her head in a rush. Countless calligraphy lessons where her mother leaned over her, long hair brushing against Brynn's back and cheek, making Brynn trace a practice pattern that had elements of the stencil before her. Learning cross-stitch with her mother and repeating a portion of the pattern before her hundreds of times in quick succession. The peculiar way her mother patiently taught her to braid her hair; it was after a fashion of the pattern on the wall before her.

The song blared in her mind.

Memories continued to fly. All with the pattern and always with her mother: the way they laid out the garden rows, the way they wove baskets, the odd interlacing of threads on the loom, the sand art, the flower arranging, even the way her mother liked to arrange the furniture in a room! It was all part of the grand and complex pattern clearly displayed on the wall before her. All those memories of her mother had elements of the pattern, but none had the complete pattern. This pattern on the wall was complete. It was whole. It was balanced. It was perfect. There was something about the pattern that was very powerful, but in an inexplicably subtle way. The more Brynn focused on the pattern, the more her mother's song wanted to play itself in her head. Suddenly Brynn realized that the pattern and the song were related. *No! They were the same!* The song was the pattern and the pattern was the song. She could virtually see the notes in the pattern.

A breathtaking realization struck Brynn. Everything her mother had taught her throughout her entire life had a hidden, deeper meaning. Her mother spent her whole life trying to teach Brynn to recognize *this* pattern, without ever actually showing it to her. Everything she thought was happening when she was with her mother wasn't really as it appeared on the surface.

Her head still dangling upside down off the edge of her bed, Brynn knew that her mother had put this pattern here, wrong side up, for her to notice and recognize in a moment of reverie. It was positioned in a calculated manner to be hidden from notice from anyone looking at it in any way but the way Brynn was looking at it now; on her bed, head dangled upside down: a perspective that Brynn, and only Brynn, would ever have. *This pattern was a message to her from her dead mother!*

Instinctively, Brynn reached out toward the pattern and placed her finger in the center of it. She traced the complex pattern from center to edge with the unconscious surety of an expert who had done a task so many thousands of times before. But Brynn had never traced this exact pattern. Indeed, she had never even seen the whole pattern all together before now. All she had ever known were pieces and parts of this pattern. But all those lessons over the years, lessons she didn't even know she was getting, had taught her how to recognize, to understand, to trace this pattern. And she did so with absolute fluidity.

Brynn gasped in amazement as she completed the trace. The pattern seemed to take on an iridescent shimmer for a moment and then with a click and a near silent pressure release of dank air, a rectangular shape appeared around the pattern and a secret door swung inward.

Brynn rolled over and stared through the opening into the darkness, her mouth agape. With the pattern now out of her sight, she realized that her mother's song had vacated her mind.

1st Day of Summer – 2:30 PM – Needle's Home in the Kuma – 11 Hours Before the Earthquake

"Does a symbol of three eyes mean anything to you?" Brynn asked Needle.

"Wha--what?"

Brynn saw that she had hit on something meaningful to Needle. Her hunch was paying off.

Brynn looked around for a blank parchment. Silly her. There wouldn't be any parchment here. She knelt down onto the dirt floor and drew a simplified version of the symbol of the eyes.

"But--? How can--? Where did--?" Needle stammered.

"I take it you have seen it?"

"Never you mind!" Needle scowled. "What does all this have to do with my father?"

"What is she doing?" Needle's mother demanded. She was leaning forward in her rickety rocking chair, opaque eyes darting furiously as if they were antennae desperately searching their surroundings.

"Nothing, Mother. She's just drawing symbols in the dirt."

One Week Earlier – 84th Day of Spring – 7:30 PM – Brynn's Bedroom

Brynn slid off the bed to her feet. A distant musty smell came to her from within the passageway. She picked up the lantern from her vanity and held it aloft to illuminate the gloom. The light showed a cobweb-filled passage angling downward. How was it possible that this secret passage had been here in her room for her whole life and she had never known about it? Her heart raced as she steeled herself and took several tentative steps forward into the murk. A tarantula the size of her palm skittered toward her as she reached to clear the cobwebs ahead of her. She squealed aloud and stomped it reflexively, feeling its guts on the ball of her bare foot and the ticklish crevices between her toes. Brynn grimaced and wiped her foot on the hard stone entrance, scraping away sticky entrails. Under normal circumstances, she would never tread in a place like this, but the idea that her mother wanted her to find this passage drove her beyond any fear of this dark place.

She stepped cautiously down the passage, which soon descended more steeply into what looked like red sandstone. Clearly, this old passage descended into the rock of the Middle Steppe. The air was thankfully cool, after the oppressive heat of the house upstairs.

The passage was damp. Brynn guessed that by the southward direction and descending slope, it must continue below the pond in the Middle Steppe, or at least very near to it.

By and by, Brynn came to stairs leading down, hewn out of the sandstone. The odor reminded her of the privy as she descended. The stairway ended, dropping her into a long dark tunnel filled with brackish water. Brynn glanced around, reflexively attempting to find an alternative to wading into the black pond. As she took in her surroundings, her eyes landed on a black iron catwalk about two feet wide that was bolted to the side of the tunnel, just above the fetid water.

She breathed in through her mouth, but that was just as bad, because she could almost taste the rot and stink on her tongue. She made her breathing as shallow as possible.

There was nothing for it though. She certainly wasn't going to stop now. She stretched her leg across the gap between the last sandstone step and onto the catwalk to test its strength. Rats scurried from the shadows ahead as the catwalk creaked under her weight. It held, so she placed both legs on the catwalk and began moving across, holding the lantern before her. She paid close attention to every groan in the metal that might announce her plunge into the sewage below.

After about a hundred paces, the iron catwalk ended. The tunnel ran on, but she would have to step into the sludge to continue. She hesitated a moment, then hiked up the hem of her silk robe and stepped her bare foot into the muck. It was cool and rose to her mid-calf.

She swished forward for twenty paces as the passage sloped slightly upwards. The filth grew shallow until she was walking on the cool sandstone floor of the passage. She crept ahead another one hundred paces until she spied something at the edge of her lantern light.

Maybe this wasn't so smart. Ahead of her was a wooden bench. At the foot of the bench, formed directly into the sandstone of the passageway, was a basin of water. This water looked surprisingly fresh and cool.

"Where am I?" she wondered aloud. Somehow it was reassuring to hear her own voice. Her heart was beating fast. The clear water was inviting.

Not to drink. She wasn't thirsty. She wanted to clean her dirty feet. So she paddled her feet back and forth in the basin, and watched as the sludge slipped off them. In moments, they were clean.

To her amazement, the water then shimmered and was sparkling clean again.

How? She had never seen anything like that. Some magic must be at work here.

She looked around. What now? The tunnel ended in a blank wall next to the bench and basin. Then she noticed something. There, on the wall, just beyond the basin, was a glowing symbol formed from phosphorescent lichen, in the distinct clover pattern of three eyes. The symbol was simple, yet it was elegant in its simplicity. The symbol was symmetrical, almost as if it had been painted on, as opposed to being a natural growth of lichen. As she looked at the symbol, she heard an odd tune play in her mind. It was much simpler than the song she heard when she had looked at the pattern on the wall by her bed. Somehow, this new tune was connected to this new symbol. She looked over both shoulders. She was alone, except for the rats.

A small one came chittering up toward her. *Brazen little thing.* She reached out and grabbed it by the tail and flung it away back toward the muck. *That would teach a rat to bother with her.*

She turned back to the wall and instinctively traced the symbol with the tip of her index finger. This time she wasn't surprised when it flashed for an instant and the outline of an unseen door appeared and swung inward. Fresh dry air came flowing toward her and she gulped it greedily.

She held her lantern ahead of her but it would not penetrate the murk beyond the secret door. The thought that her mother had intended for her to find this, and pass this way, came to her mind and gave her confidence. She stepped through the doorway into the darkness.

1st Day of Summer – 2:35 PM – Brynn at Needle's Hovel – 10 Hours and 55 Minutes Before the Earthquake

"You're a witch!" Needle's mother cried suddenly, preempting Brynn as she was about to respond to Needle.

"A witch! She's a witch, Needle! She consorts with elder beings from the outer planes! She meddles with patterns and sigils! She dances with madness!" the old crone cried.

Brynn felt her anger rise. She really didn't like the old hag and needed to speak with Needle out of earshot of his mother. Once again, the deep impression that she was meant to meet this boy and that she would need his help rumbled through her thoughts. She passed her hand over the sand, rubbing out the eyes she had drawn. The old woman wouldn't recognize a witch sigil even if she *could* see.

"Needle, I know we just met, and under strange circumstances I admit, but I really must speak with you. Will you walk with me? Escort me back out of the Kuma while we talk?"

One Week Earlier – 84th Day of Spring – 7:45 PM – The Secret Desert

As Brynn stepped into the dark passageway, her eyes recoiled at a sudden brilliant flash of white light. She instinctively covered her face with her forearm. After a moment, the pain from the flash subsided and she opened her right eye ever so slightly. Brynn's mind stumbled over itself in confusion. One moment she was stepping into a black passageway and the next she was standing here--wherever 'here' was. She had the distinct sense that this was magical space.

Before her was a barren desert of red-orange sand. About fifty paces ahead was an ornate rolltop desk of curious craftsmanship. Very old by the look of it and made from a dark wood she did not recognize. The rolltop was pulled closed, all the way down. Directly beyond the desk, she guessed about another fifty paces, was a black stone monolith that looked to be a bit taller than she was and several feet wide. It looked as if some type of symbol had been etched into the black stone, but she couldn't make it out from this distance.

She looked around her and saw sand with gently rolling dunes bordering on every side. The desk seemed to be stationed in the deepest part of a natural bowl depression between rises of dunes on all sides. Directly behind her stood another monolith of smooth polished black rock, and she immediately understood it was the doorway through which she entered. Upon it was engraved the exact same symbol of the three eyes she had seen on the wall in the sewer.

Brynn looked up at the sky. The desert where she found herself was light but not bright. It was as if it she was in the middle of an overcast day, yet the sky was deep blue. Much bluer than she had ever seen. There wasn't a cloud in the sky, but there was also no sun. Where was the light coming from? Brynn noticed that there was no wind either. This was odd. In Demon's Bluff, the wind was a virtual constant. Some days were blustery, blasting everything with wind-driven sand. Even on the calmest of days, there was a slight breeze. Brynn breathed in deeply through her nose, trying to smell the familiar smell of sage and desert blooms, but there was none. The air was dry and fresh, but totally devoid of any scent whatsoever. It was also quite cool, much cooler than the desert she was used to. Brynn couldn't make out any sign of life in this place but herself.

Brynn wondered what was beyond the rim of dunes that surrounded her. She set her lantern down in the sand and walked to her left, up one of the dunes. She felt a flush of excitement. Glancing behind her, she saw drivels of sand still flowing in the trail of footprints she left behind her. She struggled up the dune, starting to sweat, even in the cool air.

She eventually arrived at the crest of the dune, hot and out of breath. She could feel the blood rushing in her temples. She looked down the other side of the dune, into another bowl depression. From her high vantage, she had a commanding view. In the center of the valley of sand below here was *another* rolltop desk. It was flanked at some distance on either side by black monoliths. She stepped down several paces into the new depression to get a better look. Were those footprints leading off from the left monolith up the dune directly across from her?

Realization dawned on her and she whirled, kicking up sand as she did so. She scrambled back down the dune the way she had come and up the other side. When she reached the crest she looked across to the rim directly across from her, near the crest were deep footprints in the sand. The sand was still cascading near the topmost print, looking for a place to come to rest.

What was this place? Did her mother really intend for her to come *here?*

She half marched and half slid back down the dune, directly toward the rolltop desk.

1st Day of Summer – 3:30 PM – The Kuma – 10 Hours Before the Earthquake

Brynn felt better walking through the Kuma this time with Needle by her side. He wasn't very big, but he did exude a level of confidence that she could feel. It calmed her down. Oh, there were still just as many stares as before, and she could not help the feeling that she was drawing too much attention. But with Needle walking along with her, the stares seemed less threatening.

"There sure are a lot of people watching us, Needle."

"Yeah, that's to be expected, I suppose. Not many Buerdeleise ever venture into the Kuma. Especially one like, well you know, like you." Needle looked around briefly as if to verify what he already knew. He stopped suddenly as he was looking back over his shoulder intently.

"What's the matter?"

"Huh--nothing, I just thought I saw a sudden movement when I turned. Like someone jumped off the road. You're really not safe here, you know?"

Brynn rolled her eyes. "You think? Of course I'm not safe here. Let's get moving. Besides, I felt like somebody was following me all the way to your house. Thanks for walking me out."

"So, you think your mother and my father knew each other?" Needle sounded incredulous.

"Yes. There is no doubt."

"So, how do you know this?"

"I'm not sure how to ask this Needle, but can you read?"

Needle's look told her that he wasn't offended, but he was clearly amused by her assumption.

"Here," she said, hoping his reaction meant indeed he could read. "This was among my mother's things." She handed him a well-oiled rolled parchment that she had kept in a pocket inside her cloak. He unrolled the faded yellow page.

Needle was shocked. "This is in my father's handwriting!"

One Week Earlier – 84th Day of Spring – 7:55 PM – The Secret Desert

Brynn scanned the sand around the rolltop desk as she approached it. The reddish sand had only slight areas of unevenness but they were smooth and rolling. There was no sign of footprints or disturbance of any kind around it. Where the desk met the sand there was no indication that the sand had ever been blown against the sides where it should have collected in drifts. There were no drifts and no hint of a breeze. It made no sense. If there had ever been footprints here, they could only be erased by the wind. But any wind would have caused sand to collect in drifts against the side of the desk. It defied logic, but then again, this entire place defied logic.

And Brynn liked it. For the first time, she sensed something about this place. Peace. Tranquility. She felt it in her bones. This was some type of resting place, between worlds. It was *crazy.* And she knew instinctively that most other people, other than herself, would feel incredible anxiety, perhaps to the point of insanity here. But something about her mother's hidden instructions to her all her life prepared her for *this place,* and prepared her to receive a peaceful feeling from it. This was where she was *supposed* to be.

She turned her attention back to the desk. There was a gnarled wooden chair tucked up to it. She pulled this out and sat down upon it. Then she reached for the notch at the bottom of the dark wooden slats interlocking the rolling closure of the desk. As she lifted it open, a familiar smell surprised her. She had not smelled it for well over a year. It took her just a moment to realize that it was the distinctive sweet-spice perfume of her mother. Brynn mused for a moment on how an old familiar smell could trigger memories so intensely. She smiled as she recalled a memory with her mother.

Brynn's mother sometimes wore perfume made of rare desert ghost flowers. Once, she had taken Brynn with her for a full day's walk in the desert. They had paid the exorbitant fee and ridden the magical lifts to the top of the mesa and walked for miles past the graveyard and then through sagebrush and scrub oak toward the western end of the mesa where they hunted for the desert ghost flowers from which her mother made the perfume. They were very rare flowers with a distinctive sweet smell and a delicious spicy undertone. Brynn was instructed on where they grew and how to find them as they clipped almost two dozen of the bluish blossoms. Her mother had been careful to show Brynn how to harvest the flowers without hurting the rest of the plant.

As they harvested the ghost flowers, Brynn had smelled deeply of the blossoms many times. The smell in the desk transported her back to that day like no other memory trigger could. She remembered how her mother had told her that the desert ghost had a curious property. After being harvested, their petals would slowly transform from blue to a pale white and then would ultimately turn transparent. By the end of their day of hunting for the blossoms, they had started to turn to a paler shade of blue, from the deep blue that they were before picking. It was a rare sight.

Slowly turning away from her reverie, Brynn expected to see something that would further remind her of her mother under the rolltop, but she was immediately disappointed. There were two books held securely by a couple of polished sandstone rocks serving as bookends. The books were both clearly ancient, hundreds, maybe thousands of years old by the look of them. The perfectly dry air of this strange place must have helped in preserving them. The books looked as if they were hand constructed, being a thick collection of parchments covered by slats of golden-hued wood. The binding was made by several holes drilled near the spine edge of the books through which a dark cord was threaded and tied tight.

Brynn marveled at the odd workmanship as she pulled one of the books for closer inspection. The cord that secured the binding was made of some type of plant fiber that Brynn had never seen before, and it was expertly braided in the same pattern that her mother had taught her since she was a young girl. There was no title or other identifying marks on the book cover itself.

Excitement welled up inside Brynn as she paused before opening the book. She paused to savor the moment and decided to explore the few remaining contents of the desk before taking her time with the books.

There was a small circular piece of wood about the same diameter as Brynn's thumb. Brynn picked it up and examined it. Curious. It was a token of passage for the lifts.

The wizards who made their homes in the cliffs that towered over most of Demon's Bluff had constructed a system of magically powered elevators that they would use to ferry themselves up and down the cliff face. They had built them cooperatively, apparently at great personal cost. They allowed the others the use of the lifts, but the fee was outrageous and could only be paid by those with means. Brynn had ridden them a few times, most recently to her mother's funeral atop the mesa.

The token had silver inlaid in the wood on one side with some simple marks that meant something to the wizards. Brynn casually flipped the coin over and was surprised to see a sigil drawn on the back in black ink. She studied it. It was not overly complex and it was different from the sigils she had seen recently. But she had seen it somewhere before. *But how was that possible?* It was drawn on sloppily, as if done in haste. Try as she might she could not recall, but she was certain that she had seen it before. She pocketed the token and turned her attention to the rest of the contents of the desk.

There was a stack of parchments and a quill accompanied by a squat stoppered bottle of Iron-Gall ink. She flipped through the stack of parchments and every one of them was blank. The paper was old and of the highest quality that Brynn had ever seen. It was papyrus hammered from reeds, and it had yellowed with age. Brynn knew that paper of this quality would cost a fortune, even for her family.

As Brynn returned the stack of parchment, she noticed a small indentation on the desktop that had been initially covered by the stack of parchments. She set the stack aside and slid her finger into the depression. It had a catch underneath that formed a small handle. She lifted up and opened a compartment, the lid of which appeared seamlessly integrated into the desktop. As she opened it, the sweet-spice smell of ghost flower wafted up overpoweringly. Inside the small concealed compartment were two small glass bottles that contained a blue inky liquid and several long flat sticks, each with a cluster of short steel needles set perpendicular to the wood on one end. Each stick had differing amounts of needles. Brynn recognized the tools. She had seen them being used in one of the tent stalls that was set up one year during the Festival of Drums in Demon's Bluff. They were for tattooing.

Instinctively, she unstopped a bottle and took a tentative sniff. Sure enough, this was the source of the ghost flower smell. It was pure and it was concentrated. The ink was still very blue. Perhaps the color was preserved from fading through some alchemical process? She smelled deeply of it again. It was the smell of her mother. *But all this would mean....*

Brynn did not want to think about it, even though the shocking truth was undeniable. It was said that witches tattooed themselves with mysterious magical sigils to protect them and give them magical power. If this hidden place was indeed her mother's, and these tools were used by her hands, then it could only mean she had secretly been a witch.

But she knew her mother. She had spent hundreds of hours watching her mother dress and ornament herself for fancy dinners and she had never seen a sigil tattooed on her. She forced herself not to think about it for the moment. She replaced the items and shut the compartment. She returned her attention to the books. She carefully lifted the cover of one of the two books, and flipped through the pages.

Whatever she was hoping to see in the book, she was disappointed. The entire book held page after page of what looked like genealogical information. Every page was sketched full with family trees. The handwriting changed constantly, often several different sets of writing on each page. All told, there must have been many dozens of hands that had added to this book. Perhaps well over a hundred. Brynn flipped page after page, glancing at a few of the names on each. None of them meant anything at all to her. As she flipped the last page, however, a name certainly caught her eye. It was *her* name! Brynn Vallant. Above it was her mother's name, and then her grandmother's name. Her name had been written in her mother's handwriting, but it wasn't really her name. She was Brynn Bygrave, daughter of Duke Dagorn Bygrave. But her mother had written her name as "Brynn Vallant".

Blodwynn Vallant
|
Elowynn Vallant
|
Brynn Vallant

What was Vallant? It was a name she had never even heard before. It wasn't even mother's maiden name. Could this genealogy follow a matriarchal line? With a secret surname handed down from mother to daughter? *Very strange.*

Brynn flipped the pages one last time to verify that there was nothing else of interest here. It was what it appeared to be, it was just page after page of recorded lineage of what looked like several families.

She turned her attention to the second book. It was something very different indeed. She thumbed through it and saw sigils, pages and pages of sigils. No words, no descriptions, just pattern after pattern after pattern. As she flipped through the pages, different tunes started to play in her head, each competing to be heard. Every pattern had a song of its own.

In many of the patterns toward the front of the tome, she could see elements of the pattern her mother had taught her. In later pages, the patterns grew far more complex. They often had the base pattern her mother had taught her, but incorporated new patterns, variants and new elements. The further she flipped through the pages, the more difficult the sigils became to look at. They were confusing and made her eyeballs hurt and her temples begin to throb. The base of her neck grew tight as the cacophony of discordant melodies played all at once in her mind. She flipped back to the patterns at the beginning. The confusion melted away and the patterns were beautiful and inviting, represented by simple and memorable songs.

As Brynn wondered what all this might mean, she noticed the very last page in the book of sigils had come loose, and was protruding from the rest of the pages at an irregular angle. She turned the book over and lifted the back cover. The page slipped out and fluttered down to the sand at her feet. The page did not have any holes drilled in it for binding. It was also of a different manufacture than the rest of the parchment of the book. Clearly, it was not a page that had come loose, but rather a single sheet that had been tucked in. She picked it up and turned it over. It was a letter addressed to her mother, written in a distinctive boxy scrawl.

1st Day of Summer – 3:45 PM – The Kuma – 9 Hours and 45 minutes before the Earthquake

Needle's pace slowed and he ultimately came to a stop as he read the letter Brynn handed him.

Elowynn,

I fear things grow dark. Signs of the return of the Cult of Yex abound, as you know, but worse I think we are betrayed again, and I think I know who it is. Already our group of three has been reduced to two and it is yet too early for replacements. Someone has been following me recently. I was cornered in an alley by a man that I did not recognize. He underestimated me. I beat him and escaped. It is imperative that we speak ... If only there was a way to also speak with our fallen comrade from beyond the realms of death...The signs become clearer each day, but we have no help and no answers. I believe we must risk a meeting. But we must be careful, as I fear we are both in danger.

- Kemano

- The Society of Eyes

Brynn watched Needle's face as he read the letter.

"My father couldn't have written this." Needle's voice was not confident.

"I thought you said it was his handwriting?"

"Well no--yes--it is. But I know my father. He wouldn't say this, wouldn't write this."

"I know the feeling, Needle. In just the last week, I have learned that my mother was not at all who I thought she was. I thought that she was just, you know, my mother. But clearly there was a secret part of her life that I am just learning about. I denied it for several days, but it's true. I think I am the only one in my family who knows what I have discovered."

Needle just stood there in the middle of the dusty alley and stared at the letter.

"Why do you think I came seeking your father, Needle?"

Needle looked up at her, but still said nothing.

Brynn went on. "When I asked around the Kuma for him today, I was told he's been missing for a year. My mother was murdered a year ago."

Needle looked at her with genuine empathy. "What happened?"

Brynn swallowed. "She was murdered by an Agrabi man, an intruder into one of the towers of our estate."

"Who was the man? Did you see him?" Needle asked.

"I-I don't know." Brynn felt as if Needle was trying to stare right through her. His dark eyes seemed to widen. He was intensely studying her face. She could not hold his gaze and looked away. "I didn't see him. My brother told me that he--he fled."

Needle seemed lost for a moment and looked at the ground pensively. He looked back up at her with his big eyes. The contrast of the whites of his eyes to the olive dark skin of his face was startling.

"So what do you want from me, then?"

"Don't you see?" Brynn asked. "It's in that letter. My mother and your father. They knew each other. They were the last two members of something called *The Society of Eyes*. My mother is dead, your father is missing. They were connected, Needle. And so are we."

One Week Earlier – 84th Day of Spring – 8:55 PM – The Secret Desert

Brynn double-checked the desk for any other hidden caches and satisfied that there were none, turned her attention to the monoliths. She surmised they were some type of magical portal that was activated by the proper tracing of a sigil. She had entered through the first monolith and decided to have a look at the second. Was it the way back? Or did it lead someplace new entirely?

This second monolith appeared to be identical to the first from which she entered in all respects except for the sigil etched in the black stone. The sigil on the first monolith was the pattern of the three eyes. This sigil, however, was far more complicated. It was larger and had more intersecting lines. The arcs doubled back on themselves at odd angles.

Brynn soon realized that her head was cocked at an angle just like that of a dog hearing a sound it didn't understand. She was trying to find the center of the pattern, the starting point that she could trace, but she just couldn't. A cacophony of discordant musical notes played in her head, like a troupe of bards warming up their instruments before a performance at the Festival of Drums. None of the notes made sense with each other. Her head was hurting. She felt dizzy and plopped down in the red sand and closed her eyes.

Soon she was feeling all right again. But the sigil on that monolith was beyond her comprehension. If this monolith was the way back, she was going to have a problem. But there was no cause for panic just yet. She knew she could trace the sigil on the first one. So she walked back to the first monolith, through which she had originally entered this weird desert landscape.

To her great relief, when she traced the eyes sigil on the stone it flashed and the monolith shimmered as a ripple raced across its jet black surface. She reached for her lantern that she had left in the sand and touched her toe to the surface of the monolith. Sure enough, it slipped right through as if there were nothing there. She stepped partially through and pushed her face into the blackness. There was another flash of white light. She held her lantern aloft and breathed a sigh of relief to see in the dim light the sandstone passageway with the bench and the basin. She smelled the stink of the sludge and heard the squeaking of a rat. She couldn't have imagined she could be so relieved at those sounds and smells. She was back.

1st Day of Summer – 4:00 PM – The Kuma – 9 Hours and 30 Minutes Before the Earthquake

"Ok," Needle admitted as they stood together in the alley, the letter still clutched in his hand. "It seems we are connected somehow. But I don't see what that means. What do we do about it?"

Brynn looked into his dark brown eyes. "There are things about our parents, Needle, which we did not know. But I have this feeling in my gut. I need you to trust me when I say that I think our parents intended *us* to be the replacements mentioned in the letter from your father."

"How can you possibly know that?" Needle demanded. He obviously didn't share the same feeling.

"I never realized it before, but my mother was training me, teaching me things. Preparing me for something that she felt she could not explain to me. She was killed before she could tell me. Something tells me it was probably the same with your father and you."

"That is just a guess! You actually have no proof of that," exclaimed Needle, his voice just a little too loud. They must have looked an odd pair standing on the border of the Kuma and the Lower Steppe: a scrawny Agrabi boy and a poorly-disguised Buerdeleise girl arguing in the middle of the dusty road.

Needle quickly glanced around. People were staring, but that was all. "Sorry. I--I just miss my father. This is a lot for me all at once. What do you want of me?" he said in a much quieter and careful tone as they started walking again.

Brynn walked at his side. "I am sorry, too. I hope your father is alive. If he is, he has answers that we desperately need to know. I think my mother deliberately left some things for me to find. Among them, I found that letter from your father. I have spent the last several days searching all over my family's estate for more clues about my mother. But I haven't found anything more yet. There is only one more place for me to look. And I want, I mean, I would like your help."

"What do you mean, 'your family's estate'? Are you from one of the noble houses?"

"My father is Duke Bygrave."

"*Dagorn Bygrave?*" Needle's face jutted forward as his eyebrows rose in unison.

"You seem surprised," Brynn said slowly, suddenly wary. The look on Needle's face was one of extreme agitation and confusion. She worried she had said something wrong.

"It's just that I was planning on trying to see him tonight," he said. "To sell him those old artifacts on the table in our house."

Brynn was shocked by this. "What makes you think that my father would want to buy those?"

"My father was an artifact hunter. He took me with him into

the desert sometimes to find relics from an old religion from thousands of years ago. Dagorn wanted them and paid my father for them for years and years."

This could not be true. She knew her father and he had no collection of such things. "My father? Dagorn Bygrave? Up on the Middle Steppe?"

Needle nodded.

Over this past week, intricate webs of thoughts and beliefs had been rearranging themselves and establishing connections in ways Brynn had never dreamed. This was apparently one more spindly fiber floating across her consciousness to create this as yet incomplete new pattern. Nothing was as she had believed it. She felt unsteady on her feet, her heart beating irregularly.

Somewhere in the distance to the south of them in the Kuma, a dog began barking furiously. Soon several other dogs joined it and barked continuously for what must have been more than a minute before they settled down. The two young people listened without looking at each other.

"Never heard anything like that before," Needle stated flatly when the dogs stopped barking. He started to walk again, crossing from the Kuma into the southwestern section of the Lower Steppe on their way toward the Middle Steppe. The sheer cliff that backed the Middle Steppe jutted toward the sky. Its long shadow was extending across all of Demon's Bluff, bringing relief from the desert sun.

Brynn walked at Needle's side, letting him contemplate the meaning of all this. Finally, he seemed to come to a conclusion and stopped. He said, "I will help you if you think it will help find my father. But what do you want me to do?"

Brynn hesitated. She didn't know exactly how to put her plan into words. The idea had come to her over the week, but now that she was going to speak it aloud, she felt her confidence wane. Still, it felt right. It was the same feeling she had that Needle and her were supposed to meet. She decided to tell him anyway. "I want to, I need to--to visit my mother's grave..."

She paused. Needle didn't seem surprised. He just stared at her.

"I have to see it," Brynn continued. "I can't really explain why, but I think there might be clues on her funerary box that will help us. Maybe even to help find your father. Or learn more about him, at least. I know it sounds crazy, Needle. But for reasons that I can't explain, you are the only one I can trust right now."

"So she is entombed in one of the mausoleums up on the plateau? The Bygrave Mausoleum, no doubt?"

Brynn nodded, a bit surprised. "You've heard of it?"

"Just today, in fact," Needle said with a worried look. "Which makes this day even crazier than it was before."

Brynn wasn't sure how it could get crazier. She continued, "I was sobbing at my mother's funeral and wasn't paying a lot of attention to what was happening. I didn't realize that things were not right until this week when I thought about it more. She had been wrapped from head to toe in bandages. I need to see her."

"Like a mummy? But that's an Agrabi custom, before we send bodies down the river."

"Yes. Funny it did not bother me at the time. I guess I wasn't thinking clearly. It was a small private ceremony: my father, brother, me and a few servants. I think somebody was trying to hide something by covering her up. I need to know what that something is. It is why I need to open her sarcophagus and why I need your help. I am not strong enough by myself."

Needle frowned. "You shouldn't keep bodies like that," he said. "It's better to send them down the river, away from the town."

Brynn shook her head. She wasn't going to argue with him about the customs of their people. Besides, it didn't matter.

The dogs started barking again.

"I'll do it," Needle said. "I'll meet you up there. At midnight, at the Bygrave Mausoleum."

They reached the border between the Lower and the Middle Steppe. The Middle Steppe was really just a heap of boulders and rubble that had sloughed off the cliff. It was nestled right up against the cliff face and other than the wizard homes burrowed into the cliff face itself, it offered the best view out over Demon's Bluff, the lazy Demon River and the desert further to the east.

"I'm glad you will be there. Thank you, Needle," Brynn said. She felt the sincerity of her own words and knew again that this was the correct pattern to follow. "I can make my way from here. Thank you for walking with me."

"See you tonight," he said, waving his bony, hard-worn hand at her.

CHAPTER SIX
Waiting for Darkness

In time, our spies discovered what bolstered the wizards of the Cult of Yex. They had somehow acquired a most pernicious drug: a dark red moss, which so far as we knew, grew only in the depths of the Abyss itself. How they came to possess it we never learned, but it empowered the spells of the cult's wizards. But at what cost to them, we could only speculate.

-Archmage Gadrax Von Torinovo

1st Day of Summer – 3:30 PM – Needle's Home in the Kuma – 10 Hours Before the Earthquake

Letharchenel fixed on the most decrepit hovel he had ever seen, at the very edge of the desert sands in the southern end of Demon's Bluff. And to think he had supposed the boy Cael was living in poverty. King Tharchelon must have a good reason to want these children dead.

He shrugged. He was the king's assassin and he had his orders. Their time had run out. Finding this place had been more difficult than he anticipated. It took him well into the afternoon.

He slunk across the dirt road, unseen by any denizen of this indigent slub. He slipped silently past the bundle of boards that served as a front door into the mud shanty. He grasped the hilt of one of his daggers in his right hand and laid the flat of the knife against his forearm under his linen sleeve. His face would be the last Needle would ever see. Just like so many before him that had died by his blade.

However, Needle wasn't home. Only an ancient olive-skinned blind woman rocked back and forth in her chair in the heat of the afternoon. Needle's grandmother, he wondered? He could see the milky white cataracts that completely clouded her vision. He expected that her hearing might have grown more acute to compensate, nevertheless she was completely unaware of his presence. After all, how could she have heard him? He had made no sound.

He looked around the hovel. It was almost bare, except for a table filled with treasures that seemed terribly out of place. He could take his fill, but now was not the time.

He could kill the old woman easily of course, but better not to give Needle cause to be cautious if he found the old woman dead. He wouldn't suspect his fate if he came home and found her just as he left her.

The assassin slipped out as stealthily as he had slipped in. He flipped open the parchment again and considered his last two targets. Brother and sister he guessed: Brynn and Mallet Bygrave. Needle would get a few extra hours to breathe.

CHAPTER SEVEN
heart of Darkness

The free city of Demon's Bluff has thrived for thousands of years in the inhospitable desert for three reasons. First, the Arcanus Navitas, the flow of magical energy that only wizards can sense is, for reasons not well understood, more concentrated around the plateau. Wizards flock to Demon's Bluff for the same reason that the Cult of Yex built their ancient citadel atop the mesa. Second, Demon's Bluff is a crucial trade hub connecting the ancient caravan route to the commerce of the Demon River. Known only as 'The Road,' it is the only overland trade artery between the western desert and the kingdoms of the east. Finally, the seasonal floods of the Demon River bring rich silt of glacial runoff from the far northern ice. Combined with innovative irrigation and a system of dikes to keep the town safe, Demon's Bluff is an agricultural oasis.

-Return of the Cult of Yex, by Caed the Chronicler

1st Day of Summer – 9:00 PM – Demon's Bluff Middle Steppe – 4 Hours and 30 Minutes Before the Earthquake

Mallet Bygrave walked with the deliberate gait of a man determined to confess the greatest of crimes: murder.

At fifteen, he was far too young to bear such a burden. There was only one person he could think to turn to: his father. But his father was also the last person he wanted to tell. His father was increasingly quick to anger. *He could disown me,* Mallet realized. *But I did what I did. There is no taking it back.*

Worse, this wasn't the first time he had killed someone. The first time, a year ago, had been justified. He had no doubts about that. He had his father's approval, even his tacit praise.

But today's altercation seemed now like a horrible mistake. Would his father again justify him? Or would he fly into a rage? Dagorn Bygrave was a complicated man, more so since the death of his wife, Mallet's mother.

The sun was setting in the west, though the fury of its heat remained and reverberated among the red sandstone boulders crowding the winding road he walked up toward the Middle Steppe. Unlike most, Mallet liked the heat, but now it seemed to drain his will and amplify his thirst. A hot desert wind kicked up from the southwest as he plodded along. He leaned on the haft of his glaive and could hear the ringing of its curved blade as the sand blasted it. He caught the scent of sage and pinion pine as wind-driven sand stung his bare scalp and shoulders.

His white cotton pants and flaxen cord belt flapped in the wind as he bowed his six and a half-foot frame against it, seemingly impervious to the sirocco's assault. He rarely wore a tunic and today was no different. His muscular shoulders, chest and back were deeply tanned, as was his face. He liked to labor shirtless down at the docks bucking bales of cotton, tobacco and other goods. His clean-shaven scalp was also a deep, burnished brown. Despite his youth, a week's scraggly growth of dark whiskers, some bleached red by the sun, bristled all over his jaw. Many people often mistook him as one of the olive-skinned Agrabi natives, though he was much taller and his facial features were clearly Buerdeleise: blue eyes, narrow nose and square jaw.

A sudden powerful gust erupted in a cacophonous howl, as if trying to prevent him from returning home and facing his father. He raised his arm to cover his face from the enveloping dust, but he could not keep it from blasting its way into his nose and throat.

He strode on against the storm and could just make out a brown-robed young Agrabi boy being propelled toward him by the wind, arms flailing, out of control.

Mallet grunted and took one step to the left. Lowering the arm that shielded his face, he hooked the boy by the waist, startling him. The boy screeched and fought against him, but Mallet pulled the boy close to him, enveloping him in his own body, as he turned his back to brunt the storm.

"It's okay," Mallet said soothingly. The boy stopped fighting. As quickly as the wind had come, it died, leaving dancing dust devils skittering across the road and disappearing like startled lizards melting into the landscape.

Mallet took a cautious breath. The air was still laden with reddish dust and the smell of desert sage and pinion was gaining strength. He tried to swallow the dry desert taste away, but could barely generate enough saliva. He brushed dust from his face and arms as he tried in vain to swallow again. Thirst was common in the desert; especially on hard days of work at the docks, but Mallet had rarely been as thirsty as he felt now.

"Go on," he said to the boy. The boy looked up at him, muddy tears drying on his cheeks. He turned and fled down the road without so much as a thank you.

Mallet resumed his troubled thoughts and his journey to face his father. What would he say? He imagined him standing resolute against the wind in his blue silk robe, sandaled feet, and a crystal goblet of wine imported from the vineyards of Taglyon. Mallet shivered despite the heat. Was it fear of facing his father? Or was it something else? There was something strange about this evening, something portentous, ominous. It felt like the night his mother died.

He looked up at the towering bluff for which his city was named. Somewhere up there on the mesa, his mother was entombed in his family's mausoleum. He scanned the highest reaches of the cliffs, covered in the catwalks, ladders and lifts. The famed wizards of Demon's Bluff made their homes and laboratories in caves honeycombed into the cliff face.

Mallet's family and the other high-born of the city lived in the Middle Steppe, the elevated area between the base of the cliff and the rest of Demon's Bluff below. The Middle Steppe was perched on a jumbled mass of rocks that had cascaded down from the cliff above eons ago, creating a smaller, rougher plateau. It was this elevated perch upon which the nobility of Demon's Bluff had established their dominion over the inhabitants of the city. Large ducal estates dotted the whole district.

Cedars, mesquites and pinion pines survived and even thrived in the Middle Steppe district, but were rare in other parts of the city. A spring-fed stream, called the Demon's Race, cascaded down over the edge of the mesa in a splendid rainbow-hued misty waterfall. It provided clean water to the trees and nobles who lived in this privileged place before it eventually wound through the Lower Steppe below and trickled into the Demon River.

Mallet cringed. His family *was* nobility, but they were now among the lowest of the noble families in Demon's Bluff. His father had told him grand stories of the past when the Bygraves were among the wealthiest and most dominant. There had been a time when his family's name had been feared. But now the mealy Bygraves were a few wrong moves from removal from the Middle Steppe.

Mallet and his father shared a single-minded obsession to return the family to glory. What happened on the docks today, however....

He quickened his pace. The shadow cast by the mesa stretched now to the eastern horizon, shading the town and desert beyond in gray. He passed the stunning wrought iron gates of the Grimwise estate and came to the lane just past their eight-foot stucco walls.

As he walked, he put his hands in his pocket and found the black pouch he'd put there earlier. He took it and poured the contents into his other meaty palm. Twelve silver moons. Curious.

He turned right, and presently the lane began to descend slightly. From his vantage, he was looking straight east. He felt a strange yearning as he gazed out to the shadowy dunes beyond the river. He remembered his father once saying that their ancestors had come from the east, long, long ago.

He could see the lazy Demon River chugging along in the wide, gentle curve just beyond the dikes that protected the Lower Steppe of Demon's Bluff from regular floods. Docks and piers jutted into the river like the remaining teeth of a smiling old Agrabi woman. That was where he worked every day, learning and minding his father's shipping affairs. He grimaced. It was on those docks that he had committed both of his crimes, his first a year ago, and his most recent this very day.

He could just see the Bygrave warehouse from here, on the river directly east, near the cluster of docks where it had all gone so wrong this morning. The city sprawled out beneath him; the merchant district in the center of town surrounded by countless roads and cottages that sprawled in every direction, the irrigated farms to the north, the rows of shanties in the Kuma to the south, like desperate fingers reaching straight into the desolation of sand. The whole of Demon's Bluff was beginning to come alive with lanterns and candles like twinkling stars in the twilight.

Directly ahead of him at the end of the lane, clinging to the edge of a narrow gully strewn with sandstone boulders and overgrown with cedar, was the family estate. The Bygrave estate was rundown and humble by comparison to the rest of the estates on the Middle Steppe, but one day it would all be his. He had only one sibling, his sister Brynn, making him his father's only heir. Would it all be lost when he confessed to his father?

The estate consisted of three old adobe buildings with roofs topped with faded red clay shingles. The first and largest building was the main house, with three different towers over two stories high, providing excellent views of the city below. A smaller building toward the back housed the servants while the building to the left housed the horses, carriage and various tools. The entire estate was ringed with a wall made of mortared sandstones, badly in need of a coat of stucco.

Mallet followed the road, which was scattered with red pepper pods, to the front gates. Pepper trees lined the lane and Mallet batted their leafy branches with his hand as he walked under their green fronds. When he was seven years old, his mother had ordered the saplings and Mallet had helped plant the hardy trees all along the road. Every morning after that, until his mother had died, he had carried buckets of water from the fountain in the courtyard, watering all twenty-six of these trees. Servants now tended them as he couldn't bear to do it since her death. Mallet lingered for a moment on the thought of a bucket of clear cool water. He could still taste the sand that dirtied his mouth as he swallowed with difficulty.

Even in the growing darkness, he noticed how dilapidated the wooden gates between the sandstone walls were. Though they were reinforced with decorative wrought iron, they needed repairs and a new coat of paint.

Was anyone at the gate? His father employed several Agrabi servants, one of which was to stay close and mind the gate, though that duty seemed to be regularly neglected. More often than not, the assigned gatekeeper could be found in the stable playing Agrabi tile games with the other servants.

Mallet banged on the gate with the butt of his glaive. The sound was hollow and empty. What would become of him if his father disowned him and sent him away? Humble though this property was, it was opulent compared to how most people lived in Demon's Bluff. He could always find work on the docks if it came to it, but looking up here where his family lived without him would be more than he could bear.

Could his father really send him away for what he had done? What if someone had seen and reported the murder to the town watch? Being disowned might be the least of his worries. It wasn't as if he had killed an Agrabi, he had killed another Buerdeleise, that could mean the gallows.

The gate opened and his father stood there, goblet in hand. "Come in, Mallet," he said, his voice deep with a slight vibration that meant he had been drinking, a much more common occurrence since his mother's death. He was dressed in his usual blue silk robes. His father stared at him with his small grey eyes glittering as they did with a glassy appearance when he was drunk.

Mallet felt his guts tighten from the fear of his father's reaction. He smelled the wine on his father's breath. Dagorn was unpredictable in the best of times, but Mallet feared that his most likely response to his confession would be swift and terrible. But his mother had taught him to be a man and face up to his mistakes.

He entered the old familiar courtyard. Lanterns hung from the eaves of the buildings, casting the estate in the warm, friendly glow that Mallet had known from childhood. There was a water fountain fashioned from red polished sandstone in the center of the yard, ringed by a circular red brick carriageway. Various shrubs and trees were planted throughout the estate.

Something was wrong however. There should have been the sound of gurgling as the water spouted up from the fountain in the middle and cascaded down into the tile lined basin. Instead, all he could hear were his father's soft sandaled footsteps over the bricks of the carriageway as he walked toward the fountain.

"Have you seen Wheizer?" Father asked back over his shoulder. Wheizer was his father's most trusted servant, a man whom Mallet both respected and feared.

Mallet shook his head, hearing his boots clump on the bricks as he walked with his father.

"You must be thirsty," Father said, taking a sip from his own wine glass. His black ring glinted in the lantern light.

Mallet was, and he needed an excuse not to talk for a moment, so he could gather his courage. But the stone basin in the center of the courtyard was empty. Mallet ran a finger through the thin film of gritty mud, which was all that remained at the bottom of the basin.

"The spring suddenly stopped running this morning," Father explained.

Mallet swallowed, his dry throat desperate for a long, cool drink of water. His lips were cracked; his tongue felt swollen and tasted like dirt.

"How could it stop?" Mallet croaked. "Why?"

"Don't know, but the last thing I need is the added expense of having water delivered every day. It stopped this morning. I sent servants to investigate. The spring at the Treybilcock estate stopped flowing, too." Father threw his head back and drained the goblet.

"How do we fix it?"

"I don't know. I'll send for an engineer from the cliff tomorrow to look at it. I'm not going to worry about it tonight," Father said with a shrug. "Get caught in that dust storm?" He sat on the edge of the stone basin, looking up at the first stars of the night. It was almost peaceful.

Mallet desperately wanted to quench his thirst before he talked to his father, but more, he wanted to get his confession over with. "I have something to tell you, Father," Mallet said. Turning, he sat down next his father, dwarfing him.

"Does this night remind you of anything?" Father asked.

Mallet took a long, exaggerated breath. It was one of those nights when Father was going to get melancholy. He was dangerous when he was melancholy. His mood could deteriorate quickly.

"I don't want to talk about that now," Mallet said, steeling himself for his father's possible outburst.

"Do you fear dying?" Father asked, staring into his empty glass.

That was the last thing Mallet expected him to say. Did his father already know what he had done?

"We can't pretend it didn't happen."

Mallet's mind raced. How could he know? He said nothing as he braced himself for his father's reaction to his crime.

"It was one year ago today that your mother was murdered."

1st Day of Summer – 9:00 PM – Bygrave Estate – One Year Ago

There are screams of joy, of terror of anger. Then there are screams of irrepressible loss.

"What was that?" Mallet's sister Brynn said, jerking her head up at the sound of a long horrific scream. They sat together in the spacious sitting room, arguing over the studies their mother had given them. Numbers came easy to Brynn, but she struggled to help her brother understand.

"It's Mother," Mallet said, rising so fast he sent his chair crashing behind him. Mallet had noticed that parents had the uncanny ability to discern the true meaning of their children's screams in an instant. And in this case, he instantly recognized his mother's scream and what it meant. Horror filled him. "Mother's hurt! It came from the south tower!"

"But I heard Father!" Brynn cried, following him.

Father? How could she be so obtuse? He sprinted down the hall, easily outdistancing his sister, his feet pounding on the old tile floors almost as loud as his heart. He raced up the wooden stairs and saw the door slightly ajar. Lantern-light flickered within. He lowered his shoulder, knocking the door back as he barreled into the room.

Time seemed to stop. The light from a swaying lantern revealed blood everywhere, rendering the small square room's previous function, namely dry-goods storage, all but inconsequential. The floor, the walls, the shelves with their jars, sacks of grain, crates of potatoes and other stores were all spattered with splotches of blood.

On the tile floor laid his mother, on her back. She vainly struggled for life, holding her stomach. Blood seeped between her fingers. Blood gushed from a deep gash in her throat, and her gasps for breath were mingled with a foaming, sputtering sound.

Mallet came alive. He turned and slammed the door shut, sliding the lock into place. This was something Brynn should never see.

He was not a moment too soon. Brynn arrived, pounding on the door with a series of fast, hollow thuds.

Mallet turned back to the scene. At first, all he had seen was the blood and his mother. Now he noticed other things. One, the smell of blood made the hair in his nostrils stiffen and his stomach revolt. His mouth watered like it does right before vomiting.

The next thing he noticed was his father, also covered in blood, standing to the left of his mother, bent over halfway, as if trying to regain his breath. Mallet couldn't tell if his father was wounded or just covered in his mother's blood. Several feet away, near the open window stood a short, muscular, fiftyish Agrabi man with a full wiry head of black hair, dressed in linen trousers and a tunic. The whites of his eyes were bloodshot and he looked desperate.

Shards of crystal lay on the floor, and Mallet could smell the hint of burgundy wine that had been splashed everywhere. His father must have dropped his goblet.

"You!" Father cried at the Agrabi.

Mallet looked at the man. Their eyes met just as the man turned and jumped straight through the through window, knocking one of the shutters off its hinges. He disappeared into the night with a crash of branches into the foliage below.

Brynn continued to pound on the door, screaming.

Mallet just stared at his mother as she lay dying. She had stopped moving, stopped struggling to hold her stomach. Her eyes stared peacefully in Mallet's direction and then closed for the last time.

He looked at his mother's dead body. What in the hells was happening to her? It felt grotesque to look at her this way. Common decency said he should look away. This was a sight he would want to forget for the rest of his life.

She transformed right before his eyes. Her unblemished skin began to change. Slowly the faintest of blue began to appear in blotches all over her face, arms and neck. The blue blotches slowly darkened, turning from light to a deep, dark blue. The blotches grew and filled in. They connected to each other forming insane swirls and impossible patterns. *His mother's entire body was completely covered with tattoos.* The hideous marks must have been there all along, invisible while she lived. When she died, whatever magic kept them unseen died with her, exposing the appalling witch sigils. His mother's face, his mother's beautiful face, would be gone from his memory forever. In his core, Mallet knew that anytime he tried to remember his own mother's face, he wouldn't be able to remember her the way he wanted to. The memory of her face would always be ruined by those loathsome tattoos.

Horror transfixed him as the thundering realization of what his mother truly was hit him full force. It came as a complete shock. His entire life growing up, he had never had the slightest inkling of the truth. A small part of him began to hate what his mother had done to herself. The betrayal he felt was utter. He looked at his father. Sorrow filled his eyes. His father was not surprised by her hideous transformation. He knew and it saddened him deeply.

"Father," Mallet said.

Their gazes met.

"Brynn can never know. She can never see this," Dagorn said sadly. "No one can ever know."

Mallet nodded solemnly. At all costs, Brynn must be protected from this--this abomination.

Father pointed with his left hand out the open window. "That Agrabi man killed your mother," his said in a raspy croak, tears welling in his eyes. "Find Wheizer and track him."

Mallet allowed himself one last look at his deceased mother.

What had she done to herself? His mother was a witch, universally reviled and hated by everyone. Even the Thieves' Guild and the Agrabi were tolerated more than witches in Demon's Bluff. Stories of insane witches and their abominations abounded. And now he had seen it with his own eyes. His mother was a witch. Would he ever be able to forgive her?

1st Day of Summer – 9:15 PM – Bygrave Estate – 4 Hours 15 Minutes Before the Earthquake

"You still hate me for not being able to save her?" Father asked, leaning against the dry fountain.

Mallet breathed in the hot night air and shrugged. It was complicated.

His father continued, "You remember that night." It wasn't a question. "Do you think the Bygrave name could become great again if the truth about your mother got out?"

Mallet's skin prickled in anger, though not certain whether he was angry at his mother or his father.

"You remember what we decided?" Father asked.

Mallet nodded. He remembered *that* night perfectly, and the decision he had made with his father.

"I've told no one about the... things," Mallet said. He swallowed and suddenly remembered his fierce thirst.

"We can't let it be known, can we?" Father said and he reached out and grabbed Mallet's shoulder in the dark. It was a strange decaying smell that had become all too common of late.

"I have something I need to tell you," Mallet said, pulling away from his father's grasp. He steeled his nerves. Mother had told him, *A man faces his responsibilities. A boy hides from them.* "It's about the family. Something I've done."

The air was dry and still. His father's face was cast in deep shadow as he waited for Mallet to continue.

Mallet swallowed, his mouth even drier.

The gate creaked open as someone pushed it.

"Wheizer?" Father turned toward the gate.

Mallet stood up. It was darker by the gate, but Mallet could see that it was Brynn. He knew her shape and the way she walked, even in the shadows. Mallet thought she was wearing the brown robes of an Agrabi. Her auburn hair was sweaty and tousled around her red, puffy face.

"Fetch me when Wheizer returns," Father said, walking away toward the main house.

Mallet wanted to run after him, but he hesitated. He had been so close to confessing.

"Wash your face," he said looking back at Brynn. "It's caked in dirt." As soon as he said it, he realized the fountain was dry.

"What's bothering Father?" she asked, looking forlorn.

"He wanted to talk about Mother."

Brynn put her hand to her mouth, "Oh!"

"What?"

"I haven't told you," she said.

"What?"

"Not yet," she said looking around furtively.

Mallet frowned down at his sister. He definitely had a soft spot in his heart for her, but he hated when she played these little games, dramatizing everything and trying to get him to guess what she was thinking.

"Did you see Mother?" Brynn asked. "The night she died?"

Mallet felt his stomach lurch. Why must everyone bring up that horrible night? "I told you I had, but I'm not going to describe it to you!"

His sister looked up at him. She was tenacious, he knew, and intuitive too. What was she thinking? He immediately found out, "Was there anything about her that was strange?"

You mean besides her slit throat and stab wound? But Mallet knew what she meant: the... things. Did she know about them? How could she? *I can't allow her to know that her mother was a witch.*

He realized he was more concerned with protecting his sister than the family name. He didn't want to see her get hurt. But protecting her wasn't easy with her quick mind and quicker mouth.

Mallet just didn't answer further.

Brynn, being Brynn, pressed on: "Do you remember the

family crest, etched on the lid of her sarcophagus?"

Mallet furrowed his brow and said nothing. What did that have to do with anything?

"I think Father has some kind of secret collection of old artifacts," Brynn said. The rapid fire subject changes had Mallet confused.

"What are you talking about?" he almost yelled.

"I heard it today," Brynn said quietly, leaning her head toward him conspiratorially.

"Is that where you've been, out listening to rumors?" Then he thought of what he himself had discovered today. Did his father know?

"I have to go do something important, Mallet," she said, running her fingers through her hair. "Something important that can't wait."

"So what if he does collect artifacts?" Mallet asked. *But does he do other things far worse?* "What's that got to do with anything?" He had rarely felt this annoyed at her.

"Why would he keep it a secret?" Brynn asked.

"Listen to yourself, Brynn!" Mallet exclaimed. "You're just guessing. You don't actually know anything."

She gave him a blank look.

"He's old and eccentric," Mallet said. "He worries constantly about our family's station. He is sad about Mother's murder and feels guilty he couldn't save her. He drinks too much and his temper is on edge. And you are worried that he has a secret collection? Are you mad?"

"I think Mother had secrets of her own," Brynn said slowly, as if to herself. She let her hands drop to her side. "I need to look at that crest again."

Mother was a witch, Mallet thought.

Mallet was about to respond when there was a sound as the gate clicked shut. Wheizer Rhelbog sauntered into the courtyard, easy like, his long arms swinging. He was a tall, lanky man in his late thirties with black greasy hair, a long, pointed nose and scraggly whiskers. He served as his father's right hand man, and had been around since before Mallet and Brynn were born. He also served as something of a mentor to Mallet, at least when it came to how to fight. Wheizer had taught Mallet how to fight with sword, glaive and fists. His teaching approach favored repeated and humiliating beatings until his pupil could defend himself. It had worked as Mallet had grown into a formidable warrior, but maddeningly, he still couldn't best Wheizer.

"I got to go," Brynn said suddenly. Mallet had noticed that she did not like the tall man, though Wheizer had been nothing but polite to her. Brynn walked to the main house, pulled on the decorative wrought iron ring and swung the large cedar front door open. It screeched on hinges, badly in need of oil, as she closed it behind her.

"What'd I say?" Wheizer smiled effortlessly as he came up to the fountain. He wore a simple linen tunic and pants, with a belted rapier at his waist, and tall knee-high black boots.

"It's your smell," Mallet said to him humorlessly.

"Whew! I'm sweatin' like a whore in church. Done a fair bit of running today," said Wheizer. "In this infernal heat and wind. Shouldn't it get cool when the sun goes down? What happened to the fountain?"

"Don't know," Mallet said.

"I ever tell you," Wheizer began, "how nice and cool it is down in Taglyon? Sure, it gets hot, but there is this breeze every evening, comes off the ocean and it just cools things down so nice."

"You ever seen that big castle they always talk about?" Mallet asked.

"When it's not hiding in the fog," Wheizer nodded. "Craziest thing you ever seen. I hear tell it's growing, too, just swallowing up the city a little at a time."

Mallet smiled. Wheizer was often sarcastic but once in a while he got reflective like he did actually care about the simple things in life.

"So nice and cool down there," Wheizer said.

"Father wants to talk to you," Mallet said, pointing to the door.

"I know," he said, not moving. "But your father is a patient man."

"I've never known him to be patient."

"You'd be surprised. He has more patience for long-range plans than most men could ever have."

"Well, I have to talk to him after you're done."

"Oh?" Wheizer said with a crooked smile on his thin lips. His nose twitched.

"I killed a man down at the docks today."

Wheizer's smile grew just a little. "Well, well, and not for the first time, eh?"

"Don't bring that up! He already talked about Mother tonight!"

"Why didn't you tell him about this 'incident'?"

"He wanted to talk about Mother."

"Yes," Wheizer mused, "Death is a bit of a struggle to comprehend, isn't it? But revenge not so hard. You know all about revenge, don't you, Mallet?"

"This is different! It's complicated. It concerns business."

Wheizer laughed and refused to relent on that night one year ago, "I ever tell you I was impressed with what you did? Mallet, you got a heart of darkness. Hells, you scared even me that night."

2nd Day of Summer – 3:00 AM – The Docks – One Year Ago

"By the hells, Mallet!" Wheizer said to him, putting a hand on his shoulder. The waxing moon had been three quarters full that night. Mallet dragged the barely conscious Agrabi man behind him across the planks of the docks toward the end of the pier. He and Wheizer had tracked and chased him for six hours tonight from where he had jumped through the window in the tower after he had killed Mother.

Mallet kicked the man again. "You made me chase you all night!" he snarled at him.

"Your father is going to want to talk to him!" Wheizer said.

"I didn't--do it," the man gasped. He was near unconsciousness.

Mallet flipped the man over and grabbed rope draped around a bollard. The silvery ring on the finger of the man's left hand glinted in the moonlight as he tied the man's wrists behind his back. Mallet stood, breathing hard, looking down on his prey--his mother's murderer. He kicked the man in the ribs several times in response to the rage building in him.

Blood frothed from the man's lips as Mallet sat him up.

"I don't know who you are, or why you did it, but you will pay for what you did," he hissed at the stocky Agrabi.

The man's head lolled. He looked out through unfocused bloodshot eyes.

Mallet gritted his teeth. This bastard had slit his mother's throat. Hurting the man helped fill the hole in his heart. Revenge had to be meted out.

He punched the man in the face repeatedly until he lost consciousness.

"Son of Abyss, Mallet," Wheizer said whistling as he approached, clearly impressed. Mallet turned and snarled at him as if he were a desert lion protecting a kill.

Mallet tried to take a deep breath, but his heart was beating too fast. The night air was incredibly hot, even on the river, and sweat poured from him. He hadn't known he was capable of this kind of violence. He hoped the feeling would go away soon. But he knew it wouldn't. Not until he did what he had to do. There was only one cure for a pain this deep.

His mother was dead, covered in twisted demonic symbols. He blocked himself from thinking about it. What was going on? Nothing was right and this man was somehow responsible for it all. Not just her murder, but what she was as well. Mallet knew that last part wasn't true but his mind couldn't grapple with the truth--that his mother was a witch.

He bent down and lifted the man up; an easy task for someone as big as Mallet. He looked left and right. He had no idea what time it was, but it was probably a few hours before sunrise. No one was on the pier. He looked down into the river. Moonlight reflected off the lazy flow.

The man groaned, regaining consciousness. Mallet felt a sudden resurgence of anger and hurled the bound man into the current. The splash settled and Mallet watched him drift downstream. Mallet felt tears well in his eyes and an inarticulate scream of rage erupted from his throat. He clenched his battered fists, feeling the slick blood that covered them.

The man bobbed three times and then sank down beneath the waves, disappearing into the darkness.

1st Day of Summer – 9:25 PM – The Bygrave Estate – 4 Hours and 5 Minutes Before the Earthquake

Mallet stirred from the memory.

"They say," Wheizer opined, "that once a killer, always a killer. Isn't that the way with sin? Once you taste it, it's got you and you can never let go."

"That's not true," Mallet said, though he worried deep in his bones that it might be. What happened at the docks today was kind of evidence of that, wasn't it? And if Wheizer was right, then there was something else that Mallet now feared. Being disowned by his family or hung as a murderer was one thing. But becoming a true monster, living only to kill,.. that was another.

The front door opened and Father poked his head out. "Wheizer!" he said impatiently. Mallet felt his heart clench. Father held another drink in his hand.

"I got to go, killer," Wheizer said with a smirk. "Talk to you soon."

Wheizer left and Mallet was glad. He had a terrible knot in his innards.

He knew he should go quench his thirst, but he didn't have the will to move.

Am I more worried about what I have done, he thought, or what I fear my father is doing down on those docks? What would Mother think?

He sat in the darkness on the edge of the fountain alone for a long time, musing on his mother's death and his mother's killer. He still knew nothing more than he knew that night and the cynical voice in his head was right. He hadn't even really tried to figure it out. Truth was, he didn't want to for fear of what more he might learn. It had been a year and Father hadn't done anything more either. Father was certainly right.

No one could ever learn the truth about his mother. Mallet often stopped himself of thinking about the meaning of it all. The truth was too hard.

There was an ache in his heart. Witch or not, he missed his mother. He felt her presence, smelled that sweet smell that always accompanied her. He could almost taste her cooking; almost feel her arms around his back holding him. Even when he had grown so big, she had still held him like he was precious to her.

"Mallet!" a harsh voice called. He jerked out of his reverie. It seemed like almost half an hour since Wheizer left.

"Get in here," Father called from the doorway. He did not sound pleased.

Mallet walked across the old courtyard, avoiding the missing bricks. He could smell the pepper trees again and he allowed his thoughts to linger on his mother a moment more before he faced his fate. His father held the door open for him and he passed into the deep sienna tiled hallway and down into his father's carpeted study, where Dagorn spent most of his time.

Wheizer leaned against Dagorn's large old desk, picking his teeth with a dagger. Mallet caught the pervasive smell of his father's rum and maple-scented pipe tobacco and desperately wished he was somewhere else.

"Sit down," Father said, indicating the old, scratched, oblong table surrounded by chairs covered by faded, tattered leather. A chessboard with ornate marble pieces was set up on the table. "Wheizer tells me you killed someone down on the dock today."

Mallet remained standing. He felt the presence of his mother again. Was it an illusion or his mind playing tricks on him? Either way, it didn't matter. He felt stronger.

"I did you a favor," Mallet said, taking inspiration from what he deemed was his mother's presence.

Father's face flinched ever so slightly. "Did you then?"

"Well yes, this family might have gotten in serious trouble with the town watch," Mallet said.

"Go on," Father said.

Mallet felt fear overwhelming him, but thought of his mother again. Suddenly, her presence was pervasive. *I can stand up to my father on my own,* he thought.

"Well, let me tell you about it," Mallet said.

1st Day of Summer – 12:00 Noon – The Docks – 13 Hours and 30 Minutes Before the Earthquake

It was midday, hotter than the Abyss and Mallet loved it. The Ictor had finally arrived, fully-loaded at the pier, a forty-foot long flat-bottomed barge that was sailed and push-poled up the river carrying goods from Taglyon on the southern coast. The cargo belonged to the Bygrave family and much of it had already been spoken for by merchants in Demon's Bluff. It just needed to be delivered. Mallet had been waiting all morning at the warehouse for it to arrive. He was to drive the team and wagon to make the first delivery, two dozen casks of wine.

Now that the barge had arrived, he had expect things to un-load quickly, but there were even more delays. He grew agitated and decided to head down and check things out for himself.

Mallet passed through one of the many gates in the levee wall to the southern docks. The levee wall was made of fired mud bricks and was over ten feet tall and several feet thick. The docks were moored to the levee and floated with the level of the Demon River. When the river overflowed its banks and river commerce paused, the levee gates would be sealed off to protect the town from the seasonal floods. The rich silt flooded the farmland to the north of town and on the eastern shore.

He found that the *Ictor* was the sole barge being unloaded in the midday heat. The crews of the other barges had headed to taverns to wait till later in the day.

Standing stripped to the waist, Mallet greeted Captain Gun-nar Vosc on the dock with a handshake. The captain was as salty as they came, having served for the navy of Taglyon in his younger days. He had a black wiry beard, sun squinted eyes and a tanned leathery face. His cheek bulged from a wad of tobacco.

"My father sent me down here to greet you!" Mallet said

enthusiastically, though he was lying. Father actually sent him to the warehouse to deliver the wine and to see that one or two casks made it up to the family estate.

"So Dagorn sends his pup to watch over me?" Vosc said, not entirely pleased.

"I am not here to watch, I'm here to help. What's taking so long to get those wine casks up to the warehouse?"

"Get back up to your pa. We don't need your help," said Vosc, and spat into the river.

"I got a wagon back there at the warehouse ready for these goods," Mallet explained. "I'll go get it and pick up the wine casks directly."

"I'm paid to deliver to the warehouse. My men do that, so you ain't no use to me." Mallet ignored him, turning and whistling. Five crewmen were hauling crates and casks off the barge and returning with larger crates for the next load back down river. He turned back to Vosc. "Two dozen casks."

Vosc spat on the ground and turned to his crew. "Get the wine off next. The whelp is waiting for them." The crewmen were unfamiliar to Mallet and they spoke to each other in a distinct accent. A crew from Balankov?

Captain Vosc turned back to Mallet. "Now, go on back to the warehouse, boy. Your goods'll be there shortly."

The crew was busy hauling cargo on and off the ship. One crewman carried a barrel of sea salt over his shoulder, while another crewman on the far side of the barge was splashing buckets of water over some of the crates. Another carried a large burlap sack. Two men struggled along a wide gangplank, carrying a large and ungainly-looking crate with holes drilled in the sides.

As Mallet watched, he wondered why Vosc was treating him this way. It was uncharacteristic of him. Mallet had worked on the docks unloading this barge dozens of times, and Vosc had been never been rude to him before.

"Go on now, boy. Git." Vosc was looking around nervously. He spat again.

Mallet decided to board the barge anyway. After all, didn't his family own this barge? And didn't Vosc work for his father? He turned and began to stride toward the nearest gangplank onto the barge.

"Just where in the Abyss do you think you're going, boy?" shouted Vosc, moving to block his path.

"I should ask you the same question," Mallet yelled as he shouldered his way past the captain.

"Boy," Vosc drawled in a low voice as he stepped sideways and stuck his grizzled arm out to prevent Mallet from passing him. "I ain't kiddin'. You ought to turn around and head back to the warehouse and just wait. You don't want to be sorry." Vosc spat on the dock.

Mallet ground his teeth and stared down into the captain's beady eyes. The big red-faced man was angrier than he had ever seen him. A couple of Vosc's crewmen dropped what they were doing and started heading over to investigate.

"You're not worth it," Mallet muttered as he turned to leave and scanned the barge looking for a reason that Vosc might be acting so oddly.

Mallet headed back to the gate in the levee through which he had come, brooding over Vosc's lateness and rudeness.

"Get on now, boys! We're behind schedule." Mallet heard the captain's voice trail off as he continued to fume.

There was a crashing sound. "Some damn kid busted out of a crate!" one of the crewmen called out.

Mallet strode on into the momentary shadow of the levee gate and into the bustle of the city on the other side.

Some damn kid busted out of a crate.

Mallet had worked the docks many times and had known Vosc for years. In all that time, Vosc had never treated him that way.

Some damn kid busted out of a crate.

Something itched at the back of Mallet's mind, like a splinter that he couldn't reach.

Some damn kid busted out of a crate.

Vosc was up to something, that was for sure. Mallet felt he was hiding something. And a crew from Balankov? That was certainly odd.

Some damn kid busted out of a crate.

Mallet felt quite thirsty, and headed over to a street vendor for a mug of ale. *Some damn kid busted out of a crate.* He watched as the vendor poured a mug of frothy ale from the tap of a huge barrel mounted on a handcart. Mallet paid the two coppers and prepared to savor the quenching of his thirst.

Some damn kid busted out of a crate.

Some damn kid busted out of a crate.

Some damn kid busted out of a crate.

The ceramic mug shattered on the paving stone sending the untouched ale splattering as Mallet bolted back toward the dock.

Winded, he emerged back through the levee gate, and looked to see what was happening on the barge. The crew was back to work, milling about the ship, but Vosc was on the far side of the barge, near the aft section. It looked like he was talking to someone, but the cargo on the deck obscured the view. Whatever he was doing, Vosc was still angry. He waved his arms in an animated fashion and talked with a raised voice, but Mallet couldn't make out what he was saying.

Mallet scanned the cargo on the deck for more evidence to support his new suspicion. He focused his attention on the crates with the holes in the sides. Then he saw it. Two fingers sticking out of one of the holes in the crate. Two human fingers! The white of the nails contrasted against the darker skin. Agrabi slaves!

Mallet reacted instantly. He began to stride purposely up a gangplank. "What in the Abyss is going on here, Vosc?" he boomed.

He hopped up on the deck of the barge and moved through the crates toward Vosc. The captain, red-faced and furious, was striding toward him. Mallet now had a clear view of the far side of the barge now, and all he saw was an old bearded Buerdeleise man and soaked Agrabi boy in a skiff rowing downstream, the line of a cane fishing pole dangled in the water behind them.

"I thought I told you to get out of here!" Vosc thundered. The only crewman nearby dropped in behind him, flanking him.

"What's in the crates?" Mallet asked. He had to remind himself his family owned this barge and had hired this captain.

There was a quiet moment as everyone sized each other up. If it came to blows, could he handle them both?

Mallet considered his options. He realized he was in danger and had to act now.

This might be a mistake, he thought. He lunged at the nearest slave crate stacked high on the others.

He gave it a mighty shove. It was heavy, but began to slide off. Had he heard the sound of whimpering inside?

The large crate tipped over and slid, corner first off its perch and crashed into the barge deck. It shattered sending splinters flying.

Revealed inside were six dirty, tear-stained Agrabi children in chains.

The visual confirmation of this impacted Mallet like a hammer to the head.

Vosc looked panicked. "Cover them up!" he barked. His burly crewman moved toward Mallet and the Agrabi children.

The man reached down and grabbed one of the children far too roughly by the arm. She was a young girl, maybe fourteen years old. Her mouth opened wide, revealing a startling absence of teeth as she started to bawl.

Mallet didn't think. His meaty fist flew out of its own accord and impacted hard on the man's jaw. Mallet both heard and felt the most satisfying 'crack' of his life. The man hit the deck like a sack of grain, unconscious. His jaw was broken off its hinges and hung off the side of his face at a sickening angle.

"You shouldn't have seen this," Vosc said, and there was a waver in his voice, a tremulous quality that alerted Mallet to the simple fact that Vosc was panicked and liable to do something absolutely stupid.

Which is exactly what he did--the captain dropped a small black pouch he was holding and jerked a knife from his belt and faced Mallet.

"Your father warned me never to let you find out about this," said Vosc, his voice quivering and his hand shaking. *He looks like he could use a good drink,* Mallet thought as he relaxed his body and got ready to fight. "I told you to leave," Vosc continued.

"You're a poor liar. My father doesn't know about this," said Mallet confidently as he gingerly stepped backwards, keeping his distance from the advancing blade. "How long have you been running slaves at our expense?"

"I don't aim to get caught," said the captain, still advancing, holding his blade before him menacingly.

"What are you gonna do? Kill me?" Mallet asked sarcastically. Years of Wheizer's training gave him ample confidence to deal with this old captain. The rest of the crewmen seemed to be preoccupied with the aft section of the barge. He and the captain alone faced each other on the dock side of the barge.

Mallet saw his opening. He leaped at Vosc, catching him off guard. He reached up and grabbed the captain by the wrist, holding the knife up with his left hand and punched him low in the ribs with his right.

The captain was stronger than Mallet guessed and he put all his considerable strength into his knife arm. He broke the hold Mallet had on his wrist and the blade swung down toward the younger man's heart.

Mallet retreated and the blade swung down and barely missed his chest. The captain's momentum carried the blade downward. Mallet instinctively recaptured his wrist and used that momentum and redirected the knife around and up into the captain's stomach.

Vosc made no sound as his own blade sank to the hilt into his guts.

"Gods," Mallet muttered under his breath, looking around again. What had he done? There was so much confusion on the barge.

Vosc stumbled back, pulling the knife out. Tobacco juice dribbled down his beard. He let the knife drop on the deck as he gurgled out a faint cry, then tripped on the bulwark and reeled, hands holding his stomach as he fell head first onto the dock and slipped through the gap between the dock and the barge into the river with a splash, disappearing down under the dark swirling muddy waters.

Mallet scrambled to the side of the barge, looking into the water.

Captain Vosc did not come back up.

Mallet didn't hesitate. He grabbed the bloody knife and tossed it into the water. He noticed a small black pouch lay on the planks of the barge. It was the pouch Vosc had dropped.

He picked it up and instantly realized it was filled with coins, but he didn't have time to consider it further, he shoved it into his pocket.

Mallet knew he needed to get out of there and fast, but he looked at the Agrabi children splayed and chained on the deck. He couldn't just leave them, but he couldn't save them either. He was about to leap over to the dock to put distance between him and the barge when he noticed a ring of keys hooked on the belt of the unconscious crewman whose jaw he had broken. He snatched the keys from the belt and tossed them to the oldest looking Agrabi boy. "Free yourselves and get into the water and escape. Hide under the docks," he hissed at them.

It was a terrible risk. If they caused a larger commotion than was already going on, it would increase the chance that his family would be discovered and implicated in slaving. But he couldn't just leave them to their fate. Besides, the chances of being implicated were already high.

There was nothing more he could do to help the rest of them still in crates. What would happen to them when the captain turned up missing? His heart was beating so fast he could feel it in his chest and his mouth was dry.

He leapt off the barge and hustled up the pier, trying hard to remain calm. He slowed to a walk after a while and headed back toward the warehouse. He had to settle down... to think. He thought of the look on Vosc's face, and the accusation that his father knew about this.

That could not be true, he decided as he walked in the heat of midday.

You killed another man, the sun said.

This one deserved it, too, Mallet thought back.

1st Day of Summer – 9:30 PM – Dagorn's Study – 4 Hours Before the Earthquake

"You really ought to sit down," Father said in the study.

Mallet was nervous. His father's study had seemed so huge

and the furnishings so grand when he was a small child. Now it seemed very small--confining and shabby. He pulled a chair out from the oblong table and sat down. The leather felt cool on his hot skin.

"Wheizer told me we had some trouble down at the docks today. He spent most of the afternoon cleaning it up for us."

Mallet looked over to Wheizer. He was still picking his teeth nonchalantly with the dagger. Mallet knew there was meaning in what his father was saying, but it didn't come to him fast enough.

"Mallet, there are some things you need to know. You are old enough now to help me carry the burdens of our family."

Mallet struggled to find meaning in his father's words. He couldn't have guessed at his father's next blunt revelation.

"I employ Captain Vosc to transport slaves," Father explained in a low gravelly voice. "It's a dangerous trade, Mallet, but the costs are high and the profits are low on the other merchant goods we sell. Our family has been under pressure for generations. You and I carry the burden of restoring our family to greatness, Mallet. That takes gold. Lots of gold."

The impact of what his father was saying slowly sank in. His world view was suddenly being upended.

His father continued, "Wheizer here manages the dangerous parts of our business, and up until recently I've been preparing you to run our legitimate trade. But you would eventually need to know everything. I hadn't expected it would be as soon as this, but you have created some difficulties for us in killing Captain Vosc. Perhaps I should have trusted you with this information earlier."

Mallet swallowed with difficulty--his throat was so dry. So that answered *that* question. He could hardly believe it, even though he had just heard it from his own father's mouth. He looked from his father to Wheizer. The tall man was staring at him and Mallet saw, maybe for the first time, the capacity for real malice in his gaze.

"But if the town guard finds out," Mallet said, "it would be the end of our family." Mallet was dodging the real issue, but he still couldn't fully cope with what he was being told.

"Yes," Father agreed. "The guard would come here, break

down the doors and haul me to the gallows, and probably you, too. They might spare your sister, but she'd be out in the streets."

Mallet still couldn't believe what he was hearing. "But why would you do that? Why would you put our family at such risk?"

"Don't you understand where our family would be without such dealings? The real risk to our family is not doing what we are doing now. We have no choice. Bygrave was once a great name in this city: far greater than it is now. Our family mausoleum testifies to our former greatness. The decline stops with us, Mallet. I have ambitions for so much more for our family."

"So do I!" Mallet cried with utter sincerity. But it hurt him to know his father was doing this. It wasn't right. His mother had always taught him right from wrong, and this was wrong. But then again, his mother was a witch. He had seen the proof himself. Neither his mother nor his father was what he thought they were. Maybe his mother knew of this? Maybe she had arranged it? She was a witch, after all. Mallet felt confused, bewildered, without moorings. "I have always wanted what you want, Father. But slavery? We'll be found out!" Mallet's dry throat almost constricted entirely at the thought of the hangman's noose around it.

"Don't you worry about that. Wheizer here has taken all the necessary precautions. He even kept us protected despite your stunt today. We can't just go being foolish." Father's voice was hard, slightly slurred by the alcohol and tinged with the melancholy of earlier. Mallet had the sudden realization what his father was telling him. Mallet wasn't being asked. He was being told. When his father was drunk like this he was unpredictable: maybe even dangerous. Mallet felt fear for what might happen if he told his father and Wheizer something other than what they wanted to hear. Just this morning, he had killed a man more than twice his age, but he was terrified of his father, a man half his size.

"That's the risk we take, Mallet," Father continued. "But it's a manageable risk and one worth taking. You are come of age now, Mallet. You are a hard worker, and smart. You sure as hell can fight. These are powerful assets. But you don't yet know how to take the right risks. You're like your mother in that regard, far too timid. She never understood the difference between risks you take and risks you don't. But you can learn, Mallet. We are men and we must do what is necessary for the family. Even if those things aren't pleasant."

Confusion whirled in Mallet's head. The only thing he understood was that he should do nothing to upset his father. So he just nodded.

"Your mother is gone now, Mallet, and we have to protect your sister. She is innocent and she must stay that way."

"I think she is suspicious," Mallet said, not really sure why he was volunteering this information. "She said something tonight I laughed at. She said she thought you had a secret collection of old artifacts. I didn't believe her."

Father raised his eyebrows. "I don't know how she could possibly know that. But she is right. I have kept it a secret because my collection is very valuable. And it is the type of collection, well, let's just say that some people might misunderstand."

Mallet shook his head. His mother had kept secrets and his father it seemed was keeping many of his own. Father sipped from his wine glass, then walked over to one of the bookcases. He pulled down a weathered leather tome, reached in, and yanked something. Suddenly the entire bookshelf opened like a massive door.

Mallet stood up in awe.

"Come here," Father said, pulling an oil lamp from its perch on a wall sconce. Mallet followed and felt Wheizer's ominous presence close behind him. He felt penned in, not unlike those slaves in their crates.

He entered a long secret room that was filled with polished old artifacts, mostly weapons and armor, but also such things as silver chalices, a brass brazier, jade and obsidian figurines, bucklers, amulets and other items, all clearly from antiquity. Many where hung on the walls, but some were displayed on black and red velvet-draped pedestals.

"Gods," Mallet breathed. The skin on the back of his neck grew taught. This stuff wasn't mundane. A timeless aura filled the room, an almost palpable hum could be felt reverberating against his eardrums. The air was dry and cool.

"What is this stuff for?"

"It's not for any purpose. It's just a reminder of times gone by. But like I said, some people would not understand this."

"What is that symbol?" asked Mallet pointing to a faded red symbol on a field of black emblazoned on a shield hanging on the wall. The symbol adorned some of the artifacts in the room.

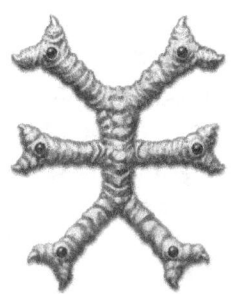

"It is the symbol of a religion that made their ancient base here atop the mesa thousands of years ago. Our family fought against them in those long ago times. I have always felt drawn to the history of our family, so I collect these things."

"Why are you showing me all this now?"

"The time for secrets between us is over, Mallet. You asked and here is your answer. Now I need an answer from you. Mallet, are you with me?"

Mallet stared blankly. "I'm not sure I...."

"You know what I mean. Are you willing to do what is necessary for the betterment of our family? To sacrifice? To do things that may seem hard or unpleasant?"

He means even to kill if necessary, thought Mallet. *I am a killer,* he realized. *Maybe Wheizer was right--once a killer always a killer.*

"Mallet?"

Mallet knew the answer. After all, didn't he kill Captain Vosc thinking that he was protecting his family? Mallet looked his father in the eye and nodded. "You know I will do anything for our family."

"Yes," Father said, as if reading his mind. "You have proven your loyalty many times Mallet. You made mistakes today, but you made hard decisions that you believed were in our family's best interest."

This was all too much. The young man felt a deep melancholy. Things had just changed forever for him. No matter what, things would never be as simple as they had been this morning as he walked toward the docks without a care. He was struck by a strange thought. "How did Brynn know?" he asked out loud.

Father frowned. "She's been poking into things she shouldn't have lately. You know I love your sister, don't you? I try to protect her and it's becoming harder and harder. She's stubborn. I need your help with her, Mallet. Keeping her safe."

Mallet couldn't disagree with that assessment, but he felt the desire to defend his sister anyway. "She wants to help the family too!"

"She is confused, Mallet," Father said. "She's a lot like your mother, rest her soul. In too many ways. She certainly wouldn't understand the risks we take or why, would she?"

"What are you going to do about her?" Mallet asked, afraid for her.

"The time is close for her to marry. But until that happens, we are going to keep doing what we have always done. Keep her sheltered. We're not going to let her find out, are we?"

"No," Mallet agreed. "Of course not." He had always tried to protect Brynn, and he wouldn't stop now. "But what if she finds out anyway?"

"If we do our duty, she won't know about our dealings, nor your mother's dishonor."

Mallet closed his eyes. What was happening? This evening was going so differently than he feared. It was worse. But somehow nothing his father was saying truly surprised him. He was torn between duty and what he thought was right. But both seemed confused; like they might be the same thing. He felt increasingly, bewildered, ill at ease.

He looked at his father and felt a touch of revulsion. He smelled the decay again. *This wasn't right. But the family....*

Father again seemed to read his mind. "I understand your reluctance. I feel it, too. I have always felt it. But we have a higher duty, you and I." He spoke with such sincerity that Mallet was moved. He was far away from the rage he had felt in killing Vosc. He shivered, and he swore he could see wisps of his breath in the cold light of this secret room.

"Mallet," said his Father, "are you with me?"

Mallet didn't know what to do.

"Give me your word, Mallet. I need to hear you say it again. Swear an oath to me."

Mallet's breath was short. Thirst clawed at his throat. He wanted to help the family so badly, and maybe this *was* the way to do it. His father was a slaver. His mother was a witch. What did that make him?

Staring into his father's hypnotic gaze, he found himself saying out loud: "Father, I am with you. What do you want me to do?"

Father smiled, "I need more."

This came as a slap to Mallet and he recoiled.

"*But he's right,*" the cynic in his mind said. "*You understand why he doubts.*"

Father turned to Wheizer and signaled. The tall man walked toward Mallet. With a rapid motion, he snatched an obsidian dagger with a hilt fashioned into the strange symbol from its display on the wall. Mallet saw the intent on Wheizer's face, so he reacted by instinct. He reached out and grabbed one of the ancient swords by the hilt and brought the blade up.

He felt imminent danger from Wheizer and swung without hesitation, willing to kill again. Wheizer had taught him much, but what happened next made Mallet clearly understand that Wheizer was far more skilled than he ever let on in their years of training together. The tall man moved with inhuman speed, stepping and turning within the arc of Mallet's blade. His left hand closed on Mallet's hand and he simultaneously bent his wrist down with incredible strength, causing the sword to fall free of his grasp. He threw his right elbow hard into Mallet's throat. The sword clattered to the ground as red hot pain exploded in Mallet's already parched throat. Continuing in his fluid motion, Wheizer took Mallet's arm and jerked it behind him in a hammerlock and slammed him hard to the stone tiled floor. Wheizer jammed his knee into his back pinning him down. It was all over before it started. Mallet lay with his cheek on the cold floor, blinking, trying to comprehend how Wheizer could possibly be that fast.

Father bent down and looked at him. His eyes reflected the flickering light in the secret room.

"I told you Wheizer was watching after our affairs. Did you know Wheizer here is a monster?"

Mallet just continued blinking, trying to restore a sense of clarity to his head.

"No, Mallet, I mean a literal monster: a dark, loathsome, soul-less monster. He has a disease, Mallet. I saved him from that. After years of searching, I found the magic that helps him control his disease. Now his disease is our family's greatest asset, Mallet."

Mallet looked up at his father. The tears in his eyes shimmered the total desolation that seared inside him.

"I trust Wheizer completely. I need the same trust in you. Wheizer here can help you earn my trust."

Mallet struggled, pushing himself up, trying to flip Wheizer from his back. The tall man was vastly stronger than he looked and easily held Mallet down. He used a leather thong and bound Mallet's hands behind his back.

Wheizer stood up next to his father. "Did you see that? He tried to kill me."

Father laughed. "Can you imagine what he will be capable of when he has it?"

Wheizer jerked Mallet up by his forearms and plopped him in a chair that Father was pulling over. Father took a silver chalice with the strange symbol emblazoned on it and held it out. Wheizer took the obsidian blade and cut deep into his own palm. A steady trickle of deep crimson splattered into the chalice.

"I'm your son!" Mallet croaked, barely able to get it out.

"Are you?" Father's voice suddenly grew hard, "You killed Vosc, one of my best men. You cost us a great deal of money today in lost slaves. Anyone else would pay with their life. You must pay with complete loyalty."

Mallet was no longer surprised, but a cold rebellion was burning in his heart. He felt his mother's presence. He wanted to say something, to spit back a reply, but his mouth wasn't working. He couldn't generate any saliva, his tongue felt swollen. He could hardly breathe.

Wheizer handed the chalice over to Father and came over behind Mallet and pulled his face back, his fingers digging into Mallet's bare scalp.

"Drink this," Father said, "and prove your loyalty to me. Don't worry. If you stay loyal, I'll help you control it, same way I did Wheizer."

Mallet stared up at his father and began to shake. He turned his gaze to the silver chalice. Something told him if he wanted to live, he was going to have to drink that blood.

Father lowered the chalice to his lips. Wheizer jammed a knuckle into the large muscle on the right side of Mallet's jaw, forcing his mouth open. Mallet wept as the warm blood poured over his lips and down his desiccated throat, finally slaking his demonic thirst. He felt his mother's terrible sadness.

Mallet stood next to his father and Wheizer. They had cut his bonds and he had stood up, the terrible iron taste of Wheizer's blood in his mouth.

Father smiled. "It's late. Go eat and drink. Get some sleep. We'll talk more in the morning. I promise to tell you more of our plans, but not tonight. Wheizer has told me some difficult news and I have to contemplate what needs be done."

Mallet nodded dumbly, drained of all will. All he could think of was that he had disappointed his mother. And now some disease infected him.

"When will I turn into a monster?"

"Soon enough," Wheizer said, and there was a nasally laugh in his voice, a deep and satisfying laugh. It made Mallet want to strike him, but he didn't dare.

"Get some sleep," Father ordered. "You gave me your word you will serve me faithfully, so don't worry about the blood. You keep your word, and I'll keep mine."

Mallet numbly stumbled from the secret room in a haze of

confusion, and Wheizer closed the bookshelf door behind him. What had just happened to him?

Mallet left his father's study and turned right down the hall toward the kitchen. He needed to drink and wash the foul taste of Wheizer's blood from his mouth, but he decided he needed to go to Brynn's room. He just had a feeling he needed to check on her. Should he tell her what Father had done to him? How had she found out about the artifacts? He couldn't shake the feeling that she was in danger for some reason.

He downed two large yeasty mugs of brown ale in the kitchen. The metallic taste of Wheizer's blood still lingered on his tongue as he headed straight to Brynn's room. He rapped on her door.

After she did not answer, he opened the door. Didn't she say she had something to do tonight? Some place to go? He breathed deep. It smelled nice in here. It was the same scent that lingered about his mother. How had Brynn known about her father's collection? Why was she dressed as an Agrabi servant?

Mallet heard some footsteps outside of Brynn's bedroom window. He walked as quietly as he could to the window and saw Wheizer striding purposefully across the courtyard. Something was wrong here.

Mallet clenched his fists, wishing he had his glaive. He ran his hand over his shorn scalp.

What had Brynn said earlier? It seemed as if she had told him something important, but he wasn't really paying attention. He had been distracted by the events of the day. *Did he remember seeing Mother when she died? Was there anything strange about her?*

His feeling that something was wrong grew. *Do you remember the family crest etched on the cover of her sarcophagus? I need to do something important. I need to see it again.*

Son of a Witch! She had been trying to tell him as they sat by the fountain. She was asking for his help but he had been too dumb and selfish to pay attention.

Brynn was about to do something incredibly stupid and dangerous.

CHAPTER EIGHT
A King's Secret

After the final victory over the Cult of Yex, Adirak sought to destroy all aspects of their vile evil. Adirak's agents tried to eradicate the red herb that the battle mages used. Adirak believed that he had obliterated all known gardens where the moss was cultivated. History shows that he was wrong.

-*Return of the Cult of Yex*, by Caed the Chronicler

1st Day of Summer – 8:30 PM – The Sacred Moss Garden in the Bystle Vale – 3 Hours and 30 Minutes Before the Earthquake In Demon's Bluff

Tharchelon, Guardian Rothin King of the Bystle Vale, slumped alone on the polished wooden floor of the holy moss garden, deep in the great Bystle Tree hollowed-out trunk. The dim yellowish light of the glowing Bystle Fruits washed over him. The ragged remainder of the Bystle Moss struggled desperately to grow back into some semblance of its former health, bathed in the life-giving yellow glow.

"Has Letharchenel succeeded?" he asked aloud. The sun would set soon and by his most generous calculation, his assassin should have had plenty of time to find and kill the young interlopers. The visitor in his dreams said they would come to take the moss from him. *Oh, the visitor in his dreams.* Why was he tormented so.

He forced himself to calm down. It was a near impossible task. It had been too long.

He pondered again, trying vainly to see over the vast distance with his mind. The deep nagging doubt told him that his assassin had not yet accomplished his task, and worse--that he would not, he could not. He was under imminent threat of losing his precious moss. That must not happen. Letharchenel must succeed in killing those four invaders.

He felt ill at ease for other reasons, too. Did the dream apparition know his secret? If so, he gave no hint. No. Tharchelon had kept his awful shame hidden from him. What would the visitor in his dreams say if he found out? For generations, the hereditary Kings of the Bystle Vale had relied on the dream visitor as an ally and advisor--except for Tharchelon. The visitor in his dreams was against him. The specter haunted his sleep and wanted the four kids from Demon's Bluff to steal his moss.

He felt a shudder of fear and a sudden strong pang came over him. He had been sitting here for what seemed like hours trying to resist, but he knew it had only been mere moments. *Damn Hell!* He could resist no longer.

Tharchelon, Rothkin King of the Bystle Vale, Sacred Guardian and Keeper of the Holy Bystle Moss, muttered a curse out loud. He reached out and grabbed a small pinch of the sacred red moss. He surreptitiously stuck it into his mouth, feeling the welcome rush of exhilaration as the bittersweet taste washed over his tongue and flooded his body.

CHAPTER NINE
Analog Cael

"That last peaceful moment in the cottage alone would ultimately become one of my most cherished memories. Looking back, it was the pivotal moment when my life would transform from what it was before to what it would become. When I departed that morning, I had no idea what I was leaving behind. I had no inkling what I would ultimately find."

-Cael Hotheway

1st Day of Summer – 6:30 AM – Boxxaway's Cottage in the Lower Steppe – 19 Hours Before the Earthquake

Cael watched Boxxaway leave the cottage through the back door, their big mastiff Dheke galloping after him. Dheke barked at Madam Dunkley's clucking chickens on his way through the backyard to the alley that wound toward the market district.

Cael sat in the familiar kitchen, boots up and resting on a ramshackle chair as dust particles swam in the beam of sunlight cascading down through the window. He looked around the kitchen where he and Boxxaway prepared and ate their simple meals. Cael felt famished just thinking about it--bread with honey and slabs of cheese--even that Agrabi cheese with the black skin of mold on it. Dates, dried fish, boiled eggs and an occasional bit of chicken or salted pork. They almost always washed down their dinner with a mug of honeyed mead or yeasty ale. His mouth was watering just thinking about it and his hunger was growing.

He felt suddenly out of place--everything seemed wrong. This was his home. And nowhere else had he felt more loved, comfortable and safe. Probably due to the intense closeness, the sense of kin he shared with his grandfather. Boxxaway understood him so well and had made this place a refuge for him.

But as of this morning, he no longer felt safe here. This was where he and Boxxaway had sat at this table on so many evenings, a lantern or one of Madam Dunkley's beeswax candles between them, heads bent reading books. They paused only to share something interesting with each other once in a while, then heads back down to reading. When one stale parchment-smelling book was done, it went back up on the shelves and another one came down to take its place.

The other rooms of the small mud brick cottage had just as many memories. The two adjoining bedrooms, where at night as a kid Cael would sometimes knock on the thin wooden wall if he was thirsty, hungry or scared, and Boxxaway would get up and come to him, knowing exactly what would make him feel better.

Then there was the small room that Boxxaway used for art as he fiddled with his hobby of painting. And of course, the room that had mostly been abandoned--the room where Cael practiced magic and where this morning he had discovered his mother and father had been murdered.

That right there was the problem. His mother and father had been murdered in this very house and the safest place in the world now felt dangerous and threatening to him.

"Stay in and get some rest today," Boxxaway had said.

But Cael knew there was no way he was staying here. He didn't know where he was going to go... just out. Maybe hang around the market district or down by the docks to watch the boats come in. But first, he was hungry. Ravenous. Dropping his feet to the wooden floor with a clunk, he got up and started digging through the pantry next to the iron-bellied stove, still warm with the embers of last night's meal.

He looked for some bread and found only crumbs. He looked for some cheese and found a small thumb-sized hardened nugget. He popped it in and his jaws instantly ached as saliva exploded into his mouth. The cheese served only to further arouse his hunger.

He found the wine skins were sagging and empty. The beer cask was empty, as well. There wasn't a damn thing to eat in the entire cottage. Boxxaway had gone off to the market, but that wouldn't do. Cael couldn't wait.

Then he heard Madam Dunkley singing softly to herself in her backyard. He leaned out the kitchen window and spied the old lady puttering about her backyard. As usual, he noticed the knobby protrusions of her shoulders and elbows. He presumed the rest of her was just as knobby, but it was hidden under the billowy silk robes she always wore. The fancy cloth was imported from Balankov, where she lived when she was a little girl. She had often told him stories of her youth there. An eruption of white erratic hair surrounded her sun-lined face. When she smiled, her wrinkles deepened into canyons.

If ever there was a time Cael hoped she had some of her famous bread baking, it was now. He grabbed his staff and ran from the kitchen, down the short hall. He paused for a moment to look into Boxxaway's art room. He was working on another piece. Once again he was painting his favorite subject: angels. His grandfather wasn't really good at art but this last painting took Cael's breath away. It was simple: just a face with a blue background. But the fierce look in its eyes and the bright tones of color were so vivid. It seemed so real. Here was an angel, some otherworldly creature from the inaccessible heavens, as fierce as he was righteous. Looking into the angel's eyes, Cael felt a thrill go through him. But his hunger propelled him down the hall, where he grabbed his cedar staff before heading out into the backyard.

"How you doing?" He waved to Madam Dunkley as he reached the western wall that marked the border between their two cottages. One of her hens jumped up on the wall, strutting back and forth, guarding her territory.

The old woman flashed him a rare smile from where she was tossing handfuls of grain to her pecking chickens. "Why Cael, what you doing about this early in the morning? You come to help me feed the chickens?" She spoke in a raspy old voice that still carried a Balankov accent.

"I was wondering if you got any of your fresh bread."

"Is that ol' bastard starving you again?" she frowned. "I don't know why he never remarried. How'd he expect to raise a boy by himself? Look at you. You're skin and bones!"

"He's doing all right, gone off to the market," Cael said.

"Well, I'll keep my opinions to myself," she said, clucking like one of her chickens. She turned and went to her back door and waved for him to follow.

Cael smiled and gave a low whistle. That old woman's small welcome meant his stomach would soon be filled with the most delicious bread and maybe even some eggs.

He hopped the fence and was greeted by her yard, which she had turned into a small farm. Chickens pecked at their grain, a small pig squelched in a corner and the goat stared at him with jaws chewing at something in the odd circular motion peculiar to goats. Cael often helped Madam Dunkley haul water from the fountain up the road for her animals and garden. She often rewarded him with her cooking.

Her rooster stood directly in his path to her back door. The hungry young man gave it a wide berth, as he used to be afraid of the golden fowl when he was a kid. He carefully picked his way through her vegetable garden, blazing a trail between the tomatoes and squash. The breeze brought him the aromatic smell of her herb garden growing just ahead.

Her mud brick cottage looked pretty much like any other in this section of town, squarely built with a thatched roof, but once, long ago, someone had painted flowers on the wooden back door. The paint was now faded and flaked.

She held the door open with a very puzzled look on her face. "Shh," she whispered and then signaled for him to follow.

He followed her into the cottage where he was hit by a panoply of smells: a hint of smoke from the cook stove, frying eggs and baking bread, all overpowered by the smell of her little dogs. Then there was a weird, ephemeral smell, one he recognized at once as being Madam Dunkley herself. He wasn't sure if it was a perfume or something else, but it always surrounded her. One of her many dogs, the furry dark one she called Houdikus, squeezed out the door as she tried to close it behind him. He had no doubt Houdikus would be scratching at the door to be let back in momentarily.

Her home was simple, with only two rooms. To the immediate left was a door to the bedroom, a room he had never seen. The rest of the cottage was one big room, which served as living room, kitchen and workroom. Madam Dunkley, all knees and elbows, walked to the long tables that ran the length of the cottage below three open windows. Candle-making supplies were littered haphazardly on the tables. There were empty earthen jars, molds, blocks of beeswax and a pile of wicks she had woven herself.

Madam Dunkley motioned for him to stand against the wall of the center window, lifted one bony arm and pointed a long finger out the window toward Boxxaway's cottage. The windows all had large reed mats rolled up above them so they could be dropped during a windstorm.

"Someone's in your house," she whispered, her eyes wide.

Cael, startled and curious, leaned his head out a bit and looked straight across the gap between the two cottages into Boxxaway's kitchen window. Something was wrong. Cael shivered as the blood drained from his face.

A small man, dressed in white linens, crept through the kitchen. He was no bigger than a child. He held a menacing dagger in one hand and a loaded hand-held crossbow in the other. His head swiveled as he studied the kitchen. He moved with such a strange grace, it reminded him a feral cat when it stalked a mouse in the alley.

Cael felt his heart thumping and pulled his head back away from the window.

Madam Dunkley expertly fidgeted with items on her table, feigning preoccupation. Her head was bent down, but she looked up toward the little man.

"Who the hells is that?"

"It's a Rothkin. Up to no good," she said.

"Rothkin?" he said. "Like one of the little beggars in the market district?"

"Shh--"

Cael tried to think why a Rothkin would be in the house. The few he had seen begging alms seemed utterly harmless. He peeked around the edge of the window again. The little man was moving slowly, looking through the house.

This was not good. Could this be the killer who had murdered his parents?

He pulled back again, his thoughts churning.

He had to look again. He suddenly smelled the bread bak-ing and remembered his fierce hunger, but he couldn't think about eating right now. He looked down at his hands. They were trembling.

"What did you do to your arm?" Madam Dunkley asked, pointing to the bandage on his wrist as she continued to non-chalantly fidget with candle supplies on the table.

He shook his head, and then quickly glanced around the corner.

The little man was gone.

"Hells!"

Madam Dunkley spared a full glance then lowered her head again. "He's in the back rooms. He's searching room to room. What does he want, Cael? Why is he—"

"I don't know!" Cael almost squeaked. But maybe he did know. Perhaps it was connected with his vision from this morn-ing? Perhaps the Cult of Yex had found him?

"What are you going to do, Cael?"

Cael looked around for some type of weapon. He still had his cedar staff, but that didn't seem enough. "What if he comes over here?" Cael asked.

She looked out again. He saw her raise her hand and wave with a smile.

What in the hells? Cael thought.

She shrugged and looked down again at her table. She grabbed a jar filled with wax and turned it over. "He saw me looking at him. What was I going to do?" she whispered.

Cael looked around in a panic. He should run. As if reading his mind, she stuck her foot out under the table and kicked him in the shin, without looking up.

"He's leaving now," she said, her voice a little louder and clearly relieved.

"What if he comes *back*?"

"He's gone, out your front door."

"He's coming over here," Cael said, assured that was the case. Their eyes were glued on her front door. Would he knock or try to force it open? They waited in silence for two tense minutes.

But he didn't come.

"You stay here," Madam Dunkley said as she walked to her front door.

She walked outside onto her front porch and closed the door behind her.

She returned moments later. "He was walking southwest. I think you are safe for now."

Cael let his breath out.

"You want to tell me what that was about? He was armed and ready to kill."

Cael shook his head. He shouldn't tell her his suspicions.

"Come here," she said. "And eat, dear. Then, tell me what is happening."

He nodded. As he ate voraciously, to his surprise, he told her everything that had happened to him this morning.

He sat at the old kitchen table with an empty plate before him and an empty mug clutched in his hand. Eggs and buttered bread filled his stomach, *but he still felt hungry*. He held out the mug hoping for some more of her black tea.

"That's quite the story," Madam Dunkley said softly, refilling his mug. "I remember your mother and father."

Cael caught his breath. He felt dizzy.

A black puppy jumped up on Madam Dunkley's lap. She picked it up and dropped it back on the floor. "It was a long time ago, Cael," she said. "They were nice, but kind of quiet. Kept to themselves. Last I recall seeing them, the woman was pregnant and close to delivering, when they said she was killed. All three of them were killed."

She looked at him pointedly.

"My grandfather came, saved me. I was the baby. He took me away, didn't bring me back for a few years."

"I always wished I could have met Kiera's little baby. And all this time, you were right here. You and your grandfather moved in when you were two, maybe three. I never would have guessed there was any connection. Your grandfather never let on. And you just found out this morning?"

Cael just nodded.

"You just watched your own parents murdered before your eyes? Oh Cael, I'm so sorry. A child should never have to witness that." She reached out and touched his face with her leathery hand.

"What am I supposed to do now, Madam Dunkley? I feel lost."

She looked to the window and Boxxaway's cottage. "I would say old Boxxaway leaving you alone there today was a mistake."

Cael nodded. He felt abandoned, alone. He surprised himself again with what he said next. "Have you ever heard of something called the Cult of Yex?"

She shook her head.

"It is an ancient religion. Evil. They are the ones that killed my parents. They thought my parents were their enemies, for some reason. I think they came back to kill me and my grandfather this morning."

Madam Dunkley just stared at him, her eyes pensive.

"What else do you know about this cult?"

"Not much. I just told you most of what I know. Grandfather says they are hidden and are trying to come back to power like they had thousands of years ago." In truth, Cael knew more than that, but it didn't seem worth explaining.

She looked at him thoughtfully for another moment.

"Well then, you have to learn more about them, don't you?"

Cael looked at her blankly.

"Go up to the Library of Mirrors and study about them. If there is anything to know about them, they will have it in that library. I don't think it is safe to stay here, anyway. At least not until your grandfather gets back."

"They'll never let me in the library. I'm not apprenticed at the academy."

"Well, let's see what we can do about that." She started digging through a large sewing basket.

Cael nodded dumbfounded. She was right. It didn't feel safe to be here, not safe at all. He thrilled at the thought of the library. He had never been there and he had always wanted to go desperately. But because he wasn't an apprentice of the Academy he couldn't go unless he paid, which was far too expensive.

Being an apprentice to an old burned-out wizard like Boxxaway apparently didn't count.

That reminded him. He clutched his pocket. Yes, the pouch of eight silver moons was there that his grandfather had given him. It was enough to get him to the top of the plateau, but not enough to get him into the library, too.

"I don't have the money to get in," he said despondently.

Madam Dunkley pulled out a small bundle of black linen. "Well, then you just need to look like an apprentice, don't you?"

Cael stood on the porch of Madam Dunkley's cottage dressed in black linen robes over his regular trousers and tunic. He carried his staff in one hand.

"There," Madam Dunkley said, nodding approvingly from in front of him. "Can I still sew or what? You look just like you walked out of the Academy! Except you should wash your face."

Cael wished he could see himself in the black robes. He had always wanted to attend the Academy but that was something only children who had money or were from the right families could do. The books he read were ones Boxxaway found or traded for in the market. Many were old and weather-beaten, some of them missing pages. He had begged Boxxaway to take him up to the Library of Mirrors, but Boxxaway had refused, saying it wasn't worth the money to go up there. Only the wizards and apprentices of the Academy were allowed in for free.

Boxxaway had never attended the Academy himself, having learned magic from his own father and had no connections up on the cliff. Thus, he taught Cael privately, simultaneously bad-mouthing the wizards of the Academy. This didn't stop Cael's daydreaming. He imagined being amongst the other students who loved magic and who would not torment him for it.

"Do you really think this will work?" Cael asked Madam Dunkley uncertainly.

"Of course it will. Those old sages up there have their noses buried in their books. Just act like you are supposed to be there."

That sounded good, but it still made Cael very nervous. What would they do to him if he were caught?

"Trust me, Cael," she said, reading his mind.

She would be in a position to know. She was the widow of old Duke Dunkley who died over twenty years ago. She used to live up on the Middle Steppe with the nobles. Rather than move back to Balankov, she had chosen to stay in Demon's Bluff, though without her husband she had lost her station. Cael knew that the nobles on the hill consorted with the wizards of the Academy often and she knew how the wizards operated. That gave him at least a little confidence in her scheme.

"I think you are ready," Madam Dunkley said, giving his face a good scrub with a wet rag.

He turned to Madam Dunkley. She gave him one of her rare smiles, reached out and patted his shoulder and nodded. "You be careful, you hear me?"

"You kidding?" he said.

She lowered her hand and stood there, looking as if she didn't know what to say. He turned away from her and began making his way toward the cliff.

He didn't look back, though he would wish he had. He would never see her again.

CHAPTER TEN
Pins & Needle

The Agrabi have never understood time in the same way as other races. The Buerdeleise see time as if it were a line. We know, however, that it does not behave that way. Time is circular. It wraps back on itself in repeating cycles. Short cycles of time repeat often inside huge cycles that span thousands of years or more. This understanding has proved useful to our people. We recognize that to know the future is to understand the past. It has taught us to be patient.

-Oral Tradition: Jaganju Ra, Agrabi Shaman

1st Day of Summer – 10:00 PM – Foyer of the Bygrave Estate Main House – 3 Hours and 30 Minutes Before the Earthquake

Twenty minutes had passed and it was growing late. Needle fidgeted with the burlap sack that held his merchandise as he sat on an ornately carved bench in the entrance foyer of Duke Dagorn Bygrave's estate. The opulence of the place stunned him. His father had never brought him here when he had dealings with Dagorn. He certainly never mentioned the wealth. In all Needle's experience, he never imagined people could live this way. At the peak of his father's prosperity, Needle had thought his family was wealthy, especially compared to how he and his mother lived now. But this! Now he realized that even when his father was doing well, before he and his mother had to retreat from the Lower Steppe to the Kuma, they had still been very poor by comparison.

The first thing Needle noticed as he was permitted to enter the foyer by an Agrabi servant was the smell of incense. How could anybody afford such a wasteful extravagance? The floor was covered in expensive sienna tiles. The chairs and divans were ornately carved and upholstered. Beautiful multi-colored vases were perched upon granite pedestals. Granite! That stone must have been brought up river from the south at unimaginable expense. It was madness! All this wealth could lift so many from the poverty of the Kuma.

He coveted such wealth for himself. This was the type of life he should be living.

"The Duke is still indisposed," the elderly Agrabi servant said, poking his head into the foyer. "It will be longer still." He disappeared as quickly as he had appeared.

Needle forced himself to concentrate on why he was here. He hefted his bag filled with the artifacts Boxxaway had given him. He needed to get a good price for this stuff.

He mentally ticked off the priorities for the money. His first priority was to rescue his mother from the poverty of the Kuma. Then he needed to pay Boxxaway his price for the artifacts. And then the most illogical expense of all: buy passage up the lifts to meet Brynn tonight. The thought of wasting money on the lifts made Needle's insides churn. Still, after what Boxxaway told him, and then Brynn. Well, the lure of possible information about his father was too much to resist.

Needle could not let Duke Bygrave get the better of him. Dagorn's reputation for driving a hard bargain was well known, especially among the artifact hunters of Demon's Bluff. Needle had out-haggled many an Agrabi boy when he was younger, trading for trinkets and collectibles, but he sensed this meeting with the Duke would be very different.

An odor from the kitchen wafted past him and his mouth began to water. The wealth of this place meant the Buerdeleise here never went hungry. Just imagine. If he haggled well, he might even have some copper stars left over for himself. He thought about the food in the stalls at the market. He swallowed in anticipation.

He was growing impatient. He remembered that sometimes his father made people wait before they haggled. At the time, Needle wondered why his father did that. Now he understood. His father was trying to agitate his competitor before they discussed price. Well, it worked. It was unnerving. Still, his father had always urged him to be patient in all things. Not to mention his mother's lessons on the great wheel of time. Some of those lessons apparently sunk in because Needle was able to breathe deeply and calm himself, just like his parents had taught him.

"Our lot will improve in time," she had said so many times he couldn't keep track. He knew what she really meant by that.

The Agrabi as a people viewed time as a huge series of repeating cycles. This was true on a cosmic scale down to an individual person and everything in between. After all, did not the stars, planets and moons behave in predictable repeating cycles? Even the comets came at regular intervals. Why should time behave any differently? Situations in a person's life repeated in the same way. Sometimes things were good. Then there would be a period of hard times and struggle, but the good times would return again in their proper season, according to the cycles ordained by the stars.

It was the reason that the Agrabi as a people accepted their lot under the yoke of virtual and sometimes literal enslavement from the Buerdeleise. It was their current role in some grand cycle and nothing they could do could change it. Their miserable circumstances would change naturally when the time was right.

According to the legends, there was a time that the Agrabi were the absolute lords of the desert and their power and wealth were known far and wide. But then, the Buerdeleise came from the east and the Agrabi hegemony over the desert began to fade countless generations ago. All Agrabi waited for the stars to signal a return to former greatness.

It was all hogwash as far as Needle was concerned. He despised that kind of thinking. He hated the idea that his family suffered and his people underwent such tribulation based on unalterable mystical circles in the sky. Such beliefs led to complacency and tolerance of injustice.

But then again, as he considered the bizarre events of the day, he could not remember a day so singularly eventful in his life. Even when his father was still around. He had been enslaved, escaped, given a fortune in artifacts by Boxxaway, given a note written by his father from a pretty Buerdeleise girl, not to mention the outlandish tale about her dead mother and a secret society. There was now a tantalizing hope that his father could be found. It had all happened on the very day that he and his mother were threatened with eviction. For the first time in almost a year, Needle had real hope. Hope for a reprieve from poverty and hope of finding his father.

Maybe there was something to the whole circle of time idea, after all. Maybe the circle of time would bring his father back to him. Wishful thinking perhaps? Needle's mind did not want to accept that he was anything other than the master of his own destiny, but what else but fate could explain the events of the day? Maybe his fortunes were indeed about to improve.

Footsteps approached from the hallway. Needle hoped it was finally Duke Bygrave coming. Instead, a tall lanky man turned the corner and strode over toward Needle. The young man looked up at the thin man, from his steel-toed boots to his bandaged hand to his rat-like face. In that instant, his heart leapt into his throat. *It was the man who had sold him into slavery this very morning!* Needle froze. All his father's lessons about how to breathe calmly were gone. His brain screamed at him to leap up and flee, but his entire body stiffened up involuntarily and his muscles would not respond.

The man flashed him a wicked grin as he recognized Needle, but he didn't break his stride at all. "Well, ain't you a slippery one," he chuckled in a nasally voice. "But I'll see you soon. Maybe sell you again."

Needle's mouth had gone completely dry. The villain strode purposefully past Needle with an evil smile on his face. He opened the door and it swung shut behind him with a heavy thud.

It seemed like an eternity before Needle could even suck in a breath of air. His mind tumbled. How could the rat-faced man be here? Why? Was he talking with the duke? Did the duke know about him? A thousand more questions pounded through his head. The improbability of the confrontation with the man refused to register in his head. Needle had no idea how long he sat paralyzed on the bench, unable to think of anything else.

Needle's heart was still racing as the old Agrabi servant peered around the corner again. "Duke Bygrave will see you now."

"Why, but you're just a boy!" the duke exclaimed with a laugh as Needle entered. Light from wall sconces reflected off the long blue silk dinner robe he wore. Sweet spice-scented smoke from his pipe curled around his slicked back salt and pepper hair as he poured wine into a crystal glass. "I planned on offering some wine to you," he chuckled, "But I wouldn't waste it on, well, a child."

"I'll have me a drink," Needle said.

The duke smiled, put the wine bottle down with a thunk on the wooden cabinet and took a sip. He made no move to pour Needle a drink.

The room was darker than the foyer, and was lavishly furnished, designed to feel cozy. He was still astonished by the vast wealth on display. Dagorn walked slowly from the wine cabinet against the wall to a desk piled high with parchment. There was a high-backed leather chair behind the desk. Above the chair, staring ominously down at him, was the huge mounted head of a desert ram. Stuffed bookshelves lined the walls throughout the room. Off to the left there was a dormant fireplace, two plush divans and a large oblong table surrounded by almost a dozen comfortable-looking leather chairs. A marble chessboard with ornate pieces sat in the middle of the table. Needle imagined this room would be wonderfully warm on the cold desert nights of winter. But clearly the fireplace hadn't been used for many months.

Needle still felt rattled from his prior encounter with the man who had almost enslaved him, but he forced himself to focus on Dagorn's face. The glass of wine obviously wasn't his first of the night. Needle assumed it would not be his last either. He was a little drunk, but it was the drunkenness of someone who had functioned perfectly well for years and years while intoxicated.

He studied Dagorn's face. Unlike his frustrating meeting with the old wizard earlier this morning, the duke's face seemed easier to read. But what Needle saw was that this man was cold and calculating.

"My name is Needle," he said quietly. "I think you know Kemano, my father." He watched for any sign of surprise on the duke's face but saw none.

"I haven't seen old Kemano for quite a while," the duke said, taking a sip of his wine. "Feels like about a year?" Needle could smell the alcohol from where he stood. "What's he gotten up to these days?"

"He's been out in a dig for months," Needle lied. Dagorn's face was a wall of stone--nothing revealed.

"That tall man that walked out a few minutes ago?" Needle asked. "I think I have seen him somewhere before. Is he an associate of yours?"

"Hmm?" said Dagorn looking up from his wine goblet. He paused for several moments. Finally he continued, flashing a hint of a grin. "Get on with it, kid. What's your business?"

"I have some artifacts," Needle stammered, abandoning his question, "you might be interested in purchasing. They are from the old Cult of Yex."

Dagorn's eyes narrowed. He stroked his goatee. "I turn down much more than I ever buy."

"I have buyers in Balankov and Taglyon," Needle explained. He rolled the sack of wares off of his shoulder and headed over to the large table by the fireplace. Next to the chessboard, he carefully laid out four daggers, a bronze dinner plate, a spearhead, a helmet with a dragon insignia, a pewter chalice and the eight other objects until all sixteen were laid out on the table. A few of the artifacts were emblazoned with the Cult of Yex symbol.

Dagorn approached the table, his feet shuffling on the carpet. Needle could smell the spice from his pipe mixed with the strong odor of wine. He stood right next to Needle. This was a problem. Needle wanted to be able to see the man's face as he looked at the artifacts. He would have to move to the other side of the table, but that would be an awkward and unjustified movement.

"I'm sorry," Dagorn said. "What was your name again?"

Needle was taken aback. Dagorn showed the slightest hint of a smile. How could he not remember his name? How drunk was he? "Uhh--Needle."

"Right. Sorry. So. This stuff just isn't that special..."

Dagorn said nothing more. How was he supposed to respond to that? It was an intensely awkward silence and Needle felt flustered.

Needle desperately wanted to fill the silence, but what was he supposed to say? He swallowed, rubbed his hands together, and coughed lightly.

Dagorn allowed himself a slight grin. The bastard, thought Needle. He's doing this to me on purpose. Needle remembered his father haggling with people in the market, often making them uncomfortable with long stretches of silence.

Needle knew he should wait, just wait it out, say nothing. But he couldn't. "Well, I think they are pretty good," he said in a rush and then cursed himself for being so stupid. If he had to speak first, why did he say something so pathetic?

Dagorn chuckled. He was toying with him.

"Where did you get this stuff?" Dagorn asked. "Your father would have never brought me stuff like this."

Needle floundered. He wondered if Boxxaway had given him junk, just to play with him. But no, that wasn't possible. Needle had spent years with his father on digs. He knew this stuff was valuable.

"My father said these were good pieces, and you would want them," Needle lied. He immediately regretted it.

Dagorn's eyes narrowed again. "I thought you said he's been gone for months."

"He sent these to me," Needle said quickly, and felt a moment of relief. It was a reasonable lie.

"He sent them to you?"

"He said to take them to you first, then to Balankov or Taglyon, if you didn't want them," Needle plowed ahead. It was too late to change the lie now.

"Travel is expensive," Dagorn said.

"Are you offering to buy?"

"This isn't what I usually buy, but..." Dagorn said. "Your

father brought me a lot of good pieces. Assuming the price was right."

"Thirty-two," Needle blurted without hesitation, suddenly excited.

"Thirty-two! I was thinking *maybe* eight," Dagorn said loudly, his face contorted into anger.

Needle recoiled. Dagorn had shifted from manipulation to bemusement to anger in a matter of a few seconds. Needle took a step back from the table and wrung his hands together. He opened his mouth to say something, but couldn't think of a single thing. He was left standing there with his mouth hanging open.

One thing did occur to Needle. The duke *was* interested. Why bother with the anger and pretense if he wasn't? Needle finally began to feel more sure. Dagorn *did* want these artifacts. It was hard to explain, but Needle knew it. This gave him a moment of confidence and when he spoke, his voice was stronger. "Help me understand your anger over my price. I mean, why even bother if they aren't worth anything? Did I misunderstand?"

Dagorn glanced down at the wine goblet in his hands for a moment and then set it down on the table to the side of the artifacts as he lowered himself into one of leather chairs.

"I thought you came to sell them?"

Needle didn't like the level of confidence that Dagorn was showing.

"I'm trying to be nice, out of respect for your father," Dagorn continued. "The bottom line is you have a couple of okay pieces here, but most of it is junk."

Needle nodded and then wanted to slap himself. He had just agreed that most of the stuff was junk.

Dagorn continued, "You got sixteen pieces here and your price was thirty-two."

Dagorn began to shuffle the items on the table into two groups.

Needle had a hard time swallowing. He didn't like where this was going.

"So, based on your price, these are two moons each."

"No, but...."

Dagorn pressed on. "I only want these four items, so that comes to a total of eight silver moons." Dagorn stood, took up his goblet again and shuffled to his desk.

Needle stared at the two groups of artifacts. Dagorn had chosen the four best pieces without error. He chose only the pieces that bore the cult's symbol upon them.

Dagorn opened the top drawer and pulled out a large black leather pouch. Dagorn opened it and started counting out coins.

Needle's eyes bulged at the fortune Dagorn had in that purse. He had never seen so much gold and silver in his life. Eight silver coins was a fortune to him and his mother! But those eight coins were needed for the lift up to the top of the plateau! He knew in his heart he could not resist meeting the girl on the plateau tonight. He would never make it the long way on foot. He desperately needed to move his mother out of the Kuma, at least back from the edge of the desert. This would leave nothing leftover. Not to mention, he owed Boxxaway!

Dagorn walked back to the table with a fist full of coins, which he slapped down with a finality that implied the negotiations had concluded and their business was over.

Needle froze. He simply could not accept such a low price. He had to have a higher price. If the duke wasn't interested at all, Needle doubted he would have wasted two seconds haggling. But Dagorn *was* haggling! Needle felt more certain.

Needle stood up straighter. He set his jaw and stopped wringing his hands.

"I'm sorry, Dagorn," he heard himself say, "but this is worth much more as a collection than as separate items. If you want just those four items that is fine, but we will have to settle on a fair price for them separately."

Dagorn's eyes narrowed and Needle expected anger.

"How old are you, kid? Seventeen? Eighteen?"

Needle smiled weakly. "My age has got nothing to do with this." He had never been mistaken for older than his actual sixteen years before.

Dagorn studied him.

Needle muddled on. "If I break up this collection, I'd have to take a trip down to Balankov to sell the rest, and given the value of the remaining pieces, it would be a hassle for me. So, I'll give you a break on the price of the whole collection if you will save me the trouble."

Dagorn said nothing.

"I'll allow you to purchase this entire collection for twenty-four."

"They aren't even worth half that, kid. I've had a rough day, and believe me, you are lucky to get an offer of eight."

Dagorn was frighteningly shrewd. Needle could not accept eight and there was only one way he was going to get a better price.

Even if it means your mother starving? he reminded himself.

Needle had to force the duke's hand. It was a terrible risk, but Needle couldn't see any other option.

Needle straightened again. "Duke Bygrave, you know and I know that this collection is worth a lot more than twenty. I'd love to sell these to you, but frankly I'd be much better off taking the whole collection down to Balankov." Needle couldn't believe what he was saying. Eight moons was a fortune.

Dagorn set his goblet down again with a clink. Needle's skin went cold and clammy. His mouth tasted sour.

Then something in Needle's brain took over. Dagorn had not sipped his wine for several minutes. He was concentrating on this discussion. Another indication that he *did* want the artifacts!

Dagorn said nothing. He was trying the silence trick again, but this time Needle wasn't going to play. He started gathering up the artifacts into the sack. If Dagorn wanted the artifacts, he would have to speak up.

Needle finished packing, and still Dagorn said nothing. He began to walk slowly to the door. *Look confident,* he told himself. Don't turn around. But as he walked, he slowed. He remembered the purse of silver and gold, Dagorn could easily afford his price. Needle knew he wanted the relics. But would Dagorn let it all go just for spite?

He grew more and more unsure by the moment, but his walk away bluff had begun. If he turned back now, Dagorn would have the upper hand, and Needle would never get the price he needed. Needle approached the door, and still Dagorn said nothing.

Needle felt as if he were about to panic. He felt bile rise in his throat, and the bitter taste spread through his mouth. He reached for the door and saw his hand was shaking. He closed his eyes and saw his mother sitting in her rocking chair, blind, hungry.

I have to take the eight, he realized. I have to.

But he surprised himself. His hand steadied and he reached out and grabbed the door. He couldn't breathe, but he kept going. He pulled the door open.

He turned and smiled, "Thanks for your time, Duke Bygrave. Perhaps we can do business sometime in the future."

The Duke neither smiled nor spoke as he leaned back in his chair and took a long gulp of wine from his goblet.

Needle knew then that it was over. The man would not buckle. Eight was it, and Needle wasn't going to accept it.

He walked down the hall toward the foyer, the door swinging shut behind him. He thought of his mother and tears began to well in his eyes.

Go back and take the eight, he thought. But he realized even that option was now gone. If he returned, Dagorn would surely offer even less.

Needle's heart sank. Sure he could find another buyer, but not tonight. He would miss the meeting with Brynn, and perhaps a vital clue to finding his father. Not to mention, his starving mother.

He trudged toward the exit, feeling more worthless than he had ever felt in his life. And that was saying something.

Damn me and my pride.

The door clicked behind Needle just as he was about to turn the corner.

"Come back in here, boy," Dagorn ordered, standing in the open doorway.

Needle wanted to breathe a sigh of relief, but knew that even that might give him away. He turned slowly, with a "what can I do for you" look on his face.

"Your father teach you to haggle?" Dagorn asked as he shuffled down the hall toward him.

You could say that, Needle thought, but he didn't actually speak.

Dagorn counted out sixteen silver moons. Needle knew his eyes bulged, so he looked away. The old man held out his hand, the silver shining in his open palm.

"Agreed?"

Needle dropped the sack and took the clinking coins in both hands. His hands were sweaty and his mouth was suddenly filled with saliva. He felt a tingle run all the way up his spine.

Dagorn picked up the sack, a funny look on his face as he stared at the money. "Enjoy that, while you can."

Needle considered that remark. What in the Abyss did that mean? He decided nothing made sense today. *Nothing at all.* Maybe he'd have to re-evaluate the whole circle of time thing, because it certainly was all coming around. Just like mother said that one day it would.

CHAPTER ELEVEN
Time Is Always on My Side

We employed various races as mercenaries as our needs grew. Of particular usefulness to us was a diminutive race from the northlands. Calling themselves the Rothkin, they were known for incredible stealth. Before the fall of the great citadel, when it appeared that all might be lost, we had to act quickly to preserve our secrets and traditions. I worked frantically to lay a foundation for the future. Among other things, I sent a Rothkin into hiding with a quantity of spores followed by more of his kind. They evaded Adirak's agents and hid away in isolation. I nurtured their culture over the eons and communed with their kings through dreams.

-From the *Lich Diary of the Archmage Xylex*

1st Day of Summer – 10:00 PM – Bygrave Estate – 3 Hours 30 Minutes Before the Earthquake

Letharchenel's crossbow was loaded with a poisoned quarrel and ready to fire. He was hidden in the shrubbery, where he had an excellent vantage of the shadowy courtyard: the largest building, the front gate and the fountain area between them.

He had watched many people come and go well past the setting of the sun. His hearing was excellent and he had overheard many a conversation. Three of his marks had been within striking distance. Mallet and Brynn had both come and gone and to his surprise, even the boy Needle had appeared at the gate. He introduced himself and asked to speak with the master of the house and was promptly escorted into the largest building.

None of them were alone for long, making it risky to strike. There were too many servants and other onlookers about. Much could go wrong. Then there was that lanky rat-faced man with the wicked rapier who seemed to pass through the courtyard regularly. Something about him felt dangerous, even ominous. It was clear from a conversation he overheard that Mallet, a giant of a boy, was wary of him. No, this walled compound was not the right place nor time to strike. Patience was an asset in his business and he knew a better opportunity would present itself.

From a conversation he overheard, he intuited that the girl was planning to visit the family mausoleum atop the bluff. By her tone, he would wager that she intended to do it this very night. A better locale he could not imagine.

CHAPTER TWELVE
The Flow of Time

A wizard, simply stated, is one who uses magic to alter or manipulate the world around him. A wizard can manipulate the elements: fire, air, water and earth. A wizard can manipulate gravity, space, thoughts and emotions. A wizard can even manipulate time itself, though most wizards never dare. The cost of altering time is far too dear.

-The Book of Eldritch Lore

1st Day of Summer – 11:00 PM – Boxxaway's Cottage – 2 Hour and 30 Minutes Before the Earthquake

Boxxaway Hotheway sat on a four-legged stool in his humble mud brick cottage, Dheke napping fitfully at his feet. He looked around the lamp-lit kitchen and couldn't help reflecting poignantly on the many memories he had in this old home. His letters were written and tucked neatly in a pack that lay on the floor. The *Lorgnettes*, protected in a sturdy scroll tube, were nestled safely in the pack, alongside the dagger and everything else he would need.

Boxxaway reflected on the improbable events of the morning; of all the times for Cael to decide to use the *Lorgnettes* to try to see his parents. The timing seemed too incredible to be coincidence. It was yet another case of something happening that he simply did not expect.

Like the odor of Bystle Fruit he noticed in the cottage earlier. Had a Rothkin entered their home this morning while they were away? If so, what did it augur? If it wasn't a Rothkin, how then to explain the unmistakable scent? These incidents were just not supposed to happen.

Years of careful planning and preparation were all predicated on his painstaking notes and understanding. He worried that these minor deviations somehow jeopardized his meticulous designs. There was too much at stake for things to go awry.

Yet, so much was happening just as he expected it would. The signs and portents were clear. The stars were right. Animals were acting strangely. Word was that springs in the area had slowed or stopped flowing altogether. Indeed, all signs confirmed it. The earthquake was inevitable. It would happen tonight.

Tonight! There was so much to do and so little time. His timing would be critical. But he felt the ache in his bones. Was an old man like him up to the task? For Cael's sake, he had to be.

He wanted to be optimistic, but his doubts lingered. The deviations were real, impossible to ignore. He thought again of the faint odor he smelled earlier. What was the cause of these abnormalities? It was as if the flow of time itself was anomalous, inconsistent. *Out of order*, the Bygrave girl would say.

The torment of worry had been too much for him. He had done something he had promised himself he would not do. He was far too old to hazard the further use of magic, but the worry of the past weeks compelled him. He had risked a few minor divinations, which confirmed his fears. Accordingly, he made adjustments to his plans. Was there more he had not foreseen?

He thought again of Cael and the others. It was much to ask of them, but at his age, what other options did he have? Were they equal to the tasks that lay ahead of them? Was he? Would he even live to see it all through to the end?

He pushed his worries aside. Everything that could be accounted for, *had* been accounted for. There was no point brooding on it anymore.

Finally, he stood up, feeling shaky. Dheke barked softly and looked up at him. Boxxaway breathed in heavily, grabbed his staff and shouldered his pack. He started to head out when he remembered the carpet. Imagine forgetting that. He stooped to roll up the tattered red rug. His old joints creaked as he straightened up to sling it over his shoulder.

He looked around the cottage with a sigh. For the second time in his life, he would never see it again.

CHAPTER THIRTEEN
Ghost of a Chance

Despite far-reaching recruiting efforts, Adirak's Alliance could not gain a numerical advantage over the Cult of Yex. When a warrior from either army fell in battle, the cult's wicked necromancers raised them to undeath. Adirak's Alliance had to kill their enemies twice and their own fallen once. The Alliance was forced to burn their fallen to save them from the foul necromancy. When it was all over, the Alliance returned to their old tradition of entombing the dead. Many of the tombs remain to this day and fears of an undead army have faded with the ages.

-Return of the Cult of Yex, by Caed the Chronicler

1st Day of Summer - 11:00 PM – The Lifts – 2 Hours and 30 Minutes Before the Earthquake

"Your mother guards a dangerous secret," the old bald wizard operating the lift said in a distant voice. Brynn took a step back from him, staring at his blank face. He looked at her through entranced eyes clouded over with swirling white mist. She had handed the strange man the wooden token she found in the rolltop desk and told him she wanted to go to the top. The old wizard fingered the silver inlaid marks on the circular disk. Satisfied, he handed the token back to her, slipped into his cloudy-eyed trance, uttered his creepy prophecy, and the lift magically began to levitate with a jerk and a shudder.

The lift reminded her of a pumpkin. It was made of tough strands of root fibers, some as big as her forearm, that arched out and up in a globe. Smaller vine-sized fibers were woven like a basket between the skeletal root strands. The floor was made of dozens of hewn wooden planks that were laid with slight unevenness. It appeared to Brynn that six or seven people would fit inside, but it seemed rickety as it creaked slowly upward. The old wizard held a lantern in one shaky, liver-spotted hand and a staff of polished dark wood in the other as he sat on a stool near the door of the lift.

"She has many secrets," the old man intoned a few moments later in a distant voice.

Brynn did not like the old man talking like this, but if he *was* talking about her mother, well, he was right. She had many secrets. Secrets Brynn intended to make her own.

"Her secret will become your secret," the old man added, as if to validate Brynn's own feelings.

She nodded, fingering the wooden disk in her hand as she rode the lift higher, staring at the sigil drawn on the opposite side in dark Iron-Gall ink. A faint haunting melody played in her head until she flipped the disk back over. When Brynn had first found the token in the rolltop desk in her mother's secret dimension, she didn't understand its meaning. Now, she was crystal clear on the message.

She had spent the past week since she had found the token trying to remember where she had seen it before, but she simply had not been able to recall where. It was like an itch in her brain that she could not scratch. She was certain that her mother had a purpose in drawing it on the token; it was a deliberate and important message to her from her mother. Until she remembered where she had seen the sigil before, it was meaningless. The memory of that sigil danced maddeningly at the edge of her mind.

Try as she might, she could not find the pattern anywhere in her home. Neither was it in the book of sigils she retrieved from the rolltop desk. It wasn't until this morning that the answer had come to her. She fell asleep last night thinking about where she had seen the pattern and woke up this morning recalling her mother's funeral. They had gone up to the Bygrave mausoleum on the plateau and sealed her in that awful carved stone sarcophagus.

As was the custom of Buerdeleise nobles, the stone sarcophagi that would become the eternal resting places for family members were prepared long before death called. Indeed, her father's sarcophagus was already prepared, with the family crest and his name already etched in the stone. As was tradition, it was the matron of the noble house who oversaw those preparations.

They had lowered Mother's wrapped, mummified body into the stone sepulcher and then Mallet, along with Wheizer, Father and a couple of servants had heaved the massive stone lid closed. It had made an awful grinding sound as it slid down and with a whoosh, sealed shut. And there, etched on the stone lid was Brynn's mother's name, *Elowynn Bygrave*, over the Bygrave family crest.

There! Enmeshed in the bas relief crest was the same sigil that had been drawn on the back of the lift token. Brynn could see it clearly now in her mind's eye. Every Bygrave sarcophagus had the same ancient family crest etched onto it, but Mother's had been modified. It was a subtle alteration that would likely never be noticed except by someone trained to see witch sigils, training that her mother had surreptitiously given to her daughter all her life.

Brynn had noticed it even then, that dreary day. It looked odd, and there had been a slight click of recognition in the deep parts of her mind. But of course, on that day a year ago, she had not considered it important and it was promptly forgotten.

This morning, as she lay in her bed, in the sudden flash of recollection, she realized how crucial it was. Her mother had a secret sigil carved *within the family crest*. Brynn *knew*--her mother had placed it there exclusively for her.

At that moment, Brynn realized her mother left her another secret message whose significance and instructions were now unmistakable. The placement of the sigil on the back of the lift token was a message from her mother. She must ride the lifts to the graveyard atop the plateau and trace the pattern of the sigil hidden on the lid of her sarcophagus. Her mother had left an ensigiled trail of crumbs for her. Nothing would stop her from following it.

However, she had felt it prudent to first search for Kemano Graji, the man who wrote the note she had found tucked under the cover of the sigil book. She found his son Needle instead and convinced him to meet her.

"A hand adorns a great weapon," the bald old wizard intoned. "It is the key to unlocking its power."

"Pardon? What does that mean?" she asked, but the old man just stared ahead blankly through his clouded eyes.

Brynn was about to pressure him for more information when his eyes unclouded and the lift slowed to a halt. A tall man opened the door and ducked his head as he moved from the iron catwalk and entered the pumpkin basket. They were only about fifty feet above the Middle Steppe. "Don't mind him," the tall man said to her with a wave of his hand. She looked up at him, noticing he was young and somewhat handsome, though he had scarring on his cheeks, maybe the remnant of childhood acne. She had seen him before, but did not know him. He was probably a member of one of the noble houses.

"Hey, Abner," the man said as he passed the old wizard a token. "Sage level, please."

The old wizard fingered the token and handed it back. His eyes clouded over again and the lift began to climb slowly skyward up the face of the bluff on its thousand foot journey to the top, passing near various iron catwalks and paths carved into the side of the cliff face. Countless doors and other entrances dotted the cliff.

"He will offer himself upon the frozen altar to atone," the old man said.

"Why does he say those things?" Brynn asked the tall man who had just boarded.

"Old Abner mumbles fortunes when he is in his trance," the man chuckled. "He's an old burned-out wizard, aged prematurely. Mostly all he's good for now is operating the lifts for the academy."

If Abner heard what the man was saying, he made no indication. He just stared at nothing through his clouded eyes.

"Well, I don't like it," Brynn said, irritated by the old man. He ought to keep his business to himself. Besides, that last thing he said didn't make any sense whatsoever.

"The scion is near," the old man muttered, as if in response.

Brynn turned to the tall young man. "Can you make him stop?"

He just smiled at her. "He's been doing that for years; he

isn't going to stop now. Everyone ignores him. It's all gibberish as near as anyone can tell."

"I've ridden the lifts before," Brynn said, "and none of the other wizards did that."

"Yep. Just old Abner here."

They rode in silence for a few uncomfortable moments as the lift rose. She looked out over Demon's Bluff. Lights all over town indicated the precise borders even in the darkness of the new moon.

"An ancient malevolence lingers below," the old wizard hissed.

Brynn could make out the Demon River below. It was easy to spot as it was a dark swath absent of light. A few lights dotted the far shore.

"Silver is prime. It is the key to this world," the hollow voice of the old wizard droned.

The old wizard's pronouncements were nonsense, but unnerving nevertheless. Brynn put her hands into her pockets. She felt the wooden lift pass and clutched it nervously.

She shivered despite the lingering heat of the night. She wore her mother's clothes: loose fitting white cloth trousers that swished when she walked. They were a little too long and the hems dragged in the dirt. She wore a beige-sleeved tunic, also too large, especially in the chest. Her hooded cloak, held around her neck with her mother's silver broach, was draped over her shoulder covering her satchel. The satchel carried ink bottles, needles and the tome filled with sigils she had gained from the rolltop desk. These things gave her comfort.

A sudden gust of wind, dry and sage-scented, struck the lift, shaking it slightly. Brynn wondered if the lift operated during sandstorms.

"The sentinels of the night will abandon their appointed posts," the old wizard muttered.

Brynn took a deep breath. This ride was out of order.

"What level?" the tall man asked. "I'm up to the sages to deliver a missive for Duke Bayliss," he continued.

Normally, Brynn would have preferred silence, but in this case she was grateful for something besides cryptic pronouncements from the old wizard.

"There is a place where nobody can find you, where all are alike," said the old man. "He will hide there."

"I'm meeting someone at the graveyard on top," she said, talking too quickly.

"Graveyard?" the man said. "Pretty scary up there at night, I would think."

"His true name reveals a great deception," the old wizard droned on.

Brynn shrugged. It probably would be frightening up there. She gripped the lift token to give her strength.

"This is your stop," Abner said to the tall man. For once, he didn't utter a fortune. The lift slowed to a stop.

The tall man smiled at the wizard as he opened the lift door and stepped out, his boots clinking on the iron catwalk. He ambled away without another word. The wind shifted and mist from the great waterfall sprinkled over them. It smelled fresh, and the coolness made Brynn shiver again. The old man came out of his trance long enough to stand up slowly, setting the lantern down on the floor of the woven basket lift. He put a hand in the small of his back and groaned as he rose. Brynn could hear his bones cracking. He grabbed the door, pulling it shut.

He sat down again and smiled at Brynn. "Next stop, your stop, the top."

Brynn shivered again and focused on her purpose. She was going alone into an ancient graveyard in the middle of a moonless night to trace a sigil her dead mother had left her. Was she crazy?

"The second cataclysm is at hand."

"Yeah, I'm sure," she muttered in response. The lift started to move again. Brynn looked out at the lights of the city again.

"My mother is dead," Brynn said to the old man for no particular reason.

He answered her immediately: "Hope springs from the second aegis which endows the scion, hidden under the nose of evil."

Brynn stopped talking, hoping it would stop the man from uttering his fortunes. It didn't. They rode up the cliff face in a silence punctuated only by the occasional baying of dogs far below, and the muttered mantras of the old man:

"All that happens now has happened before."

"In the aerie resides the lost vessel."

"The princess is possessed of kin."

"A great demon lord imbibed to his immortal tomb."

"The swamp wyrm guards over them."

"The fleet entombed emerges to resume the battle against its former foe."

"Many gates lead to many worlds."

"The forefather is freed from his prison to hunt."

"The servant will transpose his master."

Brynn let out a breath. *Was he done?*

He had one final fortune to utter: "Beware the rancor of the rat that stalks in shadow."

Brynn could make no sense of the man's ramblings, but she had an eerie feeling about the old wizard's twaddle. She had a vague sense that hidden within the incomprehensible words there was some manner of meaning, much like the meaning hidden in many of the patterns of her life.

She fingered the token in her pocket. Brynn filled her lungs with air, tasting the cool mist of the waterfall mingled with the scent of sage the desert wind blew upon them. A tingle rose up her spine. She closed her eyes.

Her mother's secret would become her secret.

"Your stop," the old man said. The lift lurched to halt. They had reached the top of the plateau.

The landing at the top of the plateau was clustered with old, whitewashed adobe buildings that formed a rough circle around a wide cobblestone-lined courtyard. Brynn had been here before and it felt like being inside a castle. She looked up and saw a town guardsman dressed in blue walking behind the ramparts above her. Had he noticed her? She thought maybe he had.

Was she even allowed up here at night?

The old bald wizard closed the lift door behind her and sat

down again on his stool. The lift slowly disappeared below the edge of the bluff. She wondered how late he operated the lift, or if any of the other lifts were still operating.

Smoky torchlight glinted off the guard's iron helm and the imposing point of his spear. His boots thumped on the stone as he walked away. Fifty yards beyond him, a huge wooden structure towered at the edge of the bluff. It was a giant trebuchet, one of several defensive siege engines atop the mesa capable of flinging fiery doom all the way to the river. His footsteps faded as he made his way in the direction of the gryphon pens. Demon's Bluff had known peace for generations; the defenses were strong.

She walked through the courtyard, surrounded by the tall white walls. Numerous lanterns, swinging in the night breeze, hung from poles. She had forgotten to bring a lantern. Would anybody mind if she borrowed one of these? There was no one around to complain.

She went through the western arch and passed into another courtyard. This was the undertaker's courtyard, where a sign carved in wood said: *Mortuary Guild.*

This was the providence of the guild of undertakers and embalmers who managed the graveyard and prepared the dead for their journey to the afterlife. It was a morbid place. Shovels leaned against mud-encrusted wagons parked next to stacks of coffins. Blank headstones, large and small, piled against each other in rows up against the buildings. The headstones were made of various types of stone, some imported and expensive. Rock chips and chisels lay strewn about.

One year ago, though she remembered few details, she came here with her father, Mallet and a few Agrabi servants. Wheizer had been there, too, for some reason. They transported her mother up the lifts in a wooden coffin and then by wagon to the mausoleum. Her mother's mummified body was transferred to a stone sarcophagus, which was then sealed with the lid carved with the family crest--the very crest she needed to see tonight. Words were spoken, tears were shed and Elowynn Bygrave was laid to rest forever.

This courtyard too was empty; no one worked up here at night.

She passed out of the courtyard leaving the buildings behind. Soon, she reached another sign mounted on a post:

No admittance to the graveyard after dark

She considered the sign. Neither gate nor guard prevented her, but fear was deterrence enough. It was indeed frightening up here, alone in the dark, just like the man said. How much scarier would the graveyard itself be? She felt like a spider had crawled up her spine. Maybe it would have been wiser to journey to the mausoleum with Needle instead of telling him to meet here there.

She steeled herself and continued down the dusty road to the cemetery as the metal wire handle of her lantern swayed and creaked. It threw dim light about as she walked into the darkness. She followed the minor curves of the old road as she walked westward and soon arrived at a wrought iron fence surrounding the entire cemetery, its great arch forming the entrance gate. She passed through and soon came to the first of many intersecting roads, called 'rows' that led to various sections of the graveyard.

The first intersection was Gadrax Row, which contained the oldest graves and mausoleums, the greatest of the noble houses of Demon's Bluff. The Bygrave mausoleum was about a quarter mile down the right on Gadrax Row. The graveled row was tidy, no weeds, as if the important members living there wouldn't allow such mess.

Even though the Bygrave family name was not what it once was, the family mausoleum kept its lofty place here among the other great houses of Demon's Bluff. It was the one place where losing your standing in the hierarchy of nobles didn't affect you. Brynn assumed this was mostly because nobody wanted to dig up five thousand years of corpses and move them to a lesser location. Besides, fortunes could change.

A desert coyote howled somewhere in the distance.

"My mother's secrets will become my secrets," she whispered to herself for courage. Hopefully, Needle was waiting for her up ahead.

She desperately tried to not remember the tales told to

frighten children, but her imagination erupted, unrestrained. The bony fingers of skeletons, raised from the grave, reached out through the dark for her throat. Ghouls hid behind every gravestone, ready to leap upon her and devour her flesh as she looked on, paralyzed with terror. Spectral forms danced at the edge of her lantern light, waiting for her to scream so they could fly through her open mouth to possess her.

Gravel crunched under her feet as she made one courageous step after the other. She mustn't scream.

"My mother's secrets will become my secrets," Brynn whispered aloud once more. She crested a low knoll and saw the great Von Torinovo mausoleum off to the left, with its awe-inspiring white pillars. It was one of the oldest in the graveyard, said to have been built at the time that Demon's Bluff was founded. Supposedly, its occupants died fighting in the great war against the Cult of Yex.

Mother feared the Cult of Yex she now realized. *So did Needle's father.* And today's surprising revelation--her own father collected Cult of Yex artifacts. What to make of that? Something about it all seemed ominous and at the same time out of order. She could sense a pattern there, just beyond the edge of her understanding.

Then again, it could all be coincidence. *Not everything means something,* her father would always say. Mother, of course, had felt that *everything* meant *something.* There were no coincidences for her.

Brynn knew that the Cult of Yex had existed, the Von Torinovo mausoleum was proof of that. However, the suggestion in Kemano's letter to her mother, that a remnant had survived over that vast stretch of time seemed not only far-fetched to Brynn but it bordered on absurd. More likely, some group of evildoers had co-opted the name to lend a little credence to their malignant designs. But on the other hand, just like her mother, Brynn could sense a pattern in the things that were happening.

What was this *Society of Eyes*? Her mother and Kemano had belonged to it and clearly it was somehow connected to the Cult of Yex.

There it was, ahead in a shallow depression. The Bygrave

mausoleum was a four-sided pyramid, made of great yellow-ish sandstone blocks. It was smaller and architecturally less intricate, but it was still grand compared to many of the other family mausoleums in the graveyard. Only the Von Torinovo mausoleum overshadowed it. The Bygraves had indeed once been more prestigious.

She knew the history of her father's side of the family, but recent events had created questions about her mother's family. What was the meaning of the mysterious name *Vallant*? Her father had recounted the history of the Bygraves to her and Mallet many times. Brynn could detect a hint of bitterness in his tone as he talked of the past when Bygrave was one of the great and powerful houses of Demon's Bluff. The Bygraves had once been guardians of the dead on the plateau, serving as the undertakers for eons; a very profitable business her father had assured them.

At some point, more than a dozen generations earlier, no one really seemed to recall why, the Bygraves had lost control of the graveyard. She had heard her father curse the weakness of that unknown ancestor. Power, he often said, was accrued through ruthlessness and bled away through weakness. She heard him tell Mallet over and over again that a single mo-ment of weakness could have ramifications that reverberated through the ages.

She walked down the road, keeping her eye on the low wrought iron fence that surrounded the vast Bygrave family plot. Beyond it she could see tombstones, some leaning at crazy angles, etched names fading from age.

She reached out her hand and felt the cool metal of the fence as she approached the entrance to the plot. She pushed and the gate opened silently until it clanged back against the pillar. The sound echoed through the graveyard, returning and fading slowly. Brynn gritted her teeth and squared her shoul-ders. This was it.

The narrow overgrown path lead straight to the granite-pillared building in front that served as the vestibule to the pyramid. Her heart leapt into her throat as her lantern flickered briefly, as if the oil inside might fail. Her fear slowly subsided as the light renewed. She looked around. Where was Needle?

Hopefully he was already here, inside the mausoleum.

"My mother's secrets will become my secrets," Brynn whispered for a third time. She knew she could turn back, but did not want to. One taste of the unknown, one alluring chime of music from the macabre and it was too late for her. It was her mother's witchcraft, the opera of the insane, the communication with the edge and the hint of danger.

Everything changed irrevocably the moment she had traced the pattern on her bedroom wall.

She shivered as she passed through the vestibule. It was predominantly Buerdeleise, but with a heavy fusion of funerary accoutrements borrowed from the ancient Agrabi. The sandstone walls were inscribed with ancient Agrabi cartouches, litanies for the dead and lamentations for the departed.

She angled the lantern upwards where great tattered papyrus ropes hung from the roofing beams like tentacles waiting to reach down and grab her. The stone ceiling, in between the roofing beams, was carved with stars and constellations in bas relief. Polished red granite pillars lined the hall and these were engraved with images of beer and bread, the rations that would be waiting for dead souls once they passed into the heavens.

At the end of the hall, a great false door was etched into the rock where the granite of the vestibule met the sandstone of the pyramid. To the left, a wide stairway led down. The pyramid itself was solid sandstone blocks. All of the burial chambers were found below it. The stair led down to the first level, which was the main level for the newly dead. From there, the stairs continued down in a rectangular spiral. Along the constantly downward slope, dear departed loved ones were stored in narrow vaults carved straight into the walls.

How far down this looping passage went Brynn had no idea, but she did know that after a number of years, the bodies in the sarcophagi on the main level were removed and taken down into the deep catacombs to make room for the newly dead. It was a convenience to the living who still mourned.

The air was stale and dry in her throat as she descended the wide stair to the opening of the main chamber. The chamber was as wide as the base of the pyramid and lined with several rows, each consisting of dozens of granite funerary boxes. Huge pillars also ran in rows, holding up the shadowy cobwebbed ceiling. The floor was smooth sandstone but covered with a layer of desert sand about half an inch thick. She felt confined here, like the pyramid could come down upon her at any moment. It smelled old.

The lantern light pricked the dark in front of her and she started to make her way down the first line of sarcophagi. She knew her mother's was about half-way down the first row. Each sarcophagus was somewhat plain; the only thing visible on the grey stone slabs was the name of the occupant and the family crest. Brynn read aloud the names of each as she passed by. She recognized only a few.

Then she saw her mother's name, *Elowynn Bygrave*, etched on the lid of a sarcophagus and a rush of emotions assaulted her. Tears filled her eyes and she wiped them away with the back of her hand. She had not been up here in the year since her mother passed and now felt very guilty for that.

My mother is buried inside this tomb, she thought. *Her body is in there, right now.*

Tears flowed freely down her cheeks. She tried to control her emotions but couldn't. Her mother was never coming back. The finality of death had struck her many times over the last year, but right now she realized it in a way completely unknown before.

Here, alone, there are no more illusions.

Mother really was dead and Brynn was never going to speak to her again. This was a truth that went deeper than just mere acceptance. This was core--fundamental, which made the connection she now felt with her mother all the more important. As she let go of her barriers and felt the loss of her mother on a true and deep level, she felt a pain she had never fathomed. The pain, sharp and piercing, had a strange, cathartic quality to it. It burned but it also healed. Brynn realized that she needed this time: alone at her mother's grave.

A new feeling arose, a connection. Mother was dead but

Brynn was inescapably linked to her. Here in this place of the dead, the living and the departed came together in a revelation of single purpose. Whatever secret path tracing the sigil on this tomb would reveal, Brynn was already walking it.

She steadied her hand and set the lantern on the sarcophagus next to her mother's. Shadows seemed to flit down the rows of stone tombs. She put her hand to her pounding heart. For a brief moment, she felt as if someone was watching her, but the sensation passed. Just the spiders skittering in the shadows.

Her mother's sarcophagus was about three feet high. Brynn walked along the narrow gap between it and the one to the right. She ran her right hand along the cool stone, leaving a trail in the dust, till she came to where the Bygrave family crest was etched into the stone.

She pulled out the wooden lift token, and that seemed to break the emotions flowing through her. Calm filled her. She looked at the sigil on the token and then studied the family crest upon her mother's sarcophagus lid; a faint haunting melody played in her mind. The sigil in the crest was as she had remembered it this morning. Intricately buried within the carving of the Bygrave family crest was the unmistakable sigil repeated on the token. She exhaled and realized that she had been holding her breath.

This was it. Her excitement surged, but at the same time, she felt calm and her thoughts were clear. All the emotional weight she had been feeling was lifted. Brynn felt a renewed sense of certainty her mother had planned this and intended for her to come here.

"My mother's secrets," she whispered.

Then out of nowhere, she was startled by a hand on her shoulder. She whirled, her heart instantly thudding. Of all people in the world, it was Mallet, her brother, who loomed over her. His normally tan face was pale as the moon, his own eyes rimmed in red. He looked awful, his parched lips protruding from the bristles on his face, moving but not saying anything.

"What are you doing here?" she demanded.

"Brynn, we got to go," he replied, turning his head back and forth as he searched the shadows.

"What are you talking about?"

"Listen to me Brynn. This is wrong," he said emphatically.

"Un uh," Brynn shook her head.

Mallet closed his eyes for a second. "Brynn, there is something you should know about Mother." His voice was soft, plaintive. It made her sad.

"I know. She was a witch."

Mallet recoiled. She could tell by his hardened face he was shocked. He was silent for several moments and she could see he was considering what to say. A parade of emotions crossed his face: anger to desperation to resignation all in one fluid series of facial expressions.

Then he sighed. "I didn't want you to find out. Father and I didn't want you to know."

"That's why she was wrapped like a mummy at the funeral, isn't it?" Brynn asked, her suspicions confirmed.

"Yeah," he said. "After she died, there were strange complicated markings--tattoos. They started to appear all over her skin, all over her face. It seemed like there were dozens and dozens of them all over her. I knew what that meant. It was horrible."

"It's why no one else came to the funeral, isn't it?" she asked.

"We couldn't let anyone know Brynn. What would happen to the family?"

"The family? Our mother *is* family! You're ashamed of her, aren't you?"

"We were just doing what we thought was best," Mallet said. "So, how did you find out, and why in the hell are you up here?"

"Mother left a message for me to find after she died," said Brynn more calmly, giving Mallet something that she knew would make his head spin. He deserved it. He should have told her the truth a year ago. They had never kept secrets before. "Mother wanted me to come here."

At first, this seemed too much for him, and he took a step back and then recovered his wits. "Message?" Mallet said shaking his head. "You can't lift that lid without me."

"Why did you come here, Mallet?" Brynn was truly curious, though she had a guess.

"I've got a really bad feeling about things."

Brynn frowned looking around. "So, you said Father knows Mother was a witch?" It was all shadows beyond the reach of her lantern.

"Father knows more than you can imagine," Mallet said, his gaze moving down as he wiped his mouth. His hand was shaking.

"How did *you* know I was coming here?" she asked, touching his arm.

"You kept jabbering about Mother," Mallet shrugged. "About the crest on her sarcophagus. You said you needed to see it again. I had some things on my mind and wasn't really paying attention. It wasn't til quite a bit later that I figured out what you were trying to tell me. Brynn, I'm getting a really bad feeling about us being here. We need to get the hells out of here. *Now.*"

"Not before I trace this sigil," she said, shaking her head.

"Someone's coming!" Mallet hissed, reaching for his glaive. Brynn turned, and saw a dancing light bobbing down the stairway. She held her breath.

In moments, Needle arrived. He walked toward them, holding his own lantern in front of him. When he arrived, he set his lantern down with a clink on an adjacent sarcophagus.

"You're a little late, aren't you?" she asked.

He shrugged.

Brynn fidgeted with her hair. Needle looked suspiciously at Mallet, then back to her.

"Who's this then?" Mallet asked, and Brynn saw he was gripping his glaive. One swing with that wicked blade and Needle would be sliced in two.

"His name is Needle," said Brynn, "and his father knew Mother. We, he and I, came here because we believe Mother left a message here, something we needed to know about what they were doing."

"What does it matter?" Mallet said, "She was a witch, for hell's sake, Brynn! We don't *want* to know what she was doing, much less what this kid's father was doing."

How could she explain to Mallet that she was not horrified by witchcraft? How to explain she was actually excited about it? That their mother was misunderstood? "Mallet, more is going on than you know," Brynn said.

"That's what I'm trying to tell you!" Mallet yelled. His voice reverberated off the sandstone walls. "Son of Abyss, Brynn! You don't know what Father is doing, you don't know who he is. We're going to get hurt, both of us, if we don't get the hells out of here!"

Brynn looked to Needle, who for his part remained calm, his face passive. No help there. She turned her head back to Mallet. "Okay, okay. Let me trace this sigil first, then we can go."

"Brynn!" said Mallet, grabbing her roughly by the arm. "What in the hells are you talking about? I don't know what a sigil is, and I don't know what you think it will do, but I do know that you could not have picked a worse time for this! *We have to go.*"

"It'll just take a moment, Mallet," she said as she jerked her arm free of his grasp and turned her back on him. She sensed him tensing behind her, but he didn't move to stop her.

"Do it," Needle said quietly.

She began to focus on the sigil and all the chaos faded as time seemed to slow. The natural symmetry of the pattern enveloped her attention. She began to hear the gentle notes of the haunting tune playing in her head. The sigil seemed to speak to her and she understood exactly how to trace it. Her finger danced on the lines, almost of its own volition.

Suddenly those dulcet notes were interrupted by a loud whoosh as something whizzed past her ear.

2nd Day of Summer - 12:30 AM – Bygrave Mausoleum – 1 Hour Before the Earthquake

Wheizer Rhelbog slowed from his run and walked the last few steps into the Bygrave mausoleum, certain that he had gotten ahead of Brynn. She was a dawdler, after all. She had no idea that he'd hitched a ride clinging to the underside of the lift right under her very feet.

He had a lot of things on his mind: Mallet mostly. Truth was, he liked the boy. He didn't care much for Brynn. She reminded him too much of Elowynn.

But Mallet, there was sand in that boy. A bit too eager to please Dagorn, but he was still young. In time, he would develop more confidence, especially after tonight. Despite a lingering morality inspired by his insipid mother, Wheizer knew that the boy *would even drink blood* to please his father. And in two weeks, he'd have a new father.

He allowed himself a smile. Nevertheless, he had a lingering doubt that Dagorn had pushed Mallet too hard. Dagorn was too quick to use his favorite tool: fear. But even Wheizer, twisted creature that he was, knew that love could be a more powerful tool than fear. He considered again that Dagorn might have handled it wrong. Deep down it worried Wheizer. He knew the boy was dangerous and would make a terrible enemy. Then again, Mallet belonged to him now, after a fashion. He smiled again.

Upon arriving at the Mausoleum, he went down to the first level where Elowynn had been entombed a year ago. He grinned as he passed her sarcophagus. Her death had made his life much less complicated. Keeping her out of their business had been a constant chore.

He found a place several rows back from her sarcophagus, hunkered down in the tiny corner and waited. He needed no torch or lantern. Since contracting his disease those many years ago, his vision in the darkness had grown amazingly keen.

Soon enough, Brynn came along. Predictably, she started to blubber before her mother's tomb. Wheizer watched her shoulders heave. After a few minutes, to his shock, Mallet entered the mausoleum.

This was deeply disturbing. First, it meant that Mallet had flat out disobeyed his father. Second, it meant that if Brynn were somehow able to discover something about her mother, Mallet would learn it, too. Of course, Brynn was definitely looking for something and Wheizer worried that it would be too easy to discover something about Elowynn that was better left hidden. That witch had lived a double life filled with secrets and lies. There was simply too much to keep hidden from anyone looking in the right places. That was a real problem. Even from the grave, she was still meddling. He might have to intervene;

not something he wanted to do. Mallet would be a problem if it came to that.

I like the boy, he thought. *I should, after all.*

Wheizer caught a faint scent carried on the imperceptible eddies in the air. He raised his head, his long nose twitching at the odor in the chamber. Someone else was coming. Brynn and Mallet were too busy arguing over their momma to notice.

A little man dressed in white linens crept down the stairs and slipped into the giant room. Wheizer watched him slink noiselessly along the rows of stone sarcophagi. He recognized him by his smell before he even saw him; he was a Rothkin from the north lands. A very slight fruity smell sometimes accompanied them and it certainly did with this one.

The Rothkin race rarely came south; usually as exiles from their great forested lands. Wheizer smiled to himself. Such journeys usually ended badly for them. The novelty of such a diminutive servant always fetched a top price in the slave market below the streets of Balankov.

One glance and Wheizer knew this Rothkin was utterly competent, a born killer, stealthy. Wheizer was certainly in a position to judge such things.

The Rothkin positioned himself silently behind a sarcophagus with a clear view of Brynn and Mallet and started pulling small objects from under his tunic. Wheizer began to creep in closer to the small man for a better view, staying hidden completely in the shadows.

You little bastard, he thought when he saw what the Rothkin was doing. He had laid four small quarrels and a hand-held crossbow neatly in front of him on the floor. He then produced a small bottle, carefully removed the stopper and set it down gingerly.

Wheizer sniffed. Arrow poison! *Purple Rhodoxanthus,* a swift and deadly killer. It was a rare and powerful toxin. Wheizer had not smelled it for years. This was serious; the little bastard intended to kill one or both of the Bygrave children.

What in the harlot-infested hells?

Wheizer slid still closer. Of all the crazy things that had gone on today, this topped them all. His mind raced, but he could not come up with any possible explanation for why this little Rothkin was here, or why he was bent on murdering the children.

The little assassin looked up suddenly as the clicking sound of boots on stone came from the stairway. What, someone *else* was coming?

Sporting a lantern in his upraised hand, Needle Graji, the scrawny Agrabi boy arrived and walked toward the other two.

Ah, of course. Wheizer had momentarily forgotten about him. The boy had a little of his father in him, no doubt about it. From arriving this morning at the Guild asking for a job, escaping from the slave crate, meeting with Brynn in the Kuma, arriving at Dagorn's with a sack full of loot, to somehow making it here, the boy's day had been at least as strange as his.

Yes, Wheizer was impressed. It occurred to him that Needle might make a good disciple after all. Maybe he should have hired him this morning? But how could he have known the Agrabi whelp was so industrious? It was too bad he had already promised Needle he would enslave him again. Wheizer couldn't help himself and flashed a wicked grin in the darkness. Besides, what else were the Agrabi really good for?

The Rothkin carefully dipped the tips of all four crossbow bolts into the poison one at a time and then laid them back down. He was clearly in no hurry. He corked the bottle and tucked it away inside his tunic. Picking up the crossbow, he silently pulled the sinew back until it locked taut. Steadily, he picked up a bolt and laid it on the groove of the crossbow, pressing the knock firmly to the tensioned cord.

Mallet and Brynn were bickering and clearly oblivious to the danger they were in. Needle just stood there watching them. Wheizer kept one eye on the children and one eye on the Rothkin. He hoped Mallet would convince Brynn and Needle to leave the tomb and go back home. That would have been the best solution to this mess, but clearly it was too late for that.

Besides, Wheizer knew Brynn would never accede to that. There was simply too much of her mother in her. Sure enough, she turned back to her mother's sarcophagus and hovered over the lid. Wheizer wasn't sure what she was going to do there, but he knew it couldn't be good.

Worse, the Rothkin was rising up to a shooting position.

The little whore raised his crossbow and aimed. Wheizer noted the bolt was intended for Mallet. This made sense. The little man was going take down the biggest threat first.

It was exactly what he would have done.

Had the poisoned dart been aimed at the smart-mouthed Agrabi, Wheizer would have gleefully allowed the Rothkin to slay the little bastard. But Mallet belonged to him now. It would be a shame to lose him before he had a chance to develop. So he pulled from his boot one of the many daggers he carried and leapt soundlessly in behind the assassin. With his left hand he grabbed the Rothkin's face over the mouth while at the same time using his right hand to pull the dagger deep and clean across the little man's throat.

Wheizer had achieved total surprise in his attack to the Rothkin. The halfling never saw it coming. In his split second of shock, he pulled the trigger of his crossbow. The bolt went wide of Mallet and nearly clipped Brynn's ear. Had it actually nicked her, she would have been dead in a few heartbeats. That would have solved a few of his problems too. Lucky for Brynn.

The Rothkin tried to cry out but his mouth was covered and his windpipe had been cut below his voice box. He sprayed out a fine mist of blood from the gash at his neck with a low hiss. Wheizer kept his hand clamped over the Rothkin's mouth as he lowered the twitching little man to the floor, trying to muffle any sound he might make. The little man desperately clutched at his neck with one hand trying to prevent his life blood from spilling over. He snatched a dagger from his belt with his other hand and jabbed it at Wheizer's face. The little bastard had skills, but he was not fast enough. Wheizer blocked the blow and grabbed his wrist.

Wheizer held him down for several moments as he bled out. The Rothkin stared hatred at him as his life ebbed away and he finally lay still. Wheizer looked up to see what the kids were doing.

That's when he saw the ghost.

2nd Day of Summer - 12:45 AM – Elowynn's Funerary Box – 45 Minutes Before the Earthquake

The sigil flashed silver under Brynn's fingers. She had been momentarily distracted by the whooshing noise but quickly refocused on the sigil. She swiftly completed the trace and the pattern seemed to glow and lift into the air, accompanied by a gentle jangle of bells. It dispersed like a sparkle on the water, momentarily blinding, then fading away gently in silver and blue hues. As the pattern faded, another bluish glow seemed to emerge from the lid of the sarcophagus: nebulous and insubstantial. Brynn's mouth opened slowly as the mirage-like image blurred, then refocused into the shape of... her mother. She floated, ghostlike, about three inches off the ground, dressed in shimmering robes. All the visible parts of her skin were covered in a scrawling maze of ink tattoos.

"Uh, Brynn," Mallet said behind her. She turned her head and looked over her shoulder. Mallet's body was facing toward the darkness from whence the whooshing noise had come, but his neck was craned over to Brynn, captivated by the apparition that floated before her.

Brynn raised her gaze and locked onto her mother's eyes. Floating before her was the ghostly apparition of her mother dressed in a flowing gown. She looked younger than Brynn remembered her.

Mother smiled sadly. She looked at Brynn, then at Mallet. She spared a brief look to Needle then returned to Brynn. "You found the messages I left for you," she said. The quality of her voice was wavering, almost like it was spoken underwater. Brynn's emotions gushed to hear her mother's voice. It seemed distant and hollow, but it was definitely hers. This was real. She had summoned her mother's ghost.

"On my bedroom wall," Brynn said. "I found the doorway to the desert. I found the desk, the books, the ink--all of it. I found them all, Mother, but I don't know what they mean."

"If you found them, then you know what they mean, Brynn. You have been on that path since birth. But I come for a greater purpose."

"And the letter from Kemano?" Brynn asked.

"Kemano," Mother said softly. "I cannot see him. But you and Mallet are still alive, still protected, so there is hope."

"What do you mean you can't see him?" Needle interrupted, taking a step toward her.

"He is not in my vision," the ghost said "But you three are. So is the fourth. The precautions were sufficient." She seemed relieved.

"Have you come to teach me?" Brynn asked.

The ghost shook her head. "You have already been taught. After all, you found me, so you know the manner of learning. I set the sigils only as a precaution of last resort in the case of my death. I placed them for you to find, to lead you here to call me to deliver a warning to you." Her voice rose in pitch, and the wavering effect seemed to worsen.

"The Society of Eyes!" Brynn breathed.

The ghost nodded. "You are the legacy of the watchers and you must know that evil times are upon you. An ancient evil called the Cult of Yex is returning." The wavering effect grew as Mother's face tightened in concentration. "You are in grave danger. Listen carefully, Brynn. We have reason to believe that someone very close, someone who is trust...."

Her words suddenly stopped. A rapier blade, glowing pale yellow, emerged from her ethereal form, straight through her chest. Her mouth opened in surprise. Her incorporeal form seemed to falter as the mist that created her started to surge out from her.

In sudden succession the three lamps exploded, Bam! Bam! Bam! Cascades of yellow sparks skittered like fireflies over the ground as the loud bangs echoed throughout the tomb, causing an immediate ringing in Brynn's ears. Brynn's heart raced like hummingbird wings and she felt immediately dizzy.

The ghost of her mother shimmered, her features twisted in agony. She called out one more time, "Beware-" and then her image brightened briefly and faded to darkness.

Utter blackness filled all the empty spaces. Nothing remained but the glow fading quickly from the rapier blade and a pair of malignant red glowing eyes standing behind where the ghost of her mother had been.

Mallet grabbed Brynn and pulled her close in behind him in the darkness. Needle's hip touched hers as he squeezed next to her. They both stood behind Mallet's bulk as he held his glaive out in front of him protectively. Brynn realized how loud her own rapid breathing sounded.

The red eyes blinked shut and were gone.

"What in the Abyss was that?" Needle asked. His voice carried an edge of panic.

"Shut up!" Mallet hissed.

"I can't see a damn thing," Needle said.

An illumination sigil! Brynn breathed in deeply, trying to control her pounding heart. She knew how to trace a light sigil, or at least she thought she did. She had been studying the ancient tome of sigils she had found in the rolltop. There were no words in the tome. Just pages and pages of nothing but sigils. It was maddening to try to decipher what it all meant. She had tried tracing the first sigil in the book and after a dozen tries, she apparently had gotten it right and it flickered with an unearthly bluish illumination. The big question was, could she trace it again from memory? And even if she could, what would she trace it on and with what? She could try to trace the sigil with her finger in the sand on the floor. But would that work? She fell to her knees and began to trace the sigil on the ground from memory. Nothing happened.

Needle bumped her, feeling blindly in the dark.

"Don't touch me," she whispered, "I'm trying something."

"What are you doing?" he hissed. She could feel the terror in his voice.

"Get up," Mallet said. "Get ready to run."

Brynn smoothed out the sand and traced the pattern again. She remembered it, or so she thought, but she couldn't see the ground upon which she was tracing, so she couldn't really tell if she was doing it right.

Nothing happened.

She felt sweat on her brow. *I will never see my mother again.*

A part of her mind intruded on her focus. Her heart skipped a beat but she bent down in the darkness and tried again to trace the sigil. She concentrated on her memory of the pattern and heard its tune playing in her mind. Her fingertip traced the pattern in a flowing, gentle script.

She hollered in triumph as the sigil suddenly flared with a silvery light on the ground; a small shock of energy flickered up her finger and into her knuckle. A soft bluish glow emanated from the sigil, casting light about in a wide radius.

She had done it.

She stood up, careful not to kick her sigil in the dust. In the excitement of her success, she had forgotten the situation. She looked up and saw the last person she expected to see.

Wheizer Rhelbog, a bemused yet calm look on his face, stood about ten feet in front of them, a rapier in his hand. "So you're a witch too, then. Your daddy will be so proud."

"Wheizer," Mallet said. He held his glaive in both hands, the wicked curved blade pointing straight at Wheizer's heart. Wheizer seemed unconcerned, but that wasn't a surprise. The man never seemed concerned.

"What in the hells are you doing here?" Mallet demanded. He felt Brynn's trembling hand on the small of his back. Mallet supposed that tears were streaming down her face.

"I should ask you the same question. Your father told you to get some rest. This hardly qualifies," Wheizer said in his high-pitched, nasally voice.

"I don't give a rat's ass what my father told me to do after what the both of you did to me tonight."

"Rat's ass," said Wheizer, chuckling. "Ironic that you would put it that way."

"What in the hells are you talking about?"

"You'll find out soon enough. Hey! Where you going, Needle?"

Mallet looked over his shoulder. The Agrabi boy had taken several steps backward, but stopped when Wheizer spoke to him, his eyes wide in fear. He didn't blink once. His left arm hung slack, but his hand twitched spasmodically. His right hand was clenched into a white-knuckled fist.

"You killed Mother," Mallet said, turning his attention back to Wheizer. He didn't have time for a scared Agrabi boy.

"Now what are you yammering about?" Wheizer was taken off guard. "You were there when it happened, Mallet. Of course I didn't."

"She came back to warn us!" Brynn screamed. "She was going to warn us about you!"

"That was your rapier. Those were your eyes," Mallet added.

"Oh," Wheizer said, scratching the greasy hair on his head with one long finger. "I see what you mean. Yeah. Well. You can't kill what is already dead. All I did was send her back beyond the realms of death. Lucky I had this blade," he said fingering the point of his rapier, its glow still fading.

"Your father gave it to me many years ago. It's a soul blade, from ancient times. Nothing else will send a ghost back to their final rest. I didn't kill her. I did her a favor."

Mallet wasn't prepared for what happened next. Brynn lunged past him with a scream of pure rage. She flung herself at Wheizer, flailing at him uncontrollably. She struck him in the chest and face with balled fists. She gouged at him with her fingernails.

Wheizer reacted with his customary poise in such situations. He stepped backward only half a step and arced his neck backward to lessen the blows. His face initially registered surprise, but quickly turned to bemusement as Brynn flailed away in futility.

"Mallet, get her off me please," was all he said.

Mallet complied and grabbed the back of Brynn's cloak and pulled her back, her arms still twirling.

"Okay, kids," Wheizer said in his high-pitched voice, "I'm done babysitting. It's time to go home. Even you, Needle, before I change my mind and you know what I'm talking about. Consider this your lucky night."

"Wheizer is right, Brynn," Mallet said. She had regained some of her composure, but her hands were still balled into determined fists. "C'mon. Let's go."

"No!" Brynn said resolutely, her voice cold and low. It reminded Mallet of his mother's voice when she had been stubborn about something.

"I came here for a purpose tonight, Mallet," Brynn continued, "And I'll be damned if I'm going to leave here before I finish it." She had stopped screaming and her voice grew calmer and more determined by the word. "You heard what Mother said. She *wanted* me to come here and I did what she wanted. Her spirit spoke to us, Mallet. Mother had more to say. And I'm going to hear it."

"The hells you are!" Wheizer said. "I don't think you understood me, girl."

"Wait a minute," Mallet interrupted, surprising himself. As much as it was abhorrent, he knew his mother had something important to say. But more than that, he realized, the very sight of his mother had filled his heart with a strange yearning. He had shoved aside the pain of losing her by focusing on her abomination as a witch, but seeing her tonight reminded him how much he loved and missed her.

"We'll go home in a few minutes," he continued, "After Brynn traces the sigil again and we have heard what Mother wants to say to us."

"Mallet," Wheizer shook his head. "Look, kid. I like you, but there are some things you have to understand. Everything changed for you tonight. You'll come to understand what I mean in a couple of weeks, but in the meantime, just trust me. You don't have a choice here."

"What are you talking about? Of course I have a choice. It will just take a few minutes." Mallet could see Wheizer growing agitated. Mallet had not seen Wheizer get truly angry very often.

"Your choices are gone, Mallet. Same as mine. What do you think happened to you tonight? Your father and I make all the decisions for you now. You have a new destiny and it lies with me!"

Brynn began walking determinedly toward her mother's sarcophagus. Mallet saw a flash of anger cross Wheizer's face.

"I said *go!*" Wheizer said pointing to the stairs.

Brynn stopped in her tracks and Mallet felt his blood rush from his head, as Wheizer *changed*. His face blurred, his body wavered, but not like the ghost. His image was solid as it morphed and pulsed like a wet butterfly emerging from a cocoon. It bristled with wet fur. His face twitched and his already pointy nose grew into a longer and pointier snout. Fangs lengthened from his mouth, dripping saliva. His eyes widened and the whites were replaced with black, the pupils replaced with a pulsing red glow.

"Son of Abyss!" Needle breathed.

Wheizer had changed into a standing bipedal rat creature that stank of sewage. He had transformed into something from a nightmare--horribly unnatural. He was neither man nor rat, but something wretched in between. His sticky saliva splattered as he spoke, his breath wheezing as it passed through his snout. "Do you understand, Mallet?"

Mallet understood. In a rush of realization he finally comprehended what had happened to him earlier in the evening. *This is the disease that is inside you.* They had deliberately infected him as a means of controlling him. Subverting his will to theirs, turning him into an evil twisted creature like Wheizer before him. He could feel the disease, pulsing in his veins, sticking in his throat, polluting his very soul. He could taste the blood again and nearly wretched.

His hands clenched around the haft of his glaive as if by their own accord as rage filled him. He felt the rush of adrenaline that presaged a fight.

"You can't kill me, Mallet," the rat creature said as if he could anticipate his next move. His speaking was nearly garbled as his rodent lips contorted over his razor fangs to form the wheezy words.

Mallet swung his glaive straight at Wheizer's head. The rat creature stood still except for raising his left arm with impossible speed to intercept the blow. The blade sliced straight into Wheizer's forearm, splitting through the exposed flesh and embedding itself deep in the bone.

Wheizer just smiled. If he felt any pain, his face didn't betray him.

"Brynn, run!" Mallet cried. "I'll hold him."

But Wheizer was too quick. He whirled and swung his rapier down upon the haft of Mallet's glaive, shattering it an explosion of splinters. Mallet could feel an unnatural strength in Wheizer.

Wheizer flicked the tip of the rapier across Mallet's chest. Any thought Mallet had about the disease that infected him making him immune to pain as Wheizer seemed to be disappeared. Adrenaline coursed through him, but he certainly felt the pain, and knew that he could be hurt. *The disease hasn't taken full effect yet,* he thought.

Blood welled across his chest. The red eyes pierced him and he knew then that he could not hope to beat Wheizer. *I've got to hold him long enough to give Brynn a chance,* was all he could think, but it seemed hopeless. He lunged forward, into the blur of Wheizer's fangs and claws. The rat man had dropped his rapier in preference for his own natural weapons.

The claws raked him, blinding Mallet with the pain of the agonizing rend. Wheizer's jaws clamped shut on his shoulder.

Mallet screamed, grabbing Wheizer by the throat and shoving him back. Skin and muscle from his shoulder trailed in bloody shreds from the rat's mouth but Mallet had the creature by the throat, his fingers clenching around the wererat's windpipe.

He saw fear in Wheizer's eyes. *Yeah, be afraid, you sick monster. I've got you now.* Maybe Wheizer could be beaten.

But then Wheizer brought his rear claws up, which had slipped free of his boots and began raking Mallet. The move was impossibly flexible. The claws tore at Mallet's chest in a flurry of shredded flesh. Mallet had once seen a sand badger get hold of a cat and he imagined the flurry of blood and fur that the badger raked from the cat must look very similar to what was happening to him right now.

He heard dimly Brynn's voice screaming in terror. She hadn't run, of course, and Mallet suddenly feared for her life. Needle too seemed paralyzed by fear.

"Run," Mallet screamed.

But Brynn didn't move. She was staring wide-eyed back toward the stairs.

Mallet followed Brynn's gaze. A Buerdeleise boy wearing black robes and carrying a staff stood at the entrance to the catacomb. He was panting and his mop of brown hair matted with sweat.

CHAPTER FOURTEEN
The Fourth Prophecy

The prophecies of the return of the Cult of Yex were uttered by the insane through the ages since the fall of the first cult. Only a few of the prophecies were recorded and were disregarded as the ranting of lunatics. History, however, showed that the prophecies held the key to understanding how the Cult would rise again from the ashes.

-Return of the Cult of Yex, by Caed the Chronicler

1st Day of Summer - 11:00 AM – Library of Mirrors – 14 Hours and 30 Minutes Before the Earthquake

At about the same time Needle Graji was being hammered into a crate on the waterfront, Cael Hotheway stood in awe at the entrance to the Library of Mirrors. He had traveled up the Dragon Way to the obelisk-lined Great Stair, the largest inclined road between the Middle and Lower Steppe. Once on the Middle Steppe, he had made his way to the majestic Dragon Academy buildings, all architectural wonders that inflicted him with a sense of awe. He longed for the power the wizards held, not just in spellcraft but also prestige.

He rode the lift partway and walked along the catwalks to the entrance to the great Library of Mirrors. No one that he passed gave him so much as a second glance. Maybe Madam Dunkley's plan would work after all.

The library was carved straight into the sandstone of the cliff face. He stood before the two huge oaken doors, more than twice his height. The doors had intricate bronze bindings and ring door pulls. The wood itself was carved with images of two dragons facing each other, one on each door.

Entering the library, he saw a great vaulted cavern hewn into the rock. Numerous large round windows were carved into the rock face to either side of the doors, allowing the morning sunlight to stream in.

Before him were countless dark round oak tables with cushioned chairs tucked into them. There might have been a hundred of the tables stretching left and right. Past this and heading deep into the cliff face were five rows of huge sandstone columns which reached more than thirty feet up to the arched ceiling.

Between the columns, running far back into the vaulted chamber, were rows of wooden bookshelves, each laden with tomes of every possible description. The shelves stretched nearly to the ceiling and Cael could see numerous ladders for accessing the high shelves stationed about.

It was the most amazing sight Cael had ever seen. He could taste the parchment, the smell was so strong and felt momentarily dizzy. Cael couldn't imagine anything more majestic than this library, but supposedly this great institution was nothing compared to the fables he'd heard about the ancient lost library of Taglyon.

The place was completely unoccupied, except for one middle-aged wizard in black robes sitting at a square desk in front of the center row of columns. He was, just as Madam Dunkley prophesied, reading a book.

He looked up absently as Cael approached. Cael put a wide smile on his face and acted like he knew exactly what he was doing. Inside he felt terrified, like he might vomit.

"Good morning, young man," the wizard said. "What brings you to the library so early? Exams to study for?"

Cael knew enough to just nod.

The man looked right back down at his book, ignoring him.

Cael shuffled past him and started walking down one of the carpeted rows between the pillars. Immense book shelves rose to the left and right of him.

He walked in a daze, having momentarily forgotten exactly why he was here. There were so many books, so many books--thousands upon thousands.

He kept walking, his boots quiet on the woven rug. As he

walked, he noticed something strange. The farther he entered the hall, the darker it should have gotten. But the hall was uniformly light.

He stopped and examined the area and noted a profusion of polished round mirrors along the ceiling and the giant columns. Sunlight from the open windows was reflected down the hall and then down onto the rows. It was amazing, ingeniously engineered with light bouncing from mirror to mirror to illuminate the place.

He felt completely at home. This is where he truly belonged. He kept going until he reached the end of the columns. There was another open space beyond the rows of books, filled with more round tables.

Past that was the sandstone wall at the end of the cavern. In the center of that wall was a small wooden door. A sign above it read: *Archives. Authorized Entrance Only.*

He turned back and realized he was completely and utterly overwhelmed. He looked back down the giant rows of books. How in the world was he going to find something here about the Cult of Yex? Where would he even start?

Surely the books had to be organized in some fashion? By perusing the books, he learned they were organized alphabetically by topic. So he started looking under Yex but found nothing. Then he looked for Cult and found nothing. After a few more slightly frustrating tries, he found a whole section of books on cults in a fairly large section of books on religion.

Finally, he found a large leather-bound tome entitled *History of the Cult of Yex. Ah ha*, he thought to himself.

He had climbed up a tall ladder to get to it and he pulled the ancient leather tome out with both hands. He managed to step down the ladder without falling, one hand on the ladder, the other clutching the heavy book. He sat at one of the round tables, choosing one in the back of the cavern for privacy.

He opened the book and glanced at the first page. The language was old and hard to understand. Many of the books over the centuries had been recopied or updated, but it didn't seem as if this one had. Deciphering the scrawl was difficult, not to mention the odd spellings of words and the new words whose meaning he just had to guess from the context.

He looked up at the sound of approaching footsteps. A group of whispering apprentices, (much younger than he was) came and sat at a table near him. He felt a moment of resentment. *Couldn't they sit somewhere else?*

He turned the page and began reading intently. The first words grabbed him:

> *The origyn of the Cult of Yex is lost to historie·*
> *How the tiny Cult grew to embroil the entire*
> *wurld in the greatest war in historie, we may*
> *never know· What we do no is that never before*
> *has such evil raigned in the land and never has it*
> *been seen again· And in that knowlidge, we can*
> *hope such evil never returns.*

Cael looked up, and realized he was holding his breath. Was it possible? Was it possible that this cult was somehow prepared to return like his grandfather said? After all these years? *Five thousand years.* None of this was new information to him, but to see it written in such an old book impacted him.

He forced himself to breathe. He began to read in earnest.

The Cult of Yex had actually begun almost seven thousand years ago, though its actual origins were misty. It was dedicated to the worship of a previously unknown demon from the planes of undeath--that unholy place of mythology most commonly known as the Abyss. The demon had many names, but the most common was simply *Yex*.

The demon communed with his wicked priests, imparting new knowledge and understandings of the arcane arts. Power mad wizards flocked to the cult, but it remained a secret brotherhood for centuries. Members knew each other through secret signs and signals and they infiltrated every organization including guilds, governments and religions. They were patient, working over centuries to get hold of the reins of power. They were successful in their slow deliberateness. Their infiltrations went undetected.

With these foundations set over the course of two thousand years, their demon patron, the great demon Yex himself, revealed his plan. The wizards of the Cult were to begin the construction of a secret planar gate, a passageway between dimensions that would allow an otherworldly being to leave the Abyss and come to the world. Rather than serve in the hells, Yex sought to reign on the earth.

Such enormity had never been contemplated before. The Cult aimed to bring the demon himself to rule personally in horror and butchery.

The gate was a huge undertaking and it took generations of time and all the resources that the Cult controlled to gather the necessary components to build it. Somewhere along the way, though the details were lost to history, the Cult erred and their plot was uncovered just a few short years before the gate was completed.

Enter Adirak of Taglyon. The great wizard Adirak forged an alliance to do battle with the Cult and root out their evil once and for all. War engulfed the entire world and Adirak and his apprentices led the fight. Adirak's armies fought all the way to the Cult's citadel atop the desert mesa above. Demon's Bluff now stood at the foot of that very mesa.

The wizards of the Cult had built their fortress citadel to house the gate at the confluence of the *Arcanus Navitas*. In the final battle of the citadel, Adirak and his apprentices fought their way past the greatest villains of the Cult of Yex and into the inner sanctum into the very presence of the now completed gate. The last surviving evil wizard, leader of the Cult, was even at that very instant bringing Yex, his demon master, through the gate into the world.

In a moment of heroism that the world could never repay, Adirak somehow managed to redirect the gate to the mysterious realms of the heavens and summoned an archangel who battled with the newly-emerged demon. It became clear that the demon, weakened from his journey, would be killed by the archangel.

The Cult's last wizard, known only to history as Xylex, knew in that instant that Adirak had defeated him. In an act of utter desperation, he sundered his staff and unleashed a powerful explosion of raw arcane energy.

In that final cataclysm of raw magic, the demon Yex was defeated but somehow preserved, imprisoned in the mists of the astral realm. The mighty mesa itself fractured and the eastern third broke free and drove itself like a dagger into the valley floor below.

The Cult was vanquished. Soldiers and camp followers of Adirak's alliance built the town of Demon's Bluff on the ruins at the base of the plateau where the eastern third of the mesa had once towered. Adirak was crowned King of Taglyon. His reign ushered in generations of peace and prosperity.

Cael sat back, musing upon this information. That was all there was. He was a fast reader, even if the words were difficult, but it had taken him many hours to complete the book. He looked around and noticed that there were a lot more people in the library now.

All of this information supported the small bits he had learned from his grandfather, which the great Cult had once made the area of Demon's Bluff their home and had been defeated here in a great series of battles on and around the great mesa. Boxxaway had made his living with Cael digging ancient artifacts from this war out in the desert and selling them to wealthy collectors up on the Middle Steppe.

The book didn't really tell Cael what he needed to know. Nothing in the book suggested the Cult would or could return. And until this morning, Boxxaway had never suggested such a thing either. The thought of the evil Cult had scared Cael as a child but that was due as much to the haunted tombs and caverns where its treasures were buried than to any real fear of their return. To Cael, the Cult had always been just some vague concept from history.

Now things were different. They *had* returned. Of this, Cael was certain. They *had* killed his parents. He had seen it through the *Lorgnettes*. Boxxaway and Madam Dunkley verified that it had happened. And now the cult wanted him dead, as well.

He slammed the book shut. Nearly everyone looked up at him as the sound echoed in the quiet library. He didn't care. The book was useless to him. He didn't need to know about the Cult from thousands of years ago. He needed to know what it was doing today.

He looked over at the door to his right. Archives. He wondered what lay behind that door.

1st Day of Summer - 11:30 PM – Archive of the Library of Mirrors – Two Hours Before the Earthquake

Cael held his breath. Throughout the day, he had continued to read other books on the Cult of Yex but found nothing essentially new. As fascinating as the history was, what he really needed was some clue as to what was going on with the Cult now.

During the day, he had noticed older wizards come and go from the archives, using bronze keys to open the door. Every time he saw one of them headed for the door he craned his head as they entered, trying to get a glimpse at what might be hidden back there. His suspicions were confirmed when he indeed got an eyeful of bookshelves back there as a limping wizard passed through slowly. The books looked old. Even older than the ones he had been examining all day.

Then, in the evening, to his amazement he noticed the limping wizard exit, but he failed to close the door properly.

Cael didn't hesitate. He abandoned the book he was reading, walked straight to the door, slipped through and closed it tight behind him. His heart was racing as he looked around to make sure he was alone.

The room was remarkably dark compared to the warm light in the open library. A single lantern sat on one of the tables, burning fitfully. The smell of ink was intense. He saw that he was in a room much smaller than the library proper. The single lantern was almost enough to light it. Sheaves of parchment, paper, bottles of ink and quills were piled high on a number of wooden tables. Past the tables, he saw the few shelves full of books he had seen through the door earlier.

He realized that any moment a wizard could come through the door. Then what would he do? What if there were magics preventing theft? What had he gotten himself into? He was compelled to go on despite the danger. He just needed to learn a bit more and would have to risk getting caught. He took the lantern and began to search the bookshelves past the scribe's work tables.

Cael breathed deep. The smell of old parchment and the alchemical odor of the ink pervaded him and made him feel at ease despite the tension he felt. He made his way through rows of shelves into the deepest chambers of the library.

His search in the archive was at first no more fruitful than his search in the main chamber had been. There were fewer books here, but many were in languages he could not read and many were so worn and faded he couldn't read them at all. Others looked like they would soon turn to dust, so brittle were the pages.

He swallowed. His mouth was dry and tasted like eggs from this morning. How long had it been since he ate? Cael rubbed his eyes. He'd been reading all day.

Cael's frustration grew. The archive turned out to be a disappointment. Cael had imagined it as a treasure trove of texts that held secrets too important for average people to know. It turned out to be a place where deteriorating books were restored, or in many cases re-copied by the scribes who toiled here endlessly. He wandered among a dozen work desks with inkwells, quills and a veritable fortune in fresh, blank parchment. There were many shelves filled with books that made their permanent home back here, but they didn't seem to guard any particular secrets. Why they were singled out for special treatment in the archive Cael couldn't guess. Perhaps he was too young to grasp their significance. At another time, he might have been more curious but he flipped quickly through book after book looking for any mention of the cult. It would seem by the lack of information that the Cult of Yex was on the verge of being forgotten.

Books on alchemy, engineering, genealogy, magic, religion, planes of existence, geography, siege craft, flora, fauna and more abounded. Some pages were ornately scripted, often with colored borders and detailed illustrations. Finally, he discovered the section where history books, scrolls and other documents were kept stored, presumably awaiting some type of restoration. None of the history seemed pertinent to his need. Little if anything dealt with history as far back as the cult.

He slipped the last book he found back into place and stood there staring at the bookshelves blankly, the lantern flickering at his feet. No one had ventured into the archive while he had been back here. It was probably too late in the evening. He ran his hand through his hair and gazed around in frustration bordering on anger.

He was no closer to learning a single thing about the Cult of Yex that was useful to him. The Cult had killed his parents and now someone was trying to kill him. He was desperate to learn something that could give him some sort of advantage.

Boxxaway said he was called to serve in his father's place, but what place was that? What had his father done and why had the Cult murdered him? Why in the world was he being asked to go get help from three others, one of whom was Needle Graji, an annoying Agrabi boy he remembered from his childhood?

Suddenly, there was a sound at the door. Cael hooded the lantern and retreated to a far corner, crouching behind a pile of books and loose parchments stacked on the floor. He watched as a man with a lantern entered, sifted through some books on a table, grabbed one, then left, shutting the door behind him. It clanged and echoed in the room.

That was lucky, he thought.

He uncovered the lantern and stood up. He looked down at the stack of parchments and books he had hidden behind and almost choked. On the cover of one book was a symbol he was becoming all too familiar with.

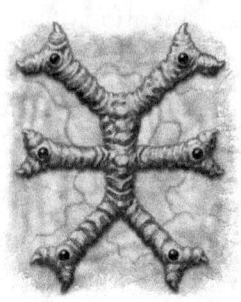

He picked up the tome. There was no title on the front or spine. He sat down cross-legged, coughing into his sleeve as dust erupted from his movements.

He opened the cover gently. There on the first page was the symbol again. The parchment was dry and brittle to his touch, and he carefully pulled the first page back and read the words written there:

> The circle of time will begin anew
> The prophecies of Yex will come to pass
> The stars will proclaim his coming
> The Codicon will be opened once more and then again
> The heir will beguile himself
> The blind think they can see, but they cannot
> The circle of time is beginning anew
> The demon sees his prison at last
> The path to evil is made clear
> The Cult of Yex is rising again
> They who are hidden shall hide no longer
> The circle of time has begun anew

"What in the Hells?" he whispered. Here then was the information he had sought: an indication that the Cult would one day return. But the passage was a riddle he could not understand. *Who* was the cult? *How* would they come back?

He turned the page and began reading with excitement. Clearly, he had discovered information about the Cult that was not contained in the traditional histories. This information was darker, more sinister. It contained prophecies and theories, and the overarching revelation for Cael. The Cult of Yex didn't die with their defeat by the alliance of Adirak five thousand years ago. They simply hid themselves, waiting patiently through the ages to re-emerge and resume their nefarious scheme. Nobody but his grandfather had ever said the Cult of Yex could return. The thought of it chilled Cael to his core as he thought of the assassin who had murdered his parents and the Rothkin who slunk through his house like a desert wolf stalking its prey.

The next page contained another prophecy scribbled in a scattered scrawl:

Accursed be the Blood of the Defiler!
Throughout the generations, even unto the end of days.
The Blood of the Defiler shall be the wellspring of resurrection
Into the bowels of the earth will the Blood go
First the Blood must fall so that the Blood can learn to fly
In the earth the Blood will learn
In the earth the Blood will choose
In the earth the Blood will fulfill its great destiny
Accursed is the Blood of the Defiler!

If that meant anything at all, Cael was at a loss. It certainly didn't clarify what he was after. He needed to <u>find</u> the Cult to avenge his parents. He turned another page:

In the day of the great cataclysm, the sundering of the earth shall be a signal to the stars in the heavens. At the moment of convergence, the circle of time shall sunder much as the earth before it, and the season of dissembling will be at hand. The season of dissembling will bring the second cataclysm, which shall be a signal to the stars in the heavens. At the moment of convergence, the great demon shall be set free. The epoch of glorious death and horror begins with the first great cataclysm. Blessed be the days of the sundering!

Cael filled his lungs through his nose and then exhaled in a rush. Clearly, there were prophecies that outlined the return of the Cult of Yex. But were they real? Or was it just the ranting of some insane remnant of the Cult, bitter about their defeat?

He pondered that for a moment. He considered his vision of the murder of his parents, and thought again of the little assassin in his house. No. It was real. He felt it with absolute certainty.

But where did these prophecies come from? How old were they? Cael was starting to get the sense that, gibberish or not, there was something more sinister at work than anyone would ever believe. He scanned the three prophecies again. They clearly meant something, but he couldn't decipher them. Then flipping the next page, he got to something more interesting. There were dozens of pages of commentaries that looked like they had been written by ancient scholars who studied the cult. Where were the scholars today? All seemed to have lost interest. Cael began to read with a growing sense of foreboding as he progressed. A clear picture began to emerge as Cael pored over the papers.

The great wizard Adirak, hero of the alliance, *did not rest* after his victory over the cult. He worked feverishly, using all his resources as King of Taglyon to track down the remnants of the Cult that were desperate to escape and go into hiding. Some said that Adirak had been obsessed with the cult, even after their defeat. He spent himself in rooting them out and establishing safeguards against what he believed was their inevitable return.

Safeguards...

Adirak was the only person who had seen Yex face-to-face in the final battle, and survived. He knew Yex's power. He knew his hatred. He knew the demon would never stop and his fanatical followers had unlimited patience. Adirak had seen firsthand the centuries of planning, plotting and maneuvering of which the Cult was capable. He knew they could try again; that they *would* try again.

Adirak's greatest fear was that the world would grow complacent and eventually forget the Cult and the genuine threat they posed. Without continued vigilance, his safeguards would fail. Adirak believed that the Cult would wait patiently until they were completely forgotten, and that would be when they would choose to return.

Cael skimmed theory after theory of who might actually

have been members of the cult, what their wicked rituals might be and where the tentacles of their power might reach. The only problem was the theories he was reading were decades old-- or centuries--or more. He didn't recognize any of the names. They didn't help him. He needed to know who members were *now*. That thought gave him a sudden chill. The Cult had acted sixteen years ago to kill his parents--and the assassin today. That meant they *were* here. There were cultists right here in Demon's Bluff, even as he sat reading. Nobody would believe it, but he knew it was true.

Then he recalled what he read in the books out in the main chamber. How for over two thousand years, the Cult had secretly infiltrated its way into the highest levels of government with their stealthy hand signs and secret symbols.

He thought of the wizards. Were there wizards even now posing as good men who were truly evil followers of Yex? And what of the dukes and other powerful men in Demon's Bluff?

Cael shuddered again, realizing something terrible. This morning he had discovered he was not safe in his own home. Such a revelation had tied his stomach in knots. But now, he realized it wasn't just his cottage that had been violated.

He wasn't safe *anywhere*.

Anyone might be a member of the cult. If they learned who his father was, and that he wasn't just Cael Hotheway, some low class Buerdeleise boy in the Lower Steppe, but the son of his father....

Cael turned the last page of the ancient tome. And there, in remarkable bone-chilling clarity was the fourth and final prophecy. He felt as if scorpions were crawling on his flesh as he read. When he finished, he had to force himself to breathe. Then he read it again.

The words on the page were impossible. Cael shuddered so hard his bones felt like they were rattling.

His mind reeled. Did his grandfather know about this?

He read it again.

It couldn't be true.

He wanted to cry.

Never in his life had he felt more lost and alone.

He needed to talk to his grandfather, to let Boxxaway know this terrible information.

At the thought of his grandfather, he suddenly remembered. He was supposed to go to the Bygrave Mausoleum to gather help from three others, Mallet, Brynn and Needle.

What time was it? How long had he been here studying these papers? He was late. He now understood that his grandfather's insistence that he go to the Bygrave Mausoleum had something to do with the all of this. The fourth prophecy made that crystal clear. He ripped all four prophecies from the book and shoved the pages in the pocket of his robes. He slammed the book shut, tossed it back on the pile and raced for the door.

CHAPTER FIFTEEN
Earthquake

Few foresaw the destruction that came upon Demon's Bluff an hour and a half after midnight on that hot summer night. Fewer still understood its true meaning.

-Return of the Cult of Yex, by Caed the Chronicler

2nd Day of Summer – 1:00 AM – Bygrave Mausoleum – 30 Minutes Before the Earthquake

Cael's voice rang out strong and commanding: "*Hold!*"

Cael surprised himself. He didn't think he had air enough in his lungs to utter the final incantation trigger, much less maintain his concentration enough to shape the magic. His voice was still reverberating through the burial chamber.

His run to the mausoleum had been a blur. His lungs burned but the words of the fourth prophecy burned even hotter in his mind. However, for the moment, even that was forgotten. His holding spell had actually worked. Under Boxxaway's tutelage, he had successfully practiced it on lizards in the alley behind their cottage but never on anything larger. To his own amazement, *the rat creature froze.*

The big boy, who he guessed was Mallet, pushed the rat thing over sideways onto the floor and then turned toward him. Three faces, illuminated by a large glowing symbol on the floor, looked up at him in surprise. Mallet wobbled but stared at Cael steadily, his bloody shoulder and chest visible through his shredded tunic. Next, he recognized the familiar face of Needle Graji. Their eyes met for a second. Needle recognized him but clearly the other two did not know who he was.

It was the last pair of eyes that enchanted him. They were

soft and green and beautiful. They must belong to Brynn. She was terrified. They all were.

He heard his own voice again: "My name is Cael Hotheway. We have to hurry. My spell won't hold that creature for long!"

Cael felt exuberant. By the heavens, his spell had <u>worked</u>. The rat creature's muscles were paralyzed. There was something else that added to his exhilaration--something about these three others. Something he couldn't explain. He hadn't seen Needle in ages and had never even met the other two, but he somehow felt a deep connection with them--almost recognition. He had a strange feeling that their destinies were somehow intertwined. But it was a distant and elusive feeling--déjà vu.

It didn't matter. He could puzzle out the meaning of that riddle later. He needed to bring them to Boxxaway.

But what about that rat man? It lay on the sandy floor bathed in the blue light from the glowing symbol. It was a grotesque thing with the form of a man but the features of a vicious, overgrown rodent. It was perfectly still, but Cael felt the malice pouring forth from it. The mere sight of such a monster filled Cael with foreboding and a flurry of questions. Where did it come from? Why was it here? Maybe they should stay and kill it while they could. That seemed the logical choice. After all, the rat creature wouldn't be held for long. Cael did not doubt it would hunt them down if it could. As he pondered, an overwhelming sense of instinct told him the priority was to get these kids down to Boxxaway.

"Come on," he said encouragingly to the others, who were alternately staring at him and the fallen rat creature with a mixture of gratitude and unbelief.

The girl looked back into the darkness beyond where the rat creature lay, then back toward Cael. She then turned and started helping the big injured boy toward the stairs.

As soon as they began moving toward Cael, he turned and started up the stairs. Holding his lantern in one hand and his cedar staff in the other, he bounded up the steps, three at a time.

He stopped at the landing on the main level and waited. His lantern threw dancing shadows on the hanging papyrus ropes and images carved onto the vestibule walls. With hands on his knees, he sucked in great gulps of dusty air.

Needle dashed up the stairs and stopped right next to him as Cael sneezed. Needle was barely breathing hard but he certainly looked glad to be leaving. Mallet and Brynn followed. The rat had really made a mess of the big boy. Cael thought he looked bad enough that he might collapse right there on the steps.

"Who are you? Why are you here?" the girl demanded.

"Well for starters, you're welcome. And I told you, my name is Cael. My grandfather sent me here to help you."

The girl was about to respond but Cael pressed on. "Look, it's a long story, but for now, let's just say that we were all supposed to be here tonight. I'll explain what I know later, but for now we must go."

He shoved the lantern into Needle's hand, "Can you lead the way? I'll help here."

He reached out to Mallet. Brynn was propping him up on his left side, the big boy's arm over her shoulder.

"Wait just one accursed minute!" the girl said angrily. "I came here tonight to speak with my mother. I summoned her spirit, and Wheizer, that thing, stabbed her ghost and she disappeared. I need to go back and try to summon her again. It will just take a few moments."

"We don't have time for that! We need to get out of here. I need to take you to speak with my grandfather."

"She should try again while we're here and that rat creature is frozen!" Needle stepped forward angrily. "I didn't get what I came for either and I'm sure you all can afford to ride that lift anytime you want, but I can't. We have to stay and do it now."

"You don't understand," said Cael. "We have to go. I don't think my spell will hold that creature for much longer." As if to punctuate the point, a strained groan emerged from the stairway.

That convinced them. Cael stepped under Mallet's right arm. "We don't have time!" He and Brynn helped him through the vestibule hall and out into the cooler air on top of the plateau. Cael noticed Brynn's perfume, even over Mallet's stale sweat. She smelled like desert flowers.

Mallet's blood seeped onto Cael's side, sticky and warm. The feeling gave him a momentary flashback to his divination of this morning. The emotions he now felt as he remembered his parent's murder made him also recollect the astounding message of the fourth prophecy and the urgency of the moment.

Pushing emotions aside, he focused on getting them off this plateau and back down to Boxxaway in one piece.

"Let's go, let's go," he repeated. He pulled Mallet along the path to the gate. Needle was ten paces ahead of them with the lantern, moving fast.

"I don't need any help," Mallet mumbled, pushing Cael and Brynn aside. He started to shuffle along by himself.

"We'll move quicker if we help," Cael said and he reached out and took Mallet's arm. "That rat creature will be free in moments." The big boy kept shuffling forward, but he didn't push Cael away again. Brynn took Mallet's other arm.

Needle apparently decided his own skin was worth more than theirs. He had expanded his lead to a good thirty yards ahead along the path back to the lifts.

"By the hells, Needle!" Cael hissed. "We can't see!"

Needle stopped and regressed back toward them several paces. Cael could see he was anxious as he looked past them back toward the mausoleum, clearly concerned about the reappearance of the rat creature. "Hurry up then!" he called.

"You two know each other?" Brynn asked as they hurried to keep up with the circle of light cast by Needle's lantern.

"Needle and I go way back," Cael nodded, remembering the first time he met 'Raju' out in the desert at Ganger's tomb. They hustled on till they caught up with Needle.

"Maybe we should get rid of that lantern," Cael said, realizing that it gave away their position.

"How we going to see in the dark?" Needle shot back.

"Do you want that rat creature to see our light?" Cael asked, looking up.

"He can smell us. Wheizer can smell us," said Mallet. "Don't matter if you are in the dark or not. He can smell my blood. I'm sure of it. Our only hope is to keep moving."

Needle gave Cael an indignant look then turned and led the way along the gravel path.

"Who is this Wheizer?" Cael asked Brynn as they helped Mallet.

"He's that creature you just saw back there," she said. "He is a man who works for my father, Duke Bygrave. He followed us up here tonight and stabbed my mother's ghost with his glowing blade. Then he turned into that creature. I've heard stories but I've never seen anything like it."

"He's a *wererat*," Needle said, looking back over his shoulder. "A shifter." His eyes were huge. "My mother told me stories about them. It's a curse, a disease that turns men into bloodthirsty rats."

"It's true," Mallet said nodding. "He's a wererat. My mother warned me about them too when I was younger."

"So I'm the only one who has never heard of this?" Cael asked, bewildered. "And you all know him? Did you know he was a wererat?"

"I should have guessed it," Needle said. "His bite is contagious, I can tell you that. In case you didn't know."

Cael didn't need to look at Needle's face to know he was staring at Mallet.

"Got me a problem then, if that's the case," Mallet said.

No one responded to that for a few moments as they hustled back up the path.

"It is probably best to stay quiet and conserve our strength," Cael said as they raced along.

Cael was breathing too hard to talk any longer. Besides, their focus should be on getting away safely. He hadn't looked behind him as of yet. He certainly didn't want to see that demonic rat creature tailing them, but he needed to know. Glancing back, there was nothing to see, which worried and comforted him, both. Beyond the light of the lantern Needle carried, there was only darkness. The wind had died down and the graveyard was silent. The only sounds were their footfalls on the gravel path and the persistent barking of dogs far off in the distance down in Demon's Bluff.

"Have you heard of something called the Cult of Yex?" Brynn asked.

Cael almost tripped. What did this girl know? "They killed my parents," he said. "Of course, I know about them. It's the reason I'm here."

"My mother was a Watcher," Brynn said. "Do you know what that means?"

Cael kept right on moving. What she was saying was of critical importance to him, especially given the message in the fourth prophecy but now was not the time. "We have lots to talk about," Cael said. "*Later.*"

"My mother--did you see her?" Brynn asked. "Her ghost?"

Cael noted the pain in her eyes. It reminded him of how he felt seeing his own parents murdered. "I didn't see a ghost; the creature was attacking Mallet when I arrived."

"How do you know his name?" Brynn asked.

"You are Brynn. Mallet is your brother. My grandfather told me to meet you both here tonight."

"Your grandfather?"

"He is an old wizard, Boxxaway Hotheway. I am supposed to bring you three with me to meet him."

Brynn looked baffled for a moment then continued. "Mother left me clues to come up here to summon her spirit and talk to her. But she disappeared when Wheizer stabbed her ghostly form. She was trying to warn me about something. Something related to the Cult and the Watchers."

"Uh huh," Cael managed. His side was bursting with a stitch and he felt like his arms and shoulders were going to fall right off supporting Mallet's weight. They kept hustling along in what turned out to be a blur in Cael's memory. Cael urged them on along the elevation changes and the winding turns of the path. He wouldn't let them stop. They kept moving till they reached the mortuary courtyard.

Cael was on the verge of complete exhaustion. His legs suddenly wobbled wildly and he collapsed in a heap with Mallet and Brynn. He felt drained from bleeding after cutting his wrist himself this morning. How must Mallet feel? Cael hadn't eaten since before entering the library and the hold spell he had cast brought his hunger back with a vengeance. The race both ways through the graveyard was more exertion than he had ever done at once. Not to mention hauling a huge oaf of a boy half the way.

As he lay there panting on the cobblestones, he became aware that something else entirely was happening--something momentous.

The ground itself was moving. It was shaking violently under them. His legs hadn't wobbled--it had been the very ground they were walking on. Only Needle had managed to keep his feet and he was looking around furtively, holding the lantern aloft for a better view.

The cedars and mesquites were swaying and the undertaker's tools clattered on the ground like jumping Junebugs. Several bricks shook loose from their mortar and fell to the ground along with sections of white plaster from the walls of the courtyard.

After several moments, the shaking settled down, but with a strange ominous promise of more to come. A cacophony of animal sounds could be heard in the distance. Mostly dogs barking furiously from Demon's Bluff below but even the gryphons screeched from their aeries off in the darkness.

"No way that just happened," Needle breathed, his eyes wide.

Cael remembered the words of the fourth prophecy.

"This isn't right," he said on the verge of panic. "We've got to get off the cliff and talk to my grandfather. Now!"

Despite their weariness, they all managed to stand and keep moving. They passed through the arch into the first courtyard. There were people here this time, milling about in little knots, heads bent together, chattering about the earth tremor. Soldiers stood on the battlements above, their gazes cast down to the town below.

Cael looked longingly at the fountain as they passed it. Gods, did he want to stop and have a drink, but at that moment the basket lift appeared, floating up from below until it hovered at ground level. The door opened and the old bald wizard inside stood expectantly. Cael's thirst would have to wait, as he felt the intense urgency of getting these three to his grandfather.

None of the other people about seemed interested in descending. Gratefully, he steered Mallet, who had started drifting toward the fountain, propelling him toward the lift. "Got to go! This is our ride!"

Mallet stumbled onto the lift and crashed against the far wall, clinging to the fibrous weave with his hands to keep himself from falling. Brynn and Needle entered next, followed by Cael, who pulled the door shut behind them. Brynn fumbled through her pockets clumsily, producing the wooden token which she pressed into the old bald wizard's palm.

"Bad things are about to happen," the old man prophesied, his eyes clouding over. "Very bad things."

"You're kidding, right?" Needle said, setting his lantern down on the wooden floor of the enclosure. The old man just stared off through murky eyes. "What in the Abyss is going on?" Needle said, directing his comments to no one in particular. "Just when I thought this day couldn't get any stranger."

The lift shifted up and down for a moment, then started its slow descent.

"He looks bad," Brynn had pulled a small knife from her satchel. She began slicing several strips off her cloak, which she wound around Mallet's bleeding chest and shoulder, binding his wounds.

"I wish I had some honey," she said. "It would help him heal."

"Honey?" Needle asked. "How is eating honey going to help him?"

"Not to eat, as a salve. It cleans the wounds and speeds healing."

Cael thought about the disease that now surely infected Mallet. If what Needle said about wererat bites being contagious was true, he didn't think honey would be enough to clean that horrible curse from Mallet's wounds. What would they do if Mallet himself suddenly turned into a wererat and attacked them?

The lift rocked violently. Something heavy struck it from above. The woven fibers of the ceiling bent down in reaction to the blow but they did not break. Dust and twigs rained on them. Cael's first thought was that the earth had started to shake again and they had been hit by falling debris.

That certainly would have been preferable to what actually had struck them. Cael looked up through the woven fibers and saw Wheizer, the twisted half-human, half-rat form staring down at them through the woven branches. Long strings of drool dripped from his open jaws and his eyes glowed red. His gangly arm stretched down into the basket and groped toward Cael, but he couldn't reach.

The hybrid rat creature moved quickly, slinging himself around to the door. Needle screamed. Brynn had just finished tying bandages around Mallet. She positioned herself in front of her injured brother, protecting him.

Cael back-pedaled from the door to the rear of the basket. Another holding spell was all he could think of, but he was in far too frantic a state to cast it.

Wheizer grabbed the door and yanked it violently. It came off with several snapping sounds as the woven fibers were rent. He tossed the door out into the open air, where it fell into the darkness. The old bald wizard guiding the lift stood up quickly, his lantern in one hand and his staff in the other. His eyes were still clouded over as he stared at nothing in particular.

Wheizer reached and grabbed him by the front of his robe and swung him out and into thin air with startling strength. The old man spread his arms and Cael's first thought was: *He's going to try and fly.* Then the old wizard dropped soundlessly out of sight, still holding his lantern and staff. Only the light of Needle's lantern remained.

Cael felt the blood rush to his head. He knew it was up to him. Mallet was injured, Brynn was shielding him and Needle was utterly useless.

Cael stared at Wheizer as he hung in the doorway of the lift. The rat creature's hind claws clung to the lintel while he held the door jamb with his left claw. His right hand swung out into the open space outside the lift. They were many hundreds of feet from the bottom. If he could paralyze the rat creature again, he would just fall from the doorway out into thin air.

Cael tried to steady his breathing, using his diaphragm to fill his lungs. He tried to let the air out slowly, through his nose but his breathing still wasn't right: it was too irregular. The slavering Wheizer was mere feet away, hanging in the doorway, a grin spreading across his grotesque face. A deep clicking chatter emanated from the back of the hideous rat's throat. Cael could not control his breathing properly. Only once in his life had he ever had to cast a spell under such pressure before.

I have to breathe, he thought desperately. He forced himself to suck in a breath of air that filled his lungs and raised his chest. He couldn't cast if he didn't calm down.

Wheizer calmly surveyed his prey, his hellish red gaze assessing Needle contemptuously. He then slowly turned to Brynn and Mallet.

Cael finally got his breathing under control and in one moment the tension flowed from him in a gush and he was filled with a sudden peace.

In this state of tranquility, he tuned to the flow of the *Arcanus Navitas.* Facing Wheizer, Cael centered himself through his breathing. Wheizer hung in the open door of the lift ready to enter and commence a gory bloodletting. The young wizard in training began to build a mental image of the effect he desired. As Boxxaway taught him, the image must be laden with details. He had to not only see it clearly but feel it. He had to feel the emotion of the spell.

He started to picture Wheizer paralyzed according to the mental pattern Boxxaway had taught him. It was the same simple *hold* spell from earlier this very night in the Bygrave Mausoleum. That time, he had been able to stand in the shadows and form the magic, taking his relative time with all the necessary details. Now however, he faced impending death by the demonic wererat leering at him. This did nothing to aid his concentration.

Much like feeling the energy flow *into* him, he now felt the *Arcanus Navitas* flow *from* him, formed and shaped by him into the mental image he had created.

The discharge of eldritch power poured from his hand as he said aloud: "*Hold!*" The magic arced into Wheizer. To Cael, the release was like a sudden respite of all burdens, a delicious liberation, followed by an immediate sadness as the power pulled a piece of his life force with it. There was an ache in his bones, a desperately clinging, greedy emotion, as if he were trying to grasp at something that was slipping away; his future. For every spell he cast, no matter how small, his life span shortened. All the possible events of his future were diminished.

How many future moments of quiet peace, love and satisfying joy had he just sacrificed? And for what?

Wheizer only laughed at him in a hollow, nasally sound. The arc of energy had entered his body but *nothing happened*. His mind had somehow resisted Cael's spell, overcoming the intention. Boxxaway had told him that strong minds could sometimes resist.

"Fool," Wheizer hissed, clearly enjoying his moment.

His gloating cost him. Mallet rose from his somnolence. He reached out and snatched Cael's staff. In one fluid motion, he jammed the end straight into Wheizer's chest. The rat man was caught completely unaware as the butt of the staff slammed into his sternum. Cael was reminded of the gaming halls down by the waterfront where the men struck ivory balls with sticks into pockets on a board. Cleanly and neatly, Wheizer was popped from the doorway and sent spinning into the free air, where he hung for just a moment before he plummeted to the darkness below with an ear-wrenching screech.

"Sorry about your staff," Mallet said, handing it back to Cael, who realized he was staring dumbstruck at Mallet.

"Sorry my spell failed," he replied, taking the worn cedar staff in his hand.

"Something's not right," Needle noted with a higher pitch in his voice.

Cael realized that yes, indeed something was not right. That something was the lift. Bereft of its operator, it was beginning to pick up speed on its journey down the cliff face. If something didn't change, they would be joining Wheizer at the bottom a lot quicker than they had expected.

Failed spell aside, Cael needed to do something. Only this time, he didn't need to cast a spell. The *Arcanus Navitas* was already bound into the woven fibers of the lift by the wizards who had joined together to craft it. He just needed to guide the magic with his mind.

He took a deep breath, again letting all of the thoughts and emotions drain from his mind like pouring mead from a mug. This time, he didn't need to touch the *Arcanus Navitas* that surrounded them, he just needed to touch the energy bound to the lift.

This was much easier to do. It was not dissimilar to what he had done with the *Lorgnettes*. He didn't need to shape the magic, it was already done for him. The wizards who made the lift had locked the levitation magic into its structure already.

He reached out and touched one of the thick sticks that formed the ribs of the cage. By connecting himself to the magic of the lift, he could control it and tell it to stop. The lift jerked to a sudden halt, sending them all to the floor in a heap of arms and legs.

"What in the Abyss?" Needle complained.

It was dark inside the lift now. The old man's lantern and Wheizer's glowing eyes were both gone and the lantern Needle had been holding extinguished itself in the sudden jolt. However, enough light came through from the city below to enable them to see. Cael clambered to his feet, making sure to stay connected to the magic of the lift. He staggered over Brynn and, holding the sides of the open doorway, peered out and down.

That was a bad idea. They hung hundreds of feet up in the air. About a dozen buildings in the town below were on fire. They must have begun to burn when lanterns and candles were toppled by the trembling of the earth earlier. Cael wobbled in the opening and pulled himself back.

"Surely that fall killed him," Needle said hopefully as he joined him in looking down. Needle seemed unfazed by the height but still a little phobic when it came to Wheizer. He looked down at Brynn and Mallet, still on the floor of the lift.

"Did you stop the lift?" Brynn asked, cradling Mallet, who looked up at him with an innocent expression of confusion on his face. Cael wondered again if Needle was right. Was Mallet a wererat already? Did it even matter? The boy had lost a lot of blood.

"I did," Cael said. "But I don't know enough to operate it properly. I can't make it run again. Look, we're close to a catwalk. We can just jump to it over there."

Mallet began to climb to his feet again with Brynn's assistance. "Let's find another lift," he said.

"My thinking exactly," Cael nodded. He turned back to the

opening. "Can you jump through there to that catwalk?"

Mallet limped to the opening and looked out. "Do you think it will hold my weight?"

That was a damn good question. The catwalk was nothing more than an iron grate and wooden handrails about four feet wide. Iron rods had been driven into the sandstone cliff face horizontally and the grates had been lain out on the rods and secured in some fashion. Along the right side were numerous openings and doorways into the hollowed out caverns beyond.

The catwalk looked sturdy enough, but Cael understood Mallet's concern. "What if the tremor weakened the moorings?" he asked.

"I'll go first," Needle said and he leaped diagonally across the opening onto the walk. He hopped up and down on the catwalk a few times.

"Nope. It's solid." Needle reached out, grabbed the levitating basket with both hands, and spun it so the opening was now facing the catwalk.

"No leaping necessary," Needle said.

Cael took one of Mallet's arms and Brynn took the other and they left the basket.

They picked their way along the metal catwalks. Sweat poured from Cael's neck all the way down to the small of his back. It was hot and the air carried a peculiar smell of sulfur. His thighs ached and his stomach burned with hunger.

There were catwalks above and below echoing with concerned voices and the sound of boots clumping on the metal grates People had also emerged from the openings on their own catwalk level and were at the railing peering down into the city. If any were concerned with the young people moving about the catwalk, they made no indication. The quake had absorbed everyone's attention.

To the left, Cael looked out over the city as they made their way through the small gatherings of chattering people on the catwalks. The scene below was bedlam. Cael now noticed more than just fires burning below. The expansive town seemed to be boiling in turmoil as gusts of steam burst from cracks in the ground and shot almost a hundred feet into the air. One geyser of steam and sand burst near the riverfront, destroying a warehouse and sending planks and shingles straight up into the air to come crashing down on and around a two-masted galley at anchor.

"Keep going!" someone shouted, pushing him in the back. Cael turned, indignant, and saw behind him a young apprentice wizard, wearing the black robes of the Dragon Academy. The boy was the same age as Cael and was in a full state of panic. Cael felt a flash of irritation. Here he was, untrained and calm, while this apprentice was erratic and fearful. The injustice of it was inescapable.

Cael let the apprentice go by. Then he saw Needle standing at the rail, his slim, long-fingered hands gripping the wooden railing. His eyes were riveted to the south end of Demon's Bluff, to the Kuma.

Cael followed his gaze. The Kuma, as blighted as the slum was, seemed to have been spared the fires and geysers.

He poked Needle on the shin with the toe of his boot. "Let's go, we need to find another lift."

"No," Needle turned to him and shook his head. "You tell me what in the Abyss is going on first."

Cael rubbed his temple. "I'm taking you to see Boxxaway. He has the answers."

"Well, I don't trust that old man and what's more, I don't trust you."

Cael was incredibly agitated. His dislike of Needle came back to him in a rush. He considered just abandoning Needle here, but Brynn came to the rescue: "Needle, neither of us got the answers we needed tonight. Wheizer saw to that. We should go with Cael. He saved us and something tells me we should meet his grandfather just like he says."

Needle just looked at her stubbornly. He turned slowly and started walking again toward the other lift.

Cael looked at Brynn and said, "Thanks."

"I want answers, too," she said.

"I wish I had them to give you, but follow me to my grandfather. He will help us."

A convocation of great winged gryphons, ridden by soldiers who were tied into leather saddles, flew down from their aeries on the top of the plateau. In the faint lantern light, they looked like a swarm of black flies at first, gliding past the cliff face.

Cael dragged Mallet along after Needle, who was moving adroitly through the clusters of people gathered to watch the chaos below. The catwalk began to sway again--another small earthquake. Dust and pebbles fell down on them from above. Somewhere below them they heard the screech of metal as a catwalk failed. Several screams accompanied the groaning metal.

"That's not good," Brynn said.

They kept moving, though the footing grew treacherous. The people on the catwalks, from students, to older wizards, to richer nobles, were beginning to panic. Their voices were rising in tone, fear overcoming sensibility.

"They are going to start stampeding if that happens again," Cael said. "We have to hurry and get the hells off this cliff face."

They quickly reached the end of the catwalk, where a small group of people gathered. Cael saw a basket lift soaring up toward them. It slowed and then stopped on their level. The basket twirled and the door opened.

The people entered the lift, and Mallet, Cael and Brynn followed. With all of them aboard, the basket was crowded. Needle squeezed in last, a look of consternation on his face as he pulled the door closed behind him and secured the latch.

The wizard controlling the lift made no effort to collect any payment but closed his eyes in concentration and the lift started down.

"Where do you think Wheizer landed?" Needle asked as they reached the bottom and disembarked from the basket. Cael also worried that the wererat might have survived the fall. An unnatural creature like that might be capable of surprises.

Crowds of sleepy people were milling about the vast complex of pale sandstone buildings at the base of the cliff. There was only one topic of frantic conversation: the earthquake.

Cael, nearly exhausted beyond the limits of his endurance, helped Mallet through the swell of humanity. Cael liberally used his elbows against the ribs of innocent passersby to help clear a path. He led them to the Dragon Way, a straight shot due east that cut through the reddish sandstone debris of the Middle Steppe. The Dragon Way was paved with sandstone bricks tightly fit together without mortar. The road ran from the ever-expanding wizard complex at the base of the cliff, turning into what was called the Great Stair, the main road descending to the Lower Steppe.

The mind is a funny thing. Exhausted, Cael noticed things he hadn't before. Perhaps it was an effect of recently tapping the *Arcanus Navitas.*

He looked at the many estates and keeps on the Middle Steppe and in the light of countless lanterns and fires, saw them in a context he had never comprehended before. They had been built upon a large section of the plateau that had broken off and fallen to the valley below. The ground here was a massive shelf of compacted rubble, ragged and rocky in several places, though thousands of years had smoothed the jumble somewhat. It was upon these jutting heaps that the nobles had built their estates. Many were constructed on and around gullies and hills formed by the uneven areas of rubble. Cael reflected on the story of the Cult of Yex he had learned earlier in the library. He suddenly understood Demon's Bluff in a historical context he had never considered before. They now stood on the rubble of a collapsed section of the plateau. In fact, the entire town of Demon's Bluff was built on the rubble of that landslide that occurred as the Cult was defeated so many thousands of years earlier. *It all happened here*, Cael thought to himself.

Seeing the new destruction of the earthquake, upon the old rubble of the collapse of the mesa, Cael felt an oneness with the ancient history. He also understood something else: his town was in danger. The thought was eerie and unsettling. These magnificent edifices of the Middle Steppe had always held for him an aura of invincibility. Growing up, Cael had dreamed of living among them. He had struggled growing up an out-cast Buerdeleise apprentice amongst a culture of lower-class Buerdeleise and resentful Agrabi. The Middle Steppe had always called to him with its shining beacon: the Dragon Academy.

That was the world Cael should have belonged to. And yet that world, the invincible pillar of his dreams, was falling into a shambles by the force of a series of earthquakes. Cael now understood how precarious it all was.

"We're going the wrong way," Mallet said to Brynn, interrupting Cael's thoughts. Mallet pulled up short as they passed a branching road. "Our estate is this way!"

"We need to find my grandfather first," Cael said.

"I must have words with my father."

"No, Mallet. That's the *last* place we should go right now," Brynn said. "Something portentous is happening and we have to do as Cael says."

Mallet wobbled on his feet, but nodded slowly. He had no strength to argue, no matter what he might really feel.

"Come," Cael said.

They continued past the throngs of people along the Dragon Way till they reached the Great Stair, where the road sloped down toward the Lower Steppe. In the very center of the Great Stair, a channel allowed the stream called the Demon's Race to flow. Left and right of the channel, great sandstone slabs formed the road, which was then lined by darker hued reddish sandstone obelisks, some of which had toppled due to the tremors.

They trotted down the decline toward the Lower Steppe. Crowds were gathered here too, forcing them to thread their way through the small pockets of people, many dressed in their sleeping robes, chattering excitedly amongst themselves. Cael marveled at Mallet's endurance. Bloodied and badly wounded, he kept moving.

When they reached the bottom of the slope, Cael felt an instant sense of recognition. Here the buildings were much more tightly packed together, made primarily of adobe bricks with wooden embellishments. The sandstone slabs gave way to hard-packed yellowy clay, mined from deep in the riverbanks. This was the neighborhood of his youth and he knew all the neighbors, the ones he liked and of course, the ones he disliked. His own cottage was only a few hundred yards down the road on the right.

Later, he would come to understand that what happened next was more than a mere earthquake. All the previous quakes were nothing more than foreshocks. Next was the real earthquake.

As an apprentice wizard, he was able to understand the world in a different way. He could comprehend layers that non-wizards never could. He could sense the lattice of the *Arcanus Navitas* effusing everything. After the earthquake, all those connections he would find were weaker. The fabric of existence would be torn, upsetting the natural order of things. The tear started in Demon's Bluff, but it would spread throughout the entire world, eventually to everywhere and every when.

But Cael didn't notice this right away. In fact, it would be quite some time before he truly understood it. What he first noticed as the earth began shaking again was his grandfather running toward them up the clay-packed road, his knees lifting high under his robes as he ran, his white beard flapping behind him over his shoulder and his eyes wide in terror. Under his right arm, he carried a rolled up rug.

He screamed as the shaking of the ground intensified, "Go back! Go back! In the name of all that is sacred and holy. *Go back!*"

CHAPTER SIXTEEN
The Return of the Cult of Yex

We will weave a fabric of lies for thousands of years. None will foresee the enormity of our scheme.

-From the *Lich Diary of the Archmage Xylex*

2nd Day of Summer - 1:30 AM – Bottom of the Great Stair

What Bannon "Mallet" Bygrave would remember most from this terrible day was not killing Captain Vosc. Neither was it his father's betrayal, nor the drinking of Wheizer's blood. It wasn't seeing his mother's ghost, or his bloody fight with the wererat. It wasn't the earthquake that destroyed half of Demon's Bluff, nor the long race to the docks after meeting the old wizard. Amazingly, it wasn't even the unexpected quest upon which he would embark that very night, changing his life forever.

What would resonate most in Mallet's memory for the rest of his life was his first impression of Cael Hotheway.

The boy was tallish and thin, much like his grandfather. Indeed, Mallet noticed that Cael was very much his grandfather's grandson. There was a clear family resemblance, despite the vast difference in their ages. *Neither were fit for labor,* as his father would have snidely observed. Mallet was certain that even a scrawny Agrabi like Needle was stronger and wirier than Cael. But what Cael lacked in physical strength he made up in resolve.

Looking back on that night, it had been Cael who led them. It was Cael who saved them. It was Cael who had appeared out of nowhere and rescued him from Wheizer's attack. It was Cael who helped Brynn carry him as they fled the graveyard, who prevented them from plummeting to their deaths in the falling lift. It was Cael who guided them down off the catwalks, who led them to the foot of the Great Stair, where his grandfather saved them from being swallowed up by the very earth itself.

Mother had always said: *There are very few true leaders in this world, and fewer still with vision.* Mallet always gravitated to people who had vision. That might explain his desire to please his father. He was certainly a leader of great vision, but his father had betrayed him--utterly. If Dagorn was a leader of great vision, it was a vision Mallet wanted no part of. Slavery. Lies. Monsters like Wheizer. Who knew what else?

But today he had met a leader of greater vision and his name was Cael Hotheway. Cael was beginning a crusade against something called the Cult of Yex, and he was going to succeed, because Mallet Bygrave decided to help him.

No, it wasn't the earthquake, the betrayal or any of the other enormously horrible things. It was his first impression of Cael Hotheway he would remember most. More than anything else for Mallet, this day marked the moment he stopped following his father and began to follow Cael.

The earth was shaking with a fierceness that was simply unbelievable, indeed impossible, to Cael. He watched the road, lit by lanterns and progressively growing fires. The street he had lived on his whole life split open like a rotting melon bursting in the summer heat. The destruction seemed to start right near Boxxaway's cottage, about quarter a mile ahead on the road from where they now stood. They had made their way a hundred yards or so onto the Lower Steppe when Boxxaway appeared out of nowhere just as the earth began to quake, screaming at them to go back, waving his arms frantically.

Cael watched awestruck as the earth heaved up and peeled back in a rush of destructive force. The first of the cottages were tossed in the air like a juggler's colorful balls during the Festival of Drums. Cael cringed as he imagined his neighbors, suddenly awakened to the terrifying experience of vertiginous flight, moments before their death.

The cottages plummeted back to earth and disintegrated into great puffs of mud-colored, brown brick smoke. The noise of the rending earth and collapsing buildings was deafening.

After the first cottages went up, a second set, including Boxxaway's cottage, went down. The earth continued to split open and the homes and buildings along its edge dropped down into the great sinkhole, leaving only little puffs of dust as evidence they had existed at all.

Madam Dunkley, Cael thought. Surely she would have been sleeping in her home with her cats. There was no way she could survive if she were inside her cottage, and there was no reason for her to be anywhere else. Cael felt numb.

From their position, just past the border between the Middle and Lower Steppe, they were still at a higher elevation than the rest of the Lower Steppe and had perfect vantage to overlook the devastation. Cael saw dozens of homes and buildings in his neighborhood destroyed in just the first few seconds, but that was only the beginning. In the firelight, the only illumination, all the dwellings looked alike. This wasn't a rich section of town and the cottages were fairly similar in structure. Only minor accoutrements, a potted cactus, a carved wooden post with a family's name on it, or a door painted red gave them any individual character. In the dark terror of this earthquake, such small individualizations were but blurs.

Cael was absolutely certain of one thing, however. This was his neighborhood and dozens of homes, including his own, had been destroyed in an instant. A dozen names of his neighbors flashed through his mind: the Pascoe family, the Longleats, the Wigweorths. Little Penelope Buldric, the toddler who played across the street from them as her mother watched over her-- most likely they were all dead now. Even their crabby old neighbor, Brock Moggs, whose voice was permanently hoarse from yelling at him and everyone else, was probably dead now, too. He would never again pound on Boxxaway's door to accuse Cael of some misbegotten deed.

He thought of Madam Dunkley again and felt a void in his heart. Only this morning, she had made him breakfast and listened to him talk about his parents. He had told her everything and she had guided him toward the library. Now the only mother figure Cael had ever really known was most assuredly dead. It left him feeling sick to his stomach but there was no time to mourn. He refocused his mind on the image of his grandfather running toward him waving his free arm like a madman.

The crack started perpendicular to the river, running east to west but then forked and split north and south. Great hunks of the town were now disappearing down the widening crevasse. A faint orange glow pulsed down in the black depths of the earth, as burning buildings fell into the great sinkhole. Steam vents spouted hot misty air in advance of the growing concavity.

A hissing sound erupted down the road and a gout of hot air and sand billowed upwards, engulfing the running Boxxaway. Cael thought for a second his grandfather was gone, roasted alive by the scalding air. But the old man emerged from the white smoke, carpet under his arm, knobby knees rising and falling.

"Go back!" Boxxaway screamed, his voice hoarse.

The crack was widening behind Boxxaway, slurping down the road and the cottages along it. Cael had no more time to think of Madam Dunkley, her cats, old Mr. Moggs or any of the rest of his neighbors.

It was time to run.

Brynn, Needle and Mallet were way ahead of him. They had turned to run while he continued watching the destruction of his old neighborhood and home. He ran as fast as he could, trying to catch up, but was passed by his grandfather. He had never seen the old man move like this. Then again, the earth had never split open and tried to swallow him before.

Needle stopped at the bottom of the Great Stair, Brynn and Mallet with him. Boxxaway arrived next, followed last by Cael. The old man bent over, starting into a major coughing fit, hands grabbing his knees.

"Do we need to go farther?" Cael yelled, watching the earth divide behind him.

Boxxaway shook his head, his eyes bulging and his cheeks red. "We are safe here," he croaked. They were now standing on the huge sandstone pavers at the foot of the Great Stair.

Cael turned back to the Lower Steppe. They all did. There were a thousand questions to ask, but none of them could form the words. All they could do was stare as the sinkhole, already more than a hundred yards wide, continued to grow and spread out across the Lower Steppe as more buildings sloughed into the great maw. The earth was still shaking violently. Some of the homes and buildings away from the sinkhole fared little better than if they had fallen in. More buildings in Cael's field of view collapsed every few seconds. The fires all around town were growing and spreading.

His anxiety grew as the terror of seeing this destruction fused with a terrible, overwhelming awe. The impact finally dawned on him that his *home* had been destroyed: the place where his parents had once lived, the place where he was born, the place that defined him. It was gone, just like that. He felt like a piece himself had been taken with it. Above it all, there was a strange foreboding about what he was witnessing. This was something... something big. The words of the fourth prophecy echoed in his memory again. He reached into the pocket of his cloak and felt to make sure the folded parchment was still there. It was.

The orange glow in the sinkhole grew brighter. Cael presumed that fires, fed by the thatch roofs of the cottages it had consumed, were burning down there. Smoke or steam or both poured out of the great chasm that was now almost a quarter of a mile in length going north to south and maybe half that east to west.

Cael had heard tell of earthquakes before but had never experienced one. He used to imagine what it would be like to be in one--what damage it might do. But he never could have conceived the devastation spreading out before him.

A thundering crash sounded behind them, punctuated by screams. Cael turned. One of the great obelisks that lined the Great Stair had come crashing down. A single poor soul was crushed under the great weight, his arms and legs peeking out. Amazingly, he was still alive but even dozens of people wouldn't be able to lift the rock off of him.

Cael turned his attention back to the town. The split in the earth suddenly shot toward them like a lightning bolt. He tensed, holding his breath. A sudden gust of steamy air ruffled his mop of brown hair and he staggered, tasting blood in his mouth. He had bitten down on his own tongue.

This was it. *Time to die.* He heard the phrase in his head in his grandfather's voice. It was what the old man often said before he killed one of Cael's pieces in their frequent games of chess.

The split came right up to the foot of the great stair and stopped just short of where they stood. More of the obelisks tottered.

Cael had thought for sure they would be swallowed up by the rapid expansion of the sinkhole, but to his amazement they had been spared.

Cael desperately wanted to backpedal to safety but something caught his eye as he looked down into the orange glow of the mists below him. Was there a shape down there in the mist? He bent down slightly, squinting to peer deeper into the abyss.

He heard chimes--distant, elusive. There was a voice. Did it whisper his name? Or had he imagined it?

He bent closer, putting his hands on his knees. There was definitely a shape down there through the smoke. He couldn't figure out what it was. But he was definitely hearing chimes. He heard the whispering voice again. What was it saying?

The words of the fourth prophecy came to him again in a rush and he understood now with startling clarity.

Needle stared south toward the Kuma. From what he could see, the Kuma did not appear to be as badly damaged as most of the rest of the Lower Steppe. He strained to see to the southern edge of the Kuma, to his home. His thoughts were only of his mother. Was she safe? Based on how the Kuma looked, he figured she was. But it was difficult to tell by firelight alone. The quake was subsiding and the sinkhole was growing more slowly and seemed to have stopped moving toward the south. It was only growing northward. One thing was for sure. Demon's Bluff would never be the same again.

He reached out his hand and grabbed Cael, who was staring stupidly down into the abyss. "What do we do now?" he asked.

Cael jerked up, his eyes were blank.

Needle jabbed Boxxaway with his thumb, but the old man was not in speaking condition yet. His coughing had stopped but he was panting desperately.

"We're safe here," Cael said finally. "At least for the moment."

Needle shook his head and looked south again. Why the holy hells was he standing here with these two? He had *hated* Cael and Boxxaway, and now he was somehow back with them again. What connection did they have with Brynn, whose mother had known his father?

They had been so close to getting answers. The ghost of Brynn's mother, covered in those awful tattoos, was warning them about someone before that rat creature dispatched her. Maybe the ghost knew something about his father?

A scream broke his concentration, and Needle turned to see a cottage on the edge of the sinkhole to his right erupt in flame. A Buerdeleise woman ran out holding a baby in her arms, both consumed in flames. A cask of lamp oil must have exploded. The woman ran directly out into the gap and disappeared down into the orange glow below, burning like a torch, her scream echoing up to them. The roof of her cottage, now a roaring inferno, groaned, sagged and slid down after its owner.

"Is there anything we can do?" Brynn asked as she stood to Needle's left. Mallet sat on the ground, staring out at the destruction with his teeth clenched. He ran his hand over his bald scalp. Brynn stood above him, one hand on her brother's shoulder. Her green eyes were wide and rimmed with tears. The hood of her cloak was back; the glow from the fires made her hair seem as if it was aflame. The trembling of the earth finally settled.

"Yes," Boxxaway croaked, in answer to her question. "Survive. You must survive. I believe this destruction was meant to kill the four of you specifically."

They all stared at the old man, still bent over, his beard trailing on the ground.

"The Cult of Yex has returned," he said. "This is their doing.

I'm sure of it."

If someone had told Needle this morning that the forgotten Cult of Yex, whose artifacts he had dug out of the desert with his father, was going to return and that they specifically wanted to kill him, he would have laughed.

Had it not been for the destruction around him, he would have laughed now. The old man was ranting. The stress of the situation had pushed him too far. The Cult was gone; it had been gone for eons. Even if it wasn't, who was *he* that they should care about *him*? It was crazy talk. Crazy conspiracy talk from a crazy old man. There was no connection between the earthquake and the cult. Besides, he had other things far too important to worry about now, like finding his father and helping his mother. Somehow, this Brynn girl's mother was connected to his father. At the thought of Brynn's mother, Needle considered the message she had delivered. Had she said something about the Cult returning? Maybe.

No matter. He had another priority bigger than finding his father; his mother needed him. The Cult of Yex and its supposed return was low on his list of concerns. But Needle could see right away that Cael bought Boxxaway's theory completely. For that matter, it looked like Brynn was swallowing it too.

"How could they do something this big?" Cael asked. "I mean, if they have this kind of power."

It was more than Needle could bear. "Oh, wake up, Cael. Don't you see what's going on here? I don't know why I didn't see it earlier today at the river. He's gone stark raving mad." He flashed a quick angry look at Boxxaway. "You really want to know where the Cult is, Cael? They are out there!" He pointed east out into the desert. "The Cult is gone. Dead. Dust. A few artifacts are all that's left of them."

Nobody said anything.

"The Cult caused the earthquake?" Needle went on. "Can you even hear yourselves? I'll tell you what caused the earthquake. A reckoning. A reckoning caused it."

Cael and Boxxaway stared at him like he was crazy.

He smiled. Maybe he did believe that nonsense his mother had always spouted about circular time.

"Yeah, it's the world's way of fixing things," Needle kept

pressing. "Fixing what the Buerdeleise have wrought."

"Needle!" Brynn breathed.

"It's not *fixing* anything," Cael shook his head. "Look around. It's killing people."

"Needle is right," Boxxaway interrupted. "About this being a reckoning, at least. But it's not the type of reckoning you think, Needle. It *is* the Cult of Yex, and they *have* returned. They have been waiting and planning a long, long time. They have brought powerful magic to bear. Don't be a fool, Needle. They most assuredly want *you*. They fear you."

"Yeah, well, I got to go," Needle said, feeling that he didn't fit here with these people. They were different, and so was the nonsense they believed. Magical earthquakes caused by a dead Cult in order kill him. He laughed aloud, though it sounded more like a gritty snarl. "I'm going to go find my mother and make sure she's safe," he announced.

"Your mother is taken care of," Boxxaway said through heavy breaths. "The Kuma was spared and I sent a parcel to her this afternoon."

Needle just stared at him through narrowed eyes.

"And the mausoleum tonight?" Boxxaway asked.

Needle shook his head, "I learned nothing there, and wasted a fortune in the process."

"And you will learn nothing in the Kuma. Did I not just save your life?"

"I wouldn't have needed saving if you hadn't sent me to the mausoleum in the first place!"

"Needle," Brynn said, "you know you were supposed to be up there tonight. It is not his fault that you didn't learn more about your father. Something tells me Cael's grandfather can help us. We should listen. Look around you, Needle. Something is happening. Something part of a larger pattern."

Needle folded his arms and leaned back, looking at Boxxaway expectantly.

"Time is short," the old man said seriously. "A man named Danilus waits for the four of you at the northernmost dock on the river. He will take you up river for a time. Demon's Bluff isn't safe for you right now."

Boxxaway was about to continue when Needle shook his

head. "No. I'm done. Do you get it? I'm done. Finished." The more he talked, the more he felt anger building in his heart. This whole situation was ridiculous. His mother needed him. She was all he had left.

"I'm outta here," he said, and with that, he turned and started running as fast as he could up the Great Stair. Once back up on the Middle Steppe, he would turn south and find another way down into the Lower Steppe and the Kuma, on a road that was not blocked by the sinkhole.

"Needle!" Boxxaway called after him.

He did not look back.

Cael didn't say anything aloud, but he was conflicted at seeing Needle go. He had been wary of Needle since they first met those many years ago. In truth, he never really liked him, but he felt some sadness nonetheless.

"Needle!" Boxxaway called again, but his voice trailed off, a worried look on his face.

"What happens now?" Brynn asked.

His grandfather wore a worried look and was silent for several seconds. "Needle is crucial to our cause, but there is no other option now but for you three to continue without him. Perhaps I will be able to convince Needle to rejoin us in a few weeks."

"But shouldn't we just go after him now?" Brynn asked.

"Time is too short," Boxxaway sighed. "He always was an impulsive kid."

Cael turned his gaze to the south, to the Kuma, and a question came to his mind. Why did the Kuma look safe? The Abala Ku, the section of town north of the Kuma where the Agrabi mainly lived, looked safe, too. In fact, it was only the center section of town, *his* section of town that had been swallowed up. Many Buerdeleise were dead and dying. *Mainly* Buerdeleise, as it looked as if the Agrabi had been spared. It didn't seem right or fair. It should have been them.

Hells, he thought looking up the Great Stair. It should have been the nobles of the Middle Steppe, too. Wouldn't Demon's Bluff be better off without them? If it was a reckoning like Needle had said, it was reckoning the wrong people.

"I was right in discerning that tonight would be the night. The Cult has returned," Boxxaway explained, reaching out and grabbing Cael's sleeve. He spoke also to Brynn and Mallet. "And I knew you four, well three, would all be in danger." He stood up a little straighter now, and his blue eyes flashed with clarity.

"My name is Boxxaway Hotheway. I'm Cael's grandfather. You must be Brynn, and you, my boy, are Mallet. You don't look good, if I might say. What happened?"

"It's worse than it looks," Mallet said, dragging himself to his feet.

"Why us?" Brynn asked, helping her brother stand. It was a good question, Cael thought. What threat were they to a power that could crack open the earth and swallow a city?

"Tonight I saw my mother's ghost," Brynn continued. "She tried to talk to us, but her ghost was attacked by a wererat before she could say much."

Boxxaway frowned. "A *wererat*?"

"Cael saved us," she said.

Cael looked to his grandfather and then remembered the prophecy. He had to tell him about it, but now didn't feel right.

"Grandfather, I went to the library today," he said.

Boxxaway looked surprised. "The library?" he said lowering the roll of carpet he held under his right arm. Once on the ground, he used his feet to kick it open. Cael blinked. It was the old ragged carpet from the kitchen of their cottage.

"I found something you should know about," Cael said. "Brynn and Mallet too, even Needle."

Boxxaway nodded, reached out and took Cael's sleeve again, "There will be time for that later. Our time is very short. Listen to me, all of you. The Cult of Yex is real and they have chosen tonight to begin their return to the world. They can still be stopped and I need your help. There are matters that require my attention shortly and you must attend to some matters of your own. You are not safe in town right now."

Cael noticed that Brynn was nodding. To his amazement, she accepted what his grandfather was saying.

"Your uncle Danilus waits for you at the northern most dock, Cael. I wish I had the time to tell you more. But get yourselves to that dock. You've been there before. Danilus will help you. He will tell you more."

As if to illustrate his point, an aftershock started shaking the ground again. Screams echoed in the distance and a section of buildings on the northern edge of the sinkhole slid into the great chasm.

"I know you have questions," Boxxaway said. "There is not time for them now and some cannot be answered, but Danilus will answer what he can. Remember that one thing is important above all: *You must survive, and in order to survive you must flee now to the northern dock.*"

"But Grandfather, what are you going to do?" Cael asked, confused. "We can't just leave you here."

"I have survival of my own to worry about, not to mention other matters which require my attention to the south in Taglyon," Boxxaway said. He was dead serious, but there was a wry grin on his face. "Demon's Bluff is not safe for any of us at the moment. If the world is to have any hope, all of us must stay alive."

"*Taglyon?*" Cael said surprised. "Why Taglyon? Why can't we just go with you?" He had never been away from his grandfather for more than a few days. But his grandfather had a way of getting his point across with a mere glance that meant he would brook no argument. Cael wanted to disagree, but fell silent instead. Boxxaway said go north to the docks and there they would have answers. More than anything else, he wanted answers.

"Answers at the dock," Cael said absently, looking out across the sinkhole. They would have to find an alternate route back up the Middle Steppe and then back down on the north end. Now that the earthquake was over, the chaos of the aftermath was evident. Fires burned everywhere. Persons wailing, signaling immeasurable loss came from all directions.

"Keep yourselves safe," Boxxaway said, his grin fading. His eyes glittering dangerously as if to say: *Don't you dare get yourself killed. More depends on you than you know.*

Cael felt that burden placed squarely on his shoulders but

he didn't complain. Complaining is something Needle would have done if he were still here. "We'll make it. We will survive." He turned to Brynn and Mallet. "Ready?"

Given Needle's reaction, he wondered briefly if they would abandon him, as well. He imagined how this must all appear to them. If he were in their position, would he follow? Maybe Brynn wanted to go see her father? Maybe Mallet did, too. It seemed reasonable to return home to loved ones in a time like this. Maybe Mallet should return home for attention to his wounds. They were either not as severe as they looked or the boy was the toughest person Cael had ever met. What was more, they were nobles and their home hadn't just fallen into a sinkhole. Their home was safe; their *people* were safe. It would make sense that they would return to their safety and abandon him to his destiny alone. At the thought of destiny, Cael thought of the fourth prophecy again and he knew the answer. They would go with him.

Mallet and Brynn nodded emphatically.

"What about Needle?" Brynn asked.

Boxxaway sighed with a look of consternation. "I don't know. It's wrong. You will have to get along without him. I don't suppose there is anything that can be done about him."

Cael looked south to the Kuma where Needle had gone.

Boxxaway stepped onto the unrolled red carpet. A few golden threads woven throughout caught the flickering firelight. Cael had never noticed the golden threads before when the carpet had been in the shadows of their kitchen. Boxxaway lowered himself carefully into a sitting position, his red tattered robes spilling around the edges of the carpet. He looked up at Cael and grinned his yellow-tooth grin. "Get yourselves to the docks, and quick." His grandfather's smile was familiar and comforting.

The earth rumbled again, not less than half a mile away, a gout of flame erupted into the sky.

Boxxaway closed his eyes and Cael felt a vibration of energy from the carpet. Cael marveled. His entire life that little patch of rug had been lying in the kitchen and he never suspected it was magical. The carpet stiffened and Boxxaway grabbed the edges of it, his eyes opening. The carpet vibrated into the air and lifted skyward. Boxxaway's beard and robes billowed behind him as the glow of the fires in the city lit him for a few moments before he disappeared into the backdrop of the starry sky.

Cael looked down to Mallet, who had slumped back down to sit on the ground. He was looking after Boxxaway, amazement on his face. Mallet met Cael's gaze. A thousand questions rose in his mind but he put them aside. There was no time. Cael reached out his hand. "To the docks."

Cael took Mallet's hand and pulled him to his feet.

"How we gonna to get to the docks?" Mallet asked, looking at the road ahead that had been swallowed by the great sinkhole.

Cael pointed back up the Great Stair.

He nodded, still gripping Cael's hand firmly. Mallet let it go with a final squeeze and a grin. "We better hurry then, because Wheizer may still be out there."

Cael's face hardened at the mention of Wheizer. *Good*, Mallet thought. The truth was, in his own mind at least, Wheizer was a far bigger threat to them than the earthquake or the sinkhole. Heading to the north dock and leaving town sounded like a dandy plan to Mallet. The thought of seeing his father or Wheizer tonight both sickened and frightened him.

"Surely he didn't survive that fall?" Cael asked.

"I hope you're right, but an unnatural creature like that? You never know." Mallet thought of the disease that surely coursed through his own veins even now. What would become of him? He knew he had been infected even before Wheizer had bitten him. He could still taste the blood on his tongue. He spat to the side.

The mere act of turning his head to spit intensified the pain in his shoulder. Could he even make it to the docks in his condition? His right arm ached where Wheizer's fangs had pierced deep into his shoulder. Plus, Wheizer had raked his chest from neck to waist with his hind claws, shredding him. He felt the throb of his own heartbeat in the pain of his wounds. Just breathing in and out felt like someone was sawing on his chest with a rusty knife.

Brynn's impromptu bandages had helped, but some of them were starting to seep through with blood. He had lost a lot of blood, and something more. He wasn't sure what it was, but he had a distinct sense of loss. It felt like something had been taken from him, something he hadn't noticed he had. Now that it was gone, he could feel its absence, whatever it was.

Right now, he needed to get to the safety of the northern dock. That meant going back up the Great Stair, back toward where Wheizer had last been.

Mallet knew Wheizer--knew his tenaciousness and knew that if he had indeed managed to survive the fall from the lift, Wheizer would continue to pursue them. Deep down, Mallet had no doubts. Wheizer was still alive.

What would Wheizer tell his father? Where was Dagorn right now? Sitting on the overlook outside his bedroom, drink in hand, watching the destruction below? Was he worried about the people? Mallet didn't think so. He was probably only worried about how this might affect his business and his plans. Likely, he was also considering any possible advantages he might find in such a disaster.

The taste of blood on Mallet's tongue intensified--the blood his father forced him to drink, the blood that would turn him into a monster. Was he destined to be another henchman for his father just like Wheizer? What was it Wheizer had said? *He had no more choices. He no longer belonged to himself.* Not if Mallet Bygrave had anything to say about it! Monster or no, he wouldn't return to be his father's servant.

Every muscle of his body ached and the smoky air made it difficult to breathe. Mallet faced a cold truth. He might not survive the night. At least it would deny his father that victory.

Looking at Cael, he felt a strange and compelling sense of hope. Cael would lead them in the right direction. If he died tonight, Cael would keep his sister safe. Right now, Mallet knew their best hope lay in following Cael Hotheway.

Brynn watched as Cael led the way up the slope on the right side of the Great Stair. He had an arm around Mallet's waist, though her brother seemed to be bearing more of his own weight. She followed behind them.

"I think it's finally finished," she said. The earth was completely still for the first time in... well... she couldn't judge how long the earthquake and subsequent tremors lasted. Five minutes? Ten minutes?

Cael didn't look back. He just kept stalking up the road, weaving in and out of the knots of people huddled together, their faces glowing orange from the fires below, their voices a mixture of sobs and terror.

"When we get to the top," Cael said, "we'll have to head north along the Middle Steppe. From there, I think there are two or three roads that wind down into the Lower Steppe north of the sinkhole. We just got to make sure we go far enough that we don't come down near it."

"What about Wheizer?" Mallet asked.

"He's dead, Mallet!" Brynn said. "There is no way he survived that fall, and good riddance if you ask me." Brynn shuddered to think what his body looked like smashed at the bottom of those cliffs.

Mallet didn't reply; he just kept stumbling along with Cael. Brynn knew she was right, but why was Mallet so concerned that he might still be alive?

Her mother once asked her what she thought of Wheizer.

"I don't like him," she said much too quickly.

"May I ask why?"

"I don't know," she had said. "I never thought about it. He's too sarcastic, I suppose. And too serious, he's boring."

"He's dangerous, Brynn." Her mother paused, then chuckled, but her eyes didn't laugh along with her. "And you think he's boring?"

Recalling that conversation, Brynn finally understood that her mother was warning her about Wheizer all those years ago.

It always bothered her that Mallet adored him. He liked the rat-faced man because he respected his strength. Wheizer always made her uncomfortable. She saw her father's calculating ambition in Wheizer, but he had other repulsive traits, too: swagger and sarcasm being the main two of many. And this very night she recognized another frightening characteristic: ruthlessness. It worried her that Mallet seemed to be on his way to following that same path, but any faults he had were covered up by the simplest of emotions she knew he possessed: love.

The earth began to tremble again and small groups of spectators raised their voices in worry. The wind gusted and the smell of smoke and sulfur invaded her nostrils.

"Stop," Cael said, splaying his legs to keep from falling. Brynn braced herself behind Mallet as they fought to keep their footing. Some of the people around them began to scream.

"Look," Cael said, and above them they saw another one of the obelisks totter and then fall across the Great Stair fifty feet in front of them. It broke into several large segments with a thunderous sound that hurt Brynn's ears. The debris lay across the slope and a large piece fell into the central canal that channeled the Demon's Race. The stream, now diverted, began to well up and around the debris of the fallen obelisk and flow down either side. Immediately behind where the obelisk had stood was statue of some great ancient hero. Brynn never cared for such old stories but most men and boys would know his name. His hair was long and braided and his face was covered with a curly beard. He was naked to the waist, and held a lightning bolt above his head as a weapon. Whoever sculpted him was a genius, capturing the essence of determination in the man's face.

Yet no amount of determination could stop this statue's eventual fate as the aftershock continued to rock the land. The statue fell, shattering in a thousand pieces upon the stair below it.

The heroes of old were fallen, Brynn had the immediate thought. *Who would step up to replace them?*

"This way!" Cael called. Despite the shaking beneath their feet, he led the way to the edge of the Great Stair where they stopped and looked back for a moment.

Halfway back up the Great Stair they now had a much better view of the Lower Steppe and it didn't look good. The city of Demon's Bluff stretched for miles along the Demon River, from the Kuma on the southern edge where the desert rose in elevation at the very beginning stages of the Ankin River Gorge, to the brewery district on the northernmost end of town. From there, the buildings gave way to the endless miles of grain fields of the fertile Demon River Valley.

The sinkhole opened roughly in the center of the Lower Steppe, crossing the Dragon Road, which ran from the Academy at the base of the cliffs, down the Great Stair due east through the market district all the way to the river. The sinkhole was over a quarter of a mile in length, north to south. It was wide in the middle and narrower on each end. The widest point was where it abutted the Great Stair and swallowed the Dragon Road. The Demon's Race, flowing down the Great Stair, poured right over the edge into the unknown fiery depths. If the water had any effect on the fires below, Brynn couldn't detect it. The sinkhole had stopped growing on the south end, but the current aftershock caused earth on the north end to peel away and slide into the yawning abyss. The sinkhole was already huge. How much bigger could it get?

When the aftershock subsided, Cael led them off the Great Stair into the jumbled mass of gigantic sandstone boulders that sloped steeply between the Lower Steppe and the Middle Steppe. He quickly found a narrow winding path that ran through the rock of the slope. It felt like they were entering a narrow canyon. The boulders rose ten feet or more to either side.

"The slope must be riddled with canyons like this," Mallet said. "What if we get lost?"

"When I was younger, I used to play here. We chased Agrabi kids through here," Cael said. "This path winds northward. We should stay off the Great Stair. I think this path will take us north past the sinkhole."

He entered the canyon between the boulders. Mallet leaned on boulders for support as he went next, followed by Brynn. The path had a sandy floor. It normally would be pitch dark in here at night, but the light from the burning city gave the appearance of twilight.

The boulders they passed were covered with carvings. Over the centuries, people had used knives or sharp rocks to carve their names, initials or witty epithets into the sandstone. Brynn noticed several crude comments and drawings mingled among them as well.

They hiked about three quarters of a mile through the narrow confines when another aftershock began. Cael lost his footing and fell to his knees on the sandy floor. Dust and pebbles fell on them from above. Mallet sneezed three times in rapid succession.

Brynn managed to stay standing, covering her face with her sleeve. "What if this canyon collapses on us?" she asked, feeling a claustrophobic sense of panic building. "I think we should get out."

"Indeed," Cael agreed, his voice was raspy from the dust he had inhaled. The ground continued to shake and more dust and pebbles fell from above. A loud crack echoed above them and an avalanche of rocks began to fall.

"Back, back!" Cael screamed, pushing Mallet, who had turned around and was shuffling as fast as he could back toward Brynn. Brynn backed up, watching the canyon collapse ahead of them. The sandstone crumbled. Another great crack echoed and a great cloud of dust billowed out, engulfing them.

For a moment, she was completely blind, forced to close her eyes. Mallet ran into her and she would have fallen, but he grabbed her arms to steady her.

The earth stopped shaking and Mallet let go of her. She raised her sleeve over her mouth and opened her eyes. They were standing inside of an orange, fire-lit dust cloud. Brynn's eyes welled up from the stinging dust.

"No going that way," Cael pointed north, the direction they had been headed, as the dust began to clear.

Indeed, the way ahead was entirely filled with rubble. Unless they wanted to try and climb over the unstable rocks, the path was blocked.

"We aren't going south either," Mallet said, pointing back the way they came. It too was choked with rubble.

"This way," Cael said, pointing east to a large crack where a boulder had broken in two. "Another passage opened up."

"We don't know where it leads," Brynn said.

"It leads down toward the Lower Steppe," Cael said, "which is eventually where we want to go. Come on!" The narrow slot he had discovered was freshly made by the earthquake. Mallet would have to turn sideways to fit and the ground was strewn with rocks, which made the footing treacherous.

Cael entered without looking back. Mallet went next, followed by Brynn, her eyes burning. The new canyon was darker and she kept her hand on Mallet's back to help steady her over the rocks.

They wormed their way through the canyon without speaking. The only sound they made was their breathing and the sound of their feet on the rocks, but the ambient noise of the chaos in Demon's Bluff was ever present: screams, barking dogs and the crackling of fires. Brynn feared the downward sloping path would dead end and they would be forced to go back or try and climb up. Mallet was in no condition for a climb. Still, they pressed on, until they emerged finally on the Lower Steppe.

The orange light from the fires lit their faces and they could feel the radiant heat. They emerged a few hundred yards from the western edge of the sinkhole.

"It just keeps getting bigger," Brynn said. The sinkhole had grown further northward. The houses here were tightly clustered together. A wave of fire was spreading through them, igniting their thatched reed roofs and sending flames licking skyward.

"This way," Cael pointed north. Cael led them north from the edge of the slope along some narrow dirt lanes until they reached a throng of people trying to put out cottage fires on the south side of the road.

Brynn kept an eye to her right, where the fires were moving like a wall toward them. It occurred to her that the sinkhole was less of a threat than the fires.

They kept moving, both she and Cael helping Mallet, who was slowing visibly. But Cael wouldn't let him rest, not that Mallet would have asked.

He led them north, and slowly, they outpaced the flames.

"This way," Cael pointed to the right as a lane twisted to the east. "We need to cross the city now and make the docks."

"Are we far enough north?" Brynn asked. They could not see the sinkhole from where they stood on a narrow lane clustered with mud brick homes to either side.

Cael didn't answer. He just turned east, hoping they'd traveled far enough north that they could now cut safely toward the docks. Cael pulled Mallet after him. Brynn paused for one moment to try and catch her breath. She never felt so tired in her whole life. But Cael wasn't stopping, so she forced herself to run after them.

The earth began to rumble again. A cottage ahead of them crumbled and collapsed. More screams filled the night as cottages just ahead of them started to sink down out of sight. Cael had turned east too soon. The sinkhole was expanding north across their path. She felt as if sand filled her feet and she couldn't move. The sinkhole's northern tip was only two house lengths away from them. The earth was still shaking.

Brynn felt Cael grab her arm and propel her north along an intersecting road. Mallet waited for her, his hand outstretched. She took his large hand and he pulled her north.

"Wait," she said. She pulled back and turned toward the sinkhole. Cael stood in the center of the lane at the very edge of the where the sinkhole reached. The glow of fires from below silhouetted him in his black robes as he stood at the precipice looking down.

"Cael!" she screamed.

He looked back over his shoulder and waved frantically for her to keep running. "Get to the docks!" he screamed. Then he turned back to the hole, which had expanded to mere inches from the edge of his boots.

"Come on!" Mallet cried. "He said to get to the docks." He pulled Brynn around and up the road. Brynn realized she should be helping him, and she put her small shoulder under his arm and tried as best she could.

They ran along about fifty yards up the road, stopping only once to look back.

Brynn squinted. The smoke was thick; wind was whipping up flames that were taking the houses to either side of them. The heat was incredible. The sinkhole seemed to be expanding again, splitting the lane in two toward them.

Cael was nowhere to be seen.

At first, Mallet couldn't move. Cael was gone and he felt paralyzed. Brynn jerked on his arm and pulled him around. "We have to keep going, Mallet."

She was right. It wasn't safe here, but his heart felt like a stone in his chest. His shoulder ached, his chest burned and his legs felt rubbery.

Cael had fallen into the sinkhole.

Brynn pulled her brother up the lane, away from the impending flames. He had to lean on her and he didn't know if she could take his weight, but he had no choice. He felt dizzy and weak.

I'm not going to make it, he realized.

Brynn kept him going as they traveled north. They managed to stay ahead of the flames and the sinkhole. They came to the Alabaster Way, a major thoroughfare that wound from the Northern Docks through the brewery district. Some of the breweries had business with the Bygrave family and Mallet recognized where he was.

"Right," he pointed. "The docks are this way."

The Alabaster Way was crowded with people and animals moving toward them, heading away from the sinkhole. Mallet fought through this momentum of people, wagons and livestock. The din was incredible and the air was choked with smoke that burned his lungs.

"There it is," he said, catching view of the dike wall ahead of them.

The crowds thinned here, and when he and Brynn reached the dike wall gate, they were mostly alone. Soldiers patrolled the walls above, their eyes riveted to the south where the fires raged.

The great gates in the dike were open, the spring flood season had passed and the Demon River ran lower in its banks. On the other side of the thick wall, wooden docks floated along the entire length of the levee, able to rise and fall with the annual floods.

Mallet led the way through the open gate, where a single man stood in the shadows. Mallet felt his gut tighten. Something was familiar about the way the man stood.

As he stepped closer he recognized Wheizer Rhelbog.

Chapter Seventeen
Rat Race

"We all lost everything, before we found each other."

-Raju "Needle" Graji

2nd Day of Summer - 1:20 AM – Dragon Academy Gardens

He couldn't remember where he was. Hells, he barely remembered who he was. Being in hybrid rat form did nothing to promote the use of lucid faculties, and plummeting hundreds of feet to a crushing impact hadn't helped either. That will tend to distract even the most rational and disciplined minds.

Then he remembered the trees: eucalyptus. He called them 'gum trees' when he was little because of the sap that poured from the gaps in their bark. He always loved the smell of eucalyptus trees. He remembered citrus groves, and the cypress and cedars. And his favorite, the date palms. He loved the feel of the bark on a date palm; he used to climb them as a child to get their sticky fruit.

Dozens of these trees shaded the landscape of the Dragon Academy buildings at the base of the cliff. In his great fall, that several hundred-foot plunge from the lift basket, Wheizer remembered how peculiar the trees looked from above as he hurtled toward them. It occurred to him that it was a rare and fleeting perspective.

Lucky, he had thought... I'll land on a tree and break my fall.

Only he managed to miss every single tree and branch and land, not in the wading pool several feet away to his right, but on the manicured lawn.

It was told in myth that the *wererats* could not be killed except by silver. Wheizer knew this not to be true. His body was not immune to injury, nor was it immune to pain. But the pain he was experiencing right now was more than he ever had to bear. He had blacked out on impact. The shaking motion of the ground intensified his pain and dragged him back to consciousness. He had no idea how long he had been out, but he was amazed that he survived.

Yes, he was vulnerable to silver weapons and some types of powerful magic. But other things could kill him, too. For example, there was a cobblestone pathway just a few feet away to his left. That might have killed him had he landed on it. He suspected that he had come very close to dying when he hit the much softer lawn. It was soggy from its proximity to the pool. Even his *wererat* rapid healing would have been overwhelmed--rapid healing even more enhanced because he happened to be in hybrid form when he hit. Fire could kill him, too. Many of his kindred *wererats* had been burned at the stake over the millennia--not something he ever intended to experience. Not if he could help it. But death in fire might actually be balmy and pleasant when compared to his current agony.

There was no telling how many of his bones were broken. But as he lifted himself to look around, he could hear a deep grinding sound as he rotated his head. The awful noise was accompanied by pain that rocketed up into his brain. In that brief moment of self-examination, he was horrified by what he saw. His abdomen had split open and some of his intestines had spilled out. His legs were broken in numerous places. A jagged bone protruded from his left shin, right through his rat hide. He had broken both arms, probably a dozen ribs, and from the sound of it, his neck. A rib stuck out through his chest. Blood bubbled around it with every breath he took. The vision in his left eye was dark on half his field of view, and the other half was tinged in red. He had bitten almost clear through his tongue. He didn't need to look at his reflection in the wading pool to know he was bleeding from every orifice in his head. He could certainly smell the metallic odor of blood inside his nasal cavity. And there was another smell, a distinctly unpleasant smell.

Yep. Sure enough. On top of it all he had defecated and pissed all over himself. Perfect.

As he lay there, he could feel the healing at work. He felt warmth in the injured areas and the pain began to abate a bit as he healed, though he had some problems. His rapid healing didn't re-arrange or set his broken bones. It just knitted them back together as they lay. He couldn't correct all these problems, but he needed to fix a few of them. He winced in advance at the pain he was about to put himself through.

He realized his right wrist was broken as he used his hand to gather his guts and stuff them back into the split in his abdomen. He nearly blacked out from the pain as he used his left thumb to push his protruding rib back into his chest. After several short gasps, he was ready for his shin bone. He used the claws on his right foot to dig into his left foot. He arched and stretched his right leg out. His shin bone slipped back through the open wound with a slurping noise. The pain was intense. He knew the bone wasn't set properly, but at least it wasn't poking out anymore.

The earth trembled again briefly as he lay back and let the healing continue for a few minutes. He could hear the wind stirring in the Eucalyptus leaves and its medicinal odor filled his nostrils.

After several minutes, he heard a whispered conversation toward one of the buildings. Two black-robed men were standing a few dozen feet away from him on the walk. They were looking right at him. He knew they were staring at a wererat who had somehow managed to survive what should have been a fatal fall, and the more he healed, the more worried they got. He could see that on their faces. It wouldn't be long till one of them decided that they needed to finish what the fall did not. And if one of them was a wizard, Wheizer knew he was going to be toast. And really, what were the chances? This was the Dragon Academy, after all.

He had no doubt that a competent wizard would take one look at him and unleash a magical firestorm. And in his current condition, he could not exactly fight back. He might be seconds away from experiencing his biggest fear--being roasted alive.

So, even though he was still far from whole, he did what he knew he had to do. He shifted form once more, but not into a man. He used the little-known third form of the *wererat*. He shifted into a two pound, worm-tailed sewer rat.

All his half-healed wounds carried over to his new form, and he imagined that as he scurried away, he looked like a rat on the verge of expiring: hunched back, broken and crooked legs and mangy fur matted with blood.

When he shifted back to the size of a man he found himself freed from his clothing, but he remembered his rapier. It was the only thing he carried that he would need. The two black-robed men started walking toward him. He didn't have long. If his thinking was impaired as a hybrid, it was even more so in the form of an actual sewer rat. Still, he knew who he was and what he was doing. He grabbed the leather-wrapped hilt of the rapier between his teeth, and to his relief, it slipped free of his belt and clothing with ease. It was extraordinarily difficult and painful as he scampered across the dark lawn dragging the unwieldy weapon along with him.

The two men shouted and began running toward him, but he headed for a nearby cedar hedge. He wove between the bases of each bush until he came to a startling obstacle. It was the bald wizard he had thrown out of the lift basket. He had landed face first, spread-eagled onto the hedge. Cedar branches had impaled him in several places and he was suspended by the branches just a few inches above the ground where his blood pooled in the dirt.

Wheizer turned to move around the obstruction and saw that the old wizard had died with a peaceful look on his face. How nice. The two young wizards were pursuing him through the hedge, but they stopped when they saw the old dead wizard.

"What in the hell's is going on?" he heard one of them say.

"It's an old man."

"It's Abner!"

"What in the name of the Abyss? They both must have fallen from the lift during the quake."

Their conversation continued, but Wheizer knew that the old bald wizard's corpse had provided him the cover he needed and they wouldn't pursue him further.

On the other side of the hedge, he found another yard. He scurried along for several minutes until he found a shadowed corner of a building that seemed safe and there shifted into his human form... naked.

He started to move. His knees wobbled and he whirled his hands in a circular motion to keep his balance. He surveyed himself. His bones had knitted, but few were set in any semblance of straightness. His back was hunched and the bones of his arms and legs were crooked. Walking would be a problem. There was still a great deal of pain, but it was much subdued from what it had been. He needed to wait a while longer to heal before moving.

He slumped down, leaning his shoulder against the wall. He gripped the hilt of his rapier; the feel of it comforted him. He needed to think, and he could do that most clearly in his human form. His first notion was to figure out what in the hells was occurring around him. There had been a series of earthquakes, and the distant sounds of bedlam drifted to his ears. The first tremor had happened while he was still on the mesa.

Most of his life, he experienced quick flashes of intuition and right now he had one. The earthquakes weren't over yet. There were more to come. Something was happening. Today had been unlike any other, and the shaking of the earth was part of it.

Not that he worried too much. You didn't get to be who he was without learning to roll with the punches.

But others would not so easily deal with such a large disruption to the routine. He thought first of Dagorn. His mentor and savior would not be pleased with the turn of events: neither the earthquake nor the situation with Mallet.

Wheizer did not want to disappoint Dagorn. It was only eight years ago that Wheizer was a pustule on the backside of society, a lowly thief infected with lycanthropy that he could not control. He used to dread the full moon. He resisted with all his might, but in vain. He shifted uncontrollably and murdered anyone around him. He always awoke from his murderous rampages with only the vaguest recollection of what he had done. Not that it ever really bothered him much. After the first time it happened, that is. After that, his biggest concern was how terribly vulnerable he was. One day, he surmised, the town guard would eventually figure it out and he would be hunted down and burned at the stake. That was the inevitable end he imagined for himself until Dagorn saved him.

Dagorn saved him by patiently teaching him to control his transformations. It took a long time, a lot of effort, and a great deal of willpower, but Dagorn was finally successful.

Now Wheizer was in complete control of his changes, and he could shift in the blink of an eye, managing it perfectly. In fact, he could sit in a crowded tavern drinking ale on a night with a full moon, and other than a few twitches, no one would even know how he had spent those horrible full moons years ago. Or the fate of anyone near him.

It was Dagorn who had helped Wheizer turn an overwhelming liability into the ultimate asset. With the disease under his complete control, he was able to bring to bear powers that were almost superhuman. Take the events of this very night. He could shift at will to intimidate his foes, and empower him in combat. The wound Mallet managed to inflict on him with his glaive had healed before he caught up to them on the lift. But best of all tonight, he had survived a fall that surely would have killed him. He should have ended up like the old bald lift operator. But here he was, alive, breathing, and healing. Indeed, Wheizer owed everything to Dagorn for helping him manage his disease.

He couldn't wait to see the look on Brynn's face when she saw him. And that Agrabi kid, Needle. Wouldn't they be surprised?

This led Wheizer to think of Mallet. As of tonight, Mallet was infected. And the big lug might be physically strong, but it took mental discipline and training to control a disease like lycanthropy. And Mallet could not do that without his and Dagorn's help. Normally, Mallet should not 'rat out' for a while (as his kindred called it.) Not until the next full moon, about a fortnight away. But great moments of stress could force the change to come precipitously. And what could be more stressful than these earthquakes? Or seeing the ghost of his mother?

And if Mallet shifted right now, well, that would be a problem, wouldn't it? He would kill everyone around him, including his sister Brynn.

It would take him years to recover from the guilt of murdering his own sister, if he recovered at all. And Wheizer was in a good position to judge such things. He forced his mind back on track before it went too far down a road he never wanted to revisit. It was all about mental discipline.

Mallet could eventually deal with the guilt of murdering other innocents. He already had a killer instinct, which was very promising. Killing Vosc hadn't fazed him much, but killing his sister.... He'd be utterly useless for years, maybe worse.

Let's face it. Wererats swam in a sewer of loathing and self-hatred; it was the nature of being a lycanthrope. But Mallet--the poor fool would drown in it. Probably end up killing himself. What a waste.

He had to protect Mallet, his new progeny, from killing his sister. He had to find them and bring them home safely.

What if they had returned home already?

He considered that for a moment. His intuition told him Mallet would not return to Dagorn, at least not yet. Bigger questions needed answers, too. What was that Agrabi whelp doing up there? Why had Kemano's son turned up three times today? And what was he doing with Brynn? That was a connection from the past that made him very nervous. He knew it would concern Dagorn even more. They were up to something and Mallet was getting dragged into it.

And then there was the whole business with Elowynn's ghost. That dumb whore had actually returned from the grave.

Good thing he had decided to follow Brynn and was there to put a stop to it. No telling what that cow would have said. The less those kids knew about Dagorn, the better off everyone would be.

He shuddered to think about what might have happened had he not been there. Well, nothing did happen, so best not to think on it. But that thought brought him back to the urgency of the moment. There was still plenty that could go wrong tonight.

Wheizer morphed back into hybrid, half-man, half-rat form, which gave him a boost of energy and further sped his enhanced healing. He then ambushed a solitary apprentice running through the gardens, knocked him unconscious, and stole his black robes. They were too small, but he had to wear *something* as he ran back to the Bygrave estate.

He needn't have bothered. As he ran, a massive quake struck. Between the dark of night and the confusion of the quake, no one even noticed him. Everyone on the Middle Steppe was focused on the quake and the havoc that ensued. Most folks were looking down to the Lower Steppe and didn't even notice him as he raced along in hybrid form. Even with his bones mended improperly, he was able to maintain his balance on the quaking ground and still run twice the speed of a normal man. He couldn't spare a moment to watch the destruction. This was exactly the type of stressful event he feared might force Mallet to shift. Perhaps it was still too soon for the curse to take hold of the boy, but best not to take chances.

He returned to Dagorn's Estate. It had been largely spared of serious damage. One of the circular towers had partially collapsed, and a few bricks had shaken loose. Nothing too bad, but then again, the ground was still shaking. He was there for less than two minutes. Just long enough to throw on a proper pair of trousers under his newly-appropriated robes and verify that neither Mallet nor Brynn had returned. No real surprise. Should he talk to Dagorn?

Not yet, he decided. Better to just bring the two children home and then explain what happened. Besides, it drove him crazy when Wheizer's own men asked for instructions on a problem they could damn well solve themselves. Dagorn only needed be involved if Wheizer couldn't solve this, and he had no doubt he could solve it.

So where would Mallet go?

Given the circumstances, he could think of no place for certain Mallet would go. There were a dozen places he *might* go, but he didn't have time for a dozen places. And Brynn. That was a laugh. He never wanted to understand her well enough to figure out where she would go in a situation like this. No ideas either on the other boy, the one who fancied himself a sorcerer. He had never seen him before. How did he fit into all of this?

And that left Needle: Kemano's son. Wheizer couldn't help himself. He indulged a big rat-faced grin filled with razor-sharp teeth. Needle had told him this morning *exactly* where he would go in a situation like this earthquake.

Needle, during any kind of disaster, would return to his hovel to tend to his momma. It was exactly that sort of weakness that made him hate Needle even more. He was really going to enjoy selling that little guttersnipe into slavery again.

Would Mallet go with Needle? Not sure on that one. Based on what he saw in the mausoleum, he didn't think so. It looked like they had met there for the first time. Brynn might go with him, though. Either way, it was the only lead Wheizer had in finding Mallet. The quake was still going strong as he left the estate and headed to Needle's house in the Kuma for the second time today.

The first time, he had followed Brynn there and crouched below the back window as they talked. He had learned a great deal about Dagorn's daughter--information that was both interesting and disturbing. He had been afraid that the little dog that went after him would give him away with its pathetic yapping, but its neck broke easier than Wheizer had estimated.

What new disturbing and interesting information would he learn on his second visit?

2nd Day of Summer – 1:40 AM – The Great Stair

Needle ran up the Great Stair, leaving Cael, Boxxaway, Brynn and Mallet. He darted around a fallen obelisk and the knots of people, who, contrary to all logic and reason, seemed to be edging closer to the great sinkhole. It was as if the attraction of looking into it was greater than the imminent danger it represented. Everyone was gathered together in groups: Agrabi servants here, Buerdeleise nobles there. No one was alone. This wasn't a time to be alone. They whispered, their voices sounding like water flowing over rocks, a constant babble of words that couldn't be understood, but could be felt. The tenor was fear and awe.

Needle felt the pull, not so much to ogle the destruction like the people around him, but rather a pull back to the people whom he had just abandoned. Everything in his brain *knew* that leaving them was the logical thing to do. But then why did it *feel* so wrong? His mother would have called it *goin' 'gainst the cull*, her slang for fighting against the inevitable circles of time that were so intrinsic to the Agrabi way of thinking.

Needle just called it *stupid*. It was letting emotion rule his heart instead of logic ruling his mind. Besides, implicit in the Agrabi way of thinking was the idea that everything that happened was destined to happen, and Needle hated the idea that he wasn't truly in control. As far as he was concerned, he was the author of his own destiny.

It was a belief shared with his father.

It was a belief he would question from this evil night forward, and it had started with the fact that he just couldn't shake the feeling that leaving was the wrong thing to do.

The earth was still shaking, though not as severely as before, when he reached the top of the Great Stair and paused to look down at the city. From this vantage, the sinkhole looked like a giant gash in the earth. Its depths were shrouded in orange mists and its circumference was lit by raging fires. The smell of sulfur and smoke made his eyes itch and his nose run. His mouth was filled with an acrid taste.

He turned left along a narrow frontage road that hugged the edge of the Middle Steppe. The smoke in the air made it hard to breathe as he made his way. He realized that his head still ached where he had been smashed with the wooden pole at the river, and his thighs and calves burned from so much walking and running today.

"Heavens protect me," he muttered aloud, then mentally castigated himself for using a Buerdeleise entreaty. He had survived a very rough day and that whole thing with Wheizer weighed heavily on his mind. The man was a wererat: of all things--a *rat.* Damn good thing he was dead now. At least one thing good had happened tonight.

After ten minutes of running, Needle found a road that led safely down through the Abala Ku to the Kuma. He looked down into the southern portions of the Lower Steppe. The sinkhole did not extend this far. The homes here seemed relatively intact. The quake had stopped, for now. Several groups of Agrabi were working to douse fires. He felt as if he should stop to help them, but he continued to trot along, anxious to get to his mother.

As he got farther into the Lower Steppe, the crowds of people began to get larger. Most of them were moving south, away from the sinkhole which lay to the north of them. He drifted south with the crowds until he reached the road that branched southeast into the Kuma. Few people were entering the Kuma, even with a sinkhole and raging fires to propel them.

It was never safe to walk the rutted roads of the Kuma alone, and less so at night. Yet tonight was different. The roads were littered with people oblivious to him, holding aloft lanterns or torches that flickered and spit in the wind, looking fearfully toward the glow in the north. Most people seemed to have no idea that a sinkhole had opened up in the center of the city. But they knew something bad had happened.

Needle didn't stop to enlighten anyone. He just kept running, hoping not to twist an ankle in the darkness. He soon reached his home. Everything looked all right from the outside.

He opened the door and entered the small adobe cottage. His mother rocked gingerly in her old rocking chair, next to an open window, listening to the sounds of the chaos that came faintly from the north. The room was dark except for the light which shone into the window from the outside. Of course. Why would a blind woman need a light?

"Needle, that you?" she asked.

"I'm okay," he said, coming to her side. He knelt and took her worn hands into his own.

"What's going on out there? It sounds like the hells have come a-calling."

"It's bad, Mother," Needle said. "The earth opened up, swallowed half the district next to the Great Stair."

"Hach!" Mother exclaimed gleefully, pulling one of her hands away from Needle's grasp and slapping her thigh with it. "Done serves them right. Did the Middle Steppe go, too? Did them nobles go down?" As always, she delighted in the fall of any Buerdeleise.

"Hit by the earthquake, some towers fell, but nothing bad."

"Pah!" she was disappointed. "And our people? The Kuma? The Abala Ku?"

"Don't know for sure, but it seems safe."

She was quiet for a few moments as she considered it all.

Needle was relieved that his mother was safe. He fingered the coins left in his pocket and, despite the horrors of the day, knew he and his mother would be okay. At least for a while.

"Someone brought us food and a pouch filled with coppers," she said, motioning over toward the table. Needle's eyes had adjusted to the light and for the first time he noticed a wheel of cheese, several dozen loaves of hard bread, a sack of dried figs and a few flasks of wine. And sure enough: a leather pouch. He could smell the food and realized how incredibly hungry he was.

He lit the lamp on the table and peered in the pouch. Sure enough, it was filled with copper coins.

"Who in the Abyss?" Needle asked, his eyes opening wide, though he already knew the answer. Boxxaway had told him.

"Said his name was Danilus," Mother said. "He smelled funny. I thought he came to rob us."

"Boxxaway," Needle muttered under his breath.

"Tell me where you been all night," Mother said, her voice going lower.

"It doesn't matter now, does it? I was with that Buerdeleise girl that came earlier. She said she could help me find Father. She took me up the lifts to the graveyard."

"Needle!" she exclaimed.

He knew she would react this way, but he didn't care anymore. No point in lying to her. With the money in his pocket and more money and food on the table, they had a chance for a new start. He wasn't going to waste it.

"I didn't learn a single thing about Father," he said, and realized how heavy those words made his heart. He was giving up his obsession with finding his father, and with it, all his hope. The time had come to put his childhood behind him and take some responsibility. This day had been a serious wake up call. The only reward for his hopes was disappointment. "And I am going to stop looking for him."

"You are a good boy, Needle." she squeezed his hand. "Tell me what happened."

"The worst of it was that I saw a creature straight out of the Abyss. You remember those stories you told me of the wererats?" Even mentioning the word made his spine stiffen and his skin break out into gooseflesh. Seeing Wheizer shift into a rat creature was an image that would haunt his dreams. "He came after us, but it's okay now. He fell off the lift from near the top of the mesa."

She squeezed his hand again. "You're okay. You're safe here." Her attempt to comfort him was laughable, but he couldn't help feeling better.

He pressed on and quickly recounted the events of the night. Meeting and dickering with Dagorn, getting the silver to ride the lifts, then meeting Brynn and Mallet at the mausoleum, seeing the ghost of Brynn's mother, seeing Wheizer turn into a rat, the fight with him on the lift, and then of the run down to the Great Stair and the meeting with Boxxaway, and his request that they head to the northernmost pier and meet with Danilus at the granary dock.

"And you didn't go with them?"

"No. You've been right since father disappeared. It was just a bunch of Buerdeleise foolishness."

Mother was quiet for a moment, rocking back and forth. The chair creaked. "Under my bed, get the cloth satchel under the mattress. I got something important for you."

Needle stood up, but then stopped. Something felt wrong. Had he heard something outside? The din of the earthquake and its destruction could still be heard to the north. But this had been something different.

He listened but heard nothing. He must still be feeling jittery from the events of the day.

Shrugging, he went to the table. He broke off a piece of cheese and stuffed it into his mouth. The taste was incredible, a rich smoky flavor. It was good Agrabi cheese. Boxxaway had said that he would send help to his mother, but Needle couldn't believe he had actually done it. It was enough to shake his lack of confidence in the old bastard.

He reached her bed, lifted the flimsy straw filled mattress and pulled out the satchel hidden there. He had seen it before, but had never looked inside. He brought it back to her and put it into her hands.

She opened the satchel and felt around.

"What is it, Mother?"

"Patience," she said.

Finally, she pulled out a small narrow object wrapped in white linen. She put the satchel down on the floor and set the object in her lap. Carefully, she unrolled the linen until she revealed a small dagger with a silver blade.

Needle's first impulse was anger. Here they were starving and in poverty, and his mother had a silver dagger worth enough to ease their burdens for a year. But her next words softened his heart.

"This silver dagger was your father's," she said, handing it to him. He took a step back, reverentially holding his father's blade. "I have been waiting to give it to you."

"But why now? Why tonight?" Needle took the dagger and felt the weight of it in his hand. He examined it. It wasn't fancy. It had a simple but elegant blade free of tarnish and a hilt wrapped in black leather with a polygon fashioned of silver for a pommel.

"Not much can hurt a wererat, Needle--but *silver can*," his mother continued.

"But I don't need it now. He's dead. He fell hundreds of feet." Needle's skin tightened at the mere thought of Wheizer.

As if answering a summons, their cottage door flew open. Needle turned and the blood drained from his face as his mind was forced to confront the impossible. Standing six feet tall, yet hunched over as he entered, Wheizer Rhelbog sauntered into the room, in full half-rat/half-man horror. His red irises shone faintly, while the whites of his eyes were riddled with bloody veins. His elongated snout was rimmed with sharp teeth. Rivers of saliva ran down the runnels between his lips and teeth and spilled down onto the floor.

His body was badly misshapen. The fall from near the top of the cliff had not killed him, but he had not walked away unharmed. His back was humped and his arms and legs were bent at awkward angles. His face was puffy, with purple splotches and great tufts of hair missing. His chest rose and fell slightly with each rattling breath. He wore black trousers under black robes. Needle could see the tip of his rapier hanging from under his robes.

"You almost disappointed me," Wheizer said, his voice much more guttural than it was when he was in human form. "I couldn't find you in all the confusion, but I figured Needle will come home to his momma. As I waited out back, next to that rotting corpse of a dog I killed earlier today, I started to worry you weren't coming. But then you did come back, just like I knew you would." He laughed--a sick, evil laugh.

"And you thought I died. Tsk, tsk, tsk. That hurts my feelings, Needle. I always keep my promises."

Wheizer just stood there with his red-eyed, rat-faced smile, waiting for a response, but Needle couldn't move. He couldn't even breathe. He was cognizant of the fact that the held the silver dagger in his hand, but fear paralyzed him.

"What's the matter, Needle? Rat got your tongue? I came back to keep my promise. You know, to sell you into slavery again."

Needle knew Wheizer was toying with him. The rat man was really enjoying this moment. Needle thought of the dagger in his hand, but still couldn't move. His brain still couldn't deal with the fact that this creature--this monster--had survived and had come straight here to torment him again.

"You don't know it, but you already performed your first act of service as my slave. Brynn and Mallet are heading to the granary dock at the north pier, you say? Very interesting. I'd thank you for that information, but you need to get used to the life of a slave. A master never thanks his slave, Needle." Wheizer's impossibly large grin grew even wider.

"Don't be worried, though. I'll come back for you after I deal with them."

Needle desperately wanted to move. But it was as if the wererat had cast a paralyzing spell on him more powerful than Cael could have done. Some part of his mind was free to analyze what was happening, and he was screaming to himself: *MOVE! USE THE DAGGER! MOVE!!!*

But he couldn't. It was the most agonizing experience of his life. It had happened to him before, with the zombie rats in Ganger's tomb and even this morning on the barge. The Abyss be damned and double damned. He wanted to jam the point of the silver dagger up under this bastard's chin and up into his brain. Wanted to more than life itself.

But he was too afraid.

But then his mother woke him up. "Use the dagger, Raju!" she said. "Take it and strike true! It's silver!"

Needle felt a grating anger at his mother. Didn't she realize he already knew that? Didn't she realize he would move if he could?

Wheizer threw his head back and laughed. "Silver? I see you holding that dagger, boy. Do I look afraid to you?" He moved close to them and leaned forward in front of his mother. He opened his mouth wide and a single strand of saliva dripped down. She turned her face up to him and his hot breath blew her wispy white hair back.

She shrieked, "You ain't gonna get me, you devil! My soul is clean! Get on out, you motherless rat!"

Wheizer screeched in her face, his voice rising from deep in his lungs.

He was just a few feet away. Needle could reach out in a fast motion and jam the dagger into Wheizer's heart. But still, he couldn't move.

Mother stiffened suddenly, arching her head backwards. She grabbed her left arm with her right hand with a panicked look on her face. She made a strange gurking noise, then pitched forward out of her chair, almost colliding with Wheizer, and hit the floor of the hovel with a sickening thud and the crack of breaking bone.

Wheizer took a step back, looking momentarily confused. He looked from Needle to his mother on the floor, realization dawning on him.

"I scared the bitch to death!" he said bemusedly. "I've never done that before. This is a memorable day indeed." Then he shrugged and strode toward the door. He stopped at the lintel and turned back to Needle. "I'll see you soon," he said nonchalantly and disappeared into the night.

Needle stared at his dead mother in shock. He shook her but she did not respond. He held his hand in front of her face to feel her breath and there was none. She lay on the floor staring straight up at the ceiling, her white eyes blind not just to light, but now to life.

I'm not ready for my mother to die, Needle thought. Now that Wheizer was gone, he should be crying, but there were no tears.

I'm a coward, he thought. *Wheizer stood over her, I had this dagger, and did absolutely nothing about it. I'm a coward.*

Needle stood up in stunned silence. A series of memories flashed through his mind. He remembered sitting at her feet as a child, listening to her stories, remembered her laughing. He remembered how she was when she could see, and remembered her looking at his father with resentment when he told her they were going out on another dig.

Then he remembered something that almost broke his heart. After his father had disappeared, his mother would bend over her son's bed, her old hands smoothing back his hair, her voice softly singing an out of tune lullaby to him. He was too old for lullabies, but he allowed her to sing them, pretending to be asleep. They both knew he was pretending to sleep, but they both didn't care.

Always she ended by whispering: "Don't you worry, Raju. You still have me. You will always have me."

Raju 'Needle' Graji looked at the dead body of his mother and realized he no longer had her. He was totally and utterly alone in the world.

Needle was drained of all emotion. His father was gone, and now his mother was dead. And he was a coward. Maybe that was the worst part. *I was afraid. I could have saved her, but I was afraid.*

She might have died anyway, he thought.

But you didn't even try, another part of his mind said.

He thought of the Agrabi circle of time that his mother so believed in--the idea that patterns in life repeated at regular intervals. It meant that choice didn't matter, and that destiny was inviolate. And he rejected it all.

I have a choice, he thought.

He heard the words of his father in his head: *You have a choice, Needle.*

"Yes I do," he said aloud. Something changed in him. He gripped the dagger. When put in the context of the Agrabi concept of destiny, he grew angry. *I don't have to be paralyzed. I don't have to let him win.*

He picked up his mother's satchel, went to the table and stuffed the satchel with bread, cheese and a flask of wine. He added his silver moons to the pouch of coppers. He slung the satchel over his shoulder.

He walked with a purposeful stride outside of the hovel and looked eastward down the lane. He glanced back and saw the pathetic rose bush. He saw the only rose, its petals still tightly packed together. His heart started to ache. He broke the rose off low on the stem, piercing his thumb on a thorn. He walked back into the hovel and laid the rose on his mother's unmoving chest.

He knelt and kissed her forehead, touching the wrinkled skin, brushing her white hair back with his hand, then turned, the silver dagger in his hand, and left the cottage. He would never return.

Chapter Eighteen
Am I Evil?

Looking back at the whole tale, I find it most interesting that evil is over and over again excused. There are those who believe there is no such thing as evil, that people are misunderstood. I have no such misconceptions.

-From the *Lost Journal of King Adirak of Taglyon*

2nd Day of Summer – 3:00 AM – The Granary Dock

"You need to go home," Wheizer said to Mallet and Brynn. He leaned against the side of the gap in the dike wall, one leg across the other, his hands folded on his chest. He was dressed in a black tattered linen robe. His filthy bare foot tapped impatiently on the cobblestones.

Mallet could *not* believe Wheizer was here. *How had he found them?* He took Brynn by the arm and pushed her behind him.

"I don't want to talk to Father right now," Mallet said.

Wheizer lowered his arms and took a step away from the inside of the gate so that he stood in the very center of the gap. He emerged from the shadows. He was a mess. He was hunched over and his limbs were bent at unnatural angles. There was dried blood all over him. He grimaced and blinked slowly.

Two men in white robes ran past. One of the men carried a large wooden chair with a checkerboard pattern on the cushion. They split apart and walked around Wheizer, each to one side.

"You're like me now," Wheizer said slowly. "Look up there? Do you see that moon?"

Mallet looked up. He already knew it was a moonless night. The stars were periodically obscured by the smoke from the fires raging throughout the city.

"In two weeks," Wheizer continued, "the moon will be full. And unless something aggravates you before then, and causes you to change early, you'll change on the night of the full moon. I see you protecting your sister. But if you shifted now, Mallet, you wouldn't be able to protect her. You'd kill her and shred her body into unrecognizable ribbons. You've seen the slaughterhouse where they kill the pigs? Yeah, that's what you would do to your sister. You'd kill anyone around you. You'll go on a rampage, and murder and mayhem will follow. You'll awake in the bushes, with cuts and scratches, but you won't really be hurt, until you realize with stark and sudden clarity what you've done, and who you have murdered. This *will* happen, you have to believe me. *I know.*"

Mallet sucked his breath in. He felt like he wanted to vomit. He considered Wheizer's blood. He had drunk Wheizer's *blood!* If that hadn't done the job, then the bite on the shoulder was a guarantee. He was already infected. Nothing could stop it.

He turned back to Brynn and for once, she was speechless. She looked up into his eyes.

"I can't go back," Mallet said. "Not yet." He thought of Cael and the directive from his grandfather to head north and come to this granary dock. To find... Uncle Danilus, was it? It didn't make sense, but in his heart, he felt it was the right thing to do.

"Your father is the only person who can help you," Wheizer said. "He can help you control the disease. Help you retain your sanity and your control."

"Like the control you showed attacking me?"

Wheizer laughed. "You have no idea the control I used with you. Be serious, son. Do you want to kill your sister? Do you not see what happened to this city? Your father needs you now more than ever."

Those words cut Mallet to the core. His father needed him. He had always tried to be important to his father. And now, as a wererat. he might gain more approval. And with both he and Wheizer having this power--well, who could really stand in their way? Wouldn't their family be able to take advantage of this earthquake and gain both power and prestige?

"You are a liar," Brynn said suddenly, coming out from behind Mallet.

The sounds of the cataclysm echoed dimly around them. Screams and yells filtered through the smoky haze. The night air was hot and Mallet felt sweat running down his back. More people passed, heading out to the docks, hoping for safety on the waters of the Demon River.

"No," Wheizer said very solemnly. "No lies. I assure you, Mallet is infected, and in two weeks, he will shift, and if you are there, he will kill you, Brynn."

Brynn shook her head. "He will control it."

Wheizer laughed. "It can't be controlled, Brynn. Believe me, without the right help, it can't be controlled."

Mallet shook his head. *What if he couldn't?*

Brynn looked up at him and met his gaze. There, in her eyes, he saw simple faith. She believed utterly that he could control it, that he was going to be okay. He wasn't sure where that faith came from, but it was there. He looked back at Wheizer.

Wheizer smiled. "You don't have a choice, Mallet. I'll drag your big ass back up to the estate with your sister. Do you understand?

Mallet didn't like those words.

"Is this what Mother would have wanted for the family?" Brynn asked.

Of course, she would bring up Mother. No, Mother would not have wanted this. She never would have wanted her son to turn into a murderer, a slaver or a wererat. Brynn, with that awful witch magic, had summoned their mother, who had tried to warn them about *someone*.

It's Father, he thought. *She came to warn us about him.*

"Wheizer," Mallet started, standing a little straighter, though the effort caused needles of pain to shoot through his shoulder and his chest.

Mallet was going to continue talking, but he saw something that left his jaw hanging open. Walking purposefully up behind Wheizer was none other than that dirty little Agrabi kid Needle, striding through the crowd. Something had greatly changed in the boy in the hour or so since he had left them on the Great Stair. The boy's face was hardened, and his eyes were wide with ferocity.

Wheizer noticed Mallet looking behind him and turned just in time to see Needle lift a silver dagger. The light from the fires behind them glinted off the blade like morning light on the ripples of the river. Needle plunged the dagger into Wheizer's chest. Wheizer screamed in a high-pitched whine cut short by a gurgling frothing sound as blood spewed up out of his mouth.

An older man in long nightclothes turned his head as he strode by, but then he just kept walking.

Wheizer Rhelbog fell to the ground, twitching. Needle stood over him, the bloody dagger trembling in his jittery hand.

"Go!" Brynn screamed, and pushed Mallet from behind. Mallet didn't move at first, too fascinated by the sight of Wheizer's seemingly mortal wound. Brynn kicked his shin, hard.

With Brynn leading him, they ran as fast as they could past the fallen Wheizer. Mallet stopped about ten feet past Wheizer and turned to find that Needle hadn't moved. He stood still, his fists clenched in white-knuckle rage, staring down at Wheizer.

Cael emerged from the smoky city like a panther, his black robes flowing. He skidded to a halt on his heels in front of Wheizer. "Hells," he said, looking at the twitching man. Then he grabbed Needle by the arm and propelled him along through the gate in the dike wall. He pointed to the left when he saw Mallet and Brynn and screamed, "The granary dock is this way! It is the northernmost pier!"

Mallet turned and started to move, but then stopped. He had been here before. A year ago, this very night, he had chased the man who murdered his mother. That man had come to the north docks and had run all the way to the northernmost dock. And there at the end of the pier, Wheizer had knocked the man down. And after that, well, after that, Mallet had taken care of it. He had beaten him, tied him up and tossed him into the river to drown.

Why do I feel like a knife just traced its way up my spine? Mallet shivered.

2nd Day of Summer – 3:05 AM – The Granary Dock

Cael pushed Mallet and Brynn while simultaneously pulling Needle along the dike wall northward until they reached the granary dock. He herded them down the pier, their feet clumping on the wooden planking. They passed milling groups of murmuring sailors readying their vessels, and panicked groups of bystanders, many still dressed in their night shirts, clutching odd belongings. A one-mast boat lay tied alongside the end of the pier.

Uncle Danilus, wearing his customary floppy hat, stood on the pier next to his sailboat, his lanky frame bending over as his hands quickly unwound the rope from the bollards. He smiled at them, his teeth visible through the thick scruff of his red beard. Dheke, Boxxaway's great grey mastiff, barked madly at his side, his hackles raised.

Cael couldn't have been happier to see him if he had been his own flesh and blood kin. His boat was about thirty feet in length, with a cabin, a single sail in the center and a deck both fore and aft.

Out of breath, the teenagers reached the boat.

"You'unz finally got here!" Danilus said, his voice booming and his smile wide. "Hop aboard! Hells, who is *that*?!"

They all looked back as one. Stumbling down the dock was none other than Wheizer himself. He was in human form, limbs bent and twisted, walking like a toddler, each step deliberate and made with great effort. The front of Wheizer's robe was covered in a darkened wet patch. Blood frothed from his mouth, dripping from his chin.

Cael pushed Mallet onto the deck. Mallet snapped out of staring at Wheizer and turned to lift Brynn off the dock and onto the boat next to him. Needle was still staring, mouth agape, at the bloody horror stalking toward them.

Cael tossed his staff onto the deck, grabbed Needle and shoved him aboard. Danilus braced himself against the deck and pushed off. The craft began slowly drifting away. With both hands on the railing, Cael hopped over. Dheke deftly leapt the gap; Danilus came last, and with a final kick off, the boat drifted away from the edge of the pier and into the current of the Demon River.

They looked back as a bloody twisted Wheizer doddered, as if in slow motion, up to the edge of the pier. The rage built on his face as he realized he was arriving too late. The gap between the edge of the pier and the boat had grown too wide.

He screamed in frustration, a great nasally, inhuman scream. "I'm still alive! You hear me, Needle! *I'm still alive!*" Blood frothed from his mouth with each taunt.

Another boat passed between them and the pier, blocking their view of Wheizer. It was a grain barge loaded with refugees trying to flee the city for the seeming safety of the river. When they once again caught sight of the pier, Wheizer was ambling back toward the burning city.

"Impossible," Needle said, his voice quavering almost as much as his hands shook, both of which were clasping the silver dagger in front of him like a sword. "He was dying on the ground." He turned to Cael. "If you hadn't grabbed me, he would have stood up and killed me."

"Well, then I got there just in time," Cael smiled, and for the first time actually felt some sort of bond with Needle Graji.

"Where were you?" Brynn asked, coming up to Cael's side. "You just disappeared back there!"

Cael shrugged. He had some thinking to do before he answered that question.

2nd Day of Summer – 2:45 AM – Edge of the Sinkhole

Cael stood at the edge of the sinkhole, the city burning around him. Mallet and Brynn had left him as they continued toward the docks, and it was good that they had.

All doubts he had about the veracity of the fourth prophecy had vanished. It was true: completely and utterly true. The implications were more than his mind could bear.

CAEL.

He heard his named called from the depths of the chasm. He knew it was soundless and only he could hear the call in his mind, but it was no less real. The orange fiery mists of the pit swirled and he thought he could see a demonic visage forming in the smoke. Or was it just a trick of the light?

CAEL.

He inched closer, feeling the irresistible pull. His mind felt as clouded as the smoke and mist in the great gulf below. The voice called out to him and he yearned to heed the call, to give himself to that seductive clarion. The words of the fourth prophecy surged through his mind.

CAEL.

He leaned over the edge of the great chasm, looking deep into its maw. It wanted him, and somewhere deep inside him, he wanted it. He crept forward, feeling suddenly relaxed, as if accepting the inevitable. He allowed himself to slowly begin to fall forward when a hand suddenly grasped his shoulder and pulled him back. "Don't."

Cael snapped out of his trance and turned to see his grandfather, Boxxaway Hotheway, standing next to him. The flying carpet lay on the road ten feet behind him. His eyes were rheumy from the smoke. He coughed.

"It's calling to me," Cael said.

"I know," Boxxaway nodded.

"It's all true," Cael cried, almost panicked. "I read a prophecy in the library tonight. I went there and found an ancient book of prophecies on the Cult of Yex. It said that the Abyss would call out to me and it was my destiny to heed the call of evil." Tears filled Cael's eyes. He was trembling.

Boxxaway's eyes were wide with surprise, but his grip on Cael's shoulder was firm. He took Cael by the hand and led him away from the edge of the great pit.

"It wants me," Cael whispered, tears streaming down his face.

Boxxaway then smiled and Cael's heart lightened. "It will not have you," he said, his voice soft and reassuring. Cael felt immeasurably safer. "I know it calls to you, but you don't have to answer."

Cael felt the pull of the sinkhole less with every step they took away. "But the prophecy said it was my destiny!"

"There is one thing stronger than destiny, Cael."

Cael blinked the tears from his eyes. "But destiny is destiny. I have no choice!"

"It is true that destiny is a powerful force Cael. But neither force of fate nor power of destiny can defeat the most powerful weapon *you* possess: the resolve of your freewill." Boxxaway waved his hands in front of his face to fan away a billow of smoke that drifted by his head. Dogs were barking all over the Lower Steppe.

Cael took comfort in the reassuring words of his grandfather. The call of the sinkhole had abated. He felt a surge of strength flow through him, clearing his mind. He knew there was truth in Boxxaway's words.

"Well, then we have won, haven't we? You helped me resist the call and the Cult can't come back now."

"I'm afraid it's not that simple, Cael. I suspect you will continue to feel the pull of that call. The Cult has waited for five thousand years and won't give up now. They will never relent. The Cult will continue to call to you, and you must continue to be strong."

"But why me? I'm nobody!"

"You aren't nobody, Cael. Don't you understand? You come descended from a long line of guardians who have existed through the generations to protect against the second rise of the Cult of Yex.

"*The Society of Eyes*! The symbol of eyes we saw on Ganger's tomb!"

Boxxaway nodded. He was looking more ragged and tired than ever. But a strength emanated from him and Cael could feel it. "Your father was one of them, and so are you. Your father was killed by the Cult and they consider you to be their greatest threat. For them, the only triumph better than killing you is co-opting you. I fear that the temptation you felt is only the beginning of your tribulation."

"Then, you knew! You knew of the prophecy all along! Why didn't you tell me?" Cael felt a sudden flash of anger.

"Yes, I have known of the prophecy for some years now. I was waiting until you got older to tell you. When I found the prophecy in that library when you were younger, I realized the time of the cult's rebirth was upon us. I hoped against hope that this would be delayed until you became a man, that you would be spared this burden at such a young age. But sadly, you are still a boy. You will have to carry the burdens of a man, Cael. You and the other three hold the key to defeating the cult."

"But that isn't what the prophecy said. It said we would unleash Yex on the world!" The smell of acrid smoke stung Cael's nostrils.

"Why would the Cult be concerned with you, Cael?" asked Boxxaway, his wizened face illuminated by the flickering yellow-orange light of the fires burning throughout the town.

"I--I don't know. I don't understand."

"Don't you see that the Cult fears you, Cael?" Boxxaway said with a cough. "They have always feared you. Deep down, they know that you and the others are the only ones that have the power to thwart them. They killed your parents. They tried to kill you, and failed. They can jabber about destiny in their prophecies all they want. But they know that they cannot bend your free will if *you don't let them.*"

"But the prophecy said—"

"I know what the prophecy says. If destiny were such a force, why would the Cult bother with such prophecies? Don't you see? That prophecy exists to try to make you believe you have a destiny you can't control. The Cult are masters of deceit Cael. You must never give in to their lies."

Cael felt buoyed by his grandfather's words. They made sense... perfect sense. "But must I resist that call all my life? I don't think I'm that strong. The voice from that pit holds some strange power over me. It felt--it felt--irresistible. I'm not strong enough. I can't do it!"

"You must be strong, but only for a time." Boxxaway paused as a cohort of the town watch ran by, weapons drawn. "We must remove the source of your temptation. I am formulating a plan. I have been for years. It is bold, but it's our only hope. We must take the fight to Yex. He is the source of the Cult's power. Without Yex, the Cult is nothing.

"*Kill the demon*? Is that even possible?" asked Cael, incredulous. A strong gust of wind whipped up around them. Embers from the fires nearby climbed higher in the sky.

"I think it may be. I have more research to do, but legends say the demon is imprisoned on the astral plane, where he is weak. The Cult is trying even now to free their demon master." Cael could see that Boxxaway was breathing hard. Due to the noise around them, he was having to talk louder than he was normally accustomed and it was a strain on him.

Boxxaway continued, "They can only succeed if we fail. But now is not the time to discuss this. That time will come. For now you must trust me--and trust in yourself. Your will is stronger than anything the Cult can throw at you. Don't forget that." A flaming building near the edge of the sinkhole to the south of them collapsed, send flaming planks and debris into the gaping chasm.

"The town watch. We must tell them the Cult is returning! They will help us!"

"The Cult has waited five thousand years to return now, Cael. Can't you think of why?"

Cael just stared blankly, a dozen emotions clouding his mind.

"The Cult is forgotten, Cael. The town watch will do nothing. And even if they were inclined, look around you. What could they do?"

Cael knew his grandfather was right. The Lower Steppe looked like the Abyss itself. Buildings had collapsed in every direction. Fires raged. Panicked screams swirled through the air like the smoke rising above the fires. All this paled in comparison to the devastation of the great sinkhole: hundreds of feet across. Many people had been swallowed up by the earth: perhaps over a thousand. Their cottage was gone. Madam Dunkley and mean old Moggs, both were swallowed up by the earth, surely dead. Cael felt numb.

"Besides," Boxxaway continued. "the Cult's ways are devious. Who is to say that they haven't already infiltrated the nobility or the town watch? How can we know which of the dukes can be trusted?"

Cael's shoulders slumped. It was as if the weight he carried had been lifted for a moment and then dropped back upon him.

"It falls to us, Cael. I am too old, but I will give my life to help you, if needs be."

"I will try, Grandfather." Cael gave a resigned nod, but the words of the fourth prophecy kept ringing in his head... *Cael will fulfill his destiny and will answer the call of evil.*

"Go now and catch up to the others. Find Danilus on the northern dock. All will be made clear in time," Boxxaway said as he slowly began to lower his old frame down to sit on the carpet.

"But where will you go?" asked Cael.

"I am close to making a plan, Cael, for you and your fellows. You must trust me. I must fly to Taglyon to see if I can find help there for our cause. I will meet you back here in Demon's Bluff when you return."

"What about Needle? He left us."

"I wouldn't worry about that. He will make the right decision. Go now, and make haste."

Cael began to turn and jog northward, giving the sinkhole a very wide berth. *Cael will fulfill his destiny and will answer the call of evil.*

Stopping suddenly, Cael turned back to Boxxaway. "Grandfather?"

"Yes, Cael?"

"Am I evil?"

Boxxaway just smiled a grandfatherly smile. "There is good and evil in all of us, Cael. Which path we follow is not a matter for fate or destiny to decide."

Boxxaway closed his eyes for a moment in concentration and the carpet began to slowly levitate off the ground. It turned and flew upward toward the southern sky.

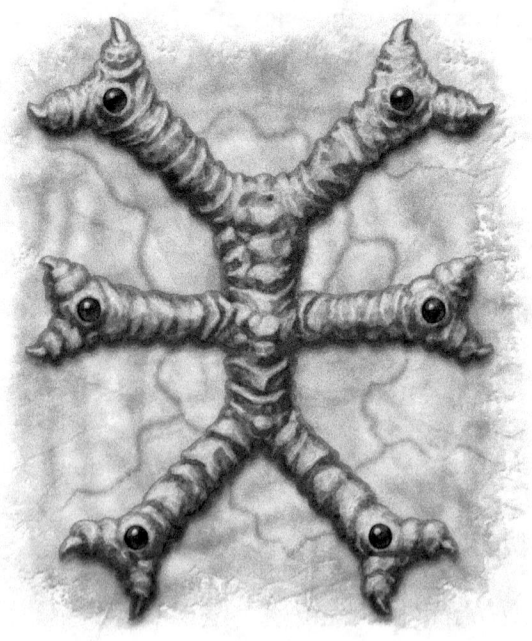

The story continues in:

PROPHECIES OF OLD
Cult of Yex Saga: Part II

DEAR READER

We sincerely hope you enjoyed Second Cataclysm. If you did, please consider leaving a review on Amazon or another bookseller's platform. Each review helps us spread the word to other readers.

And if you get a chance drop by www.CultofYex.com or our Cult of Yex Facebook Page. Say hello make a connection. We love to hear from our readers.

Author's Note

Jason F. Smith

Years ago I read some advice by comic book writer and author Peter David to people who wanted to write. I don't have the actual source of what he said anymore, but he said something like this: "So... you want to write? You've read a comic or a novel and said to yourself... 'I can do better than that.' Well it's just that simple: If you want to become a writer, then just do better than that."

Any story written seems to me to be an act of hubris. You are playing creator, with characters, setting, and story. And you have the nerve to write it down and give it to the world. You are saying I can do better.

And that's how this story started. We just sat down one day and said: 'Hey, we can do better."

But having the determination to do better is useless unless you have a story to tell, and thankfully the Universe delivered. I had a dream shortly thereafter wherein the entire story was discovered intact and downloaded into my head. I called Parker the next day, and he went to work outlining a secret document called The Cult of Yex Story Bible, making sense of the often confusing dream.

All that was back in 2000.

Fast forward 15 years... and the dream has become a glowing digital reality (if you are reading this on a digital device) and a firmly compressed slice of trees (if you are reading the physical book).

Who to thank in all this? First of all, I need to thank my writing partner, Parker. He took a leap of faith when I told him this could be done and went to work. He ground onward while I went through some major upheavals in my life and he put a mind boggling amount of just pure WORK into the project. I think he sometimes worked in front of his computer screen until his eyes started bleeding. There would be no *Cult of Yex* without his dedication and determination.

But where did all this inspiration start? I would have to say Tolkien started the whole thing for me. Other authors followed including the children's author Paul R. Fisher's *Ash Staff Trilogy* (an underrated series, highly recommended for younger kids), Lloyd Alexander's *Prydain 'Chronicles* following the adventures of young Taran Wanderer. C.S. Lewis influenced me with *The Chronicles of Narnia*. Later, more adult authors that influenced me include David Eddings (*The Belgariad* and *Mallorean*), Tracy Hickman and Margaret Weis (*Dragonlance*), and Stephen R. Donaldson (*Thomas Covenant the Unbeliever*). Stephen King's entire body of work became ever more influential, as he taught me about being fearless.

Modern TV (and we are living in a true Golden Age) that influenced me and deserves a nod of thanks include the shows: *The Sopranos* (which started it all), *Sons of Anarchy, Lost, Battlestar Galactica, Breaking Bad* and *Mad Men*. Some of these shows are not perfect, but I learned as much from their imperfections as from what they did well.

A special thanks to three authors who have helped me: First goes to Orson Scott Card, with whom I corresponded for years on the subject of politics, religion, but mostly on writing. His advice has been instrumental in making me a better writer. David Farland (David Wolverton) also contributed through correspondence and a lunch, and he read earlier manuscripts and gave great encouragement. John D. Brown is a fellow author and good friend of mine. When we aren't debating Cogito Ergo Sum, we are talking writing and how to give readers the best experience possible. John thinks totally differently from me, which is a great help in looking at things from different angles. If you get a chance, check out his novels.

Editor Sol Stein's books were also influential.

A special thanks goes to my son Simon Asher who read much of what was written as it came off the presses and took long walks with me, debating certain elements of the story. More than one solution to writing problems was offered by him.

And a most special thanks to my wife Jennie, co-conspirator, aiding and abetting in all things magical.

C. Parker Garlitz

Okay, here's the deal. I have some agonizing form of OCD when it comes to plotting a story. I can't watch a movie or TV show or read a book without getting way too granular on the plot. Some stories are just brilliantly told, but far too many of them end up disappointing me because the plot is somehow compromised. The worst for me was the TV series *Lost*. It was such a great storytelling mechanic, such a great sense of discovery, such a brilliant Lovecraftian method of dispensing tidbits of mystery, but what a colossal disappointment with the plot in the end. The way the story unfolded, it was if the authors were making a solemn pact with me to deliver on all the implicit promises of a cohesive plot. Utter betrayal. Sadly, this happens to me more often than not.

I could never do that to a reader. I want you to know how much time and effort Jason and I put into making sure that this story delivers on all its promises. This entire thing was originally plotted as a D&D adventure. Jason and I plotted the entire story out, front to back, working thousands of hours for what is now *fifteen years*. We hammered and hammered and hammered the plot until we felt it was right. This is not a story that we whipped up on a whim. We agonized and argued and plotted over tiny details until we discovered the true way forward. The entire story from the opening scene to the last.

The point of all this is, you can trust that we will deliver on all the promises of the story, explicit and implicit.

Here is the other deal. I think Jason and I both burned out on the fantasy genre, (probably me more so). It's a beautiful, creative, immersive genre but sometimes it just plods along too slowly. We have worked very hard to tell an immersive and epic fantasy tale with the fast pacing of a thriller. Thanks to Jason for that awesome insight.

Special thanks to my daughter Raegan for all her help and suggestions.

ACKNOWLEDGEMENTS

We have to thank everyone who read and commented on the novel, including: Jennifer Stanchfield, Asher Smith, Riley Smith, Amethyst Smith, Austin Lewis, Brittany Witt, Parker Webb, Peggy Stanchfield, Dr. John Stanchfield, Jordyn Jones, Megan Dennis, Raegan Garlitz, Mary Garlitz, Carol Archer, Dave Reed, Sheriece Farr, Shane Farr, Megan Bangerter, Tyler Barnes, Kaitlin Jones, and Peter Jones.

A special thanks to Jessica Hyde Wilcox for going above and beyond as a beta reader.

Thanks to Jeremy McHugh for the art and Jennifer Leigh for the copy editing.

ABOUT THE AUTHORS

Jason F. Smith

Jason F. Smith lives in the beautiful mountains of Utah with his wife, three children, and menagerie of furry family members. Jason finds a great deal of pleasure as well as a host of ideas on his daily walks through the winding mountain paths, and is an avid lover of the magical art that we call "life".

C. Parker Garlitz

Parker is a 14th Level Nerd / 9th Level Small Business Owner, who lives in the beautiful mountains of Utah with his amazing family. Parker's fondest wish is to not be multi-classed and focus on adding more levels exclusively to Nerd. If you liked what you have read, you can help him achieve that goal. Tell your friends about the Cult of Yex.

www.ingramcontent.com/pod-product-compliance
Lightning Source LLC
Chambersburg PA
CBHW060851250626
47159CB00008B/2692